PRAISE FOR
RIDE SOUTH UNTIL THE SAWGRASS

"With sparse, honed prose reminiscent of Annie Proulx, Chapin untangles and weaves again the stories of three families as they struggle in the mire of an ever-changing landscape and seek to find their place within it."

—Steph Post, author of *Lightwood*

"James Chapin brings a fraught era and place into electrifying focus in this thrilling and torrential southern. He is definitely a writer to watch."

—Janisse Ray, author of *Ecology of a Cracker Childhood*

"*Ride South until the Sawgrass* is an engaging and rewarding debut from James Chapin, who brings to the page the intimacy and skill of a veteran imaginist. This story feels genuine and raw, and lands among the best fiction writing inspired by rugged old Florida."

—Ben Montgomery, author of *Grandma Gatewood's Walk*

"With an intimate and granular eye for detail, James Chapin gives an exquisite account of the intertwined fortunes of families and communities fighting at the margins to shape the course of history."

—Tauno Biltsted, author of *The Anatomist's Tale*

RIDE SOUTH UNTIL THE SAWGRASS

BY JAMES CHAPIN

LANTERNFISH PRESS
PHILADELPHIA

Lanternfish Press
399 Market Street, Suite 360
Philadelphia, PA 19106
lanternfishpress.com

Cover Design: Kimberly Glyder
Cover Image provided by the State Library & Archives of Florida

Printed in the United States of America.
Library of Congress Control Number: 2020930843
Print ISBN: 978-1-941360-47-7
Digital ISBN: 978-1-941360-48-4

TABLE OF CONTENTS

TO KATIE

RIDE SOUTH UNTIL THE SAWGRASS

THE MAN AND THE WOMAN faced each other on opposite ends of the crosscut saw. They lifted it up from its resting place and brought it outside. The saw was seven feet long and they carried it like a stretcher into the trees. It flexed with every step they took, and the sunlight it reflected loped and danced along the undersides of the branches.

They reached the tree. A grand old pine, dying. The man had been watching it since they first came to the clearing three months ago, when they were new to that place and new to each other. He made a notch-cut in one side with an axe and then they took up the saw together. They laughed at first and were clumsy with the back-and-forth, but soon the saw bit through the bark and into the wood.

The man and the woman pulled against each other. They were well matched. Clean chips spat from the kerf and a scent of turpentine surrounded them. They made decent progress but it was dense wood. After a hundred strokes or so the man spoke up over the noise, breathing in time with the sawblade. It was only possible to speak while pulling.

Let me know if you, he said.

What? the woman said.

Let me know if you. Want to stop.

I ain't stopping. If you ain't stopping.

Well then. I guess we'll. Keep going.

I guess. So.

Forty strokes later they were deep in the heartwood. It was not a very broad tree but it was old and the pitch had gathered down at the base. When the tree finally fell they would have a supply of lighterknot for a long time. That tree would start years' worth of campfires and cookfires and fires to heat a tub for bathing in the winter and fires to heat a tub for scalding slaughtered hogs. It contained knot to be lit at night at the sound of strangers' voices in the yard and to ward off the mince and yawp of wolves, keeping them at the treeline. And eventually, much later, a last scrap or two of that tree lost among others would start hearth fires to heat old arthritic knees not a hundred feet from where the couple now stood, young and laboring and pulling cleanly at the blade. Fifty strokes later the man grimaced or grinned through his sweat.

Lord, whoever taught you. To saw.

You know I. Lived plenty of life. Before you, Quinto. Learned a lot of things.

What? Hell. Twenty years old—

Watch out!

And the woman stepped back from the tree. The man yanked on the crosscut unopposed and stumbled backward to land on his elbows, and they both looked up.

The tree moved, tipping against the high clouds. Or maybe the treetop was holding still and the clouds were moving. It was hard to tell. They stood there for a long time puzzling over that question, looking upward at the sky.

It ain't going to, the man said, standing now.

Shh, the woman said.

And now the movement of the tree or clouds had a sound accompanying it. A groaning noise, and a pop, and then a few more pops. And then the few needles left in the pinetop shushed through the air on their long arc down to earth, which leapt a little when the old tree struck home.

Then it was silence. They looked at the pine lying lengthwise on the ground and the palmettos crushed flat under it. Then they looked across the round stump at what was left standing: each other, the two of them spotlit by a sudden opening in the canopy.

THE BARREN HERD!

NAT AND LUCY FIND THEMSELVES IN FLORIDA.

I.

NAT AND LUCY QUINTO rolled into Florida Territory before the summer rains settled the dust. They drove a third-hand oxcart which creaked at every bump. The road was little more than a deer trail: Florida was not a friendly place for wheels, not yet. But Nat Quinto didn't seem to mind. He sat at ease on the bench. His hatless head glided along as if the wagon was an old ferryboat, drifting downcontinent on a southward current.

His wife wore the hat. She sat on the wagon's tailgate. Her feet dangled off the back and swung a little in the grass wake: this might have been enough to make some women look girlish. But there was nothing girlish about Lucy Quinto. Her bearing was too firm, too gold. Perhaps the past seven days had changed her. That was how long she and Nat had been leaving down for Florida in the rickety wagon, with their few possessions sliding around in the back. Maybe the seven days had given her that look of unimpeachable womanhood—or maybe it was what she was doing with her hands. In the left hand was a knife, in the right was a dead rattlesnake. She sat there skinning it down to the flesh. The head had been crushed under wagon wheels but back of that was seven feet of good snakemeat. She butchered it with an oilcloth draped over her knees, for the blood.

This was how she ended up with the hat:

It was midmorning, they had been driving for a while. Lucy was sitting on the back and Nat was up on the bench. The ox smelled water before they did: it tossed its head to the right and huffed. Soon Nat could smell it too, sweet and fresh through the trees. 'Luce,' he called. 'There's a stream there, I can smell it. Do you want a drink?' But the ox was already turning, and before Nat could use the reins it was breaking a trail down to the water.

It was a wide creek, running amber above pale sand and the last dregs of chert off Georgia's shoulder. The oaks kept it cool and shaded except for a scrap of sunlight in the middle. 'Oh,' said Lucy, coming out from the canvas. 'Nat, this is nice. How about here? This is a good place.'

'Not here, not yet,' Quinto said. He stood and looked. 'This, it's pretty and it's clear water. But where we're going is richer and prettier and clearer.'

'Is it,' Lucy said. She had stepped into the creek.

'All of this and richer and clearer and they's herds of cows, herds of horses all running, and deer running, and flowers shooting up, and fruit trees shooting up everwhere whether you want them to or not. You'll see.'

'Soon.'

'Soon, yes, soon. A couple more days.' He coughed. 'Give or take.'

Lucy was looking around the creekbottom. Nat unhitched the ox from its yoke, watching her. 'You believe me, don't you? Luce?'

She took off her shawl. 'Sometimes I wonder if I got a choice,' she said.

'Lucy, now please, you—you do, you have one.'

She was quiet a moment, taking off her shoes. 'I believe you, Nat,' she said after a time. 'Might ask myself why, from time to time. But I do.'

Lucy stepped further into the water. Nat threw the ox's last trammels off and took it to the creek to drink. He bent down alongside the pack animal, bringing water to his face and neck and dampening himself generally. He tended to the ox a moment, filling his hat with water to wet its back. Then he looked around for Lucy.

There she was. Twenty yards downstream and all in the water, naked, nakeder than he'd ever seen her somehow, behind but not very much behind an outcrop of willows. He took a shallow breath and turned toward the wagon.

There was a small pouch up by the driver's bench and he took it down and fumbled a corn-husk smoke. He was reaching the last crumbs of the tobacco he'd bought in Georgia. Soon it would all be gone. This was bad: what then would he do, at such moments? What would he do with his hands, his shaking hands? Well, they would have to steady.

The cigarette made, he smoked it: thereby it was gone. Too quickly. He slumped against the wagon, facing away from the creek, spitting out a few stray shreds of tobacco. After a moment he turned and peered over again. That whiteness, off in the water. Bathing, wading, paying him no mind whatsoever. Maybe that was what finally moved him.

He left the ox and walked twenty yards down the creekbank and stopped directly alongside her, frankly looking. There she was. The pale back, the long heavy honeycolored hair turning dark in the seep of the creek and piled a little on one shoulder, which she had raised against him, and over which she was now staring agape as if she'd never seen the man before in her life.

He laughed at this. He stood and looked and laughed again. Then he walked into the creek, in all his cotton, as if that were the most natural thing in the world. Which maybe it was.

They made love on solid ground. Afterward they each got into their own clothes, grudgingly, after a little confusion about whose were whose. Except she kept his hat and did not return it.

They came back to the Alachua trail and headed south again. It was around that time that the wagon rolled over the snake. Lucy saw the corpse stretched out in the grass after they had moved past it and called for Nat to stop. There it lay, dead. It was true what she said, that it had never even had a chance to rattle, the poor thing.

Their wagon was rickety but it held up. It didn't have much to carry. Their larger belongings were lashed to the walls and most of the floor was taken up by a large mattress. In this way the wagon was not much more than an ox-drawn bedchamber rolling down the trail. Hanging pots and pans clanged together now and then. A crate containing a few white chickens swung from the back, like a lantern.

Nat Quinto had used all of his savings to purchase the ox and the wagon. He'd been a lumber man on the Saint Marys River in Georgia, but recession had come and broken the industry and set him adrift. He and all his fellow sawyers were turned out from the company houses and given no pay for their last thousand boardfeet. This betrayal had sent Quinto into a slow fury. He was a peaceful man at heart but he had such rages sometimes. They were very rare but burned very hot, and they often resulted in decisions such as this one: to leave that country immediately for a place where there would be no man to count on for his eating or his starving, where only God himself was exchequer. He was not sure such a place existed but he guessed it did and guessed he would die if he did not find it.

He and Lucy were recently married. She agreed to go. He got the destination from an old man at the lumbercamp who described a friendly roadhouse in the Florida territory called Mrs. Monroe's and a fair country south of that. Quinto purchased his ox and wagon in town and left the very next day. They had been traveling ever since. They did not hurry; there was no need for hurry. Neither of them required haste or speed to hold them to a decision.

Nat Quinto sat high on the narrow bench. The man was tall but narrow-shouldered; he was not imposing. When he smiled it was wide and open and crooked. His dark brown hair was of the same uncertain provenance as his surname, which had been sanded down and anglicized with a short i. Lucy cut his hair but she was not much good at it and the result made him look scraggly and somewhat boyish. All the same, he had big quick fists and no man he fought ever forgot him.

South of the creek they saw little sign of human life, save for one day when they came off the trail to eat. The pretty place where they aimed to stop was no natural opening or meadow but a Seminole cropfield. As were many other such clearings on that landscape. The owners were there tending it. When the Quintos' noisy wagon broke through the trees, half of the heads suddenly dropped below the cornstalks. The rest held still, watching. But as the wagon kept going and its two passengers gave small gestures of goodwill, the faces that had ducked out of view reappeared one by one to rejoin the others and the whole party, both African and Seminole, recommenced their labors.

Nat kept the oxwagon moving. 'They're here, then,' Lucy said, as if she hadn't already known it.

'They are,' Nat said. 'Their corn's tall, too.'

'It didn't look like they'd bother with us. Did it.'

'No, it didn't. Let's try and keep it that way.'

'How,' Lucy said, darkly.

'Same way as with anyone, I expect,' Nat said. 'By not by-God meddling with them. Not stirring things, not with a gun nor a tomachuck. Nor laying hands on things ain't ours.'

They went on in silence for a time. 'I want to ride with you,' Lucy said.

'Well then,' Nat said, glad. 'Come on.'

He did not have to stop the wagon. Lucy just jumped down from the tailgate and walked alongside the slow-moving vehicle until she came even with the front. Nat's hand was there, reached out. She took it and swung up onto the bench. The single hat was enough to shade them both from the sun if they held close enough together.

Late in the afternoon their wagon was bumping across the pinelands. It was May, and hot. The axles disliked the weather and squalled loudly. Lucy also disliked the weather or was pretending to. She was under the canvas.

There had been a dog following the wagon for a day or two. It was wild and fringe-eared, a poorlooking bitch. Every once in a while Lucy flicked a thumbnail of cornbread off of the back of the tailgate and the dog ate it with gusto. Nat wouldn't like this, but Nat didn't know. The dog followed them and fattened visibly.

Lucy had pinched and was about to throw another piece of bread when the wagon stopped dead. She froze. She listened. There were no noises, or at least no battle noises. That was what she listened for—gunshots, horse hooves, shouting. There were none of those for a long minute and so she stuck her neck out of the wagon.

To the right, nothing. To the left, nothing. Nothing but those gigantic trackless woods, the same woods she had been staring at for the past week. She got down from the wagon and went around to the front. There she found her husband in the middle of the path, staring at an oak tree. She had to squint for a moment before she could see what he was looking at.

There was a house under that tree. A danklooking structure slouching beneath the branches. Lucy squinted harder. After the week spent drifting across the pinelands, it'd been easy to forget that they were supposed to be looking for a place named Mrs. Monroe's. It'd been easy to forget such places existed anywhere on earth. But now here it was, marooned in the middle of the forest. It looked like it had drifted there from someplace else. It looked like it had been set down by the receding of the Flood.

Three horses were tied up in front of the roadhouse. So the place even had patrons, somehow. Voices floated across the distance, someone laughing like a maniac in the early afternoon. A second laugh joined in, and then a third, a woman's. But then those two dropped off and the first voice kept on laughing, the sound growing dry and hoarse and chapped in the throat. An empty bottle flew out of a window and lodged in the sand and the laugher laughed on.

Lucy Quinto left her husband peering at the roadhouse. She walked to the edge of the woods and pulled a skinny laurelcherry out of the dirt, roots and all. Then she walked back to the wagon and raised the switch and swung it down on the ox's rump with all her might.

The ox gave a groan like a big door swinging and started forward at a trot. It was an unprecedented speed for that animal. Lucy dropped the switch and swung up onto the tailgate when it came to her. She sat there for a moment in the runaway wagon, brushing the root dirt from her hands. It was not bad soil here: damp, tacky, clayey. A moment later there was a Ho! and a Hey! and wild curses from the front of the wagon. The leather traces creaked and Lucy lay back, satisfied that the wagon had regained its pilot.

After that brief pause their journey accelerated. Quinto urged the ox forward with quick flicks of the reins. So they were getting close: close to what? At one point the way became a little rough and Lucy looked out from the wagon and saw that they were no longer on a road at all. They had angled out across the pinelands, bumping over wiregrass clumps, driving past big Corinthian tree trunks broad enough to put the whole ox in their shadow.

Then as quickly as they'd come into the pines they left them again. They rolled down into a leafy hammock and came into the presence of water, the ox once again knowing it before they did. Yet Quinto did not quit there but instead drove the lowing animal around the pool of water and cussed it faster into the adjoining woods down a little deer trail amidst the snapping of saplings and the crash of brush. At last they came to a clearing.

They could hardly see what was there because it was dusk. They made a meager camp and slept in the bed of the wagon. When morning came they woke up and saw the place for the first time. The trees stood off twenty yards in every direction from the center of the clearing and there was a quilt of grasses. A lone dogwood stood in the middle, abloom like Easter.

They walked around slowly, quietly. Then Nat came back to the wagon and began pulling things out of it. Crosscut, hand-saw, axe and adze. All the tools of his old trade. He would use them to clear trees if necessary but had no special desire to do so. The tools were most of everything he owned.

The location was good. The springhead they had passed was a close source of water, and the hammocky ground would be good for crops, better than the pinewoods. It was level and plenty big enough for what little they had or dreamed of having. Quinto fixed the ox with tackle and rode it out of the clearing. While he was gone Lucy walked around the place alone, look-ing, listening.

Nat came back with four whole pine trees dragging behind the ox. He split the limbs off the young trees and piled them up for the beams of a lean-to. Lucy took a drawknife and went to gather palmetto fronds. Soon they had collected all the neces-sary materials, though the pile did not look like the makings of a house. It did not look like much of anything. They both eyed it dubiously.

They slept in the bed of the wagon while the house was being built. Nat set the pine trunks upright in augered holes. They stood there like four living trees. Between these posts they set beams, lashed together with palmetto fiber at the joints. Lucy layered the green fronds on top for a roof.

Quinto set to making a floor with split tree trunks. At the end of the second day he called to Lucy. She had been out sowing corn; she came inside and smiled. The house was bigger and squarer than their old place in the lumber town. The puncheon floor was clean and white as ivory, and the whole place smelled tremendously of pine. They brought in their two chairs and their table and just sat for a while. Then they brought in the bed.

The dog which had been following the wagon came and set up there too. It stayed on the outskirts of the clearing at first, then moved closer to the center when they did not drive it off. Eventually, Lucy confessed. 'I gave it food, Nat. Well? Do you think that's wrong? Should I of just let it die walking?' But Nat was smiling, and went to the dog and evaluated it honestly, saying it was a good thing Lucy had done. He named the dog Cadge.

All of a sudden, they had the makings of a garden and the makings of a house and a dog too. During those furious few days they had barely held a conversation. They spoke about the dog, or said small things like A little farther over there, Luce, or Plant them chickens there under the oak, or Where to put the ox pen? But there was no real conversation; they were too close for that, moving too much in unison.

It was a good season. They ate through their sacks of corn and sweet potatoes and barreled salt pork like they knew they would. But as those supplies dwindled they began to make up the difference with poke greens, hearts of palm, and cattails from the pond ground into flour, as Nat had heard it was done in Florida.

In that way their old life shaded into the new one, with added bounties. The spring ran cool and deep, with a pleasant flavor. An orange tree sprang up. Deer presented themselves for the slaughter. The chickens could not stop laying eggs. As summer ended their food stores were almost empty and the garden they had planted was not yet ready, but still they ate pretty well. Soon they would have no need for the grubby old storebought corn and potato sacks anymore.

But then it rained. Of course it did. It had been a dry and mild summer, too dry to last, too good to trust, though of course they had trusted it. First came a big tropical storm. Nat Quinto looked up one day and saw clouds massed in the east the likes of which he'd never seen before. True oceangoing thunderheads birthed in the Atlantic and bound for the Gulf with little heed for the narrow peninsula between them. When he looked up again an hour later they barely seemed to have moved. But they were moving, and by late afternoon had arrived, grim and greenly flickering, shotten with the earth's healing waters.

They sat inside listening as the rain hit. It rattled against the walls and the stiff wind toyed at the roof's edges and threatened to strip it piece by piece. The house accounted well for itself but not well enough. The water didn't pour in, it just trickled. That was how everything got wet. Clothing and bedding, tallow and wick, everything. They spent days and nights inside in the dark, on a damp mattress, eating handfuls of damp corn and a few pieces of venison and some berries. After the first four days of rain Lucy Quinto was seized with panic. 'Are we going to drown?' she asked. Everything outside of the house was water and everything inside it was becoming water too. 'Are we going to drown here?' Nat said no, they were not, but they began to see that even if God did not drown them in a flood there were other ways to die from rain. It was a matter of eating. Nat could not go and hunt—all the wild animals were cowering just like they were—and anyway his gunpowder had gotten wet. They could not start a fire to cook—there was nothing that would take a flame anywhere in that landscape. The chickens had all fled to the trees, and the ox haunted the marshes. They let Cadge the dog inside. She lay pitifully on the floor and was not dry for three days, filling the room with her smell.

None of the rains that followed were as strong as that first one. But they didn't need to be. They followed back to back over the course of a month, establishing new ponds, swelling creeks into rivers, and shrinking the earth wholesale. During the breaks Nat and Lucy would go outside to patch the roof with new fronds and Nat would hurry down to the pond to try for some catfish on his single fishhook. He couldn't cook the few fish he caught, because he could not start a fire, so instead he sank them raw into a brine barrel in the hopes that they would be edible someday.

Sometimes they sat and talked. Sometimes they just sat. Sometimes they fought bitterly. Sometimes they told each other stories about what their life was going to be like soon. And oftentimes when the rain got too loud they'd spend a wordless hour hand in hand with their eyes shut in what was unaccountable as anything other than prayer.

The rain did stop, eventually. There was one last round of storms and then it was over. The sun shone like it hadn't in weeks. Quinto went out to look around.

One half of their clearing was a little lower than the other and it had become a pond. Floating in it were the bodies of several drowned snakes and what he recognized as three of his chickens. Next to that, the smokehouse he'd been building had fallen in on itself. Worst of all—he hated to see it—was the garden. The rows ran straight down into the flooded area with the dead snakes. But even the parts still on solid ground were destroyed. The shoots of corn had bent double and turned brown. The sprigs of the sweet potatoes were plastered to the ground, signposts for untold ruin below. The squashes had just started to grow before the rains started; now they lay there like forms dredged up from the ocean's floor and deposited on land, sucked shapeless and covered in a substance like pus where they lolled on the soil, steeping in their own liquors.

Quinto took stock of all of this. Then he came back to the doorway. He sat and looked out at the reeking remains of his homestead and the man put his head in his hands and moaned like a bear.

II.

THEY DIDN'T SPEAK on the wagon ride to the roadhouse. He dismounted and lifted her down, and they still didn't speak. Walking up to the place, she hung three or four paces behind him.

They walked in through an open door which might never have been shut since the day it was hung. The place smelled of rabbit tobacco and boiled chicory. Quinto stood in the bottle-neck of the room waiting for his eyes to adjust. 'Hello,' he said after a moment.

'How do,' said the nearest person, a huddled shape at the bar.

'I'm Nat Quinto.'

'And I'm Missus Nat Quinto,' Lucy said stiffly.

'We-e-ell,' said that nearest person, his smile audible if not quite visible. 'Newcomers. Passerbyers. Guestfolk. Now ain't that an occasion for some of the old Santy Rosito Extro Viejo? Who else wants a drink? Oh, we'd better take a drink.'

Quinto ignored the offer. 'I've got some things I wanter trade for food and seed,' he said, 'or else to sell for money. Knives—skinning knife, frow, draw, butcher, and bowie knife. I'd sell any three of the five. Also got sixty feet good hemp rope.

Also got two china dishes and two china plates.' These last items represented half of their wedding gift from Lucy's aunt. If they sold them they would have exactly one dish and one plate each, no spares. Lucy had cradled them in her lap all the way to the roadhouse.

'Anyone wants to make an offer can go head,' Nat said.

The nearest man sucked his teeth. Another man belched gravely. A third cleared his throat—and now all of the occupants had been heard from.

The throat-clearer spoke. 'Thatus a fair sight of rain we got, weren't it, friend?'

Nat Quinto ran his hand down his face. 'Good God almighty,' he said, his voice almost breaking.

A tall woman pushed into the room from the back, carrying a tray of cornbread. 'A fair rain,' she echoed. 'If you lived through that you'll live yet.'

The proprietress. The tray of cornbread was very large but Mrs. Monroe carried it with one big-knuckled hand. She slid it down the bartop. 'Come and sit.'

There was no refusing this person, her strong voice and harsh benevolence. The lady of the house matched the house itself: tall and imposing, with handsome grey-black hair. The couple sat down as instructed, and the lady went to the back again.

While they ate the cornbread with gallberry honey, the other patrons talked quietly. Soon Nat started fishing around for a means to pay. The throat-clearing man saw this and spoke up again.

'Yes, a fair piece of rain, a fair piece of rain,' the man said. 'A hard rain. Even harder for any poor sap what didn't have a storehouse built and some crops saved up or didn't have livestock to eat. Any fool who'd put himself through that, I wouldn't envy such a one. No, I would not.'

Nat looked at the speaker through the murk. He was small-ish sandy-colored young man, quick-eyed like someone who has known real hunger once and not long ago. But now he wore a silk hat, with a huge red feather jutting from the band. When he threw his head back to laugh the feather went with it.

'Oh, hell,' he said. 'That's me, that's me I'm talking about. A rank fool, as usual. My whole crop's ruint, the corn's ruint, everything—everything save the rice. Thank God for rice, I guess. All the rest is done for. That's what my man tells me, anyway. I cain't be bothered with all that myself. I don't worry about a few vegetable plants more or less. Myself, all I see is cows, cows, and I never known one of them to get root rot. Do you see? I'm a cowman, that's what I am.'

'A cowman,' said Quinto. 'Well, I've an idea a cowman might have use for sixty foot Virginia hemp rope.'

The other man waved his hand. 'Poh. Ain't a need for hemp rope. I'll tell you what there's need for in this territory—decent cowhands. There's need for a fair man on the muscle. Much like you look to be yourself. A fellow who can use a dragwhip. There's need—'

'I'm sure there is,' Quinto said. 'But that ain't my concern. My concern is to part with a few of my goods, or else I'm looking to head out of this rumhouse.'

'Jake Primrose is hiring men on at a half-dollar a day,' the man continued. 'That's worth two of your little lengths of rope right there.'

There was a slow intake of breath from Lucy on her stool. Nat heard it. He shifted a little in his own seat, put his feet on the floor. 'Well,' he said. 'This Primrose sounds like a generous chap. But I cain't see as I much care what his business is, unless you hear he's looking for a good drawknife. In which case give him my regards. Gentlemen,' he said, getting to his feet. 'Ma'am.' He called toward the back. 'You'll be hearing from me about that cornbread. I'm new to this country, but you'll be hearing from me. Set it down under Quinto.' He turned and he and Lucy walked toward the door.

'I don't believe you think much of cow work,' the man called out. 'No, you believe you're too high for any such tumbling work. Fine Georgia clayeater like yourself.'

Nat stopped walking, but he did not turn around. 'I hope I'm equal,' he said, 'to whatever work they give such loud-talkers as is around here.'

'Equal, hell,' the other man said. 'You ain't equal to the pickaninny blacks my boots.'

'Pickaninny?' Nat said. 'Well. There's worse things to be.' He kept walking.

The voice called to him, high and plaintive. 'Where are you going, you skinny bastard? I intend to fight you.'

Nat stopped and let out a sigh. 'Well,' he grumbled. 'Then come out.' And he stepped through the door.

Lucy trotted alongside him. 'Hey, hey Nat,' she said. 'You, Nat.' But his jacket was already off and the occupants of the roadhouse were coming outside, with the sandy-haired man in the rear, hatless and coatless, a loopy gleam in his eye from the cupful of rum he'd just swallowed.

They circled one time, then came together. The man jabbed a right fist that crushed Quinto's lips against his teeth. Blood came quickly and the man swung again, hit Quinto's mouth again, making a wet sound, blood spattering the front of his shirt.

'There,' Quinto said, 'that's woke me.' He came forward with a grin and stepped through a punch that put his opponent lengthwise onto the ground. The man groaned and tried to raise himself but Quinto rolled him with a swift kick. Nat waited for him to stand, twitching his hands at the wrists, then caught him flat on the nose. It broke easily, like one that has been broken before and the last time not long ago. But this did not seem to bother the stranger. He stood jigging on his toes with a bright look in his eyes and his nose slightly askance. Then he sprang forward and struck Quinto twice, once in each eye. Staggered, Nat tried to catch the stranger's arms to tie him up but missed. He managed to shove off and stumble back a couple of feet. Lucy said his name, *Nat*, then again, *Nat, oh Lord, stop it Nat.*

He squinted at her, sitting high up on the bench of the wagon like a Caesar weighing fates. Then he came forward and threw a punch which originated from his own jaw and carried him through, grunting, like a man hurling shotput. It landed on the stranger's jawbone and the man fell flat onto his back. He lay there in the dirt unmoving.

Quinto watched him for a moment. Then he ejected some of the blood from his mouth and proceeded toward the wagon. He picked up his hat and gave the roadhouse men a quick wave. 'Gennelmen,' he said through thickened lips. 'Come inquire about them knives.'

He got a half-wave from one of the men busy with trying to revive the fallen combatant. The ox was not excited by the battle and it took several thumps before it started moseying down the forest road.

'Why,' Lucy was saying, 'why, you brute, you savage, you gamecock, why would ye make such a commotion as that, why would ye throw things into a jumble like that, cain't ye live among men without facing them, you bullhead, cain't ye live normal, cain't ye stand peace?' He sat and explained as best he could while she applied a rag to his wounds, with more pressure than was necessary.

'Honey, Lucy,' Nat groaned, 'he asked for it, didn't you hear him? I couldn't leave him without a fight when he asked for it so, don't you unnerstand? I couldn't, it'd be lowdown, it'd be cruel.'

'Oh, that was it? For him asking for it you mashed his nose and beat him senseless? I know you, Quinto, you put your pride into thatun. Your heart was in that, you gamecock.'

He groaned again. 'Maybe. Maybe I did. I wanted to kill the bastard. I don't know what sparked me. Something in the talk about—claiming me. The talk of hiring me on. I couldn't stand it somehow. My pride couldn't bear it, Luce. The thought of coming down here to end up a bonded man, same as in Georgia.'

'And so you beat him. For talk of hiring you a job.'

'It weren't just that.'

'How much was he trying to get you paid?'

'Fifty saints a day.'

Lucy didn't say anything awhile. Nat watched the pale flanks of the ox roll and roll them through the clinging underbrush.

Soon they were home. Nat undid the ox and left it by the ruined garden in hopes it would eat some of the slops. He brought their sellable things inside and sat at the white table with his hands in his hair and Lucy tended to him, more carefully this time.

'Primrose was the name,' Nat said. 'I bet that jackass I fought was his main man. I bet they'll come ride on me soon and give me Jesse. Well, they can give me Jesse if they want. I won't fold to them. Cain't. But damn me, fifty saints a day. And found, he said. Yah—that hurts, darling. Softer, softer, please. Good. There. Oh Luce. What'll we do. It's September. September, then October, then winter after that. We'll make it all right, it'll just be root-hog season, that's all. We knew it'd be root-hog times for us. But good God, that rain—'

'Who's that?' said Lucy.

There was a horse stepping into the clearing, two horses. It was the man from the roadhouse. Nat got his gun down from over the door, though he did not bother priming it. It would not shoot anyway, with the ruined gunpowder. He came a ways outside of the house and stood with the musket under his arm.

The man's face had been cleaned somewhat but blood still ran freely from his nose down the middle of his face. His eyes were glazed, a little flat. Someone had put the feather hat back on top of his head.

'Get out of here,' Quinto said.

'Come on, you fool,' the man said. 'I'm asking you one more time. Pack a saddlebag and mount up. We're leaving tomorrow—'

'We're leaving nowhere,' Quinto said. 'Turn your ass around. If your damned Primrose wants me he can come and get me, but otherwise—'

'Oh, for God's sake,' said the battered figure on horseback. 'I am Jake Primrose, you fool.'

Quinto glared at the two riders. His gun stayed where it was, though perhaps it tilted downward a little. 'I am Jake Primrose,' the first rider repeated. 'And you, friend, you punch like an eight-foot Irishman. I can't not have you. I've got to get you. I'm asking again.'

Still Quinto stared. The man in the hat, a giddy light in his eyes; the second stranger, with a musket sheathed in his saddle. 'Oh, come, man. Can't we talk just a moment? Just for neighborliness, anyhow?'

Lucy spoke at his back. 'Let them in, Nat,' she said.

He set his gun down on the butt end and stepped back from the door. 'One moment,' he said wearily. 'Neighborliness.'

Lucy and Jake Primrose sat in the two chairs. Nat stood, as did the second man, who introduced himself as Herb Nail. He seemed to be there mostly as an amused witness. Primrose sat talking with a fresh cloth pressed against his nose and his head tilted back, looking around the room with one eye.

'Here's how it stands, Quinto,' he said in a nasal voice. 'I have nine hunnert head in and around my marsh. That makes me a cowman of some size in this country. Came into them through a Indin I knew named Hadjo. Dear old Hadjo, blessed be his memory. The cows ain't all marked but they're all mine, all of em. Ain't it so, Herb?' He turned his good eye to the second man, who nodded.

'I own the cows, but they don't drover theyselves. I need muscle, and you, sir, represent a decent portion of the muscle to be found in this godforsaken territory. That's why I'm here.'

'Name terms,' Quinto said.

'Seventy-five cents a day,' Primrose said. 'But that ain't but the nub of it. I'll get ye a horse, yours to ride, yours to keep. And you'll work for what we all work for, which is calves. Work two months and you'll get a share of the calves we've gathered at the end.'

'Calves.'

'I'd guess at the end of the hunt you'll have around five knotheads. All told, that's a good little seed herd you stand to get. The dollars, that ain't but playstuff. You know that. It's the cattle you do it for.'

Quinto stood, thumbs in his pockets, looking Primrose in the eye.

'I have a wife, Primrose,' Quinto said quietly. 'I don't know if you see.'

'I see,' said Primrose, and smiled around at her from under his cloth.

'Shape up, man,' growled Quinto. 'I've got a wife. I won't leave her empty here.'

'Hell, man, I've got one of them too,' said Primrose. 'Have her come stay on my place while the drive is on. She can live under my roof, there's rations for—'

'Ha,' said Quinto. 'She'd never.'

'Well, then, here's all I can tell you. Take a week's pay up front. Take a week's pay and ride for supplies. That money right there, that's corn, pork, coffee, sugar. Take a cow up front too and slaughter it, there's enough beef for weeks. All that and whatever's scrounging on this plot, that'll be enough. It's only a temporary solution, it's only rations. It ain't no way to make a life. But then, neither is this.' He waved a hand over the homeplace. 'And you know it.' He met Quinto's gaze unsmiling, with his quick and clear-eyed and greatly unsentimental look of a man who has known hunger himself and not long ago.

Herb Nail came out behind them, holding two hats. Primrose took his and handed Nat the bloodied cloth from his face. 'You whipped me, Mister Quinto,' he said, 'and I thank you for it. It's been too long since anyone's tried.' He put his hat on. The two men mounted up and rode out of the clearing.

It was the smallest horse Quinto had ever seen. He said as much to the redheaded youth who handed him the reins.

'Aw heck, she ain't small. She's jist purebred marshtackie. That's the best little horse for this country you can find, runs like the wind, won't tire, won't quit. My daddy roped her daddy out of yonder marsh. They grow all up in there. Jist grow all up in there.'

The sun had established itself on the eastern horizon. Thin orange light sliced through the pines and the men moving in the barred darkness took up their movements from frame to frame as if through slits in a zoetrope: Man Leading Horse. Currying the Ponies. A Country Conversation.

'Yes sir, Mister Quinto, best horse you can find for this country, runs like the wind, won't tire, won't quit.'

With the boy's whistling praise, Quinto took another look at the animal. It was indeed short, and close-coupled. But the body was muscular and heavy in the back, ending in a set of massive hooves, good for wet ground. The neck was slender and shapely and its eyes were beautiful, though unpeaceful, rolling with a wildness barely broken. She looked like she wanted to run.

'A marshtackie, you call it,' Quinto said. 'What's her name?'

'Tell,' said a man just coming up. He rode one horse and brought another, handled both with the slow gentleness of an old liveryman. He was redspeckled like the young man, though bonier, and lacking hair.

'Thatun's name Tell. Marshtackie. The finest horse for this country. Runs like the wind, won't tire, won't quit.'

'That's my daddy,' the young man confided. 'His name's Shay Tercer. We're Tercers.'

'Is that so,' replied Quinto conversationally.

They left the pines and came up to a house. It was a cabin not much bigger than Quinto's. There was another man there, named Smith, standing quiet and sullen. It was too early in the morning for him and he yawned hugely, revealing empty gums in the front of his mouth. He closed his mouth again to reveal small piggish eyes. He and Nat Quinto and the Tercers made four.

They all turned to look at the house when the door opened. Jake Primrose stepped out onto the porch. He'd traded his feathered hat for a dark felt broadbrim, like the other cowhunters wore. He gazed around at them.

'Well, I count four. Four's good. But I hired six. Where's Little Tom and Old Rouchefort? Where are they, Oscar?'

'Coming from Missus Monroe's, I'd guess,' murmured this Oscar, a slave, who emerged from around the house.

'Pissfire,' said Primrose. 'We'll be waiting here till the jug runs out.'

Just then two more riders came slouching into the clearing. An ancient named Old Rouchefort, trailing a long white beard, followed by the mestizo they called Little Tom—not a little man at all; somebody's son, then, to have gotten that name. Little Tom was dark-skinned and Rouchefort was as white as bone, but their eyes burned the same color red.

'So I guess the jug ran out,' Primrose said.

'Hell, Jake,' said Rouchefort. 'We ain't been drinking.' He lifted his leg slowly to dismount. 'We was just saying goodbye to the boys.' He continued to be dismounting for about half a minute.

Jake Primrose came down from the porch. He approached Quinto and stuck out his hand. 'Nat,' he said. They shook. 'I'm glad to see you here.'

'Jake,' said Quinto.

The cowman stepped back. 'But where's your gun?'

''Tain't with me.'

'But I thought you'd have it, Nat.'

'It's in Lucy's hands right now, loaded, with new powder,' Quinto said. 'And it won't leave her hands for the next two months.'

Primrose breathed out. 'Well,' he said, and went over to Old Rouchefort's horse and pulled a breechloader down from where it lay across the saddle.

'My gun,' said the old man.

'My gun,' said Primrose.

'Hell, your gun,' the old man mumbled. 'Yours, yes, it is yours after all.'

Primrose brought it to Quinto and handed it to him. Nat did not take it, but the man pressed it into his arms and then stepped away.

Primrose went to look over a kennelful of dogs, examining each in turn. Then he went to where the slave was loading a mule with branding irons, circles of calf rope. He spoke to the man sharply about tying the items tighter and then stepped away.

Nat Quinto turned to the person nearest to him, Little Tom. 'Say, friend,' Quinto said. 'How did Jake come into all these cows he's got, anyhow? Do you know?'

Little Tom was tending to his marshtackie. He adjusted the saddle with slow, sure motions while the horse ate Primrose's feed.

'He got the cows off Hadjo,' he said in a soft voice. 'Indin named Hadjo. They had to leave this place quick, him and his woman. And he never put a brand on no cows, so Jake got em. Jake got em.' He shrugged the cinch tighter on his saddle.

'What happened to that Indin?' Quinto asked.

'I wish I knew.' Tom stared sadly past the saddle as he straightened it. 'My mother wisht she knew. Hadjo's kin is her kin. Or used to be.'

He moved away and Quinto looked around the yard. It was a rough simple place like any other in that territory, with a few signs of incipient wealth here and there—lace curtains billowing in a window, bright new saddle on the owner's horse. But Primrose was not as sure of himself as he had seemed at the saloon. When he handed each rider a dragwhip he did not say anything about how to use it, seeming to think that any one of them could work it as well as he or better. Soon he mounted onto his horse and left out of the clearing, toward the herds.

The others mounted up one by one and lined out after him, each at his own pace. Oscar was the last to leave; he pulled a pin on the kennel and the dog pack swelled from its hatch out into the open land, barking freely, pissing freely, roiling down the narrow path like floodwater and carrying the horses along in its froth.

They rode all morning. When they reached the marsh, the early autumn day was hot enough to crease the air above the damp bottomland. The men removed the vests and jerkins they'd worn for the cold dawn. Now in greyish shirtsleeves they stood on a small rise and looked out.

It was not as far as the eye could see—the marsh rounded off a quarter mile away in a curve of trees. But the whole area was filled to bursting with cows. Their horns showed all the way across the space, bright and glimmering.

They stood there for a while. Their party lacked one person, Shay Tercer. But then he joined them out of the woods at his placid pace. He had captured a yearling calf and draped it across the front of his saddle. The calf had given up struggling, was now just bleating. Tercer smiled around at them. 'Firstuns,' he said.

Quinto and Tercer's son, Zill, hustled off for twigs and branches. Before long they had built a fire there on the bluff and Primrose produced a brand and set it in the heart of the flames. It read $\mathcal{P}$. Old Shay Tercer sat up on his horse, watching the ceremony, his hands on the calf's flank.

Soon the iron was cherry-red and they lifted the animal down and dropped it on its side. It lay there breathing. The youth Zill pinned its hind legs and the slave Oscar pinned the forelegs. Primrose took up the brand and brought it over. The calf eyed him and as the bright $\mathcal{P}$ drew closer and closer to its skin it twitched and jerked and bucked sideways and yanked its legs free from young Tercer, who was also staring at the brand. It dug both hooves into the dirt and with all its strength bucked free from Oscar. In a second was wailing off down the slope toward the herd.

Zill wailed too and sprinted after the animal. 'Son,' bellowed Shay Tercer, but he did not listen, and first the calf and then the boy disappeared between the flanks of the herd. Shay was already after them on his horse.

No one else moved. They cursed. They stood there on the bluff and watched old Tercer ride through the midst of the cattle, watched the cattle move away from him, bellowing, confused. Jake Primrose jumped on his own horse and made to ride but Little Tom grabbed his reins and held him. 'They'll break, they'll stampede, damn you,' Primrose said.

'Hold, man,' Tom hissed. They stood watching. They could only see Tercer from the waist up as he swam among the horns. Something like a yell or scream reached their ears and they all cursed again and Primrose tried to ride down again but still Little Tom held him.

Then Tercer wheeled around and started back toward the men gathered on the bluff. The cows parted before him and hustled away, moaning. When he reached the edge of the herd they saw the boy. Tercer had caught his son up and slung him over the front of his saddle, just as he had carried the calf, and was holding him there by the belt as they rode out of the herd. Tercer came up the bluff but did not stop where the others were. Instead he rode straight into the trees. There was a sound of shouting, and then a sound of blows being exchanged, one for one. This went on for only a few seconds before it stopped and was replaced by the sound of hard open weeping.

The others took seats by the tree trunk and attempted conversation about other things. Oscar paid the least mind of anyone, did not even bother with talking but only whittled at a piece of wood. A few minutes later old Shay came out from the trees. There was a little bit of blood under his nose, which he had smeared away with a shirtsleeve, but his face was once again placid, composed. He went over to his horse and with a slight frown began coiling a length of rope that had become disheveled on his ride.

Something must have passed between him and Primrose because Primrose stepped away into the trees himself. He was there a few minutes and then reemerged with his arm over young Zill's shoulder. 'All right, boys,' said Primrose, smiling at them and winking.

The young man fastened his gaze on the dirt one yard in front of his feet and allowed himself to be walked over to his horse. His shirt had come out very badly from his adventure, shredded along the back by cow horns, ripped at the collar by his father. He came and stood by his horse with his hands in his pockets, looking out at the marsh with a fat lip.

'Well,' announced old Tercer. 'Don't know what the hell we're waiting on to get to work.'

'By God, Shay, you've said it,' said Primrose gaily. 'Yes sir, let's start her up, yes sir.' The elder Tercer was already hunkering down onto his heels with a dry stick, and all of the hands approached to watch him scratch a diagram in the loose dirt.

The party split into halves, each one taking a portion of the dogs, keeping them in check with whistles and quick words. The two groups came midway along the marsh on opposite sides of the herd. At the signal of a waved hat a rider on each side rode out across it, cutting a moat through the mass of cattle. The others waited on the bluff with the dogs and as the herd began to part and scatter they took up their whips and received the slowly fleeing cows with cracks and pops. They funneled them into a broad column, the dogs doing as they had been bred to do, racing among the many legs to nip and harry them into order, the cowmen calling them off when they'd pursue the odd maverick into the woods. The men whooped and the cattle stamped a deep channel in the sodden ground, shaking the earth enough to make the brittler leaves fall off of nearby trees. The twenty dogs' barking and the eight men's whooping and even the nine hundred cows' own bellowing were nearly lost in the thunder of hooves as they exited the marsh and hit the trees.

They bent the herd toward the north. Driving them was more difficult in the dense forest. The whipcracks became constant as the men used their noise to signal their positions, unable to see one another or even the cows thirty feet ahead of them in the seething underbrush. It was a half-mile of blind fumbling through the bottomland near the marsh, but finally they reached the pines. It was better there; the riders could see the length and breadth of the herd and could wave to their fellow hands a ways off.

They reached the pens in an hour. They'd have gone slower but wanted to get to them well before sunset and have all the cows secure and the gates latched by dark. They succeeded. All the cattle crashed into the big lot in a confusion of voices and popping whips and at last the heavy gate was pulled shut. The men dismounted and stood around a while in the swirling rich dust of the pinewoods, too dazed to wipe the grit from their faces, let alone to congratulate one another on what they'd done.

At twilight they sat down to some salt pork and corn pone and about ten gallons of black coffee. Little Tom had gone and found a honeycomb from a tree and they all put some of the honey into their cups. The young man in his torn shirt took his food and stalked off to sit by himself in the shadows, sullen today. His father did not watch him go.

Quinto sat back on his saddlebag, eating a piece of honeycomb. 'Aw hell, he's a good boy, Shay,' he said. 'He's a good boy, that's all. Ain't he, Oscar?'

Oscar sat with a piece of wood, working it with short, intricate movements of a knife. 'Sure he is, sure he is,' he nodded. 'Sure he is. Sure.'

Shay Tercer did not respond to them. He was standing up, pacing a little, looking out at the mass of cattle where they stood astoundingly quiet in the darkness.

'What's on your mind, old fellow?' asked Quinto. 'Didn't it go well today? Hell, I thought it was fine. All them knotheads hollering and stamping, but we held em all, ain't we, ever last one, and no mistake. One whang of the whip and those bulls just jump back in line. Eight hunnert pounds apiece but they listen to a fellow. It ain't bad work, is it? It ain't bad tusslin stuff, is it, this cow work?'

Oscar had gotten a small cut up one side of his face from a bull's horn and when he turned to speak the wound gleamed in the light. 'It's the finest work a man can do,' he said. He pronounced each word with finality.

'Hell yes, it is, I believe it is,' said Quinto.

They were all quiet for a while, chewing. Then the man Smith sucked air between his missing front teeth. 'You bet Oscar thinks it's good work,' he said. 'Old darkie gets cows at the end of it, just like we do.'

Oscar examined the pork he was eating. 'Sometimes,' he said. 'I might get a calf after the yearly drive if Mister Primrose can spare it. If it's hurt, or runty. I doctor them as I can. Managed to gather six little head, nice little head, got them out behind some swampland.'

Smith looked around at the rest of them and shook his head. 'Ain't that the damnedest. Darkie's working up a herd right aside us. It all just goes to show what type of a man we've got in Jake Primrose. What type of a heart he's got. Allowing cattle to his blacks! He's as kindly and goodly and whitehearted a gent as you'll find.'

'Whitehearted,' agreed Old Rouchefort, getting a little misty.

'I just hope you know your blessings, old fellow,' Smith went on. 'Just hope you know what a friend your black hide has got in Jake Primrose. Oh, you better keep on and service him as good as you can, service him faithful, for all the good things he does for you.'

Oscar kept whittling. 'Swap spots if you'd like it so much,' he murmured. 'Yes, it's a soft and easy life I've got here. Go on take it, yellowhead, it's ever so balmy and pleasant.'

Smith was not listening to him. He was well pleased with the speech he'd made and fell into conversation with Old Rouchefort about their employer's goodness.

Oscar turned to Quinto, who was sitting next to him. He spoke low and hurtful, nearly a spit. 'Oh, they take what they given, they take what they given, you ought to see them. Fah. I'll take what I'm given, all right. Turn me loose to shift a lick for myself and see what comes of it.'

He turned away, speaking mostly to himself now. 'I got more cows than theter Smith anyway, and he's a free man, that's the hell of it. Twice the cattleman he is. I'd move a thousand head within five years. Turn me loose to shift a lick and see.'

Quinto took another bite of his pork. 'Let me know when that happens, old man,' he said. 'We'll go halves.' Quinto sat there eating and Oscar sat there not eating and neither of them spoke anymore, side by side with their very different silences.

Primrose instituted watches. A man awake at every hour, all through the night. Little Tom had the last shift and thanks to his efforts there was hot coffee, and hoecakes and pork frying, by the time the rest opened their eyes. They got up happy and acclaimed him a great soul. After eating they each stood up with final throatfuls of the coke-black coffee and went to the pens for the second day's work, which would be branding and notching ears on the marsh herd.

Smith and old Tercer had the finer job, the earmarking. They gave each unmarked cow's ear a notch. By midmorning the ground where they stood was littered as if by the autumn of some strange tree: scraps of kiteshaped velveteen with the barest rimming of blood. The branders' job was much ruder. All day scrabbling in the dirt. Each unmarked cow or calf had to be wrestled down, branded, and moved into the next chamber of the pen. Each man took a turn as the thrower: he put one hand on each horn and gave a swift hard twist and hoped the beast would fall on its side in the dust. Each new cow that came along was a new contest, a struggle in which the outcome was not at all guaranteed. These were big animals for woods cows and not really mellowed by their time on Primrose's plush marsh. Each one's gaze was fierce and terrific even as the catchdogs held their faces in their jaws. They glared at their human combatants and no thrower could fight more than six or seven of them in a row before he would have to be spelled. Except for Nat Quinto. By reason of freshness on the job or some wellspring of strength in his lean knotty frame, he could throw cows by the tens, by the dozens—he might have thrown half a hundred at a stretch if they didn't pull him away, worried for the man. He was angry the first couple of times this happened, but after that he was more tractable and let himself be put on an easier post for a while.

They broke at noon, started back at noon thirty, and fought straight through until dusk. They didn't quit until they'd marked every one of the unbranded cows in the herd. And yet leaving the field they did not look like victors; they looked badly beaten.

A quiet supper. Primrose left for somewhere west without explanation. The men stared at their sweet potatoes. They livened up a little when the coffee jug came. Young Zill Tercer turned chatty. He had apparently forgotten how the day before had crushed him; he had sprung back upright, the way green things do. He flitted around the clearing with a mad bounce in his stride, pestering Oscar, testing Quinto, spitting in the fire, and talking assuredly about the work to come. 'This is the way to live, I say,' he said. 'I don't see why a body don't just stay out with them cows all times. I don't see why he ever goes back, a couple months on, a couple months off. I say if he likes the house he should stay at it, and leave cattle work to us who prefers it. Why would a man fool around with all them other chores, and sleep on a farm?'

'Because a man has a wife and some children,' Oscar said.

'Nuts,' said Zill, and kicked the dirt. 'That's soft talk. Darkie, you and Dad sound just the same, you could be brothers.' At this the boy rolled his eyes over to the father and turned silent. He clenched his jaw hard as if to hold back words that had already gotten loose.

But old Tercer said nothing. He did not seem to have heard. He was standing away from the fire, looking off at the quiet cattle, as he had done the night before. Just standing, an absent look on his face.

There was no sound except for the flicking of Oscar's knife in the wood. Until Quinto gathered himself and spoke up.

'In a way, I agree with the lad. This is a pretty good life. Don't you think, Shay?'

The man did not say anything.

'Hell, Shay, come and set with us. You ain't but sniffed your coffee. It's—'

'This ain't no right cow hunt,' Tercer said.

Quinto peered at him over the fire. 'What do you mean.'

'I mean it ain't no right cow hunt.'

'Shay,' said Old Rouchefort. 'Come on here, have some coffee. You—'

'This ain't the right season, to start with,' he said. 'I knowed that at the first. We're a month early almost. And then there's the new setup. Why do we have night watches? What are we watching for? I ain't never heard of sich a thing.'

'Shay,' said Old Rouchefort.

Tercer went on, his voice quavering. 'Shouldn't be no need for night watches. The cows are penned. Ain't none getting out, ain't none getting in. It don't stand to reason, unless there's a reason I ain't been told. And then—'

Oscar stopped carving. 'Come on set down,' he growled.

'And then there's the guns,' Tercer said loudly, and spat. 'There's too many goddamned guns.'

He did come to the fire, now. His horse blanket was already there.

'I'll take the second watch,' he said. 'Shake me round midnight.' He lay down, rolled away from the fire, and did not speak again.

Nat Quinto sat up at watch on a little mound near the pens. It was about two in the morning and he had his rifle across his knees and a cup of coffee in his hand. It was a good, high position, and despite the scanty moonlight it was easy to see Jake Primrose riding up on horseback.

The cattleman spoke before Quinto could. 'Where's Tercer,' he asked.

Quinto did not respond, but Primrose was not waiting for his answer anyway. He rode straight down toward the camp. 'Tercer,' he said. His voice was too loud for the night. 'Tercer, get up and speak with me.'

Quinto came down toward the campfire. Primrose was standing there talking and all of the sleeping men stirred. 'Shay. Shay, I need to speak with you about thisyer herd.'

Shay Tercer was sitting up straight and looking at Primrose, fully awake. Maybe he had never been asleep. 'What's the matter, Jake?' he said.

'The matter is my cows, man. And I've a notion you've noticed. Hell, you probably noticed before I did.'

'What've you seen, Jake?'

'I seen nine hundred and twelve cows rounded up from the marsh. Among those are exactly two hundred calves." He breathed through his nostrils. 'When I counted the marsh herd in May, there were exactly one hundred ninety-eight calves.'

'Are you sure on that count?' old Tercer said

'I am. I'm certain. One hundred ninety-eight calves in May. Two hundred calves now.'

Gap-mouthed Smith muttered, 'What the hell is the matter with one hunnert ninety-eight—'

'The matter is this, you dumb bastard,' spat Primrose. 'There's near a thousand cows in those pens. You think that between all of them they can't produce but two new calves since May? No sir, no sir. There's something doing. There's something off.'

No one had a good answer for this. They all were silent, even Tercer. 'I see it this way, friends,' Primrose said. 'There's rustlers out on this range. Not any common rustlers, either. Good ones. Or common ones with a good trick. What they do is, they scoop up my she-cows right when they're about to calf. They hold em until the calves is dropped. Then when they's weaned, they slip the mammies back into the herd and keep all the calves for themselves. Simple. Simple.' He stared around the circle, his expression triumphant. 'Do you see it like that, Shay?'

'Afraid I do, Jake,' replied the old man.

'The jack of it is, I cain't claim I'm missing any cows. Because I'm not. There ain't a cow alive with my brand on it that's missing. There ain't a mark astray, there ain't a hair of evidence nowhere. None.' He shook his head and lost some of the boom in his voice. 'But they's my calves. Mine. Ain't no mark on em don't mean they aren't mine by God and by nature. I say that brand on the mother's hide reaches inside of em, to the growing place where the calves is borne in them, and inside that to where the calves' calves is going to be, and on. That's the law of God and nature—ain't it, Shay?'

'Sure, Jake.'

This pacified him. 'Well. All right. So tomorrow, we start up on the main cow hunt. We'll be riding out across these woods, riding and herding and riding and herding. And somewhere out in these woods there's a herd of calves by themselves, just a-lay. Them boys can't have taken them far. They'll have em stashed off somewheres. So watch, watch carefully.' He got back to his horse again. 'You won't miss it. It ain't natural. A herd of calves out there without their mothers—no, you won't miss it.' Without another word he got up and rode his horse away from the campfire.

Quinto had been standing outside the fire and now he took an angle to intercept the cowman. 'Primrose,' he said. 'You, Primrose.'

He slowed. 'Nat,' he said.

'Why did you give me this, Primrose?' he asked. He held up his musket.

'Oh, hell.'

'Listen to me, Primrose. I didn't sign on to be no gun.'

'Oh, hell.'

'I'm not fooling with you, man. I ain't no gun. I ain't no militiaman. I didn't get in for that. You hired me false.'

Primrose's voice dropped half an octave. 'And what would you do about it, Nat?' He stared with his hard, unsentimental gaze. 'You've already thrown in with me. You've already took my money, a whole gold coin I believe. Why, your wife is enjoy-ing the fruits of my generosity as we speak. Yes, man, you've thrown in with me, all the way.'

'You low bastard.'

'That's ingratitude,' said Primrose, and took up his reins again. 'You ain't thinking straight about the thing, Nat. You ain't thinking about the credits and debits of it all. Go back up there and mull it over on the rest of your watch, and you'll see I'm right.'

III.

MORNING CAME TOO EARLY. No one had gotten up before-hand to make breakfast that day. No one had the strength, after the branding work of the day before. They had to help each other up from the ground, they were so sore. They made their way over to their horses and mounted up like wooden men.

They met up on the rise very greyfaced and solemn, especially Nat Quinto, who had a fearsome look. Shay Tercer once again laid out the day's work with a stick. They were going to start hunting the cows which had not been found on the marsh. There was a channel that fed the marsh from the south; they would go there first. It was a fruitful street for cows, Tercer said. They moved down the mucky channel and immediately began seeing signs of loose cattle in those woods. Then they began hearing the cattle, and finally began seeing them hiding in the palmettos.

All day long they popped cows out of their hiding places. There was no sign of the missing calves. Still it was a large yield of adults, enough to be accounted a success on any other day. They sat to eat at dusk, and despite the matter of the calves they ate heartily and recounted all of their various battles and encounters as they normally would. But the talk suddenly evaporated. One by one they stopped eating and listened. They heard wolves to the north.

Primrose got up and began to pace. It sounded like fifty wolves howling. 'Damn it, but we've got to get them,' he said. 'Those calves are out here. I know they are.'

The men at the campfire were all looking at their suppers, not at him. Primrose went on. 'Them rustlers won't leave em out here with the wolves, I don't care who they are. If they've got half a brain they'll stay with them. Yes, they'll be out, I know they will.' He clapped his hands together, and when he spoke next he spoke to the whole group.

'Boys,' he said. 'We'll go tonight. Light up some palmetto clumps and some fatwood and let's go. There ain't but two three more places on this range to hide a herd that size, calves or no. Those yellow bastards will jump off the second they see us coming, they won't be expectin us. They think I'm too soft to move on em without evidence. Well, they'll find out different. And if they don't run? Well, we'll play guns with em. Won't we, fellows?'

'Yes,' said Little Tom. 'Yes.'

'And what'll be the result o' that? Why, a set of the lowest and meanest is rid from this country forever. And that ain't just for me and my brand, that's for you and yours, your children. Do you hear me? And I say this, fellows—' he spread out his hands— 'for them that come, those calves are for the splitting. I mean split even. Each man a cut. There's a hunnert fifty head out there, certain there is, and we're eight men to share em. That's almost twenty calves a man for one night's work, and a country with a few less snakes to raise em in. Do that sound favorable to anyone?'

Little Tom had stood up and was staring across the fire at Primrose and saying *Yes, let's go.* Smith had not stood up but had put his plate aside and was saying similar things. Young Zill Tercer got up. Old Rouchefort eased his way up. Last of all was Quinto but he did get up too. And then suddenly they were all in the saddle, lighting pine knots in the campfire.

The slave Oscar cut a bunch of palm fronds and as they started out he began to light them one by one for the brief brilliant light they gave, letting them drop when they sputtered. They traveled north in this orange glow, north because Primrose said he knew a place in that direction. 'A nice little burn, about ten miles north,' he said. 'There was a lightning strike fire, jist afore that rain we had. It'll be all green grass there by now. It's where our calves will be tonight, boys, I know it, I feel it.'

They rode through twilight into darkness. The wolf cries were warped and muddled by the distance, miles and miles away. Yet as they rode on and the howls did not stop they could tell they were heading directly toward the source. Then the howls suddenly ceased and the only sounds were cicadas and the occasional barred owl and Oscar's constant shuffling of palm fronds for new light.

They found the place after midnight. It was a smallish burn a quarter-mile square, bound on two sides by a crooked creek that had stopped the fire. It was once a brushy bottomland forest but it had burned down to the grit of the soil, and now they could see straight across it to the water, they could see everything. Primrose dismounted and brought his torch to examine the ground. He could see the shoots of grass coming up from the black soil, chewed off to the nub. 'There's been something grazing here,' he called. There were clumps of manure as he strode around and he could see that they were not from full-grown cattle. 'It's calves,' he said. 'It's been our calves here.' Still they swept their torches across the waste and did not spy the animals. Oscar caught up, carrying the burning fronds. 'Where'd they go?' said Primrose. 'I can't see them. I can't see—' but he stopped.

He saw where the others were all looking, in the light of Oscar's torch. There, up in the branches, two half-familiar shapes. They looked almost like the shapes of two men in the trees but they were not, not quite. They were only the upper halves of two men.

They had been hung from their necks with thick rope. What was left of them dangled about five feet off the ground. The legs were gone. Some of their bellies were gone too.

Their light began to leave them. Oscar was backing away.

'Oscar, come back,' Tercer said.

Primrose was retching in the grass. Zill Tercer was breathing hard and high in his chest. Quinto walked back and forth holding his chin and looking. Eventually Oscar did come back.

With his light they saw the femora and tibiae and fibulae on the ground. 'Wolves,' Quinto said. 'This was wolves.' His voice was steady and it was good to be identifying things, explaining them.

'Who hung em like this?' said Primrose. 'Who? Not three feet off the ground they hung em.'

Old Tercer had advanced a few steps to where the bodies hung in the trees like ornaments, stock still, not even turning in the breezeless night, just displayed there, half-men. 'That's Case and Jones,' he said. 'Case and Jones the rustlers.'

'Yes, yes,' said Little Tom. 'It's them. That's Case and Jones. That's them two bastards.'

Primrose was done retching. He spoke hoarsely. 'The rustlers. Are you sure it's them?'

Little Tom nodded. Then he took his torch away and stepped off into the charcoal of the burn, looking left and right over the ground. As he walked he spoke, pointing at marks. 'The calves was here, not long before,' he said. 'And then look, here, in come the wolves. But by the time they come the calves was gone, they didn't find nothing. Nothing except them two thieves. They must have been hanging already.' He kept walking. 'Certain, the calves were gone. Otherwise we'd see carcasses. Yes, they were gone from here.'

He went on further. 'There were other riders too,' he called. "Other riders, I see the marks. Maybe a dozen of them. They rounded up the calves and drove em out.'

When he spoke next they could barely hear him. 'Here, thisaway,' is what he said. 'They went thisaway. The whole lot of them. Down this path.'

The rest of the men now pulled themselves away from the hanging shapes and came to where Little Tom was. They saw a little deer path which had been trampled five yards wide. 'They drove em here, drove em tight. Whoever it was. About a dozen men.'

'There they went,' said Tercer. 'Damned if they didn't.'

They stared down the black path. It was toothless Smith who finally posed the crucial question. 'Well, what in the hell are we going to do?'

Almost without discussing the twinned possibilities into which the question had split the night, they mounted up on their jumpy horses and rode down that trail.

They followed it for miles at a fast trot, not wanting to spend their mounts, not sure how far they had to go. When they realized that their trail led straight for the Saint Johns they cursed and upped their pace, but it was not long before their trail ran out dead into the big river. They stood for a moment looking out at its surface: broad, dark, quaking with cold starlight. Someone suggested they wait until day to cross. By that time dawn was not far off. They all agreed and got down off their horses. They had spent perhaps twenty out of the past twenty-four hours in the saddle. Numbly they sat down in the cool grass by the riverbank and within minutes every last one of them had closed his eyes.

A smell woke them up. Later, each man would agree that he had never been woken up by a smell before: but that was what happened, to each of them. It is one thing to be startled out of sleep by a noise, or a touch, or light in the eyes. But being woken by smell is like being jarred by something which ought not be noticed, like the earth's turning. Maybe that was what really happened, something wrong in the basic spin of things.

When they opened their eyes a stranger was sitting on a stump right in the middle of them. He was dressed in shreds of some unidentifiable brown material, a palmetto-bud hat on his head. He was looking around at them pleasantly, he had a pleasant face. But the stink overwhelmed everything. It was thick, rank, rich; it sank in the lungs and stayed there. It was an ordure of rotting leaves and spoiled flesh.

His presence was so unaccountable that none of them made a move. If he had wanted to he could have covered all of them with a gun but his hands were empty, resting on his thigh. He just sat there, smiling faintly, as they stirred all around him.

'Good morning,' he said. 'My name's Addison.' He stuck his hand out with all the fingers extended. 'Mister J P?' he asked. He swung his hand to each of them in turn. 'One of you is Mister J P?'

Primrose spoke. 'Where the hell did you come from?'

'Mister J P!' the man exclaimed. 'It's you, I'm sure it is. It's great to finally meet you. What a privilege. I feel like we've been working together already, hand in hand, like partners.'

'Now hang on,' Primrose said.

'Christ, what is that?' asked Smith, who had sat up and was looking around himself with a wrinkled face.

'Lordamercy, I don't know,' said Old Rouchefort, who was similarly affected. Each man had sat up where he'd lain down, and each man was now edging away from the stump where this Addison was.

He spoke in a high, reasonable voice. 'You were having a problem with some cattle thieves,' he said. 'Is that correct? Some fellows pulling a trick on you with calves, is that correct? Well, somebody was having that problem. Now it's solved.'

'Now hold on just a damned minute,' said Primrose.

The stranger's face turned momentarily dour. 'Their names were Dean Case and Arnold Jones. The worst sorts of men. Larcenists. Loudmouths. Utter liars. I breathe easier now that they're gone, just like you do. Just like everybody should.'

Primrose had a clenched look around his mouth as of a man who is trying to stop his own breath, but still he spoke. 'Look here, man. Addison. I don't know you, don't know your name. I don't know how you got the idea to get all confused in our business. But this were our goddamn affair. Ours to fix and ours to solve.'

The man tilted his head chidingly. 'That's what you think,' he said. 'But my friend, it's just not that simple. Once someone starts committing these crimes, why, it doesn't only hurt you. It hurts me too. It hurts my friends.' He put his hand on his chest and looked at Primrose feelingly. 'It hurts everybody.'

'Who are you and where did you come from?' Nat Quinto asked. He had edged his way over to his saddlebag and held one hand near it, poised. 'Answer.'

'Oh, the north swamp,' Addison said, 'that's where I am. Not any of these little bitty swamps around here, mind you. The big one up at the border line. Me and my friends live there.'

'Well, why don't you go and get back up in there.'

He smiled and made to stand. 'Why, sure. I think it's time we go. They'll be needing some help across the ford anyway.'

'Help with some calves?' asked Primrose.

'That's right,' mused Addison. 'There were some calves left over after this Case and Jones mess. Unmarked calves, totally unmarked. They fall to us for disposal, of course. A matter of escheat. That's a legal term.' He stood up, the shreds of cloth arranging themselves around him. 'It's only fitting, in any case. Sort of a compensation for all the work we did.'

'A compensation.'

'That's right.' The man looked at Primrose. 'Our compensation.'

'And who are these friends you keep talking about?'

Addison did not say anything. He tilted his eyes up just over the heads of the cowmen. One by one Primrose's cowmen turned their heads too. There were a dozen men, they saw, lounging in the grass behind them, like students in the back of a classroom. Black-eyed, blue-eyed, red-faced, one-eyed, long-mouthed, split-nosed, black-toothed, staring, smiling. They had been sitting there the whole time Addison spoke, as still as headstones in the long grass.

The loungers stood up to go. A rattle of scabbards and powderhorns. Addison came away to go with them.

All Primrose's men held silent, except for Quinto. 'Addison,' he said loudly.

The man turned. 'You, Addison. That were a desecration. That back there. Hanging those men like that, with the wolves.'

Addison gazed at him. 'Why, now.' He chuckled. 'Why, I suppose I should have taken the time to measure a rope just so, and set up a gibbet just so, and—'

'I'll bet you didn't even have em die by the hanging,' Quinto went on. 'I'll bet you left em alive for when the wolves came. I'll bet you wanted to see it.'

'We hung them off the backs of what they stole,' said Addison. His smile had gone away and his eyes were fixed on Quinto. 'We hung em off the backs of those calves, that's all. When the calves ran away, they hung.' He spat. 'You must be the kind of person who thinks a man shouldn't die the way he lived. You must be the kind who thinks a man deserves better than that.'

Quinto met the stare. He spoke, but it was barely a mutter. 'You watched it,' is what he said. 'You watched from the trees when the wolves came. I know you did.'

There was a dead silence for a moment. Then Jake Primrose sang out. 'Say, Addison,' he said. 'Will you sell those cows of yours? Do call on my friend Cruz in town. Do call on him and tell him I sent ye. Tell him Jake Primrose sent ye and he'll give you a sweet price to take them off your hands, I assure you. Cruz, on Treasury Street. All the luck to you, man, with your calves. All the luck in the world. And tell old Mister Cruz I say buena suerte.'

Addison acknowledged this advice like a man waking from a brief daydream. 'Oh, good,' he said; 'thank you kindly for the advice. Mister Cruz. We'll go and see him. Thank you, Jake.' There were more kind words and it was as if Quinto had never spoken. At last Addison and his men went rattling out of the clearing and the wind took the stink out across the river.

Quinto came home after two months. Lucy was standing in the doorway. Her silhouette as he approached was precisely the same as the very last glimpse he had gotten: her shoulders level, her hips straight, one hand holding the rifle angled downward, one hand raised a little as if to reach out and touch him.

But as he came nearer he saw what had changed within the silhouette. Her eyes were the same green but they were wider, brighter somehow; the hollows they sat in had darkened. And she was pregnant: her stomach swelled outward with a different life.

He got down from his horse and just dropped the reins. In the doorway they embraced, a little loosely, then separated, and then came together again. This time they held each other for a long time. And still she did not let go of the gun. She was saying something about wolves, saying it into his shirt collar, dampening it. He did not quite hear her or did not quite understand.

They came inside and sat down in their two chairs at the white table. He asked whether she'd had enough provisions for the month. She said yes. He said that was good, and they would likely not be lacking provisions from then on. She said nothing for a moment. Then said there had been a pack of wolves walking the yard every night for two weeks. Strange wolves which moved very close to the circle of her torchlight. Quinto heard her and then, as if a weight had fallen on him, he sank out of his chair onto the floor. He came on his knees to where Lucy sat and raised his dark head up into her lap. He left it there, in the meeting of the nave of her legs and the swell of her stomach. They stayed that way for a long time, her hand on the back of his head, his head half hidden, and he said that he would never again leave her like he had done, never again, no, not for a thousand thousand cows, and she confessed that she would not let him go anyway, no, not for any weight of gold, however much it shone.

BURNT FORT BLUFF

YOUNG AB TERCER DODGES ARMY SALVOES
AND THE SCALPING KNIFE.

I.

A B TERCER'S MOTHER held his head in her lap and stroked his pale hair. He could still see out the front door into the darkness, where his father stood in a patch of torchlight. He could not see many of the people who surrounded Shay Tercer there in the yard. But he could see the glint of hoops and beads and gorgets, which marked their places constellated through the dark. And the dull glow of the muskets they carried, well-oiled for a long journey.

Ab Tercer was ten years old. That night was the last time Runner's people would ever visit his yard. It was not unusual for Runner to come and confer with the person he called Sheyatercer: long gestural conversations, a few scraps of English woven in, numerous winks—old Runner had picked up the habit of winking somewhere and was elaborately fond of it. They would come from their town on the opposite side of Varnes Pond to trade horses or to offer the surplus of a catch of fish. But this now was the year of rumors and accusations. They'd been coming less often, lately. And never at such strange hours.

The boy watched as his father talked with the silver-haired chief. Even from inside the house Ab could see the fatigue on

Runner's face: fatigue before their journey even began. He swung his arm in the direction they were headed. South. And soon the meeting was over and the people were moving away from the yard and Shay Tercer came back indoors. Some of the old chief's fatigue seemed to have impressed itself on Tercer's face. He sat down in a chair and was silent for a minute before he answered all his family's questions with a single phrase: 'They're gone.'

Jane stopped attending to her son. 'What do you mean, they're gone?' she asked. 'Where are they going?'

'I don't know,' Shay said. 'I didn't ask. They're gone.'

'But what about their town? What about all that corn they just put in?'

Shay shrugged. 'They're gone. Asked me to trade for some powder but I didn't have none spare. And now they're gone.'

Young Zill, standing in a corner with tears and a kind of rage in his eyes, said: 'Good. Good. Let em go. Let em go and not come back either. They better not come back, the way they butchered those cows out by the prairie. Did you tell them that, pappy? Did you tell them if they go they better not come back?'

But again all Shay said was 'They're gone,' and stared out into the darkness.

Ab said nothing but left his head in his mother's lap, let himself be held. He did not have many days left to seek comfort there. Indeed it was the last time the boy would ever be held so closely. Maybe if he'd known that he would not have stood up and walked out the door.

'I want to see them,' Ab said. 'I want to say goodbye'. He walked down the front steps.

'They're gone, Ab,' his father tried to tell him, but the boy kept walking, past the faint light from the house and past the reach of his father's voice. He came and stood in the middle of the darkness where the Seminoles had been. The boy turned, turned, looking for some sign of them, listening for hoof-fall or tack-clink or voice. There was nothing.

He rushed away from the house and ran around the perimeter of the lake in the dark until he came to the old town. Ab stopped dead on its outskirts, startled and afraid. The moon was bright enough to see the emptiness there. All the chickees were empty and all the gardens stripped. Even the avenues of the village were perfectly bare, as if swept clean by the draft of their sudden flight. The livestock animals which had once roamed the place had vanished too: the silence was complete. There was not so much as an ember alive in the scoops outside the Seminoles' houses. They had been careful as always to extinguish their fires when they departed.

Ab avoided the old town after that. Not even a boy's love of abandoned places could make him go. He remained behind when others went to play there. But more than a year passed. Ab turned twelve and was no longer so bound by the fears and prohibitions of childhood. And one day Jude Quinto asked him to go hunting there.

Jude was enthusiastic; his older brother had had luck in the grounds of the old settlement. So the two boys were there before dawn. They stalked sightlines between the buildings and perched shivering on the raised platforms of the old chickees. But dawn came, and then full daylight, and they saw no deer. At last, with the sun up and hot enough to make them sweat, Jude let out a Shit damn and stood up noisily from his position.

'Nothing. Not even a peek. What's gotten into these deer?' Jude said. 'Nair so much as a nanny goat, and this was the best grounds before.'

Sighing, Ab got up to leave too. And that was when he looked down and saw the coals.

An old firepit had been brushed clean in front of the chickee, and a fire had been lit there recently. There was freshly charred wood in the derelict yard.

Ab did not say anything about it to Jude. He followed the Quinto boy away from the town, faintly joining him in cursing all ungulates. But he was unusually quiet the rest of that day. Close to dusk he slipped from his parents' house and went back to the ruins on the other side of the pond. He lay there in wait, much as he had done that morning.

He did not have to wait long before they came into the clearing. It was a man and a woman and a boy. They went to the chickee and set down a load of what looked like deerskins, along with some bagged squirrels and rabbits.

Ab did not announce himself, only stepped out into the open. In that instant the man and the woman and the boy all turned to look at him. The man coiled almost imperceptibly, hand at his side for some weapon he had there. But Ab made no particular movements, only stood there holding a satchel. After watching him for a long spell the man turned away and went back to his task, skinning their catch.

The son turned to the work also, though he glanced back at Ab. The woman alone did not stop staring. It was a piercing stare, with something poison in it. Ab shrank a little and nearly turned to leave. But finally he did what he had planned. He came toward them, with a small sack of cornmeal held out in front of him.

They did not acknowledge him. He made it all the way to the chickee where the family was, holding the little sack outward, but no hand reached to accept it. At last Ab just set the sack down on the platform and lamely backed away.

Ab knew these people, or knew of them. The man was Runner's nephew, a huntsman who spoke a little English. The boy's name was Fixico, and he was Ab's age; they had been born the same month on the opposite sides of the pond. There had once been a suggestion of relation or affinity between the two of them, for that reason. But all that was gone now. The past year had changed the boy utterly. He had moved past Ab, beyond him. In the hardness of his eyes he seemed almost a man.

Ab hung there limply for a moment and might finally have gone away. Instead, despairingly, he spoke the question he had come to ask, in his desperation almost shouted it: 'Where did you go?'

Now at last the man looked over at him. Something like amusement played around his mouth. 'Where did we go,' the man echoed. He repeated the question in Maskókî for his wife and son, and chuckled a little. 'Where did we go? We go where you told us to.' The boy Fixico frowned at his father's laughter and went back with his knife to their kill. 'South of the Tsala Apopka. We're there now.'

Ab frowned. It was something about the man's mocking laugh, the boy's turned back, the woman's unceasing hardeyed stare. 'Well, why are you up here, then?' Ab asked. 'If that's your land now, why are you back up here?'

The man looked at him. 'The hunt,' he said, as if to a fool.

'Why don't you jist stay down there and hunt where you are now?' Ab asked.

There was no laughter at this. The man spat a little on the ground. The son spat after him.

For the first time the woman spoke, and it too came out like spitting. 'Primrose,' she said. It was directed at Ab. She said other words, had begun talking very loudly now, all Maskókî, but with that one English name mixed in again and again as she gestured at the boy: Primrose. Primrose.

'What's she saying?' Ab asked.

The man shook his head at the woman and addressed her. 'Sheyatercer,' he said. 'Abitercer, honvnwuce Sheyatercer.' But she did not acknowledge him and went on speaking, and that same name kept coming up, Primrose, Primrose, more vehemently each time.

'Tell her that ain't right,' Ab said. 'I ain't a Primrose. I'm a Tercer. My daddy's Shay Tercer, I'm a Tercer.'

But the woman went on, insistent, waving at him and saying Primrose, Primrose, Primrose. Ab stomped his foot, balled his fist. But she would not stop calling him by that name. At last Ab was walking away from them, shouting behind himself as he went, as loud as the woman now, on the verge of tears: 'Damn you, I'm a Tercer! I'm not a Primrose! I'm not a Primrose!'

Ab went back to the old town the next morning, intending to set them to rights. But the site was deserted again. On the chickee platform, in the exact spot where Ab had set the bag of cornmeal the day before, lay a ratty-looking rabbit pelt, left there in fitting exchange.

Spring came. Ab's father and brother left for the Primrose cowhunt, as usual. With Zill gone things were peaceful around the Tercer place, and Ab had the house and fields to himself. There were occasional interruptions: Jane Tercer had many Georgia cousins, and a large proportion of these were men at loose ends who were all of a sudden coming to Florida. They came with heads full of plans they did not care to discuss and rumors they did not care to repeat. A couple of them said something about Indian lands but that was all. They'd stay for a night and leave out the next day, continuing south.

Besides these family visitors there was not another living soul anywhere on their acreage, or anywhere for a dozen miles around for all they knew, nobody to interrupt the days of planting the garden and tending the animals and Ab spending late afternoons on his grey pony chasing woods-cows or going off to swim in the spring. Then one morning there was a loud knock at the door.

It was Zill. He did not pause but spoke his piece and then turned to ride off again. 'Popswantschye,' is what he said.

Ab looked up from his work. 'Zill,' he said. His brother was riding away. 'What are you doing back aready? What about the hunt?'

'Come on. Popswantschye.'

'What?' called Ab.

Zill stopped and turned around in his saddle. 'Hellfire, where's your ears? Get up your horse come on. Pops ain't going to wait on ye.'

Ab stood, setting his whetstone down on the chair. 'But what about Ma?' he said.

'It's all right,' Zill said. 'He already sent for Tenny and Sam to come here. They're going to hep her move to Nat Quinto's place for a while. She'll be all right.' He began to move off again. 'Just get your horse come on. We're off by the marsh, the north side.'

Ab packed his kit and galloped his pony to catch up with Zill. They rode together, Ab asking the questions—how had the hunt been so far, how many cows had they gotten, why did they need him—and Zill giving short vague answers that added up to You'll see. And then they topped the rise above the marsh and he did see.

It was a tremendous herd clogging the whole quarter mile of Jake Primrose's marsh. The glinting horns were upraised and pointing all one direction, like bayonets before a battle, but the herd was not moving. They had been stopped in that place to rest and graze a spell, but they were not grazing, either. The reason was a loud disturbance in one corner of the marsh. A thousand big animals in a herd and the wildest noise came from a handful of humans around an oxcart. The two brothers drew up and Zill sat his horse to watch and Ab did too.

There was a kind of a jousting match happening, sans horses or lances. One combatant was a thin man in a cheap three-piece suit. The other was Jake Primrose. They stood a short distance apart, arguing loudly. Then they began to tilt at one another, fists balled at their sides, accelerating as they approached, their shouts also increasing in loudness, as if they meant to knock each other down by volume alone. They did not succeed in this but passed each other by a matter of inches. Then the two combatants strode off to their separate corners to turn and try again.

'Get these cows moving or it's a broken contract Mister Primrose a broken contract I tell you and a black mark on your name for the rest of time or I'm'

'Those cows won't move while there's a blade of grass still standing on thisyer spread and that's final you nogood interferin''

'You promised Saint Augustin town quick as a wink you said quick as a wink you'

'Allow greasy flearid lawyers on your drive and it all comes apart I prophesied it'

'I knew what'd come of contracting with you cheating Crackers I knew'

'Yes I'm a Cracker by God but call me a cheat just one more time'

'Here we sit like hens waiting on a fox it's disaster it's suicide'

'Call me a hen just one more time you no good son of a son'

'It's criminal I tell you it's prosecutable I tell you it's'

'You come on my range and set up shop and try'

'I know people I have friends and they will'

'If you try to move these cows it'll be'

'Skewer you flay you quarter you'

'Swear I'll bury you under the'

'Never sell another hoof'

'Chinamen on boats'

'Andrew Jackson'

and they passed each other and came apart.

They went to their separate corners for a moment. Jake Primrose's lackeys came to rub his shoulders and give him tactical advice. The man in the dusty suit had no such support. He was in conversation with a large woman sitting up on a wagon tailgate flanked by two scruffy-looking soldiers. He pleaded with the lady as she regarded him with infinite scorn.

What a lady she was. Her face was a healthy hue of pink, and she was crowned with blonde hair piled high beneath a bonnet. This structure of yellow hair and grey cotton trembled with every movement she made. She was a person of extraordinary size and strength, despite the poverty that seemed to mark her along with her dusty lawyer. And she moved nimbly as she grabbed the thin man by the collar and spun him back toward the field of battle.

It didn't help. Primrose was waiting, refreshed by a swig of rum. He won the next round overwhelmingly. The opponent was reduced to saying something about the tides of history as he slouched back toward the wagon. The pink lady had seen enough; she tapped the man out and stepped in to do her own arguing. When the joust began she charged at Primrose with a fearsome, flat-footed stride that almost made the cowman flinch and hit him with a big payload of insults. She was amazing to behold: Ab stared helplessly. Even the cows seemed to eye her with morbid interest. Every part of the woman shook with a terrible fury. Jake Primrose was only just standing his ground. She surely would have beat him if the battle had continued. But dusk was falling and soon it would be nighttime, God's little armistice. The cows could not be moved anymore one way or the other. Both sides accepted the Almighty's decision and as darkness fell they moved apart.

As they tended to their horses, Ab asked Zill, 'Who are they?'

'That's Miz Cook,' Zill said, and spat. 'We picked her up

down around Fort King.' He spat again. 'And that little twiggy feller is her lawyer. Name of Kent.'

'Hum,' said Ab. 'What's a lawyer?'

Zill did not answer. He squinted and looked down at a knot he was trying to untie.

'I mean what's a lawyer do?' asked Ab.

Zill looked up. 'Hell,' he said. 'Carries her bags, mostly.'

'But who are they?' Ab asked. 'What are they doing with us?'

'It's those cows,' Zill said, and tilted his head toward the herd. 'You think we popped that whole herd ourselves? No, fool, no. Half of em's hers. Though dear old Osceola mighten have something else to say about that.' He laughed a low-throated laugh, like a young man trying to sound old.

'Osceola?' asked Ab. 'What you mean, Zill? What're we doing?'

'Shoot, Ab, don't you see nothing for yourself? What we're doing is we're running half a thousand Seminole cows out of Seminole country as fast as we can go, that's what we're doing. We might have Osceola on our heels. Might have Wild Cat on our heels, you cain't tell. Hell, you figure they'll let us just slide away with half a thousand head?'

'We took their cows, then,' Ab said slowly. 'Good. Good.'

Zill was pulling a clove knot loose with relish. 'That lady Cook got aholt of them somehow, I don't know how she done it. Probably something with that little suit man. He talks fast enough to give them Indins a problem. Anyway they paid us to drive em for her, so here we are.'

'Good,' said the boy. 'Good. They probably stole them cows off white people to begin with.'

'Yeah, boy. That's right. We just taking em back. Same with the slaves.'

'What slaves?' asked Ab.

'The ones in the box,' said Zill. 'The—'

Just then Shay Tercer rode up to them through the trees. 'What are you two doing? Cain't you see it's sundown? And you're standing here jawing? Go on, get us some firewood. Get up, there. We cain't be running out of damned firewood halfway through the night.'

Their father rarely talked like this. Ab jumped up, and he and Zill went out to chop the wood. Before long they had collected enough. Ab helped to build the fire. Then, while the group was all occupied with supper, he crept away from the circle of firelight.

There was another such circle glowing a little ways off in the forest. Miss Cook and her lawyer were sitting there while her two soldiers brought up piles of wood. Ab slunk past them. A little further on he could see the hulking shape of the wagon. There was lettering on the side that read *U.S. ARMY.* and beneath that *PROVISIONS.* in lime paint.

There was a sound like an iron file being dragged across wood. The cart had a small grate near the top. The boy climbed the spokes of the wagon wheel to get a look. There was a shining object behind the grate. Ab squinted hard to make out what it was and then the shining object squinted too. It was an eye. Another object moved next to where he was holding onto the grate. It was a hand. The sound of the iron file got louder. It was breath laboring inside a chest. Suddenly the boy saw the whole wagon was full of hands and eyes and teeth.

He let go of the grate and fell to the ground and scrabbled backward. Someone inside the wagon started trying to talk to him in Maskókî. 'Hadjo? Hadjo?' And then another voice took up the words too, shouting them. Ab got to his feet and turned and ran away.

He ran back to the cowmen's campfire. He came to them in the middle of a conversation about weather forecasts. He stood and searched the faces one by one, looking into them, to see who else knew. In time he accepted a tin plate and sat down, staring at the plate, searching the poke greens and warmed beef as if they might help him understand.

The only other person who maybe also did not understand was Oscar's son Zech. He, too, was staring at his meal. Everyone else sat and chewed and spoke of the good spring weather and understood everything, cutting their meat with swift motions of their knives.

Before dawn the two parties woke up and made breakfast at their separate camps. Miss Cook was awake or maybe had not slept at all, she was not much for sleep. She had probably kept the lawyer Kent awake all night, too, going over details and corollaries and contingencies. Cook was the operation's motor but the lawyer Kent was its tactician. He had done some amazing legerdemain involving contracts and bad documents and false accusations. They claimed that they had given the Seminoles payment for cows and slaves, but that the Seminoles had kept all the goods and run off with the money. Typical aboriginal cunning. And Miss Cook had papers to back it all up.

A Seminole leader had indeed made his mark on the grubby papers, but the sale had never actually occurred. They had kept their cows and slaves and never taken her money. But unfortunately for the Indians, there was no evidence of this nonreceipt, and so she followed them down through Florida territory in deafening pursuit of her legal possessions. Her passion to take what was hers overwhelmed the small handful of federal Indian Agents who were supposed to stop people like her; they crumpled in front of the woman like tin.

Kent had engineered the scheme, but Miss Cook's original impulse was the critical thing. She had recognized a foundational concept of American law: whenever possible, enter into contracts with people who can neither read nor write. Miss Cook could not read or write herself, but she knew a good lawyer. Wormy little Kent was terrified of the woman and chained to her will. Entire nights passed with Miss Cook forcing him to read the contracts out loud, down to the footnotes, not allowing breaks for sustenance or bowel movements. It was a good technique, it had broken the man and made him a very effective advocate.

At first light the cows were standing wakeful and silent all around the marsh. The cowmen spread out along the edges and started to ease the herd forward. With stubborn weight it did begin to move, creakily, huffily, with the occasional bellow. The cows had not slept much. There was something bothering them.

The herd moved north, followed by Miss Cook's group, followed by the wagon that read *U.S. ARMY*. Ab was at the rear of the herd, between it and the wagons. Hours later the sun was over top of them and they had not made it very far, and Miss Cook was again complaining about the pace.

And then there began to be noises from the prison wagon. It was a kind of a song, but there was no tune: it was just five or six voices raised to a certain pitch. The rear cows in the herd balked when this noise started, but the sound of it only increased.

When noon came, the cowmen did not take lunch but just stood their horses on the edge of the herd, watching. The cows milled about and made uneasy noises. There had begun to be a woman's voice wailing also and the cows moved away, bunching in an arc as far removed as possible from the source of the bad sound.

Ab was at the rear. He watched as Jake Primrose rode his horse to where Miss Cook and her entourage lingered at the wagons. The cattleman tilted up his hat and addressed her. 'Miss, you've got to hush them up,' he said.

She was couched on a soft chair that had been nailed to the floor of her wagon, with an awning shading her. She smoothed her skirts. 'Cain't,' she said. 'Tried. Cain't.'

'Well then you've got to move that cart away from here. Move it up ahead of us. Or else have it hang somewhere behind.'

'Then how would I keep an eye on my slaves, Primrose?'

'Well, stay back with them.'

'Then how would I keep an eye on my cows?'

Primrose put his hand against his forehead. The lady kept talking. 'Well? I've got to keep an eye on them both. The cows and the blacks. You expect me to lose sight of my investiments? Ain't likely. Not me. Not Meridia Cook. I'ma keep a close watch on everthing til we're out of this godforsaken territory. Cause they're mine. Signed and titled. Ain't that right, Mister Kent? Where's those papers? Pull em out.'

Primrose removed his hat from his head. 'You've got to shut those sons of bitches up, Cook,' he shouted.

In the box cart the woman's wailing had been replaced by a man's voice speaking in high-pitched Maskókî as if reciting from a scroll. The long drone had become rhythmic, pointed, loud. 'Well, what do you suggest, Mister Primrose?' Cook asked.

'I don't know. Let them out of the wagon.'

She laughed a short laugh. 'Oh, sure. And then wouldn't we have fun getting em all back in again.'

'Well, you'd keep em in the chains, of course,' Primrose said. 'You'd—' But something in the lady's expression made him stop. 'Do you mean they're not?'

'They didn't come with chains,' she said. For the first time she looked almost apologetic.

'So they're just shut up in that box.'

'They didn't come with chains,' Cook said again. 'The Indins don't keep em that way. They have em running around loose, like they was regular folks. It's devilish.'

'Well, damn it, what do they keep yelling for? They must want something, what do they want?'

'I don't know. They've got food and water plenty. I feed my darkies,' she said proudly.

'They want something, by God. Do they speak American?'

'Mostly,' she said. 'The older ones do, sure. Some of the youngeruns speak just Indin. They walk, talk, act Indin ways. They think they're real Indins, they do indeed. Damn, they may as well be, as far as I can tell. But there's one difference, you know what it is? They're mine. Signed and titled. Pull out those papers, Kent.'

Jake Primrose stepped past her and approached the box cart. He knocked on the heavy walls. 'Hey, you all. Talk. What do you want? What do you want?' Still the singing. Louder even. Primrose pounded the wall some more and then the people inside began to beat the walls themselves, not as if to break them, but for a rhythmic accompaniment, a measured heartbeat for their song.

'Oh hell,' said Primrose. 'Oh please. Please, is there nothing you want in there? Is there nothing? You jackasses, I'm trying to help. What can I give you?'

On a slope the boy Ab was watching, terrified. 'Oh, they ain't nothing but Indins,' he moaned to himself. 'They ain't even Negro, they're Indins. Oh, they'll kill us, we oughta just shoot em, they'll kill us.'

Primrose struck the wagon one more time and then stepped back. The cows were surging, seething. You could not hear the captives all the way at the front of the herd but you could see the cows pressing from the rear where they were disturbed. Primrose got Oscar from where he was at the front keeping the cattle at bay. They galloped back to the wagons and dismounted and Primrose turned to the slave.

'Now, man. You've got to make them hear you. Please. Tell them—I don't know what. Tell them there's to be consequences don't they shut up. Explain to em, make em hear you. I don't know, Oscar.'

Oscar stood for a moment listening to the keening noise. Then he said, 'Hey, you. Hey. You all stop this. Quit this or it'll be problems. You hear the man. Look, there's soldiers out here, guns. Do you hear me?'

'Who is this?' one voice said. 'Are you Oscar?'

'Yes, this Oscar,' he said. 'You know it is. Now stop this or it'll be bad for all of us, you get me?'

But there was no answer. Only more keening music and the beating of the walls. 'Hey,' the slave said. 'Hey you in there.'

'Oh hell,' said Jake Primrose, looking off to the north and balling his hands. 'These cows are about to stampede. Oh hell. Oh hell.'

Then one of the soldiers stepped forward. He drew his service pistol and pressed it to Oscar's head. 'Try it again,' he said. 'Try it with a gun to your ear, darkie.'

'Oh,' said Oscar. 'Please. Lord. You in there. They going to kill me. Listen, you all. Hush up. Please.'

The noise did not stop. It grew louder. Jake Primrose was yelling at the soldier to put it down, put it down. The soldier just stood with the gun pressed to Oscar's head, smiling faintly as the man trembled. Then they heard a woman scream.

It was Miss Cook, up on her chair. She was facing north and pointing. 'They're running. The cows are running away. Look.'

There was shouting from the front of the herd and a volley of whipcracks, but these sounds were quickly overwhelmed by a crackling of underbrush and a deep shudder of the earth. Jake Primrose ran to his horse and Oscar did too, freed from the soldier. They leapt into their saddles, shouting. They shouted even though no one could hear. Ab shot out after them, galloping too fast for what little he weighed, jouncing wildly in the saddle. The soldier who had pointed the gun rode off too.

The cows in the front were lining out in the distance but the bulk of the herd was still jammed together so tightly that they could not run. But as the riders galloped past the middle of the herd, the stampede finally reached it and the cows began to pull apart from one another, like ice turning into water and running away from itself. They were on a long marsh but ahead was a slope up to a wall of trees and the cattle did not slow down but only ran faster to greet it. One by one the horsemen tore into the forest and were instantly bloodied from the neck up and anywhere else that bare skin showed. But past that first line of brambles the woods opened up into wide-spaced stands of trees.

They were on the right side of the stampede and could not see the front of it at all but could hear where the cowmen were cracking their dragwhips there, barely audible over the roar which set the whole landscape trembling. They ran for two miles before they caught up. Jake Primrose pointed left and began flailing his whip in front of the nearest cows to turn them. The other cowmen were already attempting to do the same but the front was too wide; any time they altered the course of one part of it, the press of cattle would flow around them. But now they were adding horsemen from the rear. Ab took up his whip and turned around in the saddle. He was galloping three horselengths in front of the stampede and looking into it was looking into oblivion. The bulls running closest to him stared dead ahead and mouthed soundlessly, and behind them followed the massive herd of cattle with the weight of a waterfall.

Ab turned forward again. His grey marshtackie was running low and limber between the trees, over roots, past stumps, negotiating the land for itself without the boy's hand. Next to him the soldier galloped on a big military horse which did not know its rider and did not know this ground. It galloped straight ahead as the soldier turned with his pistol and fired over the heads of the running cows and turned back to reload; then Ab saw out of the corner of his eye as the man came too close to an oak branch and the branch tore his neck open and the man's hands flew upward. He fell from his saddle into the roaring and was gone.

Ab faced forward. He knit his fingers into his horse's mane, fighting his own trembling muscles, urine soaking his saddle. To his right Primrose and Oscar and three others were coming parallel to the herd and bending its course to the left with a haze of whipcracks. Despite his shaking arms Ab joined them and slung his whip at the righthand flank of cows; the herd began to angle. In another mile they reached a deep black creek and the stampede coursed into it with an explosion like hot iron placed in water, and man and beast surged up the other side, dripping, carrying half the creek with them. The cowmen were turning the herd so sharply now that they recrossed the same creek a few miles further along, but more slowly this time, and past that came to a small, bald prairie where they finally halted with a lurch, a wretched sound of moaning cattle like a machine straining against itself. Then came the isolated and pitiful sounds of the blood-caked riders howling in triumph or some baser emotion with their shredded voices.

They did not even build a fire. On a rise above the herd they fell down off their horses and lay where they landed and did not get up. It was not even sleep, not at first. Each man lay there for a long time just staring upward at the sky as the stars came out.

It was past midnight when a lone rider came up. It was the lawyer Kent. He came among the bodies. 'Hello?' he whispered. 'Hello?'

Primrose spoke up, laying on his back. 'You,' he croaked. 'How'd you find us.'

'I followed the track. It took me this long.'

'I wish I'd never seen your face,' said Primrose. 'You nor your wench's.'

'You stopped them. You stopped them from running. The cattle are here.'

'That's right we did. No thanks to you or to them soldiers of yours. What happened to that one bastard, anyway? I never saw him.'

Ab was laying next to his father with his head on the man's arm. He turned and hid his eyes in his father's shirt.

'We found him,' the lawyer said. He tried to suppress a sob, but could not. 'He was there in the middle of the track, about two miles in. Trampled. Stomped flat. Flat like a, a piece of paper.' He paused. 'His name was Harper.'

Primrose did not speak for a moment. The lawyer stood silhouetted against the night sky, childish in his too-big suit.

'Where's the woman,' Primrose said at last.

Lawyer Kent stuttered before he could go on. 'Some distance—some—some distance back there,' he said. 'Made camp. We are going straight on to Saint Augustine.'

'Good.'

'Miss Cook will be sending—'

'Tell her if she comes anywhere near my drive again with those stolen Negroes I'll shoot to kill.'

Kent snuffled and spoke more evenly. 'Miss Cook will not be riding with the cattle any further. We will be in Saint Augustine in two days, and you must call on us when you arrive. In the meantime—'

'Ain't no meantime,' Primrose said. 'You'll have your cows in Saint Augustine in eight ten days. That's it. Ain't nothing more to say.'

There wasn't. The lawyer left, unlanterned as he had come, wandering back down the flat-mown stampede path in the moonlight.

Father and son were both awake a long time. The boy's eyes were hidden in the father's side, while the man's own eyes hunted among the constellations.

Tercer talked for a while, neither fully to himself nor fully to Ab. He talked about the night, about the cattle, about the slaves in the wagon, about the contract into which they had entered, its terms. He spoke slowly, bemused.

'I don't know,' he said, 'jist how I got…confused up in all this. I don't know. I cain't untie it. Stealing Negroes out of their houses. Twelve of them in a box cart. I don't—' He stopped. 'I ain't no slaver. I ain't no—enterpriser. I know that. I'm jist a cowman. All I am nor want to be.' He blew out breath. 'Then how'd I get so'—he closed his hand into a ball—'tied up?'

He was quiet a long time, thinking. When he spoke again it was with the deliberation of something worked out, a truth uncovered, unveiled point to point like beads strung along a necklace.

'You cain't stop everthing,' he began, 'that you don't agree with.' A pause. 'You learn that,' he added confidingly. 'No, you cain't stop everthing—you don't like. Sometimes it jist sorter'— he looked at the stars for the word—'gaithers you up. And so a man's got to jist muddle on. And do as he cain.' He breathed out. 'And that's the way of things.'

Having spoken this, the man went quiet, in agreement with himself and able at last to sleep.

In the morning they found the dead soldier's horse with its

empty saddle grazing near the cows. They used it to carry extra packweight, like a mule.

They spent a day rounding up the cows which had been scattered along the stampede route and returning them to the main herd. One hundred and fifty head were found in that way, with another fifty given up as lost. Then they began to move off again, north and east toward the coast, taking the drive at the pace they wanted. The noise and alarum of the stampede thrummed in their brains for a long time: they needed this rhythm, this slowness, long peaceable days in the saddle under the sun. Let Coacoochee come catch up with them any time, went the thinking. He could come and slay them to a man if he wanted but they would not hurry these cows one step.

Nine days later they walked into Saint Augustine. Primrose inquired around and soon found Miss Cook lodged in the bridal suite of the best hotel in town. In the days since they had last seen her, the lady had traded on her new cattle-wealth and slave-wealth to buy a new wardrobe, new accommodations, and a new husband. Primrose came upon them in the bridal suite. Lawyer Kent sat at an escritoire, wearing a better-fitting suit, tallying up dollar amounts. The new husband, a sleek and perfumed Spaniard with a royal title, *duque* or somesuch, was lying on a crushed-silk couch and looking at Jake Primrose as if a barnyard animal had just walked into the room on two legs. Then there was the lady herself, essentially unchanged despite her new beribboned pink dress and the new style of her hair done up in pressed curls à la grecque. There was the same fierce, acquisitive look in the eyes which she trained on the cattleman, asking him about the cows.

Primrose told her to come see them for herowndamnedself if she wanted and she did. There was a cargo ship waiting at the docks and the cowmen had counted the cattle and driven them there. Miss Cook and party followed in a covered brougham and the lady watched until every last one was on board. Only then did she instruct Jake Primrose to come and get the gold coins they'd agreed on.

When business was finished Miss Cook spoke with new gentleness. She pursed her big red lips and eyed Primrose with a look that suggested she wished she'd wedded him instead of the duque or was thinking of a way to get both. Jake for his part was trying to get away, and not slowly.

'I'm going back up to Georgia,' Miss Cook said. 'I shall find a plantation to buy. One of them big white places, you know, with a porch.'

Primrose was not answering or even looking at her, but was busy tying up his many bags of coins.

'Course there's still the matter of getting there with twelve darkies in a wagon and—' she lay her hand on one of her gold pouches— 'a ruther substantial amount of money. We lost that one soldier of course and Private Jenks cannot come past the Floridy line, and I do not mind telling you Mister Primrose that I am scurred, scurred, scurred for my personal safety. So I've talked with a company that's agreed to escort us through the rough parts of the territory, a Mister Addison.'

Primrose looked up. 'Addison,' he said.

'Yes, a Mister Addison and company,' Miss Cook said. 'It has eased me greatly. A kind of private policeman, you could say. He's for hire anyhow and has a reputation. An upstanding man. Not afraid to deal forcefully, not for protecting a lady he ain't. That's the reputation.'

'When's he due here,' Primrose asked.

'Oh,' said Miss Cook. 'Soon.'

The other cowmen had heard this talk and they looked at one another. Shay Tercer motioned for his son to get up in his saddle. The men who had not already mounted up did so now. They had sold the entire herd at the docks in order to make the return trip quicker; there was nothing left to keep them in that town. Eight men on their eight horses turned from the stinking docks and headed toward the interior at a trot.

'Goodbye, Mister Primrose,' Miss Cook called from inside the brougham.

'Good riddance,' Primrose replied, not quietly.

There wasn't much talking on the way back from town. At Primrose's they split the earnings and went their separate ways. The Tercers rode out together, still silent. It began to shower and they did not speak even to acknowledge it, allowing themselves to be soaked.

They came to Quinto's homestead in the afternoon, the leavings of the vanished rainclouds still dripping from everything with a cheersome sound in the yellow sunlight. They met Nat on the path. The contrast between him and the Tercer men was a sorry one for the Tercers. Quinto came down the path carrying a scythe: he had just finished preparing a new cropfield. His hair and skin were slicked with rain and sweat. His bright eyes looked both weary and replenished, as though he had just woken from sleep. The Tercers looked tired too, but it was a tiredness which made their heads hang and their eyes droop.

Nat sang out. 'Shay,' he said. 'Boys.' And he leaned his scythe against a tree and came and took each of them by the hand. 'Look at these cowmen.' He reached up and ran two fingers along the back of young Ab's neck. 'Look there. Some old trail dust, I believe. This boy's been riding.'

'He sure has, Nat,' Shay Tercer said.

'Good,' said Quinto. 'How was the hunt?'

Shay Tercer blew a breath between his lips. 'Long,' he said.

'Long?' said Quinto. 'Why, Shay, you ain't been gone two months.'

Tercer scratched the back of his head underneath his hat. 'It was a long trip, Nat,' he said.

Quinto looked at each of them. Shay Tercer was looking away. Zill was scowling. The boy Ab was looking back at him with eyes that were too big for his face. 'Well,' said Quinto. 'Not much to talk about on it I reckon.'

'Not much,' said Tercer, the lie plain on his face.

'Why, now,' Nat said brightly, 'I spect you want to see Jane, not me.'

'Yes,' said Shay. He did. Nat picked up his scythe and they all headed toward the Quintos' house. 'She ain't given you much trouble, has she?' asked Shay.

'Oh, no,' said Quinto, and now the lie was plain on his face too.

Before long they were on the neat acre of his home. It was raked and swept and sodded with pinestraw. It was a new double-pen house, the logs still dripping pitch where they had been cut. Chickens pecked among the dry straw or in the shade of the dogwood tree that stood in the clearing, but they all flew when there came a scream from inside the house.

It was Jane Tercer. She ran down the steps. She was swollen from crying; her hair flew behind her from a disheveled bun. In front of the horses she seemed physically torn between going to her husband first or to one of her sons. In the end she just fell on the closest horse, which was Zill's, and hugged its neck.

The Tercers dismounted and accepted their hard embraces and the tears. Ab allowed himself to be held and cried on for a long time. Shay stood back, seeming to know that he would get his share later, both of loving and of fury. She gave a little to him now, screaming at him, 'You take both my sons and don't say where to? Both my sons? Both? Oh, bless you, you're safe, you're all safe.'

Lucy Quinto appeared in the breezeway. At her side were two sons, both hers, and a daughter, not hers. Another daughter appeared. Lucy came down to try to comfort Jane, something she had plenty of practice in lately.

The mother of the spare children came around the side of the house, as did an aged granddad, drawn by the noise. They were relations of the Quintos, lodging with them. The father was off with one of the militias preparing for conflict with the Indians, and he had left his responsibilities there at that house. All of them gathered around the cowhunters hungry for news.

Quinto's young son was the hungriest. 'Weren't there Indins?' he cried. 'I heard there was Indins, Mister Tercer, Indins. Did you fight em? Did you run?'

Nat Quinto cuffed the boy but Shay Tercer had to answer. He gave a weak smile. 'Aw, stuff,' he said. 'There weren't no Indins. Don't listen to that, little man. Weren't no Indins at all.'

Now Jane Tercer started in. 'Liar,' she wept. 'We all heard you had Seminole cows with you. Seminole cows, Shay, and you bring your baby boy in on it? You drag him into your and Primrose's schemes? Zill's grown, but Ab! Ab!'

'Jane,' growled Tercer. 'Now you listen. They was jist—cows. A regular cow drive. Weren't nothing—Jane—'

The visiting family's daughter was aged about fourteen and had a devious look. She spoke up, looking under her brows at Zill Tercer, a nervous laugh in her voice.

'I heard you all stole a thousand cows out from under their noses and stole their Negroes too. I heard you robbed em blind and Coacoochee was running after you and Osceola was running after you and they was wanting to ketch you and hack you with tomachucks and—'

'It weren't like that,' shouted Shay Tercer. He ripped the hat from his head and stood glaring around at them, his benign face contorted with a rare anger. They were all silenced. 'It weren't like that,' he said again.

Jane Tercer packed up her things. They got their horses and made to head back toward their own place. Quinto walked with them a little ways down the road and then took his leave.

'Well, you all take care.' He smiled, grasping Shay Tercer's hand for a moment. 'Don't be strange to visit. We're thinking of cleaning a hog here in a week or so, will ye come? Sundy after next, will ye come?'

Tercer kept Quinto's hand for a moment. He looked down at the man and then said quietly, 'I'm sorry, Nat.'

Quinto peered up at him. 'Hell, Shay. What for?'

He looked away. 'Because there's going to be fighting,' Tercer said. 'There's going to be bad fighting. And I ain't done nothing but help it on.'

'Shay. There ain't no need to talk like that. Maybe there will, but maybe there won't. There's enough chiefs with sense—Charley Emathla, Black Dirt, all them boys. And anyway it ain't your fault if—'

Tercer went on as if the other man hadn't spoken. 'There's going to be fighting,' he said again. 'Pretty soon now. And I don't care how good you are at keeping free of things, Nat. I don't care how—set apart from things you stay. It'll take you in too.'

Quinto's face went very hard. He regarded Tercer, then turned. 'Take care, Shay,' he said, and walked back down the path.

II.

IT GOT HOTTER. It was almost summer. Some of Jane's male relations had begun to filter back up from the south, the ones who had tried their luck on the frontier. It had not gone well for any of them. They did not say much about the situation down there or express much of anything except a fervent desire to be back in Georgia. One of them could not speak at all. A cousin once removed from DeKalb County, he had sustained a mouth injury. Someone had tried to cut out his tongue and had gotten the job about halfway done. The wound needed to be packed and surrounded with cotton at all times, and for that reason his mouth was open in a perpetual O. When he first rode up, speechless and with tufts of cotton bulging from his craw, the Tercers assumed he had gone insane in Indian country. But he had made a friend on his adventures and this redheaded halfwit explained what'd happened. The two visitors came in and occupied Ab and Zill's room.

For meals they poured beef broth down the cousin's mouth. Whiskey also. The two men stayed for a week, drinking the liquor they had failed to sell to the Seminoles, cussing loudly, and sleeping during daytime. Shay Tercer stared darkly at the door every time he passed it but didn't say a word.

The visitors left eventually. There was a stretch of time when the Tercers were able to live their lives as though there was nothing going wrong anyplace on Earth. Even Zill was glad for this peace and kept quiet and tame. He and Ab fished together like they had used to do in the lengthening daylight hours. Then a messenger arrived from Jake Primrose and dismounted in front of the house calling for Mr. Shay.

It was a message going out to all of the citizens nearby. A meeting at noon tomorrow. Jane Tercer squinted. 'Jake Primrose wants a meeting, does he? More schemes, more plans for ruination. We're to go listen to ruination?'

'Where's the meeting?' Shay Tercer asked.

'At Missus Monroe's,' the messenger gasped.

'Oh!' moaned Mrs. Tercer. 'Where else, for the ruination of man?'

The Tercers were there at noon the next day. Jane came along, wearing a black bonnet and a scornful half-smile, just to see that she was right about this ruination business. They could hear before they even rounded the final bend in the road that she probably was. Many people had come early to the meeting to make a day of it, and by noon most were drunk. They stood around making political speeches to nobody or else just lay about the yard. The Tercers went straight to the roadhouse.

There was a crowd in the shadowed room. Not everyone inside was drunk. Some looked almost excessively sober and the soberest of them all was Jake Primrose. He had dressed in all the finery that Florida cattle wealth could buy a man: deer-leather boots polished to a sheen, an indigo-blue shirt bought off a Britisher, silver buttons from Argentina via Pensacola, and a hat of black felt with not one but two bird-o'-paradise feathers looming over the brim. He stood staring at the tops of everyone's heads with a stern expression. Next to him was a military officer, a round-faced captain in a blue uniform. They both remained staring at the tops of everyone's heads until finally Primrose drew a long, deep breath into his lungs to speak.

'Boys,' was what he said, dragging the word out to its greatest possible length, starting low, ending high. One by one eyes turned to him, conversations dropped, hats tipped back. After it got quiet, he said: 'One more drink.'

A roar tore the room. Men leapt, hats were thrown upward to strike the low ceiling and drop to the floor, and there were cries of 'Primrose! Primrose!' The men rushed to the bar, where Mrs. Monroe had already poured several dozen cups of rum and set them up. Shay Tercer exchanged a look with his wife and then slouched over to the bar; he returned slowly, wiping his mouth with his palm.

If this was how the meeting began, the people were optimistic about what would come next. They waited, and then Primrose drew in another long breath.

'Boys,' he bellowed again, in just the same way. 'We are going to have war.'

No one spoke. The only sound was Mrs. Monroe washing the cups in a trough.

'Now, here's a man from the Army to tell us about it. This is Capn Woodmer. Capn,' he said, and turned toward the visitor.

The man stepped forward and hid his arms behind his back. 'I am honored sirs and madams to present myself, Captain Augustus Woodmer, Second Artillery United States Army. I have taken pon myself the duty to report to you free citizens of Florida Territory.' He paused, adjusted his stance. 'The

Seminole element is showing no desire for a legal solution to their problem. Less and less they speak of cooperation, treaties, or friendship. More and more the talk is of staying in the land where their navel strings were first cut and shedding blood if necessary to do it. The call for a move west to the reservation lands was sustained primarily by Charley Emathla. But friends, Charley Emathla is dead.'

A soft moan went through the room. 'Old Charley,' said Rouchefort, hanging his head. 'Old Charley, good old Chief Charley, oh.'

The officer continued. 'He has been assassinated by the one called Powell or Osceola. His body is laying in parts unknown, unburied, for the crows. The white man's money is scattered over his body and the Indians will not approach even to bury it. Likewise the Indians will not approach the altar of good sense, and so I come to my conclusion. We are going to have war.'

The captain stepped back and said no more. There was heavy silence until finally someone spoke up from the back.

'Well, good,' said Zill Tercer, a quaver in his voice. 'Good.'

Jake Primrose jutted out his chin. 'So, ladies and gentlefolk, now we must determine what to do. Capn Woodmer has a proposal which we had ought to hear.' On the wall behind the men was a large square object covered in velvet cloth. He came and undid the velvet from its pins and pulled it away.

On a board about three feet square there was a picture of a fortress, with streaks of pastel pinks and blues. The fortress sat on a hill. On this imagined structure a golden sun was smiling and a flock of white Vs flew and an entire herd of doglike deer was grazing just outside the wall. At the bottom of the picture was lettered *FORT WOODMER. 1835.*

Captain Woodmer had taken up a reed and was pointing at various details. He spoke at an accelerating tempo. 'This is the planned defensework of Fort Woodmer in the heart of northeast Florida. You will see in its features a place of serene and healthful charm. All the rations provided our best fighting men will be provided for the commonest individual. Every last frontier pleasure is here, without any of its drear and hazard. For the gentlemen,' he said, drawing little circles with the reed, 'shooting parties from the battlements every morning and night. The deer are plenteous as flies. And they may even let you take potshots with the big ten-pounder cannon, boys! For the ladies, I am told that there are a dozen dutch ovens on order and several new-model washboards too. The houses are spacious and airy, with at least one wax-paper window each. As for the children, they will get to grow up under the stern gaze of our military men—the best exemplars of mannish virtue and uprightness. All told, Woodmer will be the finest place of resort in this territory.'

'I hear Fort King is nice,' said toothless Smith.

'Fort King is a hogwallow,' said Captain Woodmer.

For a while the audience just murmured. Then someone else spoke from the back. People turned to look at him. It was Nat Quinto. Everyone in the place knew Nat, but they were not used to seeing him in public houses—and certainly not like this, drinking rum. 'It's all very fine, very fine,' he said. 'But tell us, sir Captain. Will the fort have a French chef or jist a Castilian one? And will they be serving veal in wine or only stuffed quail?'

Jake Primrose himself seemed bemused to see Quinto. 'You heard the man, Nat. The fort will have standard rations. Fine govment rations.'

Quinto waved his hand. 'Due respect to you, Jake, but I was speaking to yon captain, and I'd be pleased just to hear from him. Unless you and the Army is speaking for each other now.' He looked at Captain Woodmer. 'What I really mean to ask, sir Captain, is what might move us regular folks to come in to your...building, there.' He gestured at the crude picture.

'Defense, sir,' the officer said. 'The assurance of defense from the savages.'

'They're coming for us, Nat,' Primrose said. 'Don't be thick. War's coming, and the skelping knife. The Red Stick has come pon this country. They'll cut the hearts out of every corpse they catch, mark me, babes and old folks alike, and drink the blood.' Murmurs and moans. An elderly woman fainted. 'They'll come for me first, because I've got the cows. But before long they'll come for every common man in the territory. War, man, war.'

'You know what's good for bringing war on, Jake?' Quinto said. 'Soldiers. You know what to build for to have people come attack ye? Walls and pickets. You know how to get people to steal and pillage from ye? Take things what used to be theirs. I figure we're doing everything we cain to bring a fine war, yes sir, a right fine war.'

'Well now,' Primrose chortled. 'Nat sounds like he's got a heart for the red Indins. Some sort of fellow-feeling with em. I swear,' he said, and lost his toothy smile. 'I swear, Quinto, sometimes you talk like you ain't no white man atall.'

'It ain't got shit to do with the Indins,' Nat said. 'Every man in this territory who knows me knows I got nothing to hide. Want something of mine? If you're a friend, ask and I'll give ye as I have. If you ain't friend, come through me and take it if you cain. But I didn't come to this country to hide in no blockhouse.

Not at all. I've not quarreled with anyone. Ain't tampered with no one's living. And so I don't plan on getting mixed up in this—' He searched for the word, and then found it. 'Ugliness.'

He stood up, a little unsteadily. 'I'm going. Don't worry, Smith,' he said to the gap-toothed Primrose partisan. 'You don't have to do nothing foolish like try to throw me out. I won't bother you here no longer, and I won't disturb you in your blockhouse neither.' And he picked his way between the chairs until he came to the door.

Then he turned slightly back toward the room, framed in daylight, straightening his hat. 'Come to think of it,' he said. 'Why don't we just let Jake have the whole place to hisself? Let him sort of spread hisself out in there, the way he likes to do. With his cows and whatnot. I think that'd be nice of us.' And he stepped out into the daylight.

A sickly, big-skulled man named Goolby stood up. 'Yes, forget the fort, folks, jist give it all to Primrose! The Indins will come first for him who's got the cows, so let old Jake take your herds—them who hasn't already done so! They'll be ten years about skelping him, tweaking out ever last hair on his head, and ten years drawing out his heart, for all the herds he's got!'

'Oh now, oh now,' Primrose said over the sudden noise of the crowd. 'Yes, yes, it's true, there's some of us men who worked for a fortune, it's true. Then there's other of us who're deer-faced yellow-legged clay-eating lie-telling runt-whelps, yes, it's true.'

Goolby was clawing and hollering to be heard above the crowd. 'All cows to Primrose, all cows to Primrose!' he said. 'They can spend a year on the forelock and a year on the pate! Let them skin the corn-silk offen his jawbone too! We're saved, folks, we're saved!'

Smith turned toward Goolby with his fists balled, ready to defend his employer's honor. But on his way he stepped on Little Tom's toe and without hesitation Little Tom clapped Smith on the side of the head. Within ten seconds the brawl became general. After one minute every last chair in the roadhouse had been smashed over someone's skull or back. It was fortunate that the furniture had been built rickety, for just that purpose. Goolby squirmed his way over to the edge of the room and with both hands held prayerwise in front of his head executed a neat swandive through the open window.

The fight lasted a long time and by the end of it many men were left lying on the floor of Mrs. Monroe's, under the influence of concussions and liquor, and did not wake up until morning.

Not everyone stayed for the brawl. Shay Tercer had ducked out before the first chair flew, with a peaceful man's instinct for coming violence. He even managed to toss both his sons into the cart before they realized what they were missing. But before he could mount up, Jake Primrose came and touched him on the elbow.

'Well?' Primrose said over the noise. 'What did you think, old boy? Fort Woodmer!' He was beaming, he seemed to think the event had been a great success. The brawl had not touched him.

'I don't know, Jake,' Tercer said. 'I jist don't like the idea of it—going in and sitting in that place. I mean, it seemed like folks didn't like the idea of it.' A bottle flew out of the open window and shattered against a tree.

'Oh, they'll come in when the time comes, just as soon as things get a little hot up here. And so will you, for that matter.' He beamed up at the Tercer family, winked at Jane.

'Maybe, Jake,' Tercer murmured. 'But I'm jist not sure.'

'Well, we've got us a cattle drive first anyhow,' said Primrose.

'A drive?'

'Hell yes, man. I'm contracted to provide six hundred head, at a sweet price too. Don't you know they'll need beef for all them people in the fort? Not to mention the soldiers. It's going to be fat times for us, Shay. All our rations provided. The quartermasters paying for our beef with paper dollars, while all day we're just sitting making money. Don't you see? Oh, it's beautiful, cain't you see it?'

'I don't know, Jake,' Tercer said, quietly but clearly. 'I don't guess it looks too favorable to me.'

But the cattleman appeared not to have heard him. He reached up and scrubbed young Ab's head as he turned to go back into the roadhouse. 'Did you know your daddy is the best cowhunter in Florida, boys?' he said. 'The very finest there is. Couldn't do a thing without him. I am lucky to have him. Lucky, lucky to have him.' And he swung back into the dark roadhouse from which bellows and crashes and cries were still emanating, raising his finger for a rum.

In the middle of a cold month they drove Primrose's whole herd north, the cows cropping the frost-stiff grass. They came to the Army supply point at Garey's Ferry and Primrose went to see the quartermaster. When he came back to his fellow cowmen, he whooped and danced despite the cold.

'He's gon take the whole herd, fellows,' he said. 'Ever last head gon stay right here under lock and key and gun and bayonet. Right here in the fences. You ever known such luck? They'll cull a hunnert every month and keep a running tally and the total will come in gold as soon as the war's over. And this war won't be no thing at all. Ain't that as simple as you please?'

'How's a war a war if it ain't no thing at all?' Old Rouchefort asked, but Primrose was tossing sacks of coins around. 'Here's our advance. We're going to Saint Augustine, boys, and we're going to buy the town. New tog and new shoes. That Fort Woodmer is gonter be a bed o' lilies, time we get done laying in it. Let's go.'

They arrived at Saint Augustine and immediately wondered if they were in the right city. The shops were boarded shut and there was no one in the streets. The men looked around for a glimpse of a Minorcan lady but saw not a single dresshem. They came down the narrow avenues, dejected, banging on store-fronts, heading toward the only place they were sure would be open, the Army store at the Spanish castillo.

They crowded into the room. The officer was an obese man with greasy jet-black hair. Primrose began talking as soon as they entered. 'You, Willikins,' he said. 'What's happened here?'

The officer looked up from a book and spread his face in a mean smirk. 'What do you mean, what's happened?'

'I mean what's happened. Where's everybody. Why ain't nothing open. I come here with my men looking for a good time of it, and ain't nothing happening.'

The man raised his eyebrows and smirked some more. 'Why, I should say there isn't. Everyone is indoors hiding, if they're here at all. The rich people left, all the merchants. Gone to Savannah, Charleston, what have you.' He spoke gleefully, the way miserable men speak when giving bad news.

'Why? What's happened? I know Emathla's killed, but what else is happened?'

'Oh, you don't know?'

'No, I don't goddamned know. What's been happening?'

'There's two families murdered in the past week. That's the report. Both homesteads burnt to the dirt. Way far north in the territory, too, not far from here. Oh yes, people are a little scary about it right now, I guess you would say, they're very scary about it indeed. Whole families burnt to ashes right there on their homeplace. Old granddad right down to the babes.'

Primrose did not speak for a moment. Shay Tercer grabbed him by the shoulder and moved him out of the way. 'Gunpowder,' he said. 'Give us gunpowder. Whatever ye got.'

But the officer looked to his book and did not answer. 'Gunpowder,' Tercer said again. 'I can't give you any,' the officer said quietly. Shay Tercer took out his bag of money and held it in front of the man. 'That's gold,' he said. 'Give me two barrels.' But the officer shook his head, looked away. Tercer continued asking for gunpowder until at last the officer slammed his fist onto the desk.

'There is no damned gunpowder,' he shouted. 'None. We have had no spare gunpowder in this place since September.'

Shay Tercer stepped back. He looked at the man, almost smiling. 'Why, you sold it to them,' he said. 'Every last barrel. Didn't you. They came up here with their deer skins and coon skins and you sold the Indins every last barrel. Didn't you, you blamed fools.'

The men exited the store. They got on their horses and galloped out of the empty echoing city.

They traveled through the night. Their route led directly past the small parcel where Rouchefort had his house. They got there and in the darkness saw the shape of Rouchefort's old shack in flames. By that light they saw his corn crib with the door kicked off its hinges and stripped clean of its contents, and his small pen with the fence dismantled and all his cows gone. The cowmen looked to Old Rouchefort but he just gazed blankly and made no motion whatsoever to turn in toward the place or even to slow down. He just rode on past and so they did too, spurring up their horses a little faster.

The cowmen got their families and moved for Fort Woodmer as soon as they reached home. When they arrived the construction was not quite finished. Some settlers remained in their wagons outside of the walls, not yet ready to go in. Probably they were weighing their options.

The place was much smaller than they had expected. It was the same as the fort in the picture, the same dimensions and particulars. But in that picture they had seen it from about thirty degrees' elevation. In real life they walked through a yard of scuffed dust which had turned to mud in places from the soldiers' latrine and entered a place which looked more or less like a large, low wooden hatbox.

There were troops already living inside, as well as the Crackers who had sold the land to build the fort. At the start of construction the place had probably smelled like pine pitch and fresh sawdust but now it smelled strongly of human beings and other animals. The new arrivals stood at the gate and looked around. An intimate ecosystem of dogs, chickens, goats, hogs, and humans had arisen, with a connective network of fleas. The animals came around the newcomers to greet them, as did the fleas. The established residents hung back, keeping to themselves, already colored grey by inactivity.

The Tercers and the Primroses arrived at the same time. Jake Primrose walked into the place and was greeted by nobody and did not appreciate the feeling. He began asking around for Woodmer. 'Where's my Captain? Where's the captain of this fort, hey?'

A barely uniformed man with grizzled cheeks and loose hair was walking past, heading toward the munitions shed with some papers in his hand. 'That's me, sir,' he said, and came over to shake hands. 'Captain Wiman, Second Dragoons. Pleasure to meet you. Bembrose, you say? Primrose? Ah. Well, Mister Primrose, good to meet you.' And the man moved off as quickly as he'd come.

'Hang on,' Primrose said, to his back. 'Where's my Woodmer? What's happened to Captain Woodmer?'

Captain Wiman sighed and shook his head. 'Died last week,' he said. 'Out cutting trees for the fort and the crosscut hit his leg. The rot spread quick. God rest him.' He kept walking.

Jake looked around, plainly confused. He seemed to be feeling a change in his situation. 'I had an arrangement,' he said. 'He was expecting me. There was to be a place prepared. Where am I to go?'

Wiman stopped, flipped among some of the papers he was carrying, looked down one of them with his finger. 'Primrose. Primrose. Ah, here. Primrose—Tent Fourteen. In that row there.' He indicated a line of canvas hovels placed side-to-side.

The cowman worked his yellow-bearded jaw. 'That it?' he said. 'Is that it?' He turned on the new captain. 'Is that all you got for the man what organized this whole goddamn show?'

Captain Wiman checked the list again. 'It says Tent Fourteen.' And he went on to attend to his business in the munitions shed.

In a little while Shay Tercer caught up with the new captain. Tent Two, the man told him.

All the cowhunters came and took up residence in the block-house. By midweek Primrose had shown enough gold to have himself and his family moved into Captain Woodmer's vacated quarters, an actual house with walls. But this did not seem to satisfy him. He brooded and paced behind the waxpaper windows.

The Tercers took up residence in Tent Two. One room, canvas. Three army cots and a shelf. Their belongings fit comfortably enough, except for Jane's cooking utensils. There was no kitchen. Meals were taken communally in the big canteen. They ate the disappointing rations all together. People cooked the occasional squirrel or possum on a private fire, but this canteen was their common fate: if it ran thin, so would they.

The inside of the square fort contained about forty tents like the Tercers'. They were arranged in rows around a central watchtower and a barracks. One entire corner of the structure was taken up by the dining area; the hospital tents occupied another, the munitions shed a third. In the fourth corner was a low, broad structure about sixty feet square. That was where the slaves were. The shelter was little more than a low, unbroken canvas roof about six feet high, supported by posts. An outsider could barely see into it an arm's-length, and its residents hung blankets over all its openings. To keep the chill out, they said. A few slaves, like Primrose's man Oscar, occupied standalone tents like the white settlers, but the majority lived in this strange shantytown. There were whole avenues inside and intersections and an apothecary after a fashion and a canteen which dispensed the food they were given by the Army. There were rumors of other structures taking shape too, possibly civic, possibly religious. But nothing was done to counteract them. The settlers could not be bothered with the raising of the slaves' spirits; they were too preoccupied with the sinking of their own.

Ab had a spot where he sometimes perched and tried to see into this big shanty. He never saw much. He went for information to Oscar's son Zech, his old associate, who was in there often. What was going on in there, Ab wanted to know. 'Oh, it's just us making do,' Zech said, 'it's just us folks making do,' but he did not meet Ab's eyes when he said this; he moved past Ab, and did not laugh and joke with him as he once did. Ab could only know what Zech decided to tell him about the place and Zech decided to tell him nothing. And so the boy could stand a ways off and peer and observe and eavesdrop and try his hardest to imagine what was taking place inside that crazyquilted warren but he would never, ever truly know.

In those early days people could leave the fort with ease. They went and gleaned the nearby fields and shot squirrel, turkey, and deer. But somehow the time spent outside in the open made the return to its confines even worse. And so eventually the hunts stopped and they stayed inside the blockhouse and comforted themselves with the idea that something would happen soon.

Troops went out, came back. Sentinels changed shifts every four hours. Meals were served morning, noon, and night, each smelling identically of cornmeal and faintly rancid bacon grease. Once a week a supply train came and delivered letters containing no news, and for the rest of the week the inhabitants would sit around talking about all the news the next one would bring. As it happens where the flow of life has stopped, the future gained terrible importance. Plans, possibilities, prophesies: they were everything, they were what people lived on. No one talked about the past because they could not bear it; no one talked about the present because there was no such thing. The whole arena of life had shifted to the future and each day became one long anticipation of itself, eventually foiled: pacing around or sitting on corn sacks, drunk by the afternoon.

Ab was too young to find fault with the adults for all this but he could not help hating it. He had one good friend: Teek Geyer's son June. He knew how to ride hogs and galloped them around the walls. He taught Ab how and they held bareback races, which attracted some attention. But this excitement would only last a little while and then the people would return to their cornsacks and rumjugs. June would keep on riding the hog slowly around the inside of the fort, alone.

Toward dusk Ab would steal out through the gate and run down the slope into the trees. Out where the breeze actually blew and the deer actually walked and there were ferns beneath the oaks. The boy would walk a ways and then lie down. He would stay there, in the absence of noise and talk, in the presence of hares. He would gaze at the fort. From there he could see how small it really was. He could walk all the way around its outer clearing in a few minutes, this little pinebox which contained his family and everyone he knew. He would sit on a tree branch looking at his whole world concentrated in that building and fight the urge to burn it down.

One day in December, Ab woke up to the sound of a woman

crying.

The sound drew the boy as if on a string, pity and terror terribly mixed within him. The sound came from Oscar's place, a few yards away. The boy drifted to the tent and in the grey morning light he found his father already standing there.

Oscar and his wife Cassie were sitting on a box. Cassie was crying. Shay Tercer frowned, asking questions. When Ab came up he heard his father say, 'Where'd he go?'

Oscar spoke quietly. 'He just left out.'

'Well, where to?'

'I don't know. He just—' The man waved one hand numbly. 'Left out.'

'So he's jist gone.'

'That's right,' Oscar said, with a strange near-laugh in his voice. 'Said he didn't care to stay on with his daddy no more. Said his daddy weren't no real man. I ain't no real man, it seems. Not to my son I ain't.' Oscar shook his head. He looked at the dirt. Cassie's weeping was an unbroken sound, long, not loud.

Ab turned and walked away from the tent. He went straight toward the southwest corner. The blankets over the slaves' shelter hung lifeless. One of them had fallen in a little and the boy tore through it and stepped inside. The place was empty, it was dead. Still there was the smell of living people, and bedding and abandoned belongings visible on the ground, and there was altogether the sense of a rapture which had taken an elect and disappeared them forever, leaving the damned behind to view the aftermath. The boy began to shake. He turned and went out the way he had come in.

It took a while for the alarm to be sounded. It was mid-morning before the soldiers began going through the place with their bayonets, shredding it as they went. The structure fell quickly. It became a pile of blankets and old tarpaulin and palm fronds and the posts which had held it up; nothing stirred underneath.

Shouts, curses. A wailing of women to soundly beat Cassie's wailing, though these were cries of fear, not mourning. They were not weeping because of personal loss. The entire slave population in that fort had been owned by only about five of the white inhabitants. Most of the Crackers could not have afforded to buy the slaves' shoes, let alone their lives, and yet they wailed after them all the same. The children were taken indoors, as if to keep them safe from some ambient evil.

Amid the confusion, a few people tried to figure out how forty people had exited the fort unnoticed. There was a raccoon hole discovered, but it was not big enough for an adult and was nowhere near the shanty. There were some ropes discovered too; they might have climbed and then rappelled down the outside of the wall. But the women, and the babies, and all the aged? The settlers were flabbergasted. A few people had considered the possibility of a few slaves trying to escape—but not all of them, and not all at once. There were calls for a search party. Captain Wiman was remarkably deaf to them. He stood listening with his arms crossed, gazing at the ruins of the shantytown. A few of the residents got guns and stomped around waving them, trying to make something happen. Then a rider raced up to the fort from the west.

It was an express from Fort Brooke near the Gulf of Mexico. The rider made no effort to keep the news quiet but was shouting almost before he got down from the saddle, news of disaster. The people stood in a ring around Captain Wiman and the messenger where they spoke.

The young soldier was almost crying. The ride through those woods had driven him wild with fear. 'A massacre. Major Dade. His entire detachment gone, wiped out, killed crossing the river. They killed em in their own blood. One hunnert seven went out and there's only two men made it back.'

Silence. The boy wheezed. 'And only one of the two can talk. They's taking musketshot out of him right now. He says there was a thousand Indins.'

Captain Wiman stood with his arms crossed. 'What word— what report is there from Major Dade?'

'He's dead.'

'Dead. What of Captain Fraser?'

'He's dead.'

Another officer broke in. 'Old Doctor Gatlin, what of him? What's he say? Old Doc Gatlin out of Springfield, what's he say?'

'Dead,' the boy cried. 'There's only two men saved and they're both privates. Only two, don't you hear me? The rest of the hunnert and seven souls is laying out by the river.'

There were other questions but the boy couldn't repeat himself anymore. They brought him coffee and tried to calm him down. The horse he rode in on died in the corral with blood foaming at its mouth, and the boy himself fell down and took ill and did not move for two days.

As for the people of Fort Woodmer, they drew back dazed. They went around like people who have had a chair pulled from under them. The settlers did not talk any more about what must have happened with the slaves. It was plain enough. There had been some form of communication between them and the Seminoles for months, maybe longer. Who knew how many times the Indians had been at their back doors at night, in the side yards, whispering. And then at some coordinated signal too subtle for the settlers' ears they had deserted. The idea of going out searching for the slaves was abandoned, of course. The fortress was adrift, surrounded on four sides by an ocean which would not give back what it had taken away.

It was the instant of the onset of the Second Seminole War. The massacre of Major Dade's soldiers was like the ringing of a bell. And if the massacre of Major Dade's command was a bell then the sudden escape of a thousand slaves all across Florida into a state of rebellion was its loud echo. And the answering hysteria of the white settlers was like the clamor of so many birds startled and lifting up from their roosts to take flight, cawing, wheeling.

III.

WHEN THE SUN WENT LOW in the west, the boy would leave the fort by the raccoon hole in the east wall. The shadow of the pickets stretched all the way down the slope to the treeline. He would scrabble through the high grass down the slope, his heart pounding. This was better than sneaking through the gate like he had used to do. The gate was always shut now and was carefully watched—everything was carefully watched, and it was even a challenge to slink between the patches of scorched earth where the sentinels lit their brush-pile fires, but he had never yet been spotted.

From out in the trees he could hear the bugle sound for evening watch and hear the voices shouting to each other to take up positions. The sentinels lit the massive brush piles they had stacked during the day. Then Ab watched the fires leap up with enough sparks to deaden the pink sunset. There was fear in the men's hoarse voices, fear of the forest where Ab now walked. The boy would observe them making their preparations, very far away and very small, and stalk among the trees like a god.

For a while the sounds to be heard were pleasant, even comforting. The whippoorwills, the bullfrogs. The horses whinnying in their corral. Drunks of the fort sealing their last quaff of the day with a fistfight. The bugler playing evening colors. June Geyer arguing loudly with someone who was not arguing back, hog or human or angel. Ab would sit under a tree and take it all in, as if it happened by his permission. But then the wolves would start howling. When the wolves started howling, the boy would go back inside.

Late one afternoon, Ab left the fort, tromped the creek, and came back to the clearing before sunset. It was a clear dusk. He saw the sentinels preparing for the night's watch as usual. But then in the quiet he felt more than heard a movement to his left. He turned and saw them: dozens of people creeping through the undergrowth toward the fort. They wore maroon and blood-red robes, their faces painted. They moved to the left and right of the tree where Ab stood, gliding as if on rails. When they reached the edge of the woods, they stopped. The Seminoles were so close that Ab could hear them whispering as they brought up their muskets. He could hear the leather of their moccasins creaking as they knelt.

Ab stood pressed against the oak. He sucked in breath and held it, certain that something was about to happen; then it didn't, and he had to let the breath out, the air shuddering between his lips. In front of him the Seminoles were waiting for something too. They crouched, sighting across the field.

A musket rang out at last. Across the field a soldier clutched his neck and fell without a sound. For an instant there was silence, and then a cry came. It was like a death-cry, but it came from the shooter, not the casualty. Mingled in it was the sound of gladness.

A pause, then a soldier shouted from up on the walls. The trees, the trees!

Now the Seminoles in front of Ab stood up and began to fire. They fired again and again, even as shots began to be returned from the loopholes in the fort walls. There were several groups of fighters ranged around the fort in a semicircle, maybe seventy in all. After the first volley half of the Indians, every other one in the line, began to duck and sprint toward the fort through the grass, heading for the horse corral.

The boy observed all this, still no more than a dozen paces behind the firing line. The Indians threw themselves down on their left sides to reload, stood up, fired again. The return fire sang through the trees, shredding leaves, thumping into logs. Still Ab stood. As one of the Seminoles in front of him was rising up to aim he received a musketball in the leg and fell back down shrieking. In a moment he pushed himself up with his hands and hopped a few yards back from the treeline and came to a patch of ground covered in ferns, where he fell down again. This brought him to within ten feet of where Ab was standing. The Indian took out a big knife from a scabbard on his waist and began laying into the wound in his thigh with the point of the blade, digging for the ball. But suddenly he stopped. With the expression of a man realizing a very curious fact, he turned up his eyes from his bloody leg and looked straight at the boy.

They held their positions for a moment: the brave with the knife poised over his wound; the boy standing against the tree, hiding his hands behind his back as if he had been caught in some mischief. Ab thought he recognized the man, but the man did not recognize Ab. Slowly the bemused expression left the warrior's face and he pulled his knife up out of the wound.

As if by previous agreement, the boy turned to run at the very same instant the Indian stood up. Neither had said a word.

Ab heard the Indian hopping along behind him on one leg, then trying the other leg, and then beginning to limp after him at a pace that was at least as fast as the boy's. They ran like this for a few yards before the warrior shouted and was answered by several voices at the Indians' front line. Other braves came running, on two good legs each. Ab dared not look back. He ran toward a distant tumbled-in sinkhole, thinking that somehow this would save him. He seemed to be running slower than he had ever run in his life.

But then a sound like a thunderclap came from the direction of the fort. A tree snapped in half behind him. The noise came again, followed by a cry among the Indians. A third crack, more shrieks, and a ten-pound cannonball came skipping through the woods a little to Ab's right. There were more blasts. The shots came through the undergrowth with a sound like a tremendous cloth being ripped. Cannonballs flew past him and still the boy did not stop running, even when he realized that the Indians were not chasing him anymore, even when he passed the place where one cannonball had finally come to rest in the loam, even when he passed from the hardwoods into a lowland bog and a country he had never seen before.

He went through the bog as far as he could until full dark and then he climbed a tree to wait out the wolves. There was no sleeping, with the cold and the noise of the wilderness all around and under him and the wolves very close, then far away, then close again. He was fully awake until sunrise and then he climbed down and kept on through the frigid bog. In the oaks on the far side he found a trail that led south, and he walked down it for much of the day until he found marks that he recognized. It was the road that led past Nat Quinto's homestead.

Quinto was a common subject of debate inside the fort. In his absence he was called insane, he was called an Indian collaborator, he was accounted a fool, he was given up for dead. But now after an hour's walk Ab had come into the man's clearing. It was bare-swept and tidy. Nat was kneeling over a dead deer with his skinning knife. His son, who was seven, hung on his father's shoulder as he worked. Both heard Ab and looked up.

'Why, Ab,' Nat said, and got up smiling. Then he said 'Ab,' again, with concern. He laid his knife by and wiped his hands on the grass. 'Simeon, get water,' he told his son, and the child ran off.

Quinto came and knelt down in front of the visitor. He tugged the left side of the boy's shirt, beneath the sleeve. There were two identical holes drilled in the cotton about an inch and a half apart. 'Why, son. What's happened?' He ran a hand through the boy's hair, next to his ear. It came away sticky with blood.

'Where else does it hurt?' he asked.

'Doesn't hurt nowhere.'

'What about this.' The man laid a finger on the left side of his face. 'You've been shot through the ear, boy.'

'Doesn't hurt,' the boy said, a little quieter this time, and his eyes began to fill.

'Well now. We've got ourselves a tough nut, Lucy. Took a bullet and barely knew it. A tough nut.'

The woman had come up in silence and was standing over them. 'He surely is,' she said. Nat Quinto looped one arm under the seat of the boy's pants and stood up with him and walked toward the house.

The house was small and clean. An infant lay in a sling. Simeon ran in with a bucket of water from the spring and stood back wide-eyed while Lucy dipped into it with a cloth to clean Ab's wound. In the meantime Nat put his finger to the holes in Ab's shirt. 'This ain't muskets,' he said. 'It's the wrong size hole for that. This looks like a big bore, like Army rifles. Boy, what's happened?' But Ab was feeling where Lucy cleaned his ear and was feeling the small notch which was missing, and he finally began to cry.

Lucy stopped Nat's questions. 'He needs to eat, and he needs to rest,' she said. 'Come on, Ab darling. Ain't no need to talk right now. Just go lie down in the back there, and we'll get you something to eat.'

They put Ab in the boys' bed, and Lucy set about fixing him a meal. She did not talk, but the busy activity of her strong arms and heavy, honeycolored hair was more soothing than talk. When Ab had finished eating, he lay back on the clean bedsheets and looked up at the ceiling, his wide-open eyes staring at nothing.

When he woke up the next morning, Ab went outside to the porch to sit. The yard was small, stamped smooth, unfenced except by a ring of pines which let in the breeze and the redbirds. Then Nat Quinto came through it too, carrying a hoe. He walked up and sat on the stoop. He produced two small oranges from his pockets, handed one to Ab, and kept the other for himself.

'I'm trying to grow china oranges. What do you think?' He

bit the thick rind open. 'They're a good investiment. No man has figured out how to rustle an orange tree yet, y'see.'

They sat for a time without talking. Minutes passed before Quinto spoke. 'We've got to get you back there. You know that, don't you? You'll plain kill your mama and daddy, being missing. You've got to go back to them.'

The boy sat glaring in the big cane chair, the linen bandage tied around his head beginning to slip. He was beginning to cry again, a little. 'I hate the damned Indins,' he hissed.

'Watch your tongue, boy. You ain't inside my wife's house but you're close enough.'

'I hate that fort too. I hate it,' the boy went on.

'Well. I wouldn't blame you there, son,' Quinto said, more quietly. 'No I would not.'

The man stood up and began to attend to two horses hitched by the porch, saddled for a journey. 'But let me ask you this, Ab. Do they feed you in there? Are you eating?'

'Yes,' the boy said.

'Well, be glad. Because that's more than we're doing around here sometimes.' Quinto drew the saddle cinch tight.

'Shoot, you fed me plenty,' Ab said.

'Well now. That was visitin food,' the man said. 'We ain't sunk so low we ain't got visitin food.'

Color had fully returned to Ab's face. Soon he got up on a horse to leave with the man. Quinto rode through the woods toward Fort Woodmer. It was afternoon when they spotted the smoke rising from the fort. They were the normal campfires and sentinel fires, nothing more than that. Quinto got down from his horse and swung Ab down too.

Ab looked down the road, the smoke a quarter mile off. 'I'm going to walk from here,' he said.

'Sure, Ab. Sure.' Quinto shook the boy's head beneath his palm. 'Give your daddy my regards. Mama too.' He started to walk off. 'But nobody else, only them.' And he got back on his horse and headed back the way they'd come.

The boy was amazed by his reception at the fort. Everyone was angry with him. They were as angry as it is possible to be with a child, they were utterly humorless. And it was not just his mother and father but strangers, too, and military men. Various punishments were suggested beyond the standard parental beating but none of them took place. Instead they just confined him and kept eyes on him all the time.

June Geyer was the only one who understood. It made sense to him, he could see the logic of the adventure. He joined Ab by the Tercers' tent, scratching his unkempt hair. 'It's horse shit, Ab. Horse shit. They ought to give you a parade. I knew where you'd gone, but I didn't say nothing. I knew you'd wanter get out there again soon as you got back.'

'I don't know, June.'

'Horse shit, Ab,' the older boy said. 'Look here.' He unbunched a dingy piece of cotton cloth. Inside were two dozen ripe blackberries, shining bright-black. 'Found me a peach patch, a peach patch, a peach!' He quietened himself with a fist balled over his mouth.

But Ab shook his head no. He did not want to go back outside of the wall; he no longer wanted to leave the fort and join with the forest. All of a sudden he wanted to do like the others did, just sit and wait. Though he did help himself to a few of June's berries.

After the horse raid an extra sentinel force had been placed by the corral and defenses were ratcheted up everywhere. But there was no big campaign to go and get the horses back, never mind the escaped slaves.

A few people interrogated Captain Wiman about this. He tried to explain why they did not act. 'We are a blockhouse force of a hundred and thirty troops, fifty miles north of the Indian borderline,' he said. 'I'd need no less than one hundred troops to search for the gang that attacked us, to overwhelm them, and to retake our horses. But those troops could search this territory for years and never find the same party. Meanwhile this fort, without its hundred avenging angels, would be undermanned and ready for the knives and muskets. Our troops would come back and find every last soul dead. And who would ride the horses then?'

All this made sense, but no one wanted to hear it. Smith bared his teeth and spoke for the people. 'You mean those Indins is free to hold my horses and paint em with their damn zigged zags and keep all my Negroes, too, doing God knows what with em?'

'Your Negroes?' Little Tom asked. 'What sorry Negro ever let emselve be kept by you?'

'Why, there was one in Saint Augustine that one week,' Goolby crowed. 'Wasn't Anna her name?'

A fortwide fistfight ensued, with the privates and some of the sergeants joining in. They were starting to get a taste of the Florida way of life, these Maine and Mississippi boys. The afternoon argument, the twilight fistfight, and then the evening apologies and embraces and rum-and-water. Unconsciousness by moonrise. That way they would not be awake to listen to the wolves.

This way of life went on for weeks. There were rumors of bloodshed elsewhere in the territory. There was news of a battle on the Withlacoochee that had not gone well for the Army. Every few days a patrol would come back in to the fort and report Indian trails spotted, or actual Indians spotted, with a few gunshots exchanged. But the Seminoles always melted away. In the meantime, the supply trains to the fort became less frequent. Beef was becoming scarce. Tobacco was chewed and swallowed instead of smoked. Supplies were being diverted farther south, where there was stiffer fighting—to Fort King, Fort Drane, Fort Defiance—and so Fort Woodmer was neglected. Inside the walls the fisticuffs became fiercer and the rum drinks heavier, to deepen and prolong sleep through the night.

Not everyone could be satisfied with this way of life. Jacob Primrose, for one. He did not enjoy rum and fisticuffs anymore. What he liked were bold strokes and big developments. Whenever Primrose was preparing to announce his latest bold stroke, he would gather a goodsized flock of children around himself, and an invalid or two: that was the sign. The more violent the plan, the more children. One February morning he came to the Tercers' tent and borrowed Ab; he already had his little daughter in one arm and his son Hadjo by his side. Old Rouchefort tagged along a few steps behind. 'Come on, Abby,' is all Primrose said. Ab came.

They headed over to Captain Wiman's quarters in a bunch. 'Tighten up there, Hadjo,' he muttered, and 'Come even with us, Ab,' and 'Quit crying, baby girl.' They arrived in a close formation, but Primrose had a casual look on his face, as if he had just been out for a midday stroll and happened to accumulate a pack of dependents.

'Good morning, Captain Wiman.'

'Good morning, Mister Primrose.'

'I want to talk to you, Captain.'

'I know you do, Primrose.'

Jake set his daughter down. 'Do you see this little girl here?'

'I do.'

The cowman took ahold of Ab's shoulder. 'Do you see this boy here?'

'I do.'

'You know, he nearabout got carried away by Indins. Near had his tender little head skelped. Except for the sovereignty and goodness of God had his tender little head skelped. '

'I see him. What are you planning, Primrose?'

'We's feeling menaced around here, Captain. That's the simple truth.'

'I feel that way too,' the captain said, shuffling some papers.

'Menaced,' repeated Old Rouchefort. 'Menaced.' He liked the word.

'It ain't safe here, Captain.'

'I'd think not, Primrose. We're in the middle of a war.'

'More has got to be done. More action. More provision. More bold strokes.'

'Ah, Mister Primrose. Your counsel is valued. But we are coming off a national lean time, as you know, and the U.S. Government is overextended—'

'Here's the tip of it, Captain Wiman. Myself and a few other of the folks here have reached out to a militia commander in the area for extra forces.'

'Militia won't be needed. We've already got a part of General Call's Florida Horsemen, you know. Those troops over yonder.' He waved his hand toward a few country boys sunning themselves next to a shed.

'I know we got them Florida Horsemen boys. We have a few Georgia Bullies mixed in too, I believe. They're all right, in their place. But the ones we want to bring in are a different sort. Their head is a man named Captain Addison and he is known to me personally as a very keen fighter.'

'Addison?' Wiman said.

Old Rouchefort came alongside Primrose. He took ahold of his arm. 'Jake,' he said quietly. 'You don't mean that, do you? Jake.'

'I do mean it, old man,' Primrose said. He shook his arm loose. 'He's who we need. He's the one to bring things to a point.'

'No,' said Captain Wiman, regaining himself. 'No. Absurd. Jason Addison is a murderer. A leader of murderers. King of them. I hear about the deeds they have committed down in the reservation land. They have done unconscionable things.'

'He's took the fight to them,' Primrose said.

'He is a curse word among every Seminole in this territory. He will bring hell down on us.'

'You're speaking of him,' Primrose said, 'like y'all ain't even on the same side.'

'It is inconceivable that he come here. Absolutely not.'

'One week of Addison here and I guarantee we'll never be harassed agin. The supply trains can start to come through smooth as creekwater. It mayen't be pleasant while he's here among us, but it will teach the Indins, I guarantee that.'

'No,' said Captain Wiman.

But it turned out that Addison and his company were already en route. Several days of debate followed about something which was going to happen anyway. Wiman spewed against the idea. We stand to make it out of this war with nary a scratch, he said, nary a scratch. All we must do is let things transpire as they will and the Indins will wreck themselves elsewhere and we will have peace. But Jake Primrose had a few of the residents bucked up: he reasoned that bringing more troops into the place could only make it safer. How could it not? Wiman and Little Tom and Old Rouchefort and other people who had actually encountered Addison argued against it passionately, and the stalwarts wavered a little. But in the end they fell back on their best point: that it was going to happen whether they liked it or not.

One morning they awoke to the sound of clanking outside the walls. There were some pleasantries, and then the gate opened. A smell which had been working its way between the fenceposts flooded into the fort, which was already no bowl of roses. Rolling with the stench came a mass of men, razorously bayonetted. At their front and center was Addison, smiling broadly. The times had been kind to him. New necklaces of silver hung next to old ones of grey twine and there were bright silk ties threaded through seamy collars. On every shoulder was a big deep-oiled musket and on every hip was a bowie knife handled with fresh white bone. Addison himself wore a fur hat of northern provenance and a beautiful shave which some poor barber had given him earlier that day. He came among the head men of the fort grinning, with his hand and all its filthy fingers extended.

'Yes, hello, Captain Addison, and it's so good to meet you. Hello to all, and what a neat little place this is! The walls, the gates, the guns. Bless me, but it's pretty. And your name, sir? Well fine, fine to meet you. You say you've heard much of me, eh? Well I hope they told the other side of it too—ha, ha! Oh, and who is this over yonder with his belly in the grass—ha, ha! Jake Primrose! Come here, Jake, let me hold you.'

'Hello, Addison,' Primrose said. He came forward with his hand outstretched but it was no use. Addison stepped past the hand and pulled Primrose in to his damp brown jerkin. The look on the cowman's face was something to behold. The variety of it: his mouth was pulled into a smile but the teeth behind it were clenched like a bear trap; his eyes were round and bright but the veins around them swelled and twitched as he tried his very best not to breathe. 'Ah, Jake, my dear friend, Jake. Here we are again, together. Oh, it's wonderful.'

'Yes sir,' muttered Primrose.

'Together again. And didn't I say it? Didn't I say we'd come together again someday, and work together like friends and brothers? Didn't I say it?'

'Yes. Yes sir.'

They finally unclasped. Primrose stepped away, letting out breath as quietly as he could. Addison took a turn around the center of the fort. 'My my,' he said. 'This is what I love to see. White men gathered together for their own protection, it warms my heart to see it. Makes you think there's some hope for this country yet.' He inclined his head in Primrose's direction. 'Don't it, Jake?'

'Yes sir.'

'Because they are out here, make no mistake. This land is just lousy with them. The savage. The larcenist, the loudmouth. Such as have no thought for laws or treaties. Don't they care about treaties? Don't they care about the rule of law? Why, we met one earlier today. Of course the treaty tells him he shouldn't be all the way up here. He knew he wasn't supposed to be here. Angie, Angie, where are you? Bring out our Indian, for these nice people.'

Addison called again for the one named Angie and in a moment she appeared from a supply cart. Amidst the weird array of human morphology in Addison's company no one had yet noticed that there was a woman. She had wild smiling eyes and was sturdy and somewhat buxom, and her hair hung around her face like tattered cloth. But no one was very surprised by her appearance, because of what she carried. On the end of a stick: a scalp of black hair. Skewered on the twigs emerging from that stick: a left ear, a right ear, a nose, and two lips. Together they made up a face. The woman held the base of the stick in her grubby fist and tilted it like a puppeteer. 'This's Brown Horse,' Angie said, and turned her puppet to face the audience. 'Brown Horse is an awful fellow.' She made it dip in toward her cheek for a kiss. 'Aw, geer off!' she squealed, and gave the phantom face a playful slap.

Addison's company rested in the fort for one day and then left again. They went out the way they had come in. They stayed gone for three nights and returned with a new set of rifles and a string of Indian horses and five blackhaired scalps on a string.

This pattern repeated: they would go out, stay gone a while, come back with some trophies and a load of what Addison called seizures. Then they would lay around the fort in a state of extreme relaxation, eating, drinking, and enjoying their piles of contraband. Then without warning they would leave again.

It was a rigid routine and to certain young males of the fort it was immensely appealing. Some of them tried to join; Zill Tercer was one. His father argued against him harder than he had ever argued in his life but the young man just sneered. His mother bawled and wailed; her last coherent sentence was, 'What about that smell, how can you stand that smell?'

Zill laughed. 'Don't you unnerstand?' he said. 'No, I spect you don't unnerstand. That smell is to keep away people like you. Those what can stand it, stand it. They don't give a damn about a little stink. Real fighting men cain't be bothered with a little thing like that. It's jist old everyday folk that care, scaredy-cats, whelps, ninnies, old goats. You get spooked off, and that's how us fighting men like it.' And with that he scoffed again and walked out. He started going out behind Captain Addison. By his second tour he had gotten his first scalp.

When Zill came back in to Fort Woodmer he did not stay in Shay Tercer's tent anymore. Instead he lay in the southwest corner with the rest of the fighters, the area where the slaves used to be. Ab went and found him there. The lad had changed utterly. Everything from the color of his hair—it appeared to be darker—down to what he did with his feet—he did not bounce them when he talked any more. It had all changed. He reclined with his elbow on a cornsack amid the awful stench and smiled at Ab.

The younger boy was shown Zill's first trophy on its mat of gristle. Ab handed it back quickly. Zill smiled some more. 'Why, I wish I could come along and kill an Indin too,' Ab said, for politeness's sake as much anything. But his brother laughed so loudly and scorned him so fiercely that Ab had to respond. 'Well, why in the hell couldn't I?' the boy said. 'I could kill me an Indin anytime. I could fight jist as good as any of you, why couldn't I join?'

Zill laughed again. 'Hah. Cause your daddy'd say no.'

Ab had to keep going. 'Hell. I don't keer—I don't keer what that old fool says. I can go if you did.'

'Don't matter what you keer,' Zill said, smiling still. 'The old fool cain't hold me. He can hold you. Hear that? He can hold you. And I bet he'll hold you til there's no more Indins in Florida left to fight.'

'Won't neither,' Ab said. He was trying to maintain a manly anger but he was almost crying. 'I'm on kill me an Indin before this war is done. You'll see. I'm on kill me my own Indin too.'

Ab left his brother and did not go back to that corner anymore. There was nothing more to talk about. His parents did not go to the encampment to see Zill, but they did ask Ab how he was doing. 'He seems all right,' Ab said. 'He's about the same.'

Addison's militiamen conducted eight of their raids out of Fort Woodmer before the Seminoles followed them back. It was late spring, one month after they had first arrived. The fighters hustled into the defenses faster than usual and shouted for the gate to be shut. Then the north sentinel cried *Indians*, and the cry was repeated by the west sentinel. In a moment the sentinel to the south cried *Indians* too.

Some of the inhabitants climbed onto the platform that ran around the wall to look. At first they did not see anything. There were shadows shifting, but that was all. Then a single figure edged out of the woods.

He did not move like a man but crouched and spun and gamboled like a wild creature. He moved until he was exposed well in front of the trees, then stopped. The figure raised his arms into the air and screamed one shrill word, traveling down the octave: *Kirr*. He was answered by a hundred voices in the forest, a guttural note struck as if from an enormous drum: *Wough*. It came again: *Kirr—wough. Kirr—wough. Wough. Wough. Wough.* Then they fired.

The barrage did not slow for the better part of five minutes. Three of the sentinels and two men inside the battlements were killed immediately and four others were wounded. The rest fell back. The Indians were emboldened to come out from the trees and advance up the slope for better aim. They were in their preferred fighting mode, naked except for a cloth around the waist, shining with black paint and sweat and blood from self-inflicted cuts. As they got closer their painted markings were visible, ornate and painstaking, bars of blood red around the mouth and black hollows around the eyes and patternings on the ribcage. As night fell the firing continued. And before long a soldier peering above the pickets called out, 'The fields, the fields, they'll burn them.' A dozen torches had appeared and were moving to where the crops stood just outside the walls. Quickly the soldiers fired and some of the torches fell to the ground, but others continued and drew through the dry field, and it burned patchily all through the night and into the morning.

That next day the Indians did not draw down or evaporate like they normally did, but remained near the fort. More warriors arrived during the course of the day. Musketballs rang against the picket walls not on the hour but by the minute. People huddled in the belly of the fort and listened for the moment when the Seminoles would flow into the place like water, swamp them, sink them.

On the second night Addison and all his company fled the blockhouse and fought their way out through the Indian line. None of them gave any notice that they were going to abandon the place, not even the new recruits whose mothers and fathers were still in the fort. They simply left. Several were killed while battling through the line, and the next day the Indians displayed the corpses. Ab watched, his face pressed to a loophole in the wall. He strained to see whether any of the pale splayed bodies looked like it might be Zill's. None of them did. All the same, the boy would never see his brother again.

It was summer now. If anyone had thought that the Indians would leave the fort alone once Addison went away they were wrong. They stayed. The area around the fort was thick with them. The woods held death. All the settlers had anymore were the four picket walls and a rectangle of dirt it contained and, above it, the immense and treeless swath of sky.

The days were hot and dry and outrageously long. The dust rose up and did not settle back down. The smallest movement stirred it, and the fort was full of people making the smallest movements. Sitting down in the shade of a shed; getting up to follow the shade as it moved. Every tree and bush had been cut down when they built the fort and all the grass was tromped away, so there was nothing to keep the dust from aspiring heavenward. It stood above the fort like mist over a lake.

It was an uncommonly dry season for that country. These were people accustomed to rains every afternoon and they were disturbed when they did not come. There was a joke: when the clouds went away, the flies came to take up the slack in the market. They provided almost as much shade. But that joke lost popularity when that cloud of flies began to spend most of its time hovering above the hospital shed.

There the surgeon worked. A small, roundheaded man, eyes flat behind round glasses. He seemed to like his job, being handy with the scalpel and the saw. He was known for carrying the musketballs he removed around in his pocket. Some were still round, others flattened or warped from where they had struck bone. They made a musical sound as he walked. Bullet wounds were the simple part of his job: being shot with a gun was child's play compared with the country's other dangers. Yellow fever had come to the fort. At first they could not tell it apart from the sweats of summer heat or the shakings of delirium tremens or the ravings of incipient madness, but it was among them. It began to kill in mid-June. At first, one person got sick at a time, but then it was two and three people a day going into the hospital. By the end of that month they had to build an extension onto the hospital to hold the afflicted.

The thing that was clear was that the summer could not be survived in that condition. They needed reinforcements to face down the Seminoles and they needed a supply train to come through successfully. Most of all they needed news from the other forts. They had not gotten word from anyplace in weeks.

For all they knew in Fort Woodmer, all of Florida had been abandoned and they were the only ones left.

Captain Wiman organized a small party of ten horsemen to ride through the Indians toward Fort Defiance. The goal was to establish communication with the nearest fort. 'If we are not back again in six days you can account me dead,' he said. He looked more cheerful saying those words than he had looked in months. The ten men got horses and rode out under cover fire from the blockhouse.

A day later they galloped back up the slope amidst the whooping of Indians. It was Wiman and only three of his men. They barely reached the fort. All three accompanying riders had received wounds in the arm or leg or face. Wiman himself was completely, amazingly, grievously unhurt. He looked at his coat and trousers, searching desperately for a hole or fray anywhere. It was in vain; he had not been touched. His face a putty grey color, the captain informed them that one brave rider had been sent ahead to Fort Defiance and they must hope to God for his survival. Then he went into his tent. Early the next morning Ab was awoken by the sound of a single gunshot inside the fort. The boy ran down the dirt avenue between the tents and arrived in time to see Captain Wiman being carried from his quarters. There was a red hole where his right eye had been. They buried his body in the southwest corner of the fort. The patch which had previously been the slaves' quarters and then the mercenaries' camp was now being used as a graveyard.

Sometimes Ab and June stood at a hole in the fenceposts, looking out. They were no longer allowed to play up on the raised platform around the inside of the wall, so they had to go to one of these unchinked places to look out of the fort. The prisoner's peer: first the right eye, then the left eye, then the right eye again. Then it was the other cellmate's turn to look out at the free world. The forest was so green, chrome green, vermiculate with lianas, strung with slanting light and birdsong. It swelled like sailcloth with breezes which did not reach the boys behind the wall. June said, 'I'm on go out there.'

Ab thought about this a moment as the other boy peered through the gap. No citizens had been outside the walls in a month.

'I'm on go out. I don't care. What's it going to do, kill me? It's jist the woods. It's jist the same woods. Look you, it don't wanter kill me. It's jist the old shady woods like ever.'

'I don't know, June.'

'It's the same woods. And weren't I bred there? And weren't I raised there? It loves me the same as ever or this jist ain't my world no more. It's pinewoods, hummock, look you! Deer there! Shit! Three-four whitetails jist a-standing there! Don't you see them? Don't you see?'

'No, I don't see, June, you're standing in the way. Move, it's my turn to look.'

The Seminoles' pressure on the fort remained constant as the heat of the summer increased. The cases of fever increased with it. Everyone was feeling themselves for the disease: a light head, a vague pain, a prickling in the back of the throat not caused by the dust, a throbbing in the ears not caused by the gunfire. Hydrophobia, alcoholism. A sense that the log walls were flexing in and out like a ribcage. A fear of nightfall and of morning.

They stared at the world around them and listened to hypotheses. The disease killing them might have been caused by the atmosphere's moisture, the temperature, or an electrical charge. It might also have been related to gaseous vapors. There was a pond a little to the west that contained dead and decaying vegetable matter, which was known to give off gases. They came to the surgeon with this idea; he nodded his round head as he listened, jingling the musketballs in his pocket. 'Perhaps, perhaps,' he said. 'I shall examine this sometime. I know of a medical journal...in the north. I will submit it to them once this is over, all of this business.' There were other theories too; these became wilder as the outbreak spread. There were suspicions of birds and suspicions of Spaniards and suspicions of magnolia blossoms and a belief that the Indians were spiriting the disease to them with their medicine satchels. The only thing certain was that there was some venom in the world around them, in the land itself.

One day it was announced that Little Tom the halfbreed had deserted the fort under the cover of darkness. It was implied that this was in his nature. A few people took the news hard. Old Rouchefort, his friend, sat down on a stump holding his chin. Two hours later he stood up again.

'Well,' he said. 'I guess I'll go too.'

A few people looked at him. Most didn't bother to even do that. But the old man walked straight toward the gate. There he simply lifted the bar and pushed it open and stepped out and shut the gate again behind him.

The few people who had noticed cursed and stood up. 'Rouchefort,' they cried, 'old man, old man.' They ran to the ramparts. When they got there, they were just in time to see the wizened figure disappearing into the trees at the bottom of the slope. They watched a long time, gazing longingly into the deep dark forest. Those who stayed long enough eventually heard a crackle of gunfire in the distance.

The next day young June Geyer left the walls of Fort Woodmer and walked into the trees. About a minute later a musket shot was heard. After this the captain who had replaced Wiman ordered a guard posted at the gate, facing in toward the inhabitants of the fort. This inward-facing soldier stood there with his musket across his chest. And yet one day later a woman climbed over the top of the picket wall and dropped to the ground outside. It was a daughter of the Keen family, aged seventeen, delirious with fever. 'It looks cool there. Cool fine shade there,' were her last words before leaving. She had barely reached the trees before there was a gunshot and a war-whoop.

They were not suicides per se. It was more like calenture, that malady of sailors in middle latitudes who fall in love with the sea or become so hypnotized by it that they mistake its greenness for rolling fields and step over the bow to walk there. So it was with the fort-dwellers that summer. The cool forest in which they sat adrift beckoned to them and so they dove in, sank beneath its shadow, were never seen again.

On the last day of June nearly half the inhabitants of the fort were infected with the fever and more were falling ill every day. The infantry force was weakening constantly; not many of the soldiers were fit for duty. Where it was not fever it was alcohol: the twin hazards of the territory. They hardly tried to raise an alarm when one or another of the settlers scaled the wall and disappeared into the forest.

On July first the new captain stood on top of a crate to make his announcement. 'Conditions have dictated that this fort is no longer habitable. We will abandon the blockhouse tomorrow morning at oh-four-hundred hours. We will repair to Fort Crabbe in the north. Make ready. What's left behind will be burned.' They packed and prepared and before the sun rose the next day they were streaming out of the gate. The troops waited for the Indians to spot them and shoot, but they never did. The caravan took half an hour to move down the slope and into the trees. When they had finally cleared the fort, the rear-guard troops lit piles of brush all along the walls, and before long the entire structure was burning brilliantly. They fled north toward Fort Crabbe in the predawn darkness, guided by the conflagration.

The Tercer family traveled near the back of the caravan. As day broke, Shay Tercer was talking to himself in a low voice. 'No, no sir,' he was saying. 'No sir. Ain't going in nowhere. We don't need to be going back in nowhere. Fort nor city nor any of it. Hell no. Sitting there, sick and waiting. Breathing that bad air. No sir, I don't think so.'

As the caravan rounded a bend in the road he took hold of his wife's hand and turned their packhorse off into the oaks. Few people saw them and none cared. Shay Tercer and his family bore off east, toward their homestead.

Tercer kept talking, his voice rising, reaching exultant notes. 'That's right. Off home. Won't no one keep us from it. Jist home, jist a plain little place in the woods. That's all I want nor need. Just home there in the pines, yessir, and the creek running, and the breeze blowing, and the horse in the grass and the cattle in the grass, and a cookfire burning.' They had maybe ten miles to go and by late afternoon had almost reached it. Ab looked around himself wildly; the woods became familiar and yet incredibly strange, the look home has after a long time gone. They were in his woods now, without a doubt: he knew those trees, he knew individual birds singing their individual songs in the trees. They passed one last bend in the road and there stood the house. Vines and dogfennel had grown up around it, but the walls were still straight and upright and pine-white. 'Yes sir,' Shay Tercer was saying. 'Home, that's all. Jist home, jist that.'

They unloaded their few belongings and swept out the house and opened the windows. Jane Tercer got the kitchen shed open and swept it. 'Ab,' Shay said. 'Go ahead and cut some wood for a cookfire. Fetch some pieces of that lighterd stump, too, to start her. I'll go see if I can find one of our chickens and we'll have it. Yes sir, a chicken dinner, why not, why not?'

Ab took the axe and the packhorse and set out. He was gone a long time; he took a circling route, going to check on all the features of his old home. After the ordeal of the fort, these things reassured him of peace and time and reason and everything good. Eventually he got to the lighterwood stump and nicked off a few pieces for kindling the fire. Then he headed back to the yard to chop the firewood.

When he came into the clearing he saw his father in profile, standing on the edge of the porch. His arms were raised to his shoulders. Then Ab saw a rush of smoke from the treeline and heard the bang of a gun, and his father stumbled as if under a heavy weight. A yell, several yells, shrill and brief, and the Indians came forward from the trees.

Ab got down from the horse and ran to the house. His father stepped in through the doorway, holding the frame. His mother screamed. Ab ran inside and grabbed his father around the waist to support him. Tercer reached for the gun above the lintel but he was weak and did not grasp it well and it clattered to the floor, breaking the hammer off of the stock. 'God damn it,' Tercer said. The Indians were coming across the yard. The man said 'Get the door,' but Ab was already latching it, and the windows too. They remained there in the darkness of the house for a full minute. Then there was a loud thud and the axe Ab had taken to cut firewood came in through the door.

The man on the other side exerted himself with a few vigorous swings and the door broke open. Shay Tercer swayed in the patch of daylight. 'Friends,' he said. 'Take anything you want. We don't want any trouble. We don't want—' and a gun clapped in the small room. Shay Tercer fell down and did not move.

Three Seminoles in maroon frocks with silver gorgets hanging on their chests stepped into the house. They glanced at the woman and the boy. Jane Tercer had taken her son to the center of the room and was clutching him hard as the warriors moved through the house, overturning furniture, breaking things, looking around. They took the food and left the rest.

An older man with grey hair motioned for Jane and her child to leave the house. Jane did not move. Then the Indian took her by the hand to lead her outside. She would not be moved. Ab said 'Mama.' She turned to see one of the younger braves raising his gun to shoot. She lifted an arm to cover her eyes and the man shot. The ball passed through her arm and struck her in the chest and she fell.

The same warrior took the butt of his gun and dealt Ab a blow to the head so that the boy dropped unconscious. He woke up seconds later being dragged across the floor by his arms. Ab yelled and kicked and the man relinquished his grip. The older

Seminole was shouting at the younger one and tugged him away through the door. Already there was the sound of crackling on the roof. The younger man left the house speaking loudly and angrily in Maskókî, and one by one their voices dwindled from the yard and went away.

Smoke was beginning to seep in at the rafters. Ab stood himself up against the wall but his legs could not bear it yet and he fainted. But as he fell he knocked over a wash bucket and the chill water revived him again. This time the boy took it slow getting up, and when at last he stood his knees wobbled but held.

He went to his mother and said, 'Mama.' Her eyelids twitched and she groaned and moved. He went to his father and said, 'Daddy.' He did not move but only lay in his blood.

'Mama, Mama, get up,' Ab said. 'We've got to get him out of here.'

Smoke began to darken the room and seams of flame were showing in the ceiling. Jane Tercer stood up like a sleepwalker, the upper half of her dress bloody. She came and even though her right arm dangled useless she took ahold of her husband's leg with her strong left hand and she and the boy together dragged Shay Tercer across the floor. They pulled him out of the flaming house and into the yard and there the goodwife put her hand to her head and fell down again.

Ab now. He walked across the yard between broken things and got the packhorse. He attached the traces to the cart and walked it over to where his father and mother lay. He let down the tailgate and laid a ramp up into the bed. Then he undid the horse and got the thickest coil of rope they had in the homestead and tied it to the harness's hames. He looped the other end under his father's arms and then the boy went to the horse and walked it forward and the rope dragged over the top rails of the cart and his father slid up the ramp. The boy took the rope and did the same for his mother. When both were inside the cart, he untied the rope from the hames and put the horse back in the traces and walked it forward from the clearing.

Ab took the straightest path away from the burning house. He kept to the open road, not bothering to conceal himself in the woods, so that his parents would not be jostled unnecessarily. As for his parents, they lay in the bed of the cart. Side by side, together. As if just starting away from the church and chaplain for their honeymoon. Though no wedding under heaven ever had such features: the bride and the groom dressed in tatters and spattered with their own blood, and the son already born and grown and holding the reins of their bridal carriage, and the smoke of their home in the treetops.

Ab drove all day and into the night. A yellow moon lit them. At some point in the dark a voice called to him from the bed of the cart. The woman's voice was very calm and very still. 'You're taking us up to the city, aren't you, Ab?' Her voice was drowsy and sweet as the boy had never heard it before.

'Yes, Mama. I'm going to try to get us there.'

'Good,' she said. 'That's good. You're a good boy. I hope you can make it, Ab. Just do your best, darling. Just do your best, that's all.'

The next day the Tercers' wagon pulled into the army garrison at Fort Crabbe. It was a bustling place and all the evacuees from Fort Woodmer were already there. In the bed of the wagon Jane Tercer was asleep and Shay Tercer was dead.

They buried the man later that day in a common site behind

the munitions shed. The boy's mother was taken into the hospital building. A surgeon gave Ab the prognosis that she would survive and be free from any permanent injuries. Good, Ab said. Then he went away. The surgeon later remarked to his steward on the remarkable lack of emotion in that boy, like many of the other children he had seen in that place. They had an incredible resilience, these children. A stoicism.

The boy found his way into the office of a corporal who had taken an interest in his case. He was a middle-aged man with a body unsuited for this territory. He was sunblistered and sweaty, always dabbing his face with a cotton kerchief. Ab came to the man's desk and looked at him with his hard blue eyes. 'I want to jine up,' he said.

The corporal peered. 'You'd like to join. By this you mean, enlist in the Army?'

'Right,' Ab said.

'How old are you, my boy?'

'Fourteen year old.'

The corporal snorted a little. 'You aren't even that, are you.'

'I'm fourteen.'

'Well sir. Well.' The corporal leaned back. 'We might be able to make you fourteen. Have you ever played a fife, son?'

"What's that?'

'It's an instrument, something like a flute.'

'What's that?'

'Hm.' The man put his hand on his chin. 'Have you ever played on a drum before?'

'No.'

'It's easy. You ever struck the side of a tub with a stump o' sassafras root before? It's the same theory.'

'I don't want that. I don't want to play no drum. I want a gun and I want to hunt Indins.'

'My boy,' said the corporal. 'My boy.' He dabbed his face with his handkerchief. 'What of your mother, your poor mother? Don't you want to stay with her in her time of trouble, and tend to her as she recovers?'

'Shit,' Ab said savagely. 'What the hell am I going to do for her? Mammy her? Ain't that what y'all doctors are for?'

The corporal sat back in his chair. His eyes changed. When he spoke, it was no longer with the gentle ironic tone used for children.

'I can get you sent down as a drummer with a detachment,' he said. 'You will be placed near the border, in the vicinity of the heaviest Indian fighting. They need people. Things happen, down there. Men fall. Muskets fall. Sometimes the muskets need to be picked back up.'

The corporal stared up at the boy. The boy stared back. The man sighed and reached into his desk and drew out a tablet.

He dipped a quill into an inkwell. 'Name, age, occupation, place of birth.'

The boy straightened his shoulders. 'Ab Tercer. Fourteen year old. Son of Shay Tercer. Occupation, cowhunter. We're cowhunters, all us Tercers are cowhunters. Born down by Varnes Pond, across from Runner's old town. Born and raised down there. Now, where do I get that drum?'

RIDE THE LONG TRAIL

*JAKE PRIMROSE'S SON RUNS OFF INTO THE HOT
POSTWAR AFTERNOON.*

I.

'**G**LORY.'

Sun came through waxpaper windows, the color of cream. Dust motes churned through the light and settled on everything, chalkdust, sawdust, ten kinds of dust, mixed and mingling. A fine layer of it coated the spectacles of the woman whose face was so close to his. The glare obscured her eyes. So he focused instead on her firm full lips as she said it again.

'Glory.'

The word was on the page in front of him. Her index finger was pressed to it. The boy sat mute in the face of his inquisitor and there was the sound of her breath swift and dry in her nostrils. The word came one more time. 'Glory.' Her round spectacles shone as she whispered. 'Spell it.'

There was no one else in the little schoolhouse. All the other students had been sent home. He had been kept late into the hot afternoon; now they faced each other over the desk, sweat beginning to dampen the lady's neck. There it was, glo-ry. *Easy words of two syllables, accented on the first.* Right after ba-ker and before ne-gro and sa-cred. All the other pupils, three and four years younger, had spelled their way down the columns in chiming singsong, while he had not once opened his mouth. Now the teacher's face hung eight inches in front of his own. 'Spell it, you great foolish clod. Spell it or I swear I will keep you here until night comes.'

He looked at glo-ry a moment longer. Then he stood up from the desk. The schoolmistress backed away, her hands raised as if to guard herself. But all the lad did was reach into the desk and take out the books. Sadlier's *Excelsior Geography*, McGuffey's *Fourth Eclectic Reader*. Then he started toward the door.

The lady blinked. 'Where are you going with those books?'

'I don't know,' the lad answered gloomily. 'I might like to read em someday.'

He put on his brown felt hat at the door. 'But you can keep that speller for someone else, Miss Lashbrook. I don't guess I'll use it anymore.'

The schoolteacher recovered herself. 'Your father,' she said after a moment. 'Mister Primrose will be furious. What will you say when you get home?'

He looked out the door, a little downcast. 'Well. I don't guess I'll go back there either.' He tipped his hat. 'Ma'am.' Then he went out. He left quickly enough that he did not have to answer the urgent question she cried after him: 'But where are you going? Child, where will you go?'

Hadjo Primrose rode south from the schoolhouse on his dark marshtackie mare. He pointed Alma away from the school, letting the horse make the pace. But Alma wanted to go too fast. He reined her back. Hadjo needed the pace to be slow, slow. Otherwise he might get someplace before he decided where he was going.

At dark he lay down by the trunk of a massive liveoak. The satchel he'd packed that morning was a frontier child's school-bag, packed for travel: it contained a drawknife, deermeat, kindling. He lit a fire and ate alone. The next morning he chose a smaller spur road off of the main highway to ride on. It was a hunter's trail, shade-dark and lovely after the bright highway. Hadjo preferred this route and his horse preferred it too, and for a while they rode gladly.

Then, at a crossing, he stopped. He gave a sudden harsh laugh and turned his horse. It was the road that led toward his father's house. It was that road.

Old Jake, now forty-nine years old. A biblical age in that young frontier. Mere cattleman no longer, since the fighting ceased he'd become a dabbler in indigo, diversified and expanding. People would say he'd changed, of course they'd say it. He'd lacked branding-smoke in his eyes too long and forgotten how to squint. Or worse: lacked the saddle between his legs too long and forgotten how to ride. Allowed his foremen and his slaves to do the riding for him and might get himself ridden someday. But Hadjo found his father unchanged. The man had never budged an inch that he could see. Mother Pauline grew steadily greyer, in face and in heart. Little sister Flora grew every day more beautiful, more violent, more swollen with passionate anger, as if siphoning it from her mother. But Jake himself did not change. The world had changed around him, for him. The house he owned and the business he conducted and the clothes he wore had gotten finer, but Hadjo was intelligent enough to disregard such details. No, if Jake Primrose had ever changed it was before his son knew him.

In the warm afternoon, Hadjo came back to where the roads crossed and took the one that led off west, away from his father's house. He let Alma step quickly, as was her nature. This time it was because he knew exactly where they were going.

Mrs. Monroe's roadhouse had a lantern burning in the window. Hadjo approached the house with a sprightly mannish pace and swung down at the hitching posts. But he stopped before the door. There was nothing forbidding about this door—it was not even closed—but something about it made him lose all his jaunt.

At last he walked in with his eyes wide and his arms hanging at his sides, bareheaded. He moved wordlessly to the stool nearest the door and sat down, keeping his hands concealed beneath the bartop. He looked like he'd never sat at a bar before, because he hadn't. It was a bad entrance, and if any of the other patrons had witnessed it he might never have recovered. He was lucky, though, because at that moment every eye in the place was trained on the far corner of the room.

There the tables had been cleared away and two people stood facing each other in a half circle of candles. From outside it had sounded like ordinary loud conversation, but it was not. They stood speaking a play. One was dressed in Periclean armor and the other wore a white robe as they did an Italianate drama with cockney accents. The man wearing a breastplate had a long false brass staff and he struck the floor with it at the start of every line. The woman opposite him made small gestures with one arm. The audience was utterly silent and the scene had the sense of an ending. At last the two players bent and picked up a poled litter, which Hadjo had not seen. There was a slender young man lying on it; this young man wore a ringleted wig and his eyes were closed and his pale hands held the top half of a sword sticking from his belly. Pericles paused for a moment and grunted after the effort of picking up the stretcher, and then, a little red-faced, spoke the last: 'Alas, alas, Greynaldo! You loved her oll too well. Now oy will bear thee graveward, where oll true lovers dwell.' And they began to move with solemn step down an aisle which cleared for them through the middle of the rum-shop. When they passed Hadjo at the very back they still wore stage-expressions, queerly blank and flat in the shadows by the door. Then they passed into the dusk outside.

As soon as they were gone, a loud cry came up across the room. A chorus of No, no! and Ah, Greynaldo! Several of the audience members leapt up and pursued the players outdoors, hoping to change the outcome perhaps. There were others who would have followed but were too overcome with tears. *Greynaldo, Greynaldo*, they moaned. They applied for comfort to the ones who were holding up a little better. There were so few solid shoulders in the place that Hadjo's was greatly needed. A little darkhaired man came to him and began dampening his shirt. The man wore a velvet hat; he held himself to Hadjo so hard that the hat tipped and slid and fell to the ground, and they were pressed bare head to bare head.

'Why, why?' the man asked. 'Why could they not be united? Why cain we never be united? Why? Oh, sweet Greynaldo...' The rum fumes were almost visible in the air. Hadjo's vision swam. 'Easy, sir,' he said. 'Maybe...maybe in the next play they'll stick. Here.' The young man helped to lift the stranger onto an adjacent stool. The man balanced there for only a moment before he slid off and plumped bonelessly to the floor. There he remained, crosslegged and crying, like a toddler deprived of its toy.

Hadjo looked around the room. There were a few pockets of sense, mostly at the tables where a woman or two were sitting. Everywhere else the clientele was helpless with grief. But just then the ones who had followed the play outside, trying to change it, returned with radiant faces. 'They will do another, tomorrow night another!' they cried. 'They'll do a second play tomorrow night! A play about Indins and savages and Edenlike romance, they said! All's not lost!'

Rejoicing filled the room. 'Another play, another,' they repeated, now weeping from gladness. Shared tears turned to shared embraces. The emotion was too much for some people. Out of the corner of his eye Hadjo saw a man near him take out a pistol. He swung aside and ducked as the man fired the gun. Smoke balled in the room and wood splinters fell from the ceiling where he had shot it.

Silence. The man standing next to the shooter clapped him on the back of the head. 'Damn it, Hart, there's rooms up there. Rooms, where people sleep, and your fool ass is down here shooting?'

Hadjo stared at the man, blinking to get the dust and gunsmoke from his eyes. 'Shee, Herb,' the gunman said unhappily. 'I thought the missus kindy sealed it off. I thought she put some old iron paneling in the floor up there to where a bullet cain't go through.'

'Yes, fool,' said the man Herb. 'But the missus said there's still no shooting allowed. It makes divots in the metal and the chairs won't sit right. She's said it a thousand times, haven't you heard the lady?'

There she was. She stood darkly eyeing the offender through the haze. The man Herb snatched the pistol away and set it down on the bartop. 'Hold Hart's iron for him, won't you, Missus Monroe? He's sorry. He's right sorry.' She took the pistol in her big-knuckled hand and slid it under the bar. 'And tomorrow he'll go up there and take up the rug and fix the divot, yes he will.'

The room had quieted when the gun fired but now talk resumed at a good steady volume. The disturbance was probably necessary to return emotions to a manageable state. Hadjo was still blinking sawdust from his eyes. The man who had scolded the shooter now turned to him. 'It tain't difficult and it tain't hard. One oughtn't shoot guns indoors. Just as one oughtn't lick the skint off a butter-ladle, just as one oughtn't kick a tabby-cat. It's only courtesy. Most especially in Missus Monroe's good house. Don't you agree? But hell,' the man said, fixing his eyes on Hadjo for the first time. 'Hell, boy. You're nair seventeen years old.'

'No sir,' Hadjo said. 'Eighteen.'

The man squinted at Hadjo. Not into his eyes, but at his face and features. 'Seventeen,' the man mused. 'A young seventeen, too.' Hadjo didn't say anything. At last the man bugged his eyes to unsquint them and straightened up. 'Well, my name's Herbert Nail. Known as Herb.' He held his hand out and they shook.

'Good to meet ye,' Hadjo said.

The handshake went on for several more seconds. The man grinned in his face fixedly, and the young man's hand was not released. In time the man said again, 'My name's Herbert Nail, known as Herb.' He grinned tighter. 'And given that I've jist kindly told you my name, how about you tell me what in the bloody thunder yours might be.'

'Ah—Hadjo.'

'Hadjo, you say?'

'Yes, yes sir. Hadjo.'

The man ungripped his hand. 'Well, Hadjo,' he said cheerily. 'I'm pleased to make your quaintance. I am.' The man leaned back, away from Hadjo, giving him space. 'And young master Hadjo, I'd like to give you a couple of points of advice, as a stranger. Do these for me. Get your hands up over the table.' Hadjo pulled his hands up and set them on the bar. 'Don't sit so darned straight.' Quickly Hadjo relaxed his shoulders and inclined about ten degrees forward. 'Where's your hat? Borrow Ziegler's.' Herb picked up the hat of the man who had fallen on the floor. He set it on Hadjo's head and squared and cocked it.

'There,' Herb said, sitting back to look at the newly outfitted youth. 'There, now you look right businesslike. Hail, fellow, well met. And now cometh the question, the profound question, the one that needs answering before any other may be posed.' He looked along the bar, and then back at Hadjo, and said: 'What do ye know of drink?'

Hadjo swallowed. They had been joined by the shadow of Missus Monroe. She stood across the bar from them, silent, separating them from the lanternlight. 'I don't know,' Hadjo said. 'I don't know what I know of drink.'

'Well,' Herb said. 'Tonight's the night you find out.'

He looked up at the lady. 'Ma'am, if I may. For this fellow here, a brace of hard-boiled eggs, a few pickled cucumbers, and plate of your delicious cornbread. And a little later on, please bring him a cup of that Santy Rosito Extro Viejo.' He patted the young man on the shoulder. 'One of them good cups, what don't go empty.'

The lady nodded and went off, taking her shadow with her. 'Thank you, ma'am,' Herb called after her. When he turned back to Hadjo after a long moment, his eyes were faintly damp.

'She's a saint, that woman,' he said quietly. 'A purebred saint.'

A little later Hadjo was staring into a slipware cup rimmed with a reddish substance that made his airways pucker and rebel. His second mouthful stayed too long on the brim of his gorge and fumigated all the bony and fleshy backways of his skull before slithering down into the esophageal black. For a moment he bore the gaping look of a diver coming up for air but no air moved in or out. 'Chicory, chicory,' someone called. 'Get him a mug of chicory. None? Ah well. Boy, bite thisyer egg, go on now.' He did and swam a minute in his own tears, looking out at the world through a waterpane, a river's skein. Grinning faces trickled into being before him, trickled away again. Hadn't someone better water his cup? Cut it a little? He'll learn tonight, oh yes he'll learn tonight.

There was laughter, rupture, four more cups of rum. Several patrons arranged themselves around Hadjo, absorbing the wild kinesis of the first-time drunk, feeling feelings they themselves could no longer feel. He laughed, he luffed. He got up and stepped to music that someone had to start singing because it did not exist otherwise. He jockeyed back and forth on the floor in contest with one of his father's bulls and then tackled a table. His chin was split open at the base and blood frowned down into his collar and he laughed and laughed. Later, after a bout of silence, he went outside. He walked about twelve paces into the darkness before falling facefirst into its breast.

The young man woke up in treemoss. He was covered and pillowed by it, good clean grey moss. Some kind soul had covered him with it. He stood up and remained standing for a long time. It was midmorning. His eyes focused on various objects, unfocused, focused on other objects. Then he lowered himself back down to the ground and lay there in the yard for two more hours, his hot eyes opening and shutting.

He got up again nearer noon and stood; his knees held. He stepped slowly to the dimness of the roadhouse. There was one person sitting inside, alone. It was his friend Herb from the night before. The man gave a quarterwise glance at Hadjo, nodded slightly, and went back to gazing at the wall. He was smoking a cigarillo and dressed in the very same clothing he had worn the previous night; perhaps he had not left the spot at all.

'I'm sorry,' said Hadjo.

The man turned halfway toward him. 'Sorry?' he said, his voice cheerful but abstracted. 'No, not at all, not at all.' He turned back toward his study of the wall.

Hadjo was already outside. He went to the back of the house and vomited in the dirt. Then he came around to the front again. With a sudden cry he ran along the hitching posts and fell on his horse's neck. Alma held the young man upright as he buried his forehead in her mane, bridling a little at the smell of his breath.

He tore the hitching knot loose and got up into the saddle and rode Alma fast from the roadhouse. A half mile away, a creek flowed, thin and clear. Hadjo went on his knees and drank. The spring-clean water with its tincture of sulphur flowed into his body and he kept drinking until he could not hold any more. With his last bit of strength he came up the slope and propped himself there and slept or almost slept for hours.

With late afternoon he improved. He ate a biscuit from his saddlebag and stood up looking strong. Alma quit grazing and looked at him. 'No more of this, old girl, no more,' he said.

They went back to Mrs. Monroe's in the blueing shadows. The young man had a small collection of coins bundled in the toe of an old sock, the bounty of a summer spent shooting Carolina parakeets with Simeon Quinto. He had never found much of a way to spend the coins, but they were more than enough for a good meal at the roadhouse and a reckoning for the night before and maybe even a bed. He stuck the socktoe back into his boot and rode up.

The building was noisy. Most of the patrons who had been there the previous night had returned or else had never left and more had arrived. The acting troupe was in the far corner, preparing the night's show. Hadjo ordered a meal, half of a chicken marinated in honey and china orange and pungent spices of a kind he had never smelled before, with greens and a paving-stone of cornbread. Hadjo started eating and did not stop for twenty minutes. When he finished he pushed the kitchen-girl a second coin for another serving—'Another?' she asked; 'Another the same,' he said. When it came he did not look up for another twenty minutes. By that time the cockney players were taking their places and Hadjo pushed back to look.

Pericles was back but now wore a variety of feathers in the red comb of his helmet. He stepped to the front of the ring of candles and spoke. 'Ladies and Gentlemen. Boy popular demand. A foinal performance, of a foine play. Boy us. The

Bomsgrove American Players. And now. The Red Strangers. Or. Theft of the Innocents.' He bowed and withdrew.

From the side door came the slow beating of a drum and the slender lad came into the room. He was dressed as an Indian of some kind. Before him marched the woman, tied up with rope, stepping in time with the drum, her arms at her sides. They reached the corner of the room where the tall actor was standing, a small axe clutched in his hand.

The actors began to recite their lines. The two men dressed as Indians dialogued and the trussed woman cringed. The crowd moiled, muttered, sniffed. A man whispered loudly. 'That's the talkingest Indin I ever heard,' he said. 'That Indin's got more words than old Senator Clay.' But the play went on and became less easily ridiculed. It was a captivity drama. The woman had been stolen from her settler family. The savages had planned to ransom her, but the taller Indian began to fall in love. He was proposing to the lovely paleface in her bondage, the woman shrinking away as he impressed his affections on her, the little axe in his hand.

It went wrong. In the midst of a dialogue, an aged man in the audience pushed back his seat and stood up. 'The Indins never carried no one off like that,' he said. 'They kilt people and burnt down houses but they never carried no one off.'

The players paused in midgesture and stared at the man. They stayed like that for a long moment. Another voice chimed in. 'That's the truth, Tilly. They never carried no one off and they sure never carried off no women.'

The players began again, stutteringly. 'B-but, Red Horn. We are so different, you and I. We come from such different circumstances—'

It went on. The Indian, Red Horn, took up the small axe and made a flailing soliloquy with it. 'And yit how can oy forget the cruelties of the past, done on moyne own family? Moy sisters six, each taken boy a white man forcibly to woyfe, made spouse most unwillingly to a palefaced ravener...'

'Like hell,' a voice spat from one side of the room. 'Like hell.'

'And so it has been for all the moons and months of moy loife,' the actor went on, loudly, 'a tale of untamed woe, for which the woild forest in moy breast calls for equal blood, equal rape...'

From another section of the room a turnip came flying. It hit the tall actor squarely on the helmet. Next, a half-eaten chicken leg soared in and struck him on the chest. 'Chroist,' he said, breaking character.

Then a young man of the Geyer clan stood up at a table near the back. 'Coop—hee!' he cried with a savage lilt and bull-rushed the stage. The players scattered. Young Geyer's cry awakened something in the audience, and many leapt up and began chasing the actors around the room in a frenzy of war-whoops and overturned tables. 'Eep—eep—ee—yahh!' went the cry. The actors were elusive and showed a native cockney wile at navigating close quarters. But they could not outfox a tavernful of thirty half-crazy Crackers. They were eventually caught and trussed up with some more rope and Pericles was scalped of the red coxcomb on the top of his helmet with his own small axe.

They were taken out to the painted wagon, where they were tossed in the bed alongside the leading lady. Young Geyer produced a torch. 'Oh, Chroist,' the tall actor said, 'oh please, no.' It looked that they were about to be burnt alive in their caravan.

'Please, no. We'll do anything. We'll sail back for Dover, we'll change to a musical revue, we'll go away forever...'

'That's right, you will,' cried Geyer. And he touched the torch to some hay which had been tied to the horse's tail. A few seconds later the cart was rocketing up the road with a whinnying and wailing. The flames illuminated the cart as it took the bend in the trail on two wheels and disappeared.

The mood in Mrs. Monroe's that night became oddly sedate. Many of the visitors had gone away, satisfied with the night's entertainment. A small number of regulars sat up, talking by lamplight. Mrs. Monroe had kept the bucket full of coins which the troupe had left behind and said that drinks were free on its account. But no one took advantage of the windfall to get drunk. They sipped moderately, conversing pleasurably.

'It's enough to make you wish the Indins were really back one night,' an old man mused. 'Jist one night. To come and skelp a fool or two and go away again. That would clean up some of the nonsense we've been seeing, lately.'

'Yes,' said another man. 'There'd be no more damnfool actors, for one.'

'No more speechmakers.'

'No more policemen.'

'No more census takers.'

'No more tax collectors.'

'No more damned tax collectors, no.'

'No more Philadelphia druggists.'

'No more Molly-tuggers.'

'No more larder raiders.'

'No more Carolina slavers.'

'No more of these bigamists what come through trying to marry everbody.'

'No more expensive Frenchwomen.'

'No more Keno sharps.'

'And no more actors.'

'That's right,' said the first old man. 'No more dratted two-faced actors. All it'd take is for old Coacoochee to come back one time and do like he done before. Just one time.' He sipped. 'By God, it reminds me of the time I was at Fort Cummings and he come in.'

'You were there?'

'I was. They come in for a parlay. In strides Coacoochee, Wild Cat. The tallest, finest-looking fighting man you ever saw, white or red. Fire in his eye. General Jesup knew he was coming and he's sitting at the table just a-shivering, and in he steps. And I swear, he's dressed top to tail like Hamlet, out of old Shakespeare's play. You know? Hamlet. Wearing hose leggings. Then in comes Horatio, with plumes in his hair. I'm told Richard the Third was there too, with a crown on.'

'I heard that.'

'They'd been outside Saint Augustine and fell on a company of actors what was coming to the city. Killed three of them and took all their costume trunks and wore them costumes through the end of the war.'

A few men chuckled; others shook their heads. 'And you can bet that city didn't have no more theatricals visiting for a long time.'

'No, no they didn't. They wasn't bothered with them no more.' The old man ate a pickle. 'It's enough to make you wish we'd kept a few of them Seminole braves around. For just sech purposes.'

There was silence for a moment. Then all of a sudden Hadjo spoke up. 'Hell, I wish they'd come back around, so I could get a chance to kill me one. I never did get to kill me one.'

This was a conversational turn Hadjo had heard many times. It was not gracefully done but it followed the usual pattern. Talk of the early days would lead to talk of the Seminoles and how things had not been so bad with them once. A tone would arise that sounded strangely unlike hatred. Then someone would have to do what young Hadjo had just done: bring the talk back to war, blood, enmity. The other talkers took their cue.

'Hell yes, that's what I was just going to say,' a man said loudly. 'Bring em back so I can get about four five more of the bastards.' He slapped his knee. 'That's all I ask ever night before I go to sleep. Lord, let just a few of them Red Sticks squeak back up north again. I've got a few things to settle about how they did my cousin Roger at Black Point.'

This was what Hadjo had unleashed. This was what inevitably had to come. Yet somehow he did not seem gladdened by it, as some men were. Or appeased by it, as others pretended to be. After a while he got up from the table and went outside. What had come over the boy? Did he take too much of the Ron Dominicano? Or had he mixed two kinds? He looked a little poorly, but he would get over it. A young man can't hold his liquor quite so well as an older. Give him time, give him time. Let him step outside.

He went on foot past where the road curved. He followed no trail, marked nothing but the stars, the moonrise. Breeze blew, a forest fire somewhere, tang of muck and hickory. He came to a marsh and stood above it. It was long and broad, dotted with cows. Just like his own marsh, the one marked with his surname on the map. The mother of all his fortunes. His father had called it that, when they stood on just such a night above just such a marsh, years ago. Thisyer's the mother of all our fortunes, son, he said. Everything I worked for and everything you stand to gain. You owe it all to this land right here. Don't let anyone tell you otherwise. Don't let anyone tell you you owe it to somebody else, or even to me. You owe it to this marsh. It birthed the grass and the grass birthed the cows and the cows make our lives. It's the fat of the land here, son, all you got to do is draw it out.

Then the boy had asked a strange question. Whose land was it before you, papa? Before us?

Jake Primrose was quiet for a time. It was nobody's, he said at last. It was just the earth.

The young man sat at the table with his hat on and his elbows out. It was not his table but it was his to use. His left hand harbored a drink.

It was October now, and Hadjo had learned how to drink. He had survived the first night's excesses and become steadier in his habits. The boy did not have the makings of a tosspot, the older men said sadly. Other roles would have to be found for him.

Others were. He became acquainted with the many enterprises of which every roadhouse is the centerpoint. He rolled cigarillos, he sharpened knives. He transferred boots from a box that read *Made in Alabama* into one that read *Made in Spain*. Most recently, he had agreed to help a man named France shoe his horses. He explained to this France that he had no experience shoeing horses but the man did not believe him. Like hell you can't shoe a horse, France said, standing over his table, rather drunk. I never done it, said Hadjo. Like hell you can't shoe a horse, the man repeated. Look here. You got clever hands. He grabbed Hadjo's right hand by the wrist and showed it. Clever hands. Tell me you can't use an iron. That's the trouble with you young chaps today. Here I stand trying to hire you a half-dollar job and you say it can't be done. Meet me at the stable first thing tomorrow, boy, and we'll do the thing.

So Hadjo went to the stable at dawn, hoping that the man had been too drunk to remember. He had not. France was standing in the yard, and when he saw Hadjo coming he turned on his heel and went inside. They spent the whole morning shoeing France's string of colts, an awful-looking group. He was having trouble selling them but declared that the shiny new shoes would 'heave them over.' The simple-minded stableboy held the reins while Hadjo raised the leg to be shod. France pruned the hoof and then drove in the nails. Hadjo was supposed to heat and widen the shoes for the broad-footed Florida horses, but he kept holding them in the fire too long. Eventually France frowned at him and told him to step away and let the halfwit do it. Hadjo was made to stoke the fire, shovel the ashes.

So it went, and Hadjo might have stayed around the roadhouse doing odd jobs for years until he fell into one that suited him. Until one day a slave named Santiago came to the roadhouse. His owner was a sweaty, dissipated person named Raulerson who'd taken a room with his family for a few days, seemingly at loose ends. Hiring out his slave was his only means of paying for it. He and France shook hands and the bondservant went to work in the stable the next morning.

Santiago was a slender and graceful person, but strong. He was a fair hand at all blacksmithing. Despite this he claimed to have barely tried it before. 'Seen it done from afar,' he said absently to Hadjo as he roused the fire. 'Just a bit, you know. You pick things up from being around shops. That's all I done.' He took ahold of a horseshoe, heated and hammered it into a right shape.

Soon France's shoeing job was finished and they went on to the next task. Several wagons around the place needed repairs and Santiago was set to it. The stableboy refused to work under the black man, spitting at the idea, and so Hadjo became his assistant by default. Santiago did the work skillfully and with disdain. 'I don't know why they're putting me on this shit,' he said, fashioning a spoke. 'I ain't never tried my hand at it at all. I'm a boatbuilder, is my trade. Boatbuilder.'

There was a long silence, one of many. Then the man cleared his throat. 'How about you, young buddy,' he asked. 'What kind of work do you do.' There was a gentleness in his voice that said he did not mind if Hadjo lied to him.

'Oh, I'm a cowhunter, mainly,' Hadjo said, putting a gruff tone in his voice.

The man just nodded. 'Cowman,' he said. 'That's good work. That's a good trade for you to be in, young buddy. I'm sure you'll do well with that.'

They worked through a long afternoon. Sometimes Santiago was cool and haughty toward Hadjo. Nonetheless he tried to teach him the work. 'No, see, you got to make the end of the spoke skinnier than the middle,' he said. 'Why would you make the middle skinnier? That's where you need the beef to be. That's right, taper off them ends. Right. Do it careful, though. Don't whittle it down too thin. It's got to fit that fitting snug. Hold on, wait—wait. All right. Look here. See how that'll be loose in the fitting? Don't want that. Hell no. That's all right, go ahead and get you another spoke length. Try again.'

That night, when they were finished with the work, Santiago received a minute fraction of the payment given to his owner. He sat down in the roadhouse to eat with it. There was one table apart from the rest in the far corner of the room, hidden from view behind a stack of barrels; he chose it automatically and sat down. He ordered liberally from what was being served that night. It cost him his whole day's earnings. When it came out he ate the grizzled goatmeat with utmost gusto, and the chicken dumplings, and the greens in potlikker, and the boiled egg, and the white beans, and the green beans, and the omnipresent cornbread, and then more cornbread drizzled with honey, filling the gaps with cup after cup of coffee and finishing with a long chew of sugarcane he produced from a pocket.

Hadjo tried to eat like him but could not. In the end he just pushed back and listened as Santiago talked through mouthfuls. 'I ain't been in Florida in the longest,' he was saying. 'Though I'm from here to begin with. As you could maybe tell. People say they take me for a Florida man. Born and raised in Saint Augustine.'

'Do you miss it?' Hadjo asked.

'Do I? Hell yes I do,' he said. 'Things was good there. When we was in that Spainish town we was nearbout free. Nearbout free. Then the Cabrey house fell on hard times, the old don died, and the doña sold us on up to Savannah. I was about your age. Fourteen. We worked on the shipyards, I was a boatbuilder by trade. Yes. But my family got sold apart there, after a while. And I got moved again. And now—well. Now you see me.' He gestured around the room with his mug of coffee. 'You see me. Next thing you know I'll be picking god-damned cotton.'

He went silent for a time. Hadjo glanced around the road-house. There were two other tables that night. Everyone was either looking at the slave or carefully not looking at him.

'You know my daddy built boats in three languages? English, Spanish, and Minorcan. Which is like Spanish but different. Three languages, and taught me in two. He's still up there, working in the yards. Seventy years old.' He smiled at the thought. But he stopped when his master Raulerson walked into the room.

Raulerson led his wife and son to the farthest end of the bar. The man was already drunk, and was sweating, though he had done no work that day. He ordered food and placed coins on the bartop for it. One by one, as if it hurt him to be parted from them.

There was silence in the room. Silence where the family was sitting, and a deeper silence from Santiago. Hadjo tried to break it. 'So what are you going to do tomorrow?' he asked.

'I don't know, young buddy.' He sucked his teeth. 'I done all the work there is to do around this place. We'll have to head someplace else, I suppose.'

'Where?'

Santiago shrugged. 'Wherever good marster leads us. I await on his wisdom. Yes indeed. The good marster always leads us aright.' He took a sip of coffee. 'I only hope he leads us someplace that has food. Not everplace we go has food, you see. But I await on his wisdom, yes I do. His deep prosperin wisdom.'

Down the bar Raulerson cast an eye at his bondservant. Then he half-turned toward his wife. 'Theter coon sure do like to damnwell talk though don't he,' he slurred at her.

'Richard,' the woman said. That was all she said.

Silence towered in the room. It lasted for a good two minutes. Santiago took small drinks from his cup and stared over its brim at the wall. Across the room Raulerson cleared his throat, a ruck of phlegm.

'Hi, Sonny,' he said. 'You, Sonny.'

Santiago kept looking at the wall. 'Sonny,' the man called again.

'I don't know who he's talking to Sonny,' Santiago said to Hadjo. 'My name Santiago. Might be there's a Sonny in the room.'

'You, Sonny,' Raulerson repeated. 'Hey. Run upstairs and fetch me a coat. My coat, boy, and be quick.'

Santiago straightened up. 'I don't know who he's talking to Sonny,' he said. 'But it sounds like old marster needs help so I'd best go help him.' He stood and went out of the room. There was the creak of his footsteps going up the stairs, then coming back down. Raulerson sat smiling at his wife and son and drinking from a tumbler of liquor.

Santiago came back with a black coat worn sleek at the elbows and brought it over to Raulerson. After a moment's pause he held the coat open. Raulerson slipped one arm into its sleeve, then the other, a look of childlike pleasure on his face.

Santiago straightened the collar on the man's neck and stepped away.

'Now hold on, darkie, you're not done,' Raulerson said placidly. 'I think little Thad is chilly too. Didn't you think about that before you went upstairs? He's cold, just like his daddy. As the father, so the son.' The boy looked at Santiago, a little afraid.

Santiago turned, his face blank, to go out of the room. As he went Raulerson kept talking. 'You know, when I bought ye they called ye a real smart boy, and quick on your feet. What happened to all that, Sonny? You ain't showed me much of that.'

The man turned. 'My name ain't Sonny,' he said. 'I don't know who you talking to Sonny. My mother named me Santiago, which means James, on account of the bible Book of James. You ever read it?' He stood there, waiting for a moment, then went on. 'No. Well, you should read it, Marster Raulerson. It's a powerful good book. Powerful good.'

The man smirked. 'Well, what do it say, boy? Tell us about it. Educate us.' He sat back with a comical air.

'Says Go to now, ye rich men. Says your gold and silver is cankered, and shall eat your flesh as it were fire. Ye have heaped up treasure for the last days.' He looked at Raulerson and did not look away.

Raulerson sat, still smirking or trying to. Santiago went on. 'Also says we count them happy which endure. And I sorter like that. Which is why I go by Santiago. For Saint James.'

'Well,' said Raulerson, 'I guess I jist like Sonny for you. And so I guess that's what I'll call you, boy. And you damnwell better not duck when I call you that name, either.'

'Why not?' Santiago said, taking a step forward. 'Why, marster, I seen you duck plenty of times when there's people calling your name. Every time we leave a town.'

Raulerson blinked. Then he sat up. There was an uncomfortable chuckle from one side of the room, a low whistle from another.

'Well,' Raulerson said, slowly. 'Well. I believe I just had my reputation spoke on.' He shook his head. 'And I don't believe I stand to have my reputation spoke on by nobody. Least of all my own damned darkie.' He stood up.

Santiago turned around, slowly. He began to walk away from Raulerson with a queasy look on his face. The man reached into his coat and was following after him with slow, rolling strides. He produced a small pistol.

'Hey now,' said Herb Nail, from his side of the room. 'Hold on now, friend.'

'Don't do that, sir,' said France. 'Don't do that in here.' But the man kept walking, gun pointing outward from his middle.

Santiago had reached the door. Raulerson called to him. 'Just you stop right there,' he told him. He did.

Santiago had gone suddenly calm. He faced Raulerson, faced the pistol leveled at his belly.

'You talk too much, boy.'

'Yes I do,' said Santiago, a raw lilt in his voice. 'Yes I do.'

'You been a lot of trouble to me.'

'More than I been good.'

'More than you been good.'

'I was supposed to help you along in business. Wasn't I? I was supposed to be your magic. Get you in with the Spainiards, and all of that. But it hasn't worked. And now you ain't rich, you the same as ever. The same, but with a slave.'

'A loudmouthed slave,' Raulerson said. He waved the gun at the man's mouth.

'And a expensive one,' Santiago said, quietly.

'I jist never thought I'd get spoken on,' Raulerson said, 'by my own damned darkie.' He took a step forward, very free with the gun now.

'So what next?' Santiago asked, loudly. 'You going to defend your honor? Don't that call for the duello? Hand me a gun, then. Hand me a gun, someone.' He cast his eyes around the room, fierce, inflamed. The place was silent. 'But no. That's against the law, ain't it. To give a Negro a gun and let him stand on his name like a man. You cain't have that.'

'Stop talking,' Raulerson said. 'Damn you.'

'I see you got bad choices, Marster Raulerson. You cain't get satisfaction from me if I cain't hold my own side of it. And you cain't jist cut me down, no. Not me, not your expensive investiment. Shoot me and you'd ruin your owndamnself.'

'You think it'd ruin me,' Raulerson said.

'I know it would. And I'd like it that way. I'd smile at it. But you won't do it.' He stared at his owner; they stared at each other.

'You're the worst thing I ever done,' Raulerson said.

'Let me go outside,' Santiago said. 'I'm going to go outside.' He turned and stepped through the doorway into the night.

Raulerson was left alone in the room for a moment with his gun pointing at nothing. Then he slowly followed the slave out the door.

'Richard,' the man's wife called, high and long. She stood up and hurried after him. The son unfolded himself from his chair and went out too. The rest of the people in the room stared at each other, or at nothing.

It came in a few seconds. A gunshot, thin and paltry in the yard.

'Oh Jesus Christ,' said France. Then came the second gunshot.

There was nothing for a while. Then, outside, a woman's weeping. It was a long sound and it persisted even as a man's voice ordered it to shut up, shut up. It didn't stop.

Inside the roadhouse people got up to leave. It resembled an ordinary closing time, but sped up. They all hurried for the back door, putting on their hats. Hadjo was the last to leave. He was searching each person's face as they exited, searching for an explanation perhaps. But then there was no one left. He stayed for a moment longer, looking at the line of abandoned cups arrayed along the bar. He looked for a long time at the cup which Santiago had been holding not three minutes earlier. The plate he'd eaten from, the knife, the dropped fork. At last Hadjo picked up his own cup and drank it down and hurried out the back door.

II.

IT WAS QUIET around Mrs. Monroe's the next day. Quiet but not empty. A few people needed to be around the place, for appearances' sake. It was not clear how they selected themselves but they sat at two tables—not the bar—and talked about the night before in a roundabout fashion. The only person who spoke straight about the thing was the stableboy. 'That feller killed his own darkie,' he said. 'Shot him clean between the eyes, didn't he! The boy talked saucy and he just shot him down. Kapow!'

France growled at him. 'Be quiet, boy,' he said. 'Why don't you go back out there to the stables. Go curry my horses.'

'Yes sir,' the boy said happily, and went.

Around noon Raulerson appeared in the roadhouse. He had a haggard appearance, bloodshot and fatigued. His wife was with him and her eyes were swollen from crying. The man stood in the doorway and addressed them.

'Pardon sirs. I'm informing every person present that my man Sonny run off last night. He acted very bad towards me and then run off. If you see him please notify the law. Some of you know his description. He is very dark, with narrow limbs. He has a mean look and a low character all around. Though he is also clever and quick to grin and talk.' Raulerson's wife gave a soft sob. The son stared blankly ahead. There was dirt on his trouser legs, and dirt rubbed into the hollows of his eyes.

'I'll be posting Sonny's description in the cities. Also with the slavecatchers. He jist run off. You'll find that all his belongings is gone from me and his horse also. He might be headed down south to Indin country. Or to the Spanish town. Or hell, he might still be lurking in theseyer woods, you cain't tell. Be careful around this place. He's a bad sort. I am going to north now to lodge a report, then back up to Georgia. Thank you gents for your help.' And without waiting for any reply Raulerson turned and walked out of the room. The wife and son trailed after him out of the roadhouse.

The sitters in the room were quiet for a long time, long enough that the clatter of the family's wagon had faded to nothing through the trees. 'Is it me,' France said at last, 'or is folks these days jist getting meaner and meaner.'

'No, there's no doubting it,' breathed an old man. 'It's a bad breed these days.'

'You know that's right,' Herb said, leaning back in his chair. 'I don't know what makes them act the way they do. No decency. I know we—' he gestured at everybody present— 'we're the ones been here from the beginning, and first got the land open, and fought through it, and beat back the Indin and all of that. But I swear theseyer Come-Latelies are meaner than we ever were.'

Somber, they drank. All except Hadjo. He was alone at a third table. His eyes were red. As the others were putting down their cups he spoke.

'What was that man's name,' he said.

Silence a moment longer. Everyone else had found their own patch of nothing to look at. Then Herb Nail cleared his throat. 'I recall it was Richard.'

'Richard, it was,' France said.

'Richard what,' Hadjo asked.

Another silence. A longer one. 'Might of been—' Herb said. 'Did he say Ronson?'

France shook his head. 'No, it weren't that. Ronaldson. I believe he said Ronaldson.'

'Hell, I don't know. I thought it was Ronson.'

'So it was Richard Ronson,' Hadjo continued, 'or Ronaldson, and he was from Georgia, he said—it was south Georgia, wasn't it? And—'

'Boy,' France grumbled.

'He was from Georgia, and they'd been at Saint Augustine, and Santiago said they were going to—'

'Damn it, boy.' France struck the table. 'What's your game? Do you want to go help him hunt his slave? No? Then sit down, and be quiet.'

'He shot him,' Hadjo said. 'He killed him.'

'Did you see it happen?' said France. 'Did you? No. You was right here in this room. Same as me. Same as the rest of us. And none of us saw anybody shoot no damn Negro.'

'Where did they take him?' Hadjo said. 'Where's he buried?'

'Young man,' France said quietly, beginning to stand. 'Someone, someday, is going to have to teach you. Teach you about talking. When to do it. When to not. Because you, son, you say nothing when it's a good time to be conversating. And then, when most people's content to be quiet, that's right when you open your mouth.' He was all the way upright now, and facing Hadjo where he also stood. 'And it's going to hurt you. And it's going to cost you. And it's going to cost others.'

'It's that easy for you, is it,' said Hadjo. 'You can sit here talking about wars and stories and who killed who. Then when there's a body shot right here on this place you cain't say nothing about it.' He looked around at them. Their faces were as motionless as if painted on wood.

'I don't believe none of your old stories anydamnway. Doubt you even believe them yourselves.' Hadjo spat on the barroom floor. Then he stepped past France. He went straight back to the rear of the room and through the door.

The lady was there, at a desk, sitting in a chair of wrought wood. Her black and silver hair was loose, as always, framing her broad face. An imposing woman, but her chair was larger, a grand dark thing carved on another continent, in another century. The only thing on the desk in front of her was a black bible. She had been reading it but now she closed the pages on her finger and looked expectantly at Hadjo.

'Ma'am, I've come about my bill,' he said. 'I'm leaving, and I'd like to settle it.'

She watched him carefully. 'There isn't one,' she said.

'What do you mean?'

'I mean there's nothing you can pay. Person or persons have been filling it the whole time you been here.'

Hadjo shook his head. 'No. I didn't need that. Why?'

'I don't know,' the lady said. 'Maybe someone with a debt to your father. Or maybe not. Maybe it's for your own sake and not his.'

Hadjo shook his head again. 'No. I didn't need that. I have

my own damned money. I can pay my own.' He lifted up his boot, to fish in it for his stash of bills.

But the lady's voice boomed out in the narrow room. 'Put that boot down, boy,' she growled at him. He did.

She leaned back in her chair. 'There's nothing for you to pay. If you don't want people's help, you'll have to go someplace else.' Hadjo stared at her. 'But I believe you were planning on that aready.'

The young man turned from the huge-fisted matron and her chair and her bible, but before he could leave she spoke again.

'They've left him on the sand ridge up yonder,' she said. 'Every person who has ever died in this place ends up on that ridge. The killers take them there. Their sin gets too heavy for them here in the forest after about a quart' mile, so they lay them up on the desert. As if the desert can conceal the fact of whatever happened down here. Sometimes it does conceal it. From us, anyhow. The earthly claybound.'

'I'm going to try and find it,' said Hadjo.

'All right,' Mrs. Monroe said. 'North a mile, then west to the ridge.'

The young man walked out through the tavern room. The conversation went quiet again until he left.

He had gone perhaps a mile when he came across the slave's old horse. It stood half-concealed in a titi thicket. The old mare had been driven loose into the woods. It was eating some grass, an empty saddle on its low-slung back. Hadjo got down and examined the animal. Then he got a lead string and tied its reins to the rear of his own saddle, and with Santiago's horse in tow he rode on.

The formation called the trail ridge rose unheralded and unexplained out of the forest floor. A chain of sandy mounds or dunes that stood as high as the pine canopy around it. Hadjo climbed up this ridge. He looked among the scraps of vegetation on the peaks, cactuses and scrubby oaks, the pools of water that lay in the troughs. After a short distance he found the little mound of earth.

They had not gone far to bury the slave. Maybe five minutes' ride along the ridge. They had scraped away enough sand to hide the body under the surface and no more than that. The mound had the unmistakeable length and width of a man, a dead man, the blank anonymity of coffins, that faceless recumbent shape of more-than-sleep. Yet the man's horse seemed to know him. It came to the mound to examine it and lowered its face to the earth. Then it stepped away.

More of the man's possessions had been scattered into the bushes nearby. Hadjo gathered them up, shirts, trousers, small tins, and put them into the horse's saddlebag. Then he came and crouched down next to the grave. The fresh-dug sand showed brilliant white in the moonlight.

Hadjo got his knife from its scabbard. He searched around in a nearby stand of trees for a piece of wood right for the job and found it, a big crooked knot dry as driftwood and shaped like a rood. On the crosspiece he carved

Santeago

Killed.

1844.

and planted it at the head of the grave.

The young man built a fire from the abundant dry wood and ate some jerked venison. Then he found himself a patch of clean needles under a nearby pine and lay himself down parallel to the dead man and the two of them and their horses were still.

In the morning Hadjo came to where the man lay and hunkered down on his heels for a time. He looked at the mound, just looked, his elbows on his knees. Then he stood and kicked the fire out.

He turned the horses north. Hadjo had never left the territory of his birth, had never set foot in the state of Georgia. Therefore he had never in his life entered the United States of America. But he was headed there now, at a trot. He set off with the sun rising on his right hand. Likenesses of the young man and the two horses were printed in the treetops to the west. Ahead of him the ridge ran off, bare and rounded, like a child's drawing of foothills. Someone or something or no one thing in particular had made a trail that ran a perfect line of best fit along the loping mounds. Common to it were the marks of deer hooves and horse hooves and bootsoles and wagon wheels and rabbits' feet and possums' feet and bear paws and fox paws and panthers' paws with the delicate tracing of the tail between the prints and the long belly-drag of tortoises and the tiny scrabblings of lizards. He rode until noon before stopping under a sand pine. He dug through his saddlebag and ate more jerked venison and some biscuit. The tethered horses stood chewing on what grasses they could find. The slave's horse was old and swaybacked but had not slowed yet in their ride. It wore its saddle well.

Hadjo stood up to look at it more closely. It was a fine saddle. Dark leather, almost purple, tooled fancywork along the edges. Hadjo reached up and undid the clasps. Slowly, as if afraid to disturb a resting place.

In one side were all of Santiago's clothes. A pair of trousers rolled, a pair of shirts. Hadjo took out an oystershell and opened it and discovered his own face looking up from a piece of polished metal, the dead man's mirror. He quickly snapped it shut and put it back.

The saddlebag on the other side held a few of Santiago's tools, a coil of fine string and some fishing hooks. And down in the bottom he felt a strange object. He took it out and looked at it. A small wooden carving of a ship. It had all of the details of a clipper to scale: foremast and aft, portholes, mizzen. On its hull was the inscription RIVER JORDAN BOATBUILDING CO. Hadjo looked at it for a long time, turning the thing over and over in his hand. Looking for an answer in it somewhere. Then all of a sudden he put it back and closed the saddlebag. He did this quickly, like a trespasser, discovered somewhere he ought not be.

The ridge flattened down into the bulk of the land. The road ran between taller trees than it had previously. Soon the trail took Hadjo away from the sand ridge altogether. The road was graded here, the streams were bridged. Though he saw no other travelers, the whole area had a clean, swept look. He came across a sign reading GEORGIA 12 MILES. UNITED STATES FEDERAL GOVERNMENT.

The Saint Marys River appeared, running southeast. Even the river seemed to have the hand of order upon it—it moved tidily toward the ocean as if it had an appointment to keep. He followed that river until he came to a small scrap of a town.

Five or six buildings faced the road with their backs to the river. It was a poor imitation of a county seat. Hadjo hitched the two horses and walked up onto the raised boardwalk that stretched along the storefronts. There were handbills posted on each of the establishments, according to their kind. The public house had notice of musical entertainments, mostly past. The drygoods store had a list of medicines to be demonstrated there, and the names of physicians. The inn had news of a bad-check passer who had recently visited the town.

But most of the handbills were tacked up on the post office: they were for fugitive slaves. Hadjo scanned them. Some were old, tanned, tattered at the edges. But others were quite recent. And the newest one was tacked up with the boldfaced title:

WANTED: ABSCONDER

Reward for negro bondservant calling himself
SANTIAGO CABREY, about 35 years of age,
middling tall and rather thinly built.

The negro is a good looking fellow, darkskinned,
with eyes narrowed at the edges almost
oriental fashion.

He has a HOT TONGUE and is
troublesome property withal.

Still he is not unintelligent and
HAS LIKELY CHANGED HIS NAME.

Any negro the reader meets may be
Santiago in cognito.

A good reward at market price will be given
if he is secured in jail so that the
owner can come and get him again.

R. T. Raulerson of Macon County Georgia.

Hadjo tore down the handbill. He stepped indoors, holding it in front of him. The office seemed empty, but there was a scratching sound off to his left. When Hadjo looked, a girl of about fourteen picked up her quill from the page.

'Office closed til my daddy gets back,' she sang. Then she returned to scratching at the paper.

Hadjo took a step forward. There were two stacks of paper in front of the girl, one blank and the other filled. He looked more closely at the stack that she had copied out. They were the advertisement for Santiago, copies upon copies.

'No,' Hadjo said, shaking the notice in his hand. 'No, this isn't right.'

'What d'ye mean?' the girl asked. 'Did they catch him aready? Drat, I just started making these.'

'No. He ain't missing. He never was.'

The girl knitted her thick brows. 'Well, that ain't what his owner said yestiddy,' she said. 'He seemed like he was missing his man right badly.'

'Santiago was killed. His owner killed him.'

The girl rolled her eyes at him. 'You're trying to tell me the man murdered his own Negro? Come on, now. Why would Mister Raulerson ruin his own property?'

She looked at Hadjo reproachfully. 'He's a man of business, Mister Raulerson is. He and my father talked all about all his business doings in Saint Augustine. Gave daddy a tip on an investment over there, matterfact. He's a man of business.'

'He shot Santiago,' Hadjo said. His voice had gone louder. 'Santiago spoke bad to him and then Raulerson went outside and shot him. Twice.'

The girl's eyes narrowed. 'Mister,' she said. 'We hain't had any problems like the one you're describing. We take good care of our people around here. They stay nicely clothed and nicely fed. Any bad use of a slave would be taken very serious.' She went back to her work. 'And any other talk—well. My daddy says that's the stuff that gets made up for Northern newspapers. By folks looking to stir up problems where there ain't any.'

'I want to talk to the sheriff,' Hadjo said. 'Where is the sheriff in this town.'

'No sheriff anymore,' the girl said, scratching along. 'No need for un. We've got a company to take care of all that now. Mister Addison's company. My daddy says they take care of the slavecatching and thieftaking and general regulating better than any sheriff done.'

'Well. Where are they?' Hadjo asked.

'Out with the hounds,' the girl said. 'Ain't no telling when they'll be back.'

'The hounds.'

'Sure. The owner left us one of that Negro's shirts. They'll be tracking his smell all over Florida.'

'Listen to me. They ain't going to find him. Santiago's dead. Raulerson shot him and put—'

Then the girl straightened in her chair. 'Why, that's them now,' she said happily. She pointed out the window, down the road.

'Who?' Hadjo asked. The girl had jumped up to go outside, and he followed her.

'Yes, yes, it's them,' she said, smiling and pointing. 'Mister Addison's company.'

The far end of the road into town was clogged with a group of riders, all sizes and all kinds, coming along in neat single file with a pack of dappled dogs. Which were beginning now to bay.

'Ooh, listen to that,' the girl said. 'Why, it sounds like they've got ahold of something. They've picked up the Negro's scent. Right here in the town!'

And indeed the dogs were beginning one by one to break into a run. There was a Hey! and a Hoop! from the gang of riders and they came faster.

'Oh Lord,' Hadjo said. 'Oh no.'

He rushed past the girl down the boardwalk and sprinted toward the two horses where he'd left them at the hitching post. He yanked each one free and jumped up into Alma's saddle. Already the hunters were coming close, the hounds scarcely using their noses anymore but simply bearing down on their target, the dead man's horse.

Hadjo cursed. He looked frantically all around the town's clearing. Then at last he cut his reins toward the river and clucked. He went toward the water at a trot, then a canter, then a gallop.

The riders called off their dogs. Three of their group came along behind Hadjo at an easy unbothered pace. They had drawn guns. Hadjo reached the edge of the riverbank and pulled Alma to a halt; the aged mare came up knickering behind.

They were at a bend in the river. The bank there was not a slope but a sheer drop of six feet. The water churned below them, already night-black though the land around it was still lit by a blueish dusk. Hadjo looked back. The three riders kept coming at that unhurried walk, plainly curious what the youth would do. He cursed under his breath. 'Well, let's go,' he said, and put Alma forward.

But they did not move. He tried again; Alma leaned forward again but still could not move. Hadjo turned around and saw the old mare standing upright, not even trying to strain against the lead rope but still stopping the little marshtackie dead in her tracks. Hadjo tried to ride forward one more time but they made as much progress as if they were tied to a tree. Finally Hadjo got his dragwhip and leapt down from his saddle. He glanced into the mare's sullen eye and then got up on its saddle. He raised the whip, cracked it. The deafening pop came from an inch behind the mare's flank and at the same instant Hadjo rammed his heels viciously into its ribcage.

The horse heaved forward. At the edge of the water the hollowed bank crumbled away, and they fell down into the river. Horse and rider were fully submerged for several seconds and Hadjo started kicking free of the stirrups so that he would not drown with the thrashing animal.

At last they broke the surface. The mare was moaning and sawing the water frantically. Alma came alongside of them, heading north for the opposite bank. But the old mare did not follow. It turned this way and that in the current, unresponsive to Hadjo's tugging on the reins. Eventually it decided to turn back and started swimming determinedly for the near shore.

The tether between the two horses drew tight. Hadjo cried out. With the old mare pulling at her line, Alma could not head for the far bank but was actually dragged backward through the water by the bigger animal. There they hung: the horses straining in opposing directions in the middle of the current, both being swept downstream. On the bank the three riders had dismounted and were walking alongside them at the speed of the river.

Then all the tension gave way. The lead rope had torn off the old mare's pommel. With a cry Hadjo leapt after the rope and grabbed ahold. Alma kept swimming, pulling him easily through the water toward the far bank. He rolled onto his back and saw the dead man's horse still swimming downstream at the same oblique angle, bobbing crazed and riderless toward the sea.

Hadjo watched the three silhouettes printed on the sky above the opposite bank. They aimed at Santiago's horse. A flare at the tips of their muskets. Two balls splashed in the water, but one struck home and the mare whinnied piercingly. The injury seemed to knock something straight in the animal. It turned around began churning for the north shore, a dozen lengths behind Alma.

Hadjo was dragging along in the black water a few feet behind Alma. At last the gunmen spotted the ripple that he pushed up as he drew through the river and they fired. The shots struck the water left and right of Hadjo; a third was close enough to splash his face. He dove under the surface then, to swim with the horse and also perhaps not to have to watch the three men as they reloaded their muskets. He cut deep under the surface and stayed there and still they nearly hit him. There were three soft thumps as musketballs hit silt.

Then he kicked off the bottom and charged up the gentle slope. His head and shoulders came above water. Alma was already on shore, stamping and flicking herself dry. Hadjo did not mount up or even lead Alma but just shoved her ahead of him into the forest. Then he scrambled after Santiago's horse where it was just starting out from the water. The musketball had grazed it along one flank. He grabbed its reins and pulled it into the trees.

Roping the horses together again, he dragged them into a dense bottomland forest. Encroaching on either side was something darker, deeper. There was not much dry ground to walk upon. Hadjo came forward slowly until they reached the absolute end of the solid land. He looked out.

'Here's that big swamp, boy,' he said to himself, breathing heavily. 'The Okefenokee. And didn't I always want to see it? Well, here it is.' And he put Alma forward.

The horses walked with swamp water up to their cannons for a while. But then the water deepened, and the surroundings rose up in a squawking and chirring and rattling discord so loud that the horses turned their ears this way and that to try not to hear it. The trees around them grew thick and buttressed. Hadjo looked around for any scrap of dry land but he couldn't see one and he was not turning back.

The place was black and dense as if the night had grown flesh and was striving against the intruders. The spiders felt like hands on him. Hadjo cowered in the saddle and looked behind at their backtrail but it seemed every bit as impassable as what was ahead. They could only go forward. Hadjo was talking to himself. 'I don't want to be here no more. I don't want to be here no more.' And yet he kept going. He rode toward the moon, even as the moon seemed to draw back from the young man and the horses and stand in cold and clinical observation of their plight.

Thirty hours later he came out on the other side of the Okefenokee. He'd lost his hat and his shirt was torn. His eye-sockets and forehead had been rubbed clean, but every other part of him was black with mud and speckled with sphagnum. The two horses were colored about the same and had a similar frightful look in their eyes from whatever trials they had shared.

Along all the plain and tidy byways of south Georgia they carried traces of the swamp's mud and ruin and disorder. He looked like a dislodged piece of the swamp itself. Two constables followed him for a while outside Brunswick. They started to come close to the young man to ask his business there. But their horses shied away, afraid of the smell. And soon they too shied away from talking to the strange young man who did not even look at them or their badges when he passed.

He washed off in the Altamaha River. After two more days on the highway north, Savannah sprouted up house by house out of a fetid stretch of bottomland. He rode into it at night. Cobbled streets, hard and dry. All of the water was sluiced away to the waiting river. He followed one of the gutters down toward it. The dingy stream trickled through a neighborhood of mismatched shacks not so different from those in his own place: doublepen cabins that might have stood a dozen miles apart, here within arms' reach of each other, built by countryfolk who were used to miles of distance but had been pressed into service in the crowded town. From time to time a sow squonked across the road, but otherwise all you could see were humans and their houses.

Then he came into Savannah proper, the platted city, its large squares. It was perfectly rectilinear and stupendously white and well-lit. The traffic of carts and carriages and muleteers moved like a geared machine. It carried Hadjo along; he stepped wide eyed and wary, and his horses were wary too. Iron tires clattered on the street, which was cobbled with the ballast stones of ships.

But the city's big white geometry began to loosen again at the waterfront. The place tended toward disorder there. Wharves clattered with boats and seethed with the tide. Hadjo found the first place with stalls for horses and took a room. The matron was no Mrs. Monroe. She leaned across the bar at him, grinning, copious. In the end he went to bed hungry to avoid her offer of complementary candied yams.

Up in the room he was awake for a long time, gazing at a beam of light on the wall. It was orange, cast from the fire in the foundry. It fell fixed in one corner of the room and never moved. Hadjo had brought Santiago's belongings up with him, for safekeeping. He set them out on the bureau. The shirts, the trousers, the tools, the little carved wooden ship. Carefully arranged, as if waiting for their owner to come and claim them.

He woke the next morning to a waxy light. Hadjo went straight down to the stables to check on Santiago's horse, and on

Alma. He was a long time currying Alma and speaking to her in the dark stall. Then he left out into bright morning by the waterfront.

The first wharf he came to had the name Stoddard in iron over the entryway. Men moved around pushing handcarts and carrying hanks of rope over their shoulders. They called to one another, their cries mixing with the gulls'. Hadjo searched for anyone who might be Santiago's father's age—seventy years old and still working, as the boatbuilder had told him on his last night on earth. But no one matched the description. And soon the foreman came up to Hadjo and asked him to state his business there or leave. He left.

For a time he kept to a precinct of stoven barrels and half-smashed crates. Soon a man with a briefcase stepped out from one of the wharves and approached.

'Pardon me, sir,' Hadjo said to the man. 'I'm looking for a fellow. A very old slave, nair seventy, working on these docks someplace. He has a son named Santiago. Do you know him?'

But the man shook his head and stepped away, staring at Hadjo over his shoulder. Hadjo followed for a few steps but could not get him to turn around. He was left standing there in the middle of the street.

There was a sound like a sneezing fit nearby and Hadjo turned toward it. Two young dockhands were laughing into their fists. It was the noon hour and they were sitting on fruit-crates with their lunches. When Hadjo went toward them they stopped laughing. And yet they did not move away—when he came close the man on the left let out a loud, ironical 'Afternoon to you, young marster.'

'Afternoon.'

'Let me explain for that gent you just met,' said the smaller youth on the right. 'It's just that folks mostly go to piss back there, where you was standing. So I guess you gave him a little surprise.'

Hadjo grimaced. The larger man on the left had gone back to tittering. The slim man on the right held his composure. 'Anyhow. Kin I help you, young marster?'

'I don't know,' Hadjo said. 'Maybe you can. I'm wondering if you ever knew a fellow named Santiago. A Negro. He built boats here.'

The two shook their heads at him and chorused Nosir, no. Santiago? No.

Hadjo pressed on. 'He had—he had a father that worked here. Old man, he must be seventy. Do you know of him?'

The two men shook their heads again, gave more Nosir nos. The fatter youth muttered: 'Does he like to peek on fellows pissing too?'

Hadjo looked up and down the waterfront. The sun was making its way toward the rooftops. With a sigh he reached into his pocket. 'Well, I don't know. Maybe this will help.' He produced the little carven boat. 'Have you ever heard of the River Jor—Jordan—the River Jordan Boat—' He stopped trying to read the inscription and simply held it out to them.

The large man squinted at the boat, then shook his head. He had never heard of any such thing. But the bony young man on the right had gone stock still.

'Where did you get that.' He stood up and faced Hadjo. 'Where.'

'It—it belonged to a slave. I met him down in Floridy, I saw him killed. It was with his things.'

'You ain't supposed to have that.'

Hadjo stared back at him. 'Look,' he said. 'I don't know what this is about. I don't know what this—this Jordan Boat Co is. All I know's that a man named Santiago had it, and now he's dead. And his people don't know what happened to him.'

The larger man was peering at his friend. 'Hey, Scipio,' he said. 'What's this about, Scip?' But he would not answer. He continued his deep examination of the young man who stood in front of them in tattered, swampwrecked clothes.

'I'll find the man for you,' he said at last. 'Or I'll find someone who will find him. But you got to give that to me.'

Hadjo pulled the object closer. 'No,' he said. 'I ain't giving it to no one. It goes to his family, with the rest of his things.'

The young man shook his head. 'But you won't never find them to begin with. You'll never find them, and you know it. Unless you give me that boat.'

'Damn it all,' Hadjo said. 'What does the thing even mean? What's the purpose of it? Tell me. If I give it to you you got to tell me.' But the skinny young man did not answer him. He only stretched out his hand.

Hadjo held the little lacquered object, turned it over and over. Then he pushed it into the other man's palm.

'Now tell me,' he said.

The skinny young man grinned at him. 'Oh, it's just a set of fellows that get together and eat sometimes. We watermen, boatbuilders, stevedores, such as that. We eat together and talk about things. Trifling things. Call ourselves that, the Jordan Boatbuilding Co. It ain't nothing for you to concern yourself over, young marster, it ain't nothing troublesome or worrisome for you. Just a few of us that set together, eating, jawing the way we do.' He smiled a little and pocketed the object, then headed back toward the gate. 'Wait here,' he said. 'When quitting time comes we'll find you.' And then he was gone, absorbed into the clatter of the wharf. His companion trailed along after him, casting confused looks back at the slovenly white youth.

Hadjo remained in the street, keeping to the shade. But where he stood he could follow the path of the skinny young man who'd spoken to him. He was a climber on the rigging, he went to the very top of a clipper which was in drydock. Hadjo watched another man climb the mast next to him and when both reached the top they paused for a time. A conversation took place there, halfway to the sky. They were talking back and forth between mainmast and mizzen. And then he saw how one of the climbers reached out his arm and pointed directly down at Hadjo.

He retrieved Alma and the old mare, then waited there through the afternoon. They were still working at the water-front, though the sun had gone down behind the buildings, though the tips of the masts were the only place where there was still sunlight. Then a bell rang. Hadjo scanned all of the faces that came streaming out from the gate, but it was only the whites, with one or two freemen mixed in. Hadjo peered inside and saw that all of the slaves were still at work. They were sharpening the tools and putting away the materials and setting things right after the mess everyone else had made. Hadjo was waiting there for another forty minutes before a husky voice shouted out. 'All right, all right, you boys go on,' it said. 'Straight home, now, and no stopping for the craps games.'

There was another perfunctory clanging of a bell and the slaves began filing out. Weary and slow, smelling of sweat and turpentine. The bony young man from earlier was one of the last out. He was walking shoulder to shoulder with an older man of broad build and wire-rimmed spectacles.

'That's him,' he said, pointing at Hadjo. 'He's the one had the Jordan boat.'

The older man had an expression of deep misgiving and yet he did not once break his stride. He passed into a sidestreet, waving for Hadjo to follow.

Hadjo did, leading the horses along the narrow way, struggling to keep up. They bore west for a mile or more before coming out on one of the last wharves on the waterfront. Here at last Hadjo's guide slowed down and spoke to him.

'It's a old boatbuilding man you're hunting, bout seventy.'
'Yes.'

'Had a son worked here too, who's gone down to Florida.'
'Yes.'

'You got news for him.'

Hadjo nodded.

'Well,' the man said. 'I guess this is your man in here.'

The place was mostly empty. Three people were standing on the dock looking at a large rowboat newly launched into the river. They were speaking together and looking down at the boat to see how it rode in the water. Satisfied, two of the people went away, which left one man standing by the water, wiping his hands clean with a rag. He was a short man, lightly built, greyheaded but unbowed. Hadjo's guide came and touched the man on the arm and said a word or two to him. Then he turned and pointed at Hadjo. The old man looked at the youth and stopped cleaning his hands.

Hadjo came across the planks. The old man held perfectly

still and silent and it was as if he already knew what the young man had to tell him, though he could not possibly have known it yet. Like the awful word had reached across that open space and seized him.

At last Hadjo was standing in front of him. 'Are you—' he said. The rest of the question would not form itself.

'My name is Seville,' the old man said. He was nodding now and would keep nodding throughout their talk, understanding something.

'Do you have a son named Santiago?'

'That's him. Yes.'

'He's dead down in Floridy and buried on a hill.'

He had said it so fast. The old man looked away. Hadjo followed with 'I'm sorry' once or twice but the man was peering off into the middle distance, to the other side of the river. Then he wiped his hands once or twice more and walked away.

There was a small stable over to one side of the place. He went into it and came out a minute later with a tall grey mule. Soon, with the aid of a stepladder, he heaved up onto its back, though other men hurried up to help him. Then he was off, at a mule's amble, through the gate and out into the city.

Hadjo followed on foot, leading the two horses along. The large man with the spectacles came too, and they walked behind the old man Seville mule-slow through the streets of Savannah. When Hadjo glanced back at the large man, he saw how his face was seized in a scowl, fierce and violent as if to clench back bitter tears.

Soon they'd come to a district for slaves and hired men where ancient shacks abutted three-story rooming tenements, and the old man went into one of the latter. Hadjo remained out in the street as the other man went in after him. Across the way was an empty broken-fenced yard. Hadjo sat down in it. He remained there, elbows on his knees, staring up at the old man's room.

An hour passed. Hadjo let his little horse roam across the empty lot. The place had more grass for the horses to eat than anywhere else he'd found in that city. He found the stump of a tree and lay back, to wait, to watch for what?

It was hours later and the moon was well up when a hand shook him awake. 'Excuse me,' a woman's voice was saying. 'Excuse me, but are you the man who came for old Seville?'

Hadjo looked around himself. 'Oh, hum. Sorry. I don't know if.'

'Well, course you are,' the woman said. 'No other white man laying down with his horse in Yamacraw. Come along, young marster, if you please. Seville'd like to speak with you.'

Hadjo looked up at her. 'He would?'

'Yes, he would,' the woman said. 'Please—go to him.' Her voice faltered a little.

Hadjo stood up and brushed himself off. He put on his hat and squared it and went on toward the old man's door. 'And don't worry about the horses, young marster,' the woman said. 'No one going to bother them here.'

He passed into the building and up a narrow staircase. There were two doors at the top; he chose the one with light shining past the jamb. When he knocked, the door swung inward, latch-less in an unbalanced frame.

The old man was sitting on the edge of his bed. He looked quite different than he had earlier. He'd lost his scowl, his hat.

His furrowed face had smoothed into a look nearly childlike in its unalloyed sadness. Yet he was not crying. There was another bed on the opposite wall and a man was sleeping on it, turned away from the light.

'I'm sorry about all of this,' Hadjo said. 'I cain't tell you how sorry.'

'Can you please tell me what happened,' the old man broke in.

Hadjo stood there, swallowed. 'He was killed,' he answered simply.

'I knew that. But can you tell me what happened.'

Hadjo nodded. 'He was shot outside a roadhouse. It was—it was his owner done it. They got to arguing and then he shot him. Just shot him.' The young man shrugged his shoulders, as if he wished there was more. 'There's news he ran away but it ain't so. They killed him and no one's supposed to tell about it.'

The old man's gaze had left the dark window and roamed around Hadjo's face for a long time. 'It's a hard thing you done to me,' he said at last.

Hadjo frowned. 'What?'

'I say it's a hard thing,' the old man said. 'See, I've been imagining my son's life. Imagining it healthy and pleasant. Maybe even free. All these years I ain't seen him, all these years he's been away. And look at me. I didn't have many more to go. It wouldn't be long now before I could lay myself down in peace. And I'd go to my death imagining Santiago's happy, healthy, maybe with a wife and sons of his own. I got good at imagining that. I could go down easy that way. But that death wasn't for mine, no. It seems that death wasn't for mine.'

'I'm sorry,' Hadjo said. 'I thought you'd want to know.' He was almost crying.

The old man looked up at Hadjo as if seeing him for the first time.

'Where did you say he's buried.'

'In the sandhills,' Hadjo said. 'It's a place they call the Trail Ridge. It's the way people ride on when they's coming down into Floridy.'

The old man nodded and got up. He walked stiffly to get a rucksack down from a shelf. Then he began to move around the sparse room, gathering up clothes and necessaries and folding them into the sack. A coin purse, a razor. Provisions from a larder. He reached over the sleeping man for a broad black hat hanging on a peg.

'What are you doing?' Hadjo asked.

'Getting ready to go.'

'Go where?'

The old man glanced at him. 'To Santiago.'

'But,' Hadjo said. 'But you don't know where you're going.'

'I'll look till I do.'

'You'll be looking forever,' Hadjo said. 'I'll go with you.'

The old man looked at Hadjo for a moment. 'You might want to think on that a while longer, young marster,' he said.

And then he had made all his preparations and was cinching the bag. Hadjo was watching him, trying to say something. 'But wait,' he said at last. 'Ain't your—I mean, ain't you got a—'

'A owner.' Seville turned to him. 'I ain't seen the lady that owns me in a sixmonth. I don't think she knows my name. I'm hired out to these docks, you see, and they send her the rent. Her slave Seville is just some numbers on a sheet to her. Yield per centum. Return on investiment. She don't hardly know I'm alive. There's plenty of us like that. But what you're really asking is, who's going to chase after me. That's the better question. Well, right now it's Saturday night. I have all this coming Sunday to walk. Then on Monday the boys at the shipyard going to tell the bosses I took sick, that'll buy me another half a day. Then by noon they'll come looking. Whoever wants to look can look, I'll be gone. I'll be with my son, then. In one way or the other.' Then, with a gesture suddenly solicitous, he held open the door and gestured for Hadjo to pass.

The young man went ahead, down the stairs and into the street. Hadjo went up to him, leading Alma and the old mare.

'I—I have his things,' he said. 'This is his horse. This is his saddle. You could ride it.'

The old man looked at the horse for a moment and felt its back. He thumbed the leather of the saddle. Then he opened the bag. In the paltry glow from the roominghouse the dead son's shirt shone pale in the murk. He touched it, ran his fingers slowly along the cloth. Then he drew back his hand. He nodded, as if understanding something, and mounted nodding up onto the old mare. Still nodding he started away down the street.

III.

I T WAS STILL DARK but the sun was beginning to announce
itself in the sky downriver. Seville wore a black coat and a
broad black hat. He pushed on through the outlying streets
of the town, which were declining into flat expansive country roads. By the time they reached the first village south of
Savannah, churchgoers were just beginning to issue from their
houses in thin black suits and yellow dresses and blue dresses.
As old Seville rode past them he removed his broad hat to
greet them severally with a graceful Sunday slowness, the once-
weekly slowness which held all those villagers in its grasp as if a
viscous substance of perfect clarity had encased everything and
everyone and all their doings, giving decorous ease to the least
movement. The old man spoke his greeting into it, loud and gentle, tipping his hat. And a good day to you sir. And a good day
to you ma'am. Beautiful isn't it. Well, it's the one the Lord has
made. I thank him for it.

After noon Seville turned off the highway and rode a ways
into the forest. He eased down from the saddle and moved
around to his bag, which was tied behind the saddle. He fished
out some cooked sweet potatoes and distributed them onto two
round wooden plates, putting a thin slice of dried salt pork on

top of each. As Hadjo rode up and dismounted, he held one of the plates out to the young man.

'Oh,' said Hadjo. 'It's all right. Thank you. I've got my own food, some.'

'Got your own food, you say?' the old man said. 'Well, it don't like you been eating it.' And he held the plate out a little farther. In the end Hadjo took it.

They settled themselves on opposite ends of a log. The old man chewed carefully; his teeth were strong but a few of them were missing. When he finally spoke it was in time with the working of his jaw.

'Oh, but I was a poor host last night, young marster,' he said. Hadjo looked at him. 'I didn't offer you a thing to eat, after all your riding. And what's more, I didn't ask your name. Did you ever say your name, young marster?'

'Don't believe I did. But it's Hadjo.'

'Ha—'

'Hadjo.'

'Hecho?'

'Hadjo. Haytch ay dee jay oh.'

'Ah. Hadjo. Why, that's a fine name. What sort of name is that?'

The young man shook his head. 'I've never quite known.'

'Well, now.' The old man sniffed. 'If you don't know, can't you at least have a story made up, handy? Some fine old lie? Young man like yourself.'

Hadjo shrugged his shoulders. 'Never managed it,' he said. 'I've never been much good at stories.'

'Well, I suppose it's something you learn.' Seville looked off into the distance for a while. 'I'm surprised you didn't pick it up from my Santiago. Now, that boy could lie some. He could lie up a nation. He could lie like a bird can fly.'

Hadjo smiled. 'He could talk, I know that,' he said. 'He told a story about his own name, matterfact.'

The old man frowned. 'His mother gave him that name. Cordelia did. I told her with a name like that he'd always be set apart from these English-type folks, and battling with them. And that's just how it fell out. Stayed that way his whole life. Battling this one, that one. White men, Negroes. Quarreling and quarreling. That's what got him sold away out of Savannah. Quarreling and quarreling.' He was quiet for a time, working his jaw. 'And that's what happened at the end. Wasn't it? It was. He said something. Spoke hot.'

Hadjo closed his eyes. 'He did—say something. Yes, he did. He spoke on his owner's name. Out loud in the public room. And he was right, too. He said the truth about that bastard.'

Seville was looking down at the ground and frowning very hard. 'Fool,' he said at last, whispering. 'Fool.' He stood up and slung the scraps of sweet potato away. Then he got up on the old mare and rode off.

Hadjo caught up with him later in the afternoon, several miles down the road. This was to be their orientation: Seville ahead, Hadjo some distance behind. Hadjo kept his eyes on Seville's board-straight back where he rode high on the saddle. Once when Hadjo drew closer he heard the old man singing. It was a long tune, low, wavering. Hadjo backed away so as not to hear it. He had not been invited to that song.

They began to pass churchgoers coming back from meeting. The people all moved a little faster now, to get home to their meals. Seville did not greet them so readily anymore. At most he touched his hat in passing, a gesture like hiding his face.

The sun dropped, stretched through the trees on their right. A small round lake shone like a medallion and Seville hupped the mare up a bluff which overlooked it. He got down from the saddle and set about collecting twigs and pinestraw, and without a word Hadjo went hunting for branches and logs. Seville soon had a small fire glowing and Hadjo brought his contributions. Their fire swelled as the sun died down. The old man set a few sweet potatoes in the ground close to the coals. Then he stretched his old legs out with his bootheels very near to the fire and sighed.

'Day's over,' he said after a long silence by the fire. 'Sunday's over.'

After a while when Hadjo did not answer this, he continued. 'It'll be a harder thing to be a runaway now. People don't pay so much mind on the Lord's day, but after that, after that—' He looked at Hadjo over the fire.

'Or didn't you know that's the word for this. Runaway.'

Hadjo snorted. 'Hell. It won't be so bad as all that. You's just an old fellow going from here to there. Won't be no trouble with it.'

The man gave a kind of a chuckle, dry and hard. 'Won't be no trouble,' he said. 'Hi now, young marster. Florida's only the next state down from here, it ain't the other side of the earth. I know things cain't be so different there than here. What, are Negroes running around without a care down in Florida, frolickin and prosperin and paying no mind? My my, that's a wonder, a universal wonder.' He sniffed.

'Didn't say it's a frolic,' Hadjo grumbled. 'I know there might be problems.'

'Well, that's good you know there might be problems,' said the old man. 'Cause I'd say problems is likely.' He took a stick and poked the sweet potatoes to turn them over.

'The only thing I have on my side is that I'm superannuated.' He said the word with relish. 'Superannuated, which is to say old and woredown. There won't be much lookout for me. Most fellows quit running away by the time they turn seventy years old.'

'Have you ever done it before?' Hadjo asked. 'Run off.'

The old man regarded him, a hard stare which lasted a long time. 'Well. That's quite a question for a young gentleman such as yourself to be asking,' he said. 'Specially one who comes from a big grand slave-holding house. Yes, I kin tell,' he interjected, as Hadjo protested this. 'I kin tell you was raised with the Negro. Yes. They's just a certain way a person has who's used to em, who have money and such to own em. The way they sorter—well, they just take to it natural, having a person around. Here's your sweet potatoes, young marster.' He plucked two out of the fire and set them on a plate for him.

'Thank you,' Hadjo said absently.

The old man looked at Hadjo over his food. 'And now I got a question for you, young Hadjo, now you've asked a few of me. How do it feel, son of a slaveholding house, to be on the helping end of a runaway Negro?'

Hadjo quickly shook his head. 'Naw. This ain't running away, what you're doing. Not like that.'

'Oh?'

'No. This is different.'

'Oh.'

'Because you've got a righteous cause to do it, see. Ain't doing it out of meanness or spite. This type of running away, it's for a good reason.' Satisfied, the young man bit down into his second sweet potato and chewed in silence. The old man nodded and did the same.

Morning came up cool and still. The little lake below the hill was hung with fog. Hadjo took Santiago's line and hook and cut a cane pole to fish with. Above the lake he dug his hand into a dark patch of soil and found earthworms just by the feel of them. Hadjo then settled himself on an outcropping and within half an hour had caught two big catfish. He rushed up the slope with them to show Seville. But when he got there the old man was gone.

Tracks led out of the clearing. A small fire had been built and then kicked out. Hadjo cast around the place and found Alma and rode out of the clearing.

He came upon the old man several miles on. When Hadjo drew alongside, Seville did not look in his direction or acknowledge him. The old man was squinting away down the road. Though he was going no faster than he had the day before, he was somehow more hurried.

'You left,' Hadjo said. 'I went down caught some fish. Here, look—' He brandished them. 'Where'd you go?'

'Right discourteous of me to've left you, young marster,' the old man said. 'I just didn't reckon I had time for a nice catfish breakfast. I's too bothered with trying to get out of Georgia alive.'

Hadjo frowned. 'Why—hell, it's just the morning—'

'I don't guess you took what I said last night too serious,' the old man said. 'About traveling on a Sunday compared to traveling on a workaday. How things ain't going to be so easy now.'

'I took it serious—'

'Of course you did,' said Seville. 'Just not serious enough. But I suppose it's my fault. I cain't expect you to know the same things, mind about the same things. Shoot, I scarcely know whether you won't throw my hide over to the paterollers if the time come.'

'I'd never. Damn it all, I'd never—'

'Young Mister Hadjo,' the old man said. 'I understand you a good fellow, you got a good heart, and so on. But I think it's best if you don't bother yourself with this—all of this business. And so I'll just go on down to my son's resting place and do my respects, and you can get on back to your home and your people.'

'No.'

The old man peered over at him. Hadjo looked a bit surprised at what he himself had said. 'No?' Seville asked.

'No.' Hadjo shook his head, firmly now. 'I ain't never going back to my home, for one thing. And as to letting you go to his grave by yourself—well, that's a fine idea. What do you propose to do, stop folks and ask em where they bury all the murdered people they don't want found? No, they'll cotch you, send you back, do their worst. And then I'll still be the only person who knows about Santiago.'

'And why's that bother you?' The old man was looking at Hadjo, reading his face.

'I don't know.' Hadjo let out a breath. He did not say anything for a long time and neither did Seville. They rode like that for a mile or more, side by side, silent. Then Hadjo lowered his head.

'He spoke truth. The way I wish I'd do. And they killed him for it.' He shook his head. 'And I walked out the back door of that building same as all the rest of them, right out the back door.'

He turned away, as if averting himself from the memory. They were silent again. The old man sat high on the old mare with his head swaying loosely, his eyes almost shut, until Hadjo spoke again.

'I got nowhere else to be,' he said. 'I just want to—' He gestured off down the road. 'Keep going.'

Seville nodded his head. 'All right,' he said. 'Then we'll keep going.'

They approached the next town south when the sun was at its peak. The old man looked up and cocked his head. 'Noon o'clock. There's that bell,' he called in a loud voice. 'Hear it ringing out the twelve o'clock hour. That's the bell says I'm a missing man.' There was no bell to be heard.

Hadjo hurried up alongside Seville. The old man took in a deep breath. 'But good God, I declare that I kindly like being a fugitive,' he said, and smiled. 'I'm my own man right now, in a way. At least until they run me down.'

'Are you so worried that they'll cotch you?' Hadjo asked. 'If you's worried why don't we go faster, and hurry down to the big swamp?'

'Oh now, wouldn't that be a sight,' the old man said. 'Old fellow like myself on a creaky mare, speeding down the road at top gallop. It'd be a marvel, and a universal wonder. The whole county would turn out to see.'

'All right, then. Why don't you travel in the trees? If you's scared to be looked at.'

'You mean lurk in the woods? No,' the old man said, shaking his head. 'It's best not to go to the woods until you absolutely got to go to the woods. Then you damnsure better be in the woods.'

They rode quietly for a while longer. 'If you only had a pass,' Hadjo said. 'Them boys would not bother you then.'

Seville peered at him. 'Now, wherever would I get a pass, young marster?'

'I don't know. Write one up.'

'Well now. Now you's talking about serious matters,' the old man said. 'Running off, that's one thing. But writing up a pass—that's another. That's death. It's sheer death for them to find you writing and making figures, using them on the white man. A doubleheaded Negro is in danger every day of his life.'

Hadjo frowned. 'I'd write one up myself, but they'd never take it. My hand ain't no good. Never has been.'

'Oh that's all right, young marster, I don't want you to get yourself troubled in that way.' Seville's voice was loud and cheerful. The town was just beginning to take shape around them. 'Now go, go on ahead of me here, young marster. Fetch on ahead of me into the town, for I don't want to slow you up with this old horse.'

It was a town with a single road, which recent rains had turned into a hogwallow. Cartwheels rutted the street with a kind of violence. Townspeople stood about on the porches of the dozen stores, stained up their shins with mud. They rested their feet on the railings and watched the travelers pass. Hadjo got a wave and Seville a nod, or less than a nod. Soon they were past the town and moving south again.

Hadjo made to turn his horse around to come back to where the old man was. But then he heard a hissing sound. Seville was making gestures at him, telling him not to stop. Hadjo strayed close enough to hear what he was saying. 'Keep on. Keep on riding, damn it. They're coming.'

'Who? Lord, man. It's broad day. What do you think's going to happen?'

But the old man had turned his head to one side. And though he barely seemed to be looking, some skill enabled him to see the backtrail and anyone following behind him. Because he said, 'That's them,' and Hadjo had to swivel all the way around in his saddle to see what he meant, as the old man said the word 'Paterollers' with cold, clipped finality.

Five horsemen had appeared a mile behind, on the edge of town. They rode in no kind of formation and with no kind of haste, about the same speed as Seville or maybe just a little faster. Seville had turned to face front again and soon Hadjo did too. 'Mightn't be paterollers,' the young man said. 'They might be just anybody riding south today. Peddlers. Farmers. Anyone, there's no telling. Not all white men on horses is a danger, you know.' But he said this to Seville while facing forward, stiff in his saddle.

Seville for his part said nothing. There was a bend in the road ahead. As soon as they were around it and the riders were out of eyeshot, the old man whipped over to the right and hurried into the woods. He went about fifty feet into the undergrowth, Hadjo following. At an open spot the old man clambered down from the top bench, holding a knife in his hand.

Hadjo cursed and made to wheel Alma away from him. Seville reached up and gripped the mare's lead halter with one strong hand, the knife clutched in the other. He reached up with the knife and plunged it into the skirt of the saddle.

He sawed upward, cutting through the seams, and tore back the upper flap. There, concealed in the grey padding of the saddle, was a pale object. The old man brought it out. It was a bundle of paper. He dug further and came out with a short hollow reed, angled at the tip and stained with ink.

The old man rushed out of the clearing. Hadjo came to look at the papers. Every piece was different: some were waterstained, some were greasy, some were jagged where they had been torn from a larger sheet, some had scraps of someone's writing already on them. A few were clean and blank. An abecedary torn from a book was among them, with the directions of the penstrokes for forming perfect letters. Hadjo turned around as Seville came back into the clearing. He was holding in his hands a shrubby plant: a pokeberry bush. He had torn it up by the roots. There at the cart he took up the knife again and began to slice off the purpleblack berries. He took a small earthenware cup and began to crush the berries with the butt of his knife. Soon he had a pool of dark reddish juice in the bottom of the cup.

Hadjo came up and began to pick berries from the bush to add them in. 'Here,' he said.

'No,' the old man said. 'No, don't get any of that dye on you. Stay out of this, damn it all, for your own sake.'

So Hadjo stood back. After laboring for a minute the old man finished and turned, appraising the sheet of paper in his hand. In dark red ink, it said:

Oct—7 1844

Please to let Seville Cabrey pass
From this Monday Oct 7 until
The up coming Sat'dy Oct 12.

Signed
Penelope T. Weiss
Savannah

The soil was white and sandy there and Seville took up a handful and sifted it over the wet lettering, then blew it off. Then he folded up the remaining papers and handed them to Hadjo. He dumped out the contents of the pokeberry cup and slung it away into the woods. It shattered against a tree.

As they rode back to the highway the old man held the sheet of paper in the air to dry, like a blazon. After it had fully dried he put it in his pocket. They were about to regain the road when he turned to Hadjo. 'Stay in the trees,' the old man told him. He did.

Seville returned to his easy gait along the road and Hadjo kept pace, away in the forest. He watched as a change came over the old man. Bit by bit he lost the square set of his shoulders and the tense driven-forward tilt in the saddle. He relaxed, shifted into an amiable slouch. He rode that way for a while, nothing more natural. And then the five riders rounded the bend behind him.

It took an agonizing length of time for them to catch up. Hadjo watched from the shadows, wringing his reins. The men came up talking amongst themselves about any number of things. But at last they reached the old slave, and quieted. A few murmurs here and there and then came Seville's jovial 'Evening, gentlemen, evening.'

One man separated himself from the group. 'Ho there, uncle,' he said. 'How you doing tonight.'

'Oh, well enough, I thankee. I's just traveling along, traveling along.' There was a big smile audible in his voice. 'And how do it find you gents.'

'Oh, we's all doing well. Just out riding, you know. Spied you coming along. And, ah, chanced amongst us, nobody could say they'd ever met you before. Have we, fellows? No. Not around here.'

'Oh, I spose not,' Seville said. 'Can't say I been acquainted. But it is a pleasure, sure is.'

A second voice jutted in. 'About to be nightfall, uncle. Where you supposed to be?'

'Well, I's just traveling down, traveling down,' Seville said, that smile in his voice. 'Heading for Florida.'

'Floridy?' the second voice said, and spat. There were murmurs from the other riders.

'Floridy,' the first man said, losing a bit of his gentility. 'Why, that's an awful long way. Hell of a long way.'

'It surely is,' Seville said weakly.

'Now, I almost hate to ask you, uncle, because it's a little discourteous according to our lights here in Glynn County. But I got to ask whether you got permission here tonight, to be going sech distances. A good written pass that might help us to see your way.'

'A pass?' said Seville, and rolled the word around as if it were unfamiliar to him. 'A pass—yes, I do have the pass. Now, now, where did I put it?' There was a rustling and the creak of saddle leather. 'Ah, there. Yes Jesus, here's that old pass.'

There was silence for a minute as the crisp sheet of paper was handed around. Murmuring as one of the riders labored to read it aloud to himself. Soon the letter had made its rounds to everyone who could interpret it and Seville thanked the man who handed it back to him.

'Well. Much obliged for letting us see it, uncle,' the first voice said. 'Lord, but your mistress must be a true charity-hearted lady, to let you away from her for so long.'

'Oh yes sir, she is, she is. A good Christian woman is Mistress Weiss, and so kind to her poor Negroes.' He turned his face up to heaven as he said her name, recollecting her charity.

'No doubt she is. Now for the lady's sake, uncle, I ought to ask where you plan to sleep tonight. Night's coming on quick.'

'Oh,' said Seville, 'I'll just go on ahead and lay me down on some plain earth.'

'Nonsense,' the first man cried. 'Why, what would your mistress say to us if we left her man to sleep out in the dirt? Fine old Savannah Negro like yourself. No, you need accommodations.'

'Why, I—'

'Yes, I think that's what we'll do. I've got an open cabin out mongst my own darkies. They might be a little common for you, old fellow, but it'll serve to spend a night.'

'But I—'

'You'd best just go on with Dollinger, uncle,' the second voice grumbled. 'You heard him say it, he's got accommodations.'

Seville resisted a little while longer. But soon he was borne along between the armed riders on a waft of tobacco smoke and light banter. The group turned north, back the way they'd come.

After several miles the man Dollinger split off toward his residence, leading Seville along with him. Hadjo followed next to the road, still in the trees, and stopped at the edge of a large farm. There were slaves moving outside a cluster of cabins in the twilight, performing their ablutions, putting out lights. In a moment he heard Seville's voice drawing nearer. It said: 'Yes, Marster Dollinger, I thank you for your kindness. Yes, Marster Dollinger, I'll stay put. No, Marster Dollinger, I won't run off nowheres, haw haw haw. I understand, you'll come for me in the morning. I'll see you then.'

Hadjo stood there. The moon came up. The slouching roofs of the settlement were revealed. The stable, the corncrib, the cabins. Then a shape detached from the buildings and came across the pale ground. It was Seville, his mare's hooves silent in the sand. He did not slow as he reached the treeline, even as Hadjo rushed over to join him.

They moved well into the woods before Hadjo found the voice to question him. 'Seville, your bag,' he whispered.

'Fuck the bag,' Seville answered.

They took parallel paths on their same-sized animals. Now they were keeping to the trees, moving fast. And the fugitive slave rode straight and tall on top of his mare like the mast of a ship, heaving forward under sail.

'We'll go up onto the road for a moment,' Seville whispered. 'Mix up our trail there in the road, and then come back down.'

Hadjo followed him onto the hard, moon-bright highway. They rode there for a quarter of a mile during which neither of them breathed much. Then Seville crossed over and down into the woods opposite. When they were once more enfolded by the forest's darkness he began to mutter, 'Oh Jesus. Oh Jesus,' pronouncing the good name with every exhalation.

They headed due south, irrespective of the roads. Over time Seville began muttering at the now-distant man who'd tried to keep him in the cabin. 'I didn't lay in your bed,' he said. 'Didn't sit in your chair. I didn't touch the plate of food you gave me, buckra. Didn't touch nothing to give you my scent. Ain't nothing in that room to follow me with. Just stood up straight in the middle of the floor, waiting on my time such as the Lord gave it. And you ain't going to summon me back, devil, no you are not.'

By daybreak they were closing in on the Okefenokee Swamp. Alma knew it and became agitated, difficult to ride. They veered coastward, moving along the edge of the swamp, that eternal home of runaways.

At the tail end of the day they reached Saint Mary's town and the ferry over the river. The boatman had just finished his last run of the day and could not be persuaded to take them over into Florida. At last Seville and Hadjo went away, cursing him under their breath. They made camp in the trees outside of the town and lay down to rest.

Hadjo dozed off in the silence. But he was not asleep for long before he roused suddenly. The moment he opened his eyes Seville began to speak from the opposite side of the campfire, like a player whose curtain had been raised.

'I was going to build myself into a ship,' he said. 'It was at the Savannah yards. A big three-masted clipper bound for Bahama. I was going to build myself into it, make a little compartment down around the starboard hull. To hide in. A door on one side to let me out. And if they found me, a door on the other side. To let the sea in. I'd of sunk it. I'd take that ship to the bottom to not go back. That was how I felt. But they wouldn't have found me, the way I'd build it. Had it all figured up with concealments and devices.'

'What stopped you from doing it?' Hadjo asked.

'Cordelia came pregnant. With Santiago. So I didn't leave, and I was glad I didn't. But now Santiago is dead. And so I examine the choices, and I tell myself. What stopped me from sailing away once is not going to stop me again.'

Seville said nothing more. Hadjo did not close his eyes again that night, only lay watching the east for the sun to appear.

The two of them were waiting at the ferrypoint long before the boatman arrived, bleary-eyed. He loaded up Alma and the mare, tying them to the rail so they would not buck halfway out in the river. Then he brought them over into Florida.

The southern bank of the river welcomed them, awash in fog. They rode all the rest of that day and the following morning, speaking little. Before noon they were passing Kingsley Pond, which meant they were nearing Mrs. Monroe's road-house. They came upon piles of shattered bottles and bent cutlery—a place for discarded things. Hadjo put Alma up to a canter because he feared Seville would pass by the grave completely. But then he saw the horse stop and its rider fall down to the ground.

Hadjo stopped several yards behind. Seville's arms were over the treebranch cross and his head was against the inscription, and he was weeping. The tears ran down the name and fate and death date

Santeago

Killed.

1844.

and they turned the dry grey wood the same color as the carven letters so that the name disappeared in the surrounding grain. And so as long as the tears ran he might have been mourning any dead soul anywhere or all dead souls everywhere or Christ himself before he arose.

Hadjo stood there behind him for a long time. Then went away. He hobbled Alma in a patch of grass, then went to fetch Seville's mare and led it there also. Then he sat down under a tree. He put his chin on his knees and remained there, not looking at the old man, not looking away from him either.

Even after he stopped weeping Seville stayed where he was. Draped over the beam, his head on the name. Hadjo got up to collect a little firewood. He led the marshtackie and the old mare down to a pond to drink. When he came back, Seville was no longer holding to the gravemarker but was sitting on the ground next to it. The old man never once looked up.

On the second day the man began to rage. He paced and kicked, churning up the sand around the grave. Hadjo was driven away. He moved further along the ridge, hoping not to hear the words. But by midmorning his stomach was groaning and he came back to check his bags for food. There was not a crumb left.

Down the hill, Mrs. Monroe's roadhouse stood unchanged. The midday lingerers welcomed Hadjo at first, until they remembered how he'd left. Herb Nail called for a toast in his honor but Hadjo barely acknowledged him. He stood silent and dire at the bar, waiting to place an order. It had only been ten days since he had gone away but anyone could tell by looking at him that it had been a long ten days. When Mrs. Monroe appeared she looked at him steadily and did not ask where he'd been or what had happened since their conversation in the rear of the house. He touched his hat and said, 'I'll have two orders of whatever's cooking today, ma'am. Two. And if I can have them bindled up, please.' She nodded and went away. Soon she came back carrying a little wooden firkin with steam coming from the lid.

Hadjo took the very last coin he had and placed it on the bar. He looked at that coin for a long time before standing up. There was another call for a toast before he left and finally he raised his eyes and said: 'Oh, hell. One drink.'

Back up on the ridge the man was still storming. Two tow-headed boys in potato-sack shirts were standing on the next dune, pointing and gawking. Hadjo chased them off with threats of violence. After they were over the next ridge he sat and ate under a tree: beef tripe and onions, a pile of greens, cornbread. He had his fill and brought the rest to the gravesite.

The old man was busy disputing. Hadjo set the little wooden firkin down in the sand behind him and started to move away. But he had not made it very far when Seville wheeled around and drew him into the argument as if he had been part of it all along.

'And what did he want with all his quarreling? And what did it ever gain him? Buried on a sandhill in goddamned Florida, that's what. Got his father sonless, got his sister brotherless. Got the whole world poorer for the sake of his pride.'

Hadjo was trying to back away. 'I'm sorry,' was all he could think of to say.

The old man pointed his finger. 'Hell, you're probably what got him killed. Is that it? And now you're remorseful over the thing, ah, poor you. Lingering around with a white fellow got him into trouble, as it always will do a Negro. Your company got him feeling fine and high and elevated and then bang! the next white man to come along cuts him down. Bang!' He clapped his hands together as he said it. 'And so there you went, galloping up to rouse his kin, all to soothe your own sorrow. Yes, I seen it before—a white man's apology is a fearsome thing, liable to break more than it's already broken.'

'No.' Hadjo was shaking his head. 'No. That weren't it. I came for his sake. Just for him. I couldn't stand him dying and no one even knew his name. I couldn't stand for him to be buried like this and no one knowing it but me, it made me sick—'

The old man smiled. 'That's just it. You think it matters how you feel. You think your sweet intention and good will matters. It don't matter a whit. Not to me. Ever piece of mercy and charity you could give me will just fall in a pile at my feet. Santiago's dead. You might like to think your work was a healing for all the evil that the world did to him, to me. It don't make a patch on it. The facts remain the same. My son is dead. The fractious untractable fool is dead. And me and the son of the damn buckra the only ones to mourn him.'

Hadjo was crying a little now. 'If he were alive you wouldn't be saying these things about him. If he were standing here right now you'd never talk to him thisaway.'

Seville stopped his pacing. 'If he was alive?' the old man said. He turned toward the grave. And all the rage and all the storming left his narrow body and his shoulders went limp. He placed his fist to his mouth, as if considering a difficult question. 'No. I wouldn't say such things to my living son. I don't suppose I'd say a thing to him besides I love you. Son, I love you. I do. I do.' He breathed. 'And did I ever say that while you was alive? Well now, I'll say it now. Son, you was the pride of my life. The glory.'

The old man knelt down to place his hand against the piled earth. Hadjo withdrew to the foot of a scraggly pine and stayed there until night, keeping vigil over the vigil.

The next morning Hadjo woke up with a smell in his mouth.

It was like flowers but there was nothing blooming on that ridge. It was a hard reek of perfume, with something behind it that cloyed like sugar but was not. And it was so thick that he was almost choking. He sat up and looked around and that was when he saw the gunmen.

They were on their horses in a ring over Seville. The old man sat there, rubbing his face. If he was startled or afraid he did not show it. He looked dazed, like he'd woken up from an odd dream.

The riders were wildly different in shape and physiognomy but they were all dressed identically in fine blue coats. And the guns they carried were all the same model gun, and it was powerful and new. Each rider's scarred or battered or fourfingered or threefingered hand dallied around the trigger.

Hadjo got up to approach them. But after only a few steps he had to stop and reel around, to go seek some fresher air. He went back and got some good breaths in him before he tried again.

As he got closer he could hear Seville, answering questions. 'No sir, we ain't been acquainted. You say it's a Mister Addison? No, I can't say I'm familiar.'

'Of course you aren't, old man. We haven't acquainted cause you haven't set foot in this country in your life, and you know it. Now why don't you save us all the hawing and jawing and tell us where you run off from.'

A man was crouching on the ground in front of Seville. Something glinted in the light. There was a knife in the man's hand. He held it loosely, twirled it, and toyed with it against Seville's throat.

As Hadjo came closer, the men noticed him. All their heads turned toward him at the same moment in well-oiled unison. 'Morning,' Hadjo called. His throat was tight.

'Good morning, sir,' one of the riders said: a young man with fair hair, the commandant of the little group. 'Maybe you can help us. You know this loose darkie here?' He pointed at Seville with the knife.

'I do know him,' Hadjo said. 'And he ain't a need for concern, I'll assure you. He ain't dangerous.'

'Dangerous by whose lights?' the young man said. 'Beg pardon, friend, but you're just as foreign to me as old Cotton here. Now, maybe you could help us to know where he's come from. And maybe throw into the bargain just who you are, hid out with a Negro way up on this hill.'

The young man breathed in through his mouth. 'My name's Hadjo Primrose, and that's old Seville. I known him a long time. Since I was younger.'

The commandant raised his eyebrows, lowered the knife away from Seville's chin. The old man breathed out, silently. The blade had drawn blood from his neck. 'Why, a Primrose,' the young man said, looking him over from head to foot. 'I'll be. You're old Jake's son?'

'That's right.'

'Why, my name is Zill Tercer, I'm a Tercer. My daddy Shay worked for your daddy in the old days. I doubt you remember him. He was a sorry old dodderer. Strange to meet you like this. What are you doing with the darkie?'

'Well. We're on business. Family business for my old papa, and it hurts me to tell it. See, we're sending old Seville away. He and I are just passing through on our way to the port. Sending him away to his new ownership, you see, and it'll hurt me to see him go.'

'Off to new ownership,' Seville echoed. A small line of blood tricked down onto his collar.

'Well, now. That's a queer thing,' the commandant said. 'You're passing through here on business for your daddy, and damned if we aren't doing the same.' He chuckled. 'We're headed to meet with Mister Primrose about some business he wants done by the Addison company. Regulating business. So we're moving along the same road contrarily. Ain't that a lark?'

'Ain't it,' Hadjo said.

'Well. I'll have to tell your old daddy that we done met you out here,' the young man said, sheathing his knife. 'You and old Uncle Seville. Won't he be amused at that.'

'He will,' Hadjo said. 'And tell him—please tell him I might be a long time coming back. A long time. Tell him not to wear himself out waiting for me.'

'I'll do that,' the young commandant said. He mounted his horse and all the other riders turned their wellbred horses to go down the slope. The scent remained behind them. Hadjo and Seville sat there in its presence for a long time. Then it, too, faded and they were truly alone, the young man and the old man and Santiago's grave, which the riders had never once noticed, looking as it did like nothing more than a haphazard mound of sand, with an old twisted tree rooted at the head.

Soon the two of them were riding away. They headed roughly toward the coast, which lay fifty miles east. Seville was quiet and abstracted. Hadjo watched the old man for a time but his expression never wavered. And he never once looked backward at the hill where he'd left his son.

Toward midday the old man spoke. 'Don't know why in the world you went and did that, back there,' he said. 'Talking about your daddy's affairs. Now you're roped into this thing. How will you go home, now you done lied on your family name? You can't, you can't go home.' Seville looked at Hadjo, but the young man was silent. 'Or didn't you think that's what would happen?'

'No,' Hadjo said. 'I was just thinking how good it sounds.'

They came up a bluff overlooking a small prairie that was full of cattle. Hadjo stopped at the overlook. Then in a moment he began to laugh. 'Hi, Seville, how are you at working cows?' he called over one shoulder. 'Because here's a mess of cows down in this prairie with my name on them.'

Hadjo rode among the cattle, Seville coming gravely along behind him. He gazed into the big wet kindly eyes, ran his hand along haunch and flank, traced the $\mathcal{P}$ repeated on the hides of all five hundred animals.

'Well? You ain't answered me, man.' Hadjo turned smiling to Seville. 'How are you at moving cows?'

Seville gawked. 'You're the one who's daddy's a cattleman, not me. Shit. Never asked you to patch a skiff.'

Hadjo spat. 'He didn't bring me near the trade. Never let me try my hand at it.' The young man looked out over the sea of horns and hides and flicking tails. 'But I'll try it now. Won't I. I will.'

With Hadjo on his marshtackie and Seville on the old mare they broke off close to a hundred head from the main herd and maneuvered them neatly up the slope into the trees. From there it was a shambles. They lost a dozen cows which turned back at the treeline and ran down to rejoin the prairie herd, irretrievable. After that they lost cows by the twos and threes to the sheer breadth of the forest. Hadjo would chase after them with abandon but rarely managed to get a single one back. In the first few hours all the most wayward animals broke away and trotted off into the pines, leaving the rest of them to this foolishness.

The herd they'd cut out was too big for two novices to drive, that much was clear. But Hadjo fought to hold it together. Lacking whips he cut a long cane, wielded it like a crozier. Seville cut one too and was gentle with it at the hips of the rearmost cows. He kept the herd moving even as it shrank. He let them make their own pace across the countryside, as Hadjo rushed around the perimeter trying to keep them bunched. Alma for her part was tireless. She galloped around and around the cattle and the long day's work did not seem to strain her at all. The herding roused something in the marshtackie horse; her mane flew wild and she tossed it.

When night came they guided the cows to a clearing and got down from their saddles with difficulty. Hadjo cussed the soreness in his legs and Seville cussed his pains louder and then cussed Hadjo for daring to cite a single ache in the presence of a seventy-year-old man. They culled a calf from the herd and killed it for meat and had a proper meal at dusk. Hadjo counted about sixty head of cattle bedding down in that clearing and accounted it a pretty good number, all things considered. They had learned plenty about this drovering business that day and would not suffer more such losses before Saint Augustine.

They woke up the next morning to find the herd reduced by half. The cows were simply gone. It was as if a rapture had taken all the righteous cattle home, leaving the heathen. In fact the cows had been disgruntled enough to simply escape in the dead of night. Hadjo spent two hours racing around the nearby woods and was only able to recover four gloomy heifers. He would have kept spinning through those woods forever if Seville hadn't shouted to him at one of his near passes. 'Get over here let's move the cows, youngblood. Time is wasting. These beeves going to get senility before we reach the market.'

They moved the cows all that day and into the next, the woods slowly whittling away the little herd they had. Hadjo began to let the forest have them, too tired to care. Finally, after three days, they entered into Saint Augustine. There were twelve cows remaining out of their original hundred. Hadjo was muddy and wild-eyed but showed a stately battered pride in his dozen head. Seville simply pursed his lips as he headed them toward a cattle broker he knew of.

The business was still there, in the same building Seville remembered from two decades before. He was surprised and gladdened at this but hid his grin as he stepped into the house. He took off his hat to stand before the sad-eyed Spaniard behind the enormous desk. 'Buenos días, señor. ¿Cómo está usted? Ah bien, bien. Sí, bien, gracias a Dios. Entonces, hace muchos años que yo viví en esta ciudad—me fuí a Cuba, a la Habana, viví muchos años en la Habana. Pero ya he vuelto a esta gran ciudad, gracias a Dios, ja ja ja. Y mi nuevo amo tiene algunas vacas, y por eso yo le dije, le dije al Señorito, Usted necesita ver al Señor Xímenez y Cabál. Solamente al Señor Xímenez y Cabál, y su honrado negocio. Sí señor, de nada. Sí, vacas Floridanas, criollas. Pero no están flacas. Al contrario, son vacas gordas, vacas bonitas, vacas fuertes. No tenemos muchas aquí—una docena. Pero hay otras, mi Dios, muchas otras. ¿Sí me explico? Sí, las tenemos por acá. Vamos, sí, vamos.

He bounded out the front door with the cattlebroker in tow, giving a large wink to Hadjo. Seville introduced the old broker to the young man and then to the cows. 'Aquí están las vacas, Señor Xímenez y Cabál. Bonitas, ¿no? Sí, gracias. Y ahora, le presento al Señorito. Mister Hadjo Primrose, el vaquero. Sí. ¿Perdón? ¿El apellido? Ah, sí, Primrose. Sí, de la familia Primrose, del gran vaquero, sí—el Jake Primrose, el famoso. Mire la marca, la J P. Mucho gusto. Y seguramente, el joven será tan grande como su padre. Ja ja ja, sí. Vamos a ver.'

Seville drummed the price for the small cluster of cows up to wondrous heights. It was all done with the understanding that the young Primrose would continue to bring his cattle to this out-of-the-way brokerage as he embarked on his illustrious career. It would be a splendid relationship. Xímenez y Cabál was giddier over this transaction than he had been over sales of five hundred head, giddier than he had been in years. He watched avidly as Hadjo signed his name in the receipt book, followed every loop of the Primrose. When it was finished he produced a bottle of Dominican rum and poured three glasses. Salud, salud.

Hadjo walked out hefting the smallish bag of coins. He went around the corner and dumped them out on top of a barrel, cackling, then parted them with the edge of his hand. The portion nearer to him he dumped into his pockets. 'That was a damned fine bit of Spanish you did there, old man,' he said. 'Good God amighty, I don't know why you ain't talked your way over to Cuba already. Wouldn't be no trouble for you.' He adjusted the mass of coins, then snapped his fingers. 'And hell, it's not a bad idea. It's not bad at all. Cuba. Cuba's where to head—Cuba, old man. Make a fortune in cows. You'll do the conversating, and I'll handle the cattle. Bring em over and market em. Live in one of them big houses they've got. You'd be free there, or near enough anyhow. And me, I'll be rich in Spainish gold. Think of it. Cuba!'

The old man did not answer. He was looking at the pile of gold coins still sitting on the barreltop. He looked at it for a long time. At last, slowly, he reached up and dragged the coins over and dropped them into his own pockets.

Hadjo was starting to walk away. 'I'm going to go along King Street, old man. Find me their best little roominghouse they've got and take a damned bath. After that I'll believe I'm going to the shops with thisyer lump—get some new shirts, some trousers, go to the hatter and buy one of them tall-belled silk items. How about you? Will you get a silk hat, old man?'

Seville was mute in the face of the young man's excitement. For a moment he looked away toward the scrap of horizon visible between the buildings, where the river melded with the inlet.

'Lord, young marster,' he said. 'I had a thought. If you really serious about this Cuba business, there's a couple matters that we oughter bash out with the broker back there. Strike while the iron is hot, you know. He might be able to advance you a few things to get started. Why don't you go on down to King Street, and I'll go do some more conversating with the old man. Everything takes time, you know, with these oldworld Spaniards.'

'Sure, sure,' Hadjo said, turning to go. 'Tell him what you got to tell him. Where'll we meet?'

'I'll meet you down on King Street, in a little while.' The old man smiled. 'Oh, it'll be no trouble to find you. I'll just hunt the best little roominghouse they've got and look for the young man wearing a clean white shirt, and new trousers, and a fine new silk hat. I'll just look for the smartdressed clever young blade, the one who's about to beat the world and stomp the devil.'

'All right, old man,' Hadjo said. 'I'll see you in a while.'

Seville watched Hadjo saunter away down the street. Then he went back around the corner to the cattlebroker's office.

He explained the situation. That the young vaquero needed the use of a small sailing vessel. That he was impatient to get some supplies for his new operation and take them down the Atlantic coast to his personal cattle range, which lay by Mosquito Inlet. Would Señor Xímenez y Cabál be able to assist young Primrose in this matter? They would only need a small boat, a piloting cutter at most.

The old broker knit his fingers and pondered and then replied that he knew just where to obtain a vessel such as that, and soon. Seville winced. How soon? he asked. For in truth the young Primrose was anxious to leave immediately—that very day, if possible! Seville had tried to restrain the young man, but that afternoon's sale had whetted him. He was hotblooded for the cattle work, he would not wait! Ah, youth!

The two old men laughed for a time, and the cattlebroker wiped his eyes with the knuckle of his thumb. Ah, it was insanity, he acknowledged. But old fellows should not stand against the insanity of the young. He would go straight to the waterfront and procure a boat. Seville took out his load of coins and set them before the man. Hopefully this would help with some of the expense, and any remainder could be covered by the next load of cattle. If Señor Xímenez y Cabál would be gracious enough to advance them the ship for a short period. Of course, the broker said. There would be no trouble affording that amount of credit to the young cattleman. It was a privilege to do business with the Primrose name. A privilege.

Xímenez y Cabál got up and put on his coat to go toward the harbor. He would not be long, he assured Seville. But in the meantime he asked if the old man would mind waiting outdoors for him to return. He did not want any of his customers to come by looking for the cattlebroker and find a black man sitting in the chair! He laughed and clapped Seville on the back and went out, locking the door behind both of them.

When the broker came back an hour later he stank of rum and had docking paperwork crumpled in his hand. He gave it to Seville and explained where the boat would be waiting. He, Xímenez y Cabál, had had the small cutter brought forth and prepared. They would have to do nothing more than cast off the ropes and they could be away that very evening. It was waiting on the very last pilings. Go, go, he told him. Go with God! Seville thanked him and departed.

It was dusk and the day's seabreeze was fading. Still the sails of the small pilot cutter caught what little air there was to catch and swelled with it. They caught the faint remainder of the daylight too. The high reaches of the canvas shone a scuffed pink against the sky's ink-blue. Seville looked up at the high canvas, admiring its color and the crisp sound it made when it luffed.

New sails on an old boat. A raggedy old cutter. It was sure to leak, at least a little. But it would get him where he was going. Seville steered the boat for the dark gap between the inlet's shoulders and threaded the shore all the way out. His hands were easy on the tiller and the line. The breeze waned but did not fail him.

THE DEVIL'S WEDDING!!

JUDE QUINTO FIGHTS FOR JUSTICE—HIS OWN WAY.

I.

S HE LEANED IN. The fence stood against her but Flora hardly seemed to notice it. The sturdy old split-rail was taller than the average height but so was she. The young lady swayed a little, gazing onto the racetrack. It had rained earlier but she'd taken no cover and her hair was streaming: she was a picture. What's more, she was drunk—drunk, the poor girl.

The blooded horses sped around the track. Their great hooves clabbered the damp sand. She put her foot up on the lowest rail. Then she put her other foot up on the middle rail and leaned in further. A voice cried out behind her but the words were swallowed in the growing din of hooves as the horses rounded the turn and lined out toward her. She swayed. Then she swung over the topmost rail.

Someone had been running toward her; they reached and grabbed at her foot. But she was already falling onto the track. When she stood up they were almost upon her. She stepped toward the charging thoroughbreds, looking very small.

It was as if a pair of hands grabbed her shoulders and pulled her backward, gently but powerfully, and she fell away from the horses' pounding trajectory at the very instant they reached her. They roared past in a froth of white sand.

A moment later two real hands came, rougher hands than the ones which had moved her before. They took her under the arms and dragged her across the track. At the fence they picked her up and almost tossed her over. She let herself be transported in this way.

'Emily, Emily,' she said to the trembling and fear-mad woman who half-carried her toward the house. 'Oh, Emily, I jist couldn't do it. It jist wasn't me, was it, Em? Though it was worth it to try, all the same.'

The maid only continued to tremblingly bear her along. Then they were in the shadows of the house. Flora swayed down the hallway, her muddy hands leaving marks all along the wall. That was when she began to cry.

'Don't let him see me like this. Oh darling, please hide me away somewheres, he don't deserve to see me like this. He don't deserve it, do you understand?'

Emily tried to hide the evidence and did a pretty good job of it. The empty bottle of brandy, the torn and dirty dress, the trail of overturned things throughout the house. She intimidated the witnesses: the horse trainers, two of whom were her brothers. It was almost a clean thing. Except for one detail. Mrs. Pauline Primrose had been home the whole time, watching her daughter through the window. Emily thought she had gone to Newnansville with her husband, but no. She had watched the whole calamity, hidden behind taffeta. When Jake Primrose got home she summoned him into her separate bedroom and told him all.

Emily had succeeded in getting Flora partway into bed. She brought honeycakes and black coffee, to work against the brandy. It didn't entirely succeed. Flora was laying sideways across the bedcover and singing a song she should not have known the words to. The song did not change when Jake Primrose appeared in the doorway. He stood there, taking her in.

'Flora, darling. What brings you abed? At this early hour.' She continued drawling her song at the roofbeam. Primrose pressed on. 'Why, it's only a little after dark. Must be something ailing you. Most times you'd still be abroad at this hour. Traipsing. Though some might call it different. Some might call it helling. But you're my daughter, so I'll not say it thataway.'

'The boy to chase them he did run. Fal de ra. And he had his great silver gun, all along the river clear. Softly my shepherdess dear. Fal de ra.'

Primrose narrowed on her. 'You've been a disgrace. The hired men are laughing. Hell, the darkies are laughing. How does it feel to have them laughing at you, darling?'

Flora sat up, suddenly. 'I like it well enough, Papa,' she said. 'I thought you must like it too. Ain't you heard them laughing at you, lately?'

That got him, with the effect of a good swift blow. 'Listen to me, you sloppy tart.' He advanced a step, through Flora's incredulous repetition of the word *Tart? Tart?* 'I don't know what you think you'll fix with this damned show. But I tell you this. If Gallatin catches wind of it I don't doubt but he'll call the whole thing off. I wouldn't blame him neither. And you know exactly what that'd mean for you. Yes, trollop, I done told you. Or maybe you thought I was abluffing.' The lip pulled back from his teeth. 'No, I'll do like I said. Did you think I'd give up, me, Jake Primrose? Did you think I'd throw up my hands?'

Flora looked at him square. 'I'll make you throw up your hands.'

'Ah, you will? And how—'

Flora had slid her palm underneath the pewter tray of honeycakes, and now, with a swift sudden motion, she propelled it at Primrose's face. The cattleman threw his hands up with a yelp. The tray itself went clattering away but the cakes struck him on the head, arms, chest. One made a round honeymark in the middle of his forehead before dropping to the floor.

Primrose swung his arms wildly as if to parry a second tray. It didn't come. He brought his arms down, glaring, and came forward with a curse. Emily had been standing in the hallway the entire time; now she rushed into the room, crying out. They reached the side of Flora's bed at the same moment and as the man raised his hand to strike his daughter, the woman cried, 'Marster Primrose!' The man stood there for a moment with his right hand raised over his left shoulder, as Flora stared up into his face, daring him, and Emily continued to weep into his ear: 'Marster Primrose! Marster Primrose! Marster Primrose!'

Then the man turned from his daughter and with one long fluid motion swung his hand all the way around at Emily and slapped her face. His name caught in her mouth and the room went dead silent. He turned and went out.

Flora did not even watch him go. She could not take her eyes off of Emily's face. The face which did not move but held with a more-than-human stillness, like a figure done in marble, delphic, peering off down the thread of time.

The morning was humid-cold. The dogs were roused, and the children. Both creatures understood that this day was important and stood around in quiet watchful packs. Lucy Quinto crammed a big midday meal into a hamper and loaded it onto the old family ox along with the empty buckets and other implements. Then they set out, Lucy walking a little bit behind, alone. She had never liked this business with the fire.

At the line they set down their tools in the firebreak they had made the day before. The children were dispatched to the nearby spring with the buckets. While they were gone, Nat and Jude went to a palmetto clump and cut a few fronds. Then they kindled a little fire.

The field was scruffy with tall grass and fennel. Awkward and oblong, it had not been used much. But Nat had signed a contract with a hog farmer for a thousand bushels this year: the patch would have to be cleared, for enough acreage. Nat and Jude stood a moment, discussing their plan. Then they each picked up a stack of palm fronds and touched one to the fire.

Nat went first. He dragged the burning frond behind him as he walked along the field's edge. The wind was from the south and it blew the strip of low flames toward the north firebreak, where it died in the scraped dirt. In a minute Jude started on a parallel line to his father, several yards deeper into the field. His tail of flame blew north likewise until it met the charred remains of his father's fire. In that way they progressed down the field strip by strip, the green fronds crackling in their hands.

The fire ran low but sometimes it would catch a clump of palmetto and surge in a quick red pillar. Then embers and ribbons of ash would go sailing high across the line, toward the trees. This was why the children were there: They would jump up and go running after the embers that drifted through the air. When a spark landed it was usually already grey and cold, but still they would take their rakes and scour the spot until no trace was left and then dump a bucket's worth of water, to make good and sure.

Nat and Jude continued carving southward into the field. When they reached the far end they were barely visible through the accumulated smoke. Lucy Quinto watched. There was no sign of them for several minutes and she stood with her jaw working. Then she set out after them.

She found father and son at the far edge of the field, sitting on a stump, finished with the job. They were simmering scraps of beef over the dying fire and sharing a smoke on Jude's illicit tobacco pipe. Lucy came upon them through the veil of smoke like a terrible angel. They looked up at her with expressions befitting such a sight. The apparition did not speak; she came directly to her son and plucked the pipe from his hand. 'What'd I say about using tobaccy,' she said to him. She dropped the pipe on the blackened ground and crushed it underfoot before starting back across the field. 'Nat, tell your son about using tobaccy, and also about trying to hide things from me.'

The two men sat together a moment in silence. 'It don't work,' Nat said eventually, shaking his head at the ground. 'It's never worth the try.'

It was midday but Flora's room was dim. The eaves and the drapes mercifully held the sun back. But they did not keep back the sounds, and every going-on in the yard clamored through the window. She listened to the crow's caw, the redbird's cheep, the blacksmith's far-off anvil clink, a call from slave to slave in the open field. Then a horse coming up the drive. A big four-gaited Morgan with a tinkling harness. Flora twisted the sheets in her fists.

Jake Primrose let his manservant greet the visitor at the door but did not stay aloof for long. The gloved slave had barely finished saying Yes sir, Marster Primrose is here, before the cattleman stepped in with his hand outstretched.

'Gallatin, Gallatin. Step in here, old boy. Come, bust the ice off them boots.'

'Good day, Jake,' the visitor said, smiling and shaking his hand.

'It's dreadful out there—come on, there's a hot toddy waiting for you, drink it before the chill gits you.'

'Thank you, Jake. Thank you. And tell me again, what makes up a—toddy?'

'Toddy, old boy, that's nothing but the simplest thing in the world. Whiskey, sugar, water. Het up and mixed into the finest fluid on the earth or in the seas. Will you take one?'

'Ah, no, no.'

The visitor was John Gallatin, a middle-aged gentleman new to Florida. His voice matched his person perfectly: thin, dry, Pennsylvanian, a little depressive, unmistakably rich. Jake Primrose walked the man into what he called his parlour.

'Yes, coffee will do better than toddies,' Primrose allowed. 'There's too much to talk about—it's coffee we need, coffee.'

Gallatin had halted at the doorway and was looking around the empty room. The bright, nervous look he had worn since coming into the house turned to a frown. 'And Miss Flora,' he said after a moment. 'Miss Flora is in, I take it?'

'Ah, Flora,' Primrose said, as if recalling a person he had not thought of in ages. 'She ain't well today. Attack o' lagrippe has her poorly.'

The visitor attempted to take this news stoically. 'Ah.' He cleared his throat. 'Well. Perhaps I could go in to her, and—just to wish her well, and give her my affectionate—'

'She's right poorly, old boy,' Primrose put in, and looked at the rich man with meaning. 'Right poorly. She needs rest, and no talk.'

'Of course,' said the Pennsylvanian, with a nod. 'Of course.'

'And anyhow, it's a boon for us,' Primrose went on with good cheer. 'It'll give us some time to talk business. To really chew things over.'

'Of course,' Gallatin said. 'Of course. A moment for business. It's a good time for that.'

Happy, brisk, and with his face set in a businesslike frown, Primrose went to a nearby table, where he unrolled a map. A fat slice of the Florida peninsula. On it, a vast hatchmarked rectangle. THE PRIMROSE-GALLATIN SECTION. The visitor stood over it, admiring. 'Splendid, splendid,' he murmured. He traced the contours. Forests, rivers, lakes. The boundaries were pin-straight, the corners sharp. Then his finger reached the southeastern part of the property.

Near a place labeled Varnes Pond there was a flaw. The square boundary was disrupted by a little indentation on the southeast corner. 'Well, it's all very fine,' Gallatin murmured. 'Only, I do wonder about this little—situation. Here.' And he pointed at the pockmark.

'Oh,' said Primrose. His face and voice fell. 'That's Tercer's.'

'Tercer,' Gallatin murmured. He waited. 'And what are the Tercers?'

'The Tercers—well, you see, they are an old family in the area. Were one,' he corrected himself.

'Were?'

'Well, it's jist a lady left now. A widder.'

'A widow?' Gallatin said. 'One widow, on all those acres?'

'Yes sir,' Primrose said. He watched as the man continued to trace the indent of the rogue property.

'Well,' Gallatin said. 'Mayhaps a widow can be persuaded to part with this little lump.'

'Of course,' said Primrose, too quickly.

'It'd make things more agreeable, I think.'

'Of course,' said Primrose with an amiable chuckle. 'Of course.' Then he fell into a glum study of this suddenly glaring blemish on his possession.

'Well, it's very fine.' Gallatin rapped the middle of the map with his palm, causing it to roll up. 'As I've said before, it's a damned generous arrangement, Jake.'

'Generous? Hell! You're the generous one for taking this she-devil offen my hands.' He laughed at his joke, but Gallatin said nothing. The thin man had gone into a reverie. He gazed up at the lintel above the fireplace, where a garish portrait hung. FLORA. He folded and unfolded his soft white hands, gazing at the image.

'Your daughter,' he murmured, 'is a treasure. She is a breath of life, of hope. She will be the bright center of my days. She will be my stay against despair. She will be the thread to hold me to life, the golden thread.'

'She'll be yours, old boy,' Primrose said. 'For whatever you need.' He clapped the man on the shoulder, confident again, and went to see about the coffee.

In the other room, the girl was pulling on her shoes. A good pair, with heavy soles. She went to her window. In the frame were two dowels that were meant to hold the window closed. She had already loosened these dowels, unbeknownst to her father; now she took hold of them with her fingernails and pulled them free. She slid the window open and dropped out.

Flora set off for the trees, fast and upright. The fair hair was loose and unkempt all around her highboned face, her blue eyes were bright and wide, the eyes that everyone called terrible—terrible in their beauty, or terrible in their accusation. She provoked powerful feelings. Where in creation had she come from, with that wayward mind, that fierce pride? No one quite knew. Her childhood, her adolescence, her entire life were sealed off from anything which could possibly have given rise to her. A house controlled by a strong, complacent father. A mother bent to her husband's will. A brother who was lost to some long dark trail, whereabouts unknown. And for close neighbors, only the family's slaves. Where in all this had she found the spirit for rebellion? Her heart's waywardness should have been crushed before she was even weaned.

It was not for lack of trying, on her father's part. Things had been bad enough between them before her brother left. But after Hadjo vanished it got worse. Old Jake had ridden far searching for his son before it dawned on him: he had been defied, and tricked out of a male heir. From that point on he never spoke the name Hadjo again. And with a terrible lurch all of his ambitions shifted to land squarely on the daughter.

She was no longer called on to work around the homestead or pitch in on the cattle work, as before. Now he needed her to be a spotless young thing, with clean fingernails and French hair. He tried to develop her in that direction. It failed miserably, and not just because she quarreled with the society girls in the Newnansville parlours. There was a deeper problem. The occupants of those parlours were real townsfolk, and Flora—Jake Primrose saw it with horror—simply wasn't. He bought her all the right dresses but her skin was too suntanned. He asked her to do her hair but it always came undone on the long ride to town. And despite the tutors he brought out to his estate over the years, her voice still stood out at society events like a plucked banjo in a room full of harps. Primrose soon gave up on the debutante idea and withdrew her from the salons. Still, the girl was too pretty to escape wide male attention in that country, and for a time Jake was afraid. But then came Gallatin.

Primrose had needed a stroke of luck, and the Pennsylvanian was that stroke. The $\mathcal{P}$ brand was in a dangerous position: Primrose had reached too far, suffered humblings. His baronetcy was tottering. Then John Gallatin came to call on Primrose about an investment proposal, spied Flora, and almost choked on his tea cake. Within a week he was whispering to Jake about marriage.

Gallatin was a rich man but personally unimpressive and physically ugly—the top half of his head was too broad for the bottom half; his skin was white and slack. Flora for her part thought him nice enough. He was quieter than most men she knew on the Florida frontier, and gentler, and he did not spit indoors. She never suspected his intentions until it was too late. Not long after he first appeared he invited the Primroses to visit his home in Saint Augustine, fifty miles due east toward the coast. He had a mansion there and had filled the place with velvet furniture and paintings of strange landscapes. And most importantly, he had a big pianoforte. Flora had heard several pianos in her life but they were all sorry, warbling instruments, audibly mildewed. But this one was new to Florida and had not yet had the chance to come untuned in the weather. What was more, it was played beautifully by a squat, tobacco-stained Frenchman who had no other purpose in Gallatin's house. Flora listened all night, rapt, an unusually beautiful light in her eyes. The big mellow instrument, the pianist's fingers flitting over the keys, the porto wine: soon she was in a sort of trance and gazed lovingly at everything, including the host. At the end of the night Primrose hustled her out of the house with an excited wink back at Gallatin.

Primrose questioned his daughter on the wagon ride home. He asked whether she would consider the man's advances. She murmured a half-conscious Yes. Maybe she thought he was talking about the Frenchman. In any case, a chain of events was set in motion, with terrible momentum, on rails greased by money and property and desire and fear. Flora woke up and found herself squarely in its path, as if she had been born on the rails.

Jude's horse was sleeping where it stood. It was very late in the night, but this was the best vantage. From the bluff Jude could watch all the fields burning at once.

The orange glow ran in parallel lines where the old crop-rows had been, ribs of fire in the blackness that revealed the framework of the earth. Jude watched it seethe. At last dawn came. He patted his horse awake and rode down the easy slope, out into the sweet-smelling smoke.

The breeze had slackened and the fire died down. The flames looked suddenly paltry in the early sunlight. He rode back to the yard. There he came across his younger brother, who was rubbing his bleary eyes.

'Jude, you never called,' he said. 'I was supposed to spell you after midnight. Why dint you call for me?'

'Ah, never mind, Dan,' Jude said. 'I just felt like watching, that's all.'

Jude got down from his horse and went to the kitchen to look for breakfast. He met his father there and the man looked him up and down.

'You stayed out all night?' he asked. 'You remember we're going to Widder Tercer's today.'

'Yes sir,' said Jude.

'It's a fair bit of work we've got. You going to be able to pull through?'

The young man puffed. 'Course.'

A half hour later they were riding north toward Varnes Pond. The infusion of coffee and lack of sleep had turned Jude giddy. He sang an aimless trailsong. He butted his horse into Nat's and tried to make it buck. Riding with his father did not turn him serious: just the opposite. He could forget the weight of his adulthood and depend on his father's for a time. Maybe Jude knew he would not have many more chances to do so.

When they arrived Jane Tercer appeared in the doorway of her house. Jude took off his hat and rubbed his hair straight. He turned solemn again: the woman had that effect on people. Nat Quinto called out brightly, but she was still wary about coming past the porch. Newcomers unnerved her. No one could fully convince the woman that there were no more Indians in the region. Nat came closer until she recognized him and knew that he was not a Seminole. She descended into the yard, saying, 'Oh, Nat, hello.'

Her round blue eyes shone. Her grey hair hung loose and long. It hung like her right arm, the one the musketball had passed through.

Her clean little clapboard house had been built near where the first one had burned down. She lived there by herself, but not alone. People visited. Old friends helped around the place. It was the work of half the county to keep the property in good working order, as it had been when old Shay was still alive.

'Hidy, Jane,' Nat said, kissing the woman's cheek. 'I brought my Jude. You remember Jude. We gonter get things ready to run a little fire through, like we talked about.'

'Fire?' the woman asked. She looked at Nat, concerned.

'Jist a little fire, like we done before. It'll clear things out in your old field, so you kin plant it. And we'll pass some through those woods to make the blackberries to come up. I know how you like your blackberries to come up.'

'Yes,' she said finally. 'That'll be good. Yes, it will.'

'Yes ma'am,' said Nat. 'And it will make it safer here in case a real wildfire blows thew. We'll plough a few fire breaks first, and then we'll go.'

'Right,' Jane said, and a change came over her, a new solidity. 'You'll need that old plough of ourn. It's in the barn over there. And you kin use the mules. Just watch the blackish one, he's blind in the left eye.'

Together the two Quintos ploughed a line around one of the widow's choked and overgrown fields and another around a brushy stand of pines fit for berries. Lastly they made a break around the perimeter of the yard. Then they put away the plough and the mules and bade farewell to the lady, saying they'd be back the next day with the fire.

After a while Jude turned to his father. 'What was he like?'

'Who? Shay?'

'Yes. I don't remember him much.'

'Shay. He was...' The man rubbed his jaw. 'Well, I'm not surprised you cain't remember him. When you're young it's sometime hard to remember a person like him. What doesn't take nothing from you, nor give you something just to soften you up. What wouldn't do a single thing for himself before he'd done five for somebody else, but quiet, always quiet about it.' He spat. 'But then you get to a certain age and that's the only kind of man you remember anymore. They start to kind of—stick out.' He looked off down the trail, much farther than they had to ride.

John Gallatin came back to the Primrose house two days later. They were no longer pretending the girl was sick, so she could not get out of it. She came in from a walk, fifteen minutes late for Gallatin's arrival. That was a decent amount of time to keep a man waiting, a nice tardiness. The mud on her dress: not so nice. Her father stared glassily at it as she came in. Gallatin took her slack arm and kissed the hand at the end of it; he did not see the mud, was incapable of seeing the mud. He sat back down and almost missed his chair. Flora sat down in her own chair and proceeded not to speak. Her gaze drifted around the place, meeting no one's, her lips closed as if against some great round word that wanted to come out.

For a long time Gallatin sat almost as quiet as she did, while Pauline Primrose recited a long, aimless opinion about the effect of last year's declaration of statehood on Florida's cuisine. But eventually he joined Mrs. Primrose in conversation, saying dreamily that the area would certainly see an increase in fine Northern jellies, aspics, and other preserves.

Flora's gaze finally came earthward. Gallatin started talking knowledgeably about the federal transition. She watched him for a moment, as she might have watched a curiously shaped cloud drift by. But then, with a shiver, she turned away. Flora had seen and could not unsee the awful truth of him: the thin hair greying around his too-wide forehead, his bony legs crossed in scarlet trousers, the soft white hands dallying a teaspoon as he regarded Flora with a fondness nearly grandmotherly, with just the faintest tinge of male sexual approval.

Jake Primrose was a skilled reader of his daughter's moods. He saw her shift in her chair like she was looking to crawl out of the room. He frowned at her, a warning that hearkened back to the monumental argument that had taken place a month ago, the morning after their visit to Gallatin's mansion. Jake had explained to Flora that she had agreed to entertain the gentleman's advances. She had expressed revulsion, of course, but Primrose brought firepower to the argument. First he gave horror stories about what the rich man might do to the Primrose name if she jilted him. He'll swamp us, Jake thundered, he'll starve me out of the ports, and it'll be ruination for this whole family, me, you, and your mother. Your poor mother! It would shake her terribly, don't you care? But Flora did not care and said that the woman could use a good hard shaking.

Next the man threatened to send Flora away if the marriage did not happen: a standard exile, north to Connecticut and a ladies' finishing school there. This suggestion seemed to scare her a little but she recovered, and hissed, Send me then, send me, I don't care, put me on a boat, I hope it sinks, then you'll be sorry.

Primrose paced. Damn me, what a fine hand I've drawn. First your brother turns cur on me, and now you turn bitch.

Flora stood up with a jolt. Hadjo never turned nothing. All he done is run off to get away from your meanness. But Primrose laughed loud and bitterly. All he done is run off? Hell, I wish that was all. But that ain't how the regulators see it. Ain't how Addison and his fellows see it. They come ask me about the boy pretty often, you know. There's warrants, they're turning over stones for him. Enticement of a slave to run away. Giving a pass to another person's darkie. I got Addison visiting my house in broad daylight, questioning me. And the hunnert head of cattle he stole off of me, me, his own goddamn father, fah! I've got a mind to tell them where he's lurking, hired on with the Forty-Four brand down near Punta Gorda. Let them go and put him in a deep hole someplace where the bastard can't bring hell on my good name.

Flora remained silent. Primrose saw he was having an effect on her at last. How come that bothers you, darling? he roared, an odd smile on his face. The boy done nothing but steal from your family. Done nothing but drag down our enterprise, and turn Murrellite with a goddamn slave. Well, for consideration of your gentle feelings I'll leave the matter alone, Flora. Let the bastard go on playing hell. But if you break this agreement with Gallatin, I'll—I'll turn him over.

It went from very loud in the room to very quiet. The girl only stared at him. You wouldn't, she said. You cain't, you wouldn't. But Primrose's face had gone rigid and strange. There was no turning back from it. He spoke quietly.

I cain, and I will. I will let them have him. I swear I will do it if you defy me in this.

Flora fell back, silent. She sat on her mattress not even weeping. Your son, she said at last.

Ain't my son, he said, almost laughing. Might be your brother, but it ain't my son. There was triumph in his face mixed with something harsher, hotter. The enormity of what he'd said had fallen on him as heavily as on Flora.

After a few minutes Primrose offered words about marriage as a duty and a convenience, nothing more. But there was no need for any of that. His threat echoed in the room, as it echoed to this day.

The conversation in the sitting room flagged a little. The three people who were not Flora shuffled and coughed. Gallatin turned to the girl, a little shyly. 'Now, that's just my perspective on the matter,' he said. 'But my view is a man's, and a man's only. If I knew how a young lady felt about it, I would have a much finer picture of the issue and would have a fuller opinion.' He paused, then added, 'about secessionism.'

'I'm sorry, but I don't know a thing about it,' Flora said. She stood up and left the room.

* * *

There was an unfamiliar covered wagon in front of Widow Tercer's house, backed right up to the front porch. It appeared to be an old Army medical transport, repainted, with a Seal of the State of Florida on its side. At first Nat and Jude Quinto just squinted at it. But then Nat got down from his horse and began walking swiftly toward the house.

He came straight up the porch steps. There was someone rummaging around inside and it was not Jane Tercer. The boot-steps were heavy and brisk. They came toward the door and Nat waited, tense, coiled. But then the interloper came out with a quick businesslike step and fixed Nat with a smile of such bland doughy cheerfulness that he stepped back, perplexed.

'Hullo,' the stranger said.

He was carrying a small side table; he set it in the back of the wagon. A round little man in starched clothing. He came back up the steps, giving Nat another broad grin.

'Who're you,' Nat said.

'Ah.' The man unfolded a piece of paper from his coat pocket. 'Are you—Mister Adolphus Snell?'

'No. My name's Nat Quinto. I'm a friend of Jane's.'

The man nodded knowingly. 'Well, that makes two of us, my good man. I'm a friend of Miz Tercer's too.' And he gave Nat a sympathizing wink.

'Where is she?' Nat asked.

'Oh, out there.' He gestured past the wagon. 'I told her I would do all the moving for her, so she could just sit comfortable in the sun for a while and rest up for the trip.' Nat stepped to the far side of the porch. Jane Tercer was sitting in a chair in the side yard. Her hands were folded in her lap and her wide eyes stared balefully.

Jude had come up to the house. 'Dad, what is this?'

'Never mind, Jude. Just stay back there.'

The round man was coming out again, carrying a pierglass this time. 'I ask this agin,' Nat said. 'Who're you?'

The man's smile flickered away for just a moment. It returned, but with a different light in the beady eyes. 'Why, sir, I already told you. I'm a friend of dear old Miz Tercer's, just like yourself. And I think you'd agree that a lady in her—situation— needs all sorts of friends. I'm taking a more active interest in her affairs, as someone must.' He set the pierglass in the bed of the wagon. When he came back up the steps Quinto was standing in the doorway.

The man made a couple of halfhearted attempts to step past him into the house but then stopped. He saw the game. He spoke to Nat in a clear, chipper voice. 'Excuse me, sir. But if you wouldn't mind stepping aside. I'm trying to do my job.'

'First why don't you tell me jist what job it is you're doing.'

At long last the smile left the man's face. 'Are you this woman's kin? Do you have legal guardianship? No? Well then I don't got to tell you nothing. Now get up out of my way, you dumb Cracker.'

Nat shook his head slowly and looked like he was going to back away. Then he shot one hand up and grabbed the stranger's neck. This one hand was strong enough to lift the man off the ground, but Nat reached with the other hand and grabbed him by the broad crotch also. With this grip Quinto hoisted the man up like a bulky firelog, walked to the edge of the porch, and slung him javelinwise out into the yard.

The man flew a fair distance and came down teeth-first in the dust. His face ploughed a furrow in the ground; he groaned and rolled over and spat out a clod of earth. But then he got to his feet. Nat hopped over the porch railing and out into the yard. It took only three steps to be on him, but the man was ready. Enraged, the stranger swung first. Nat weaved away. The man swung again, but Quinto parried the blow with his forearm.

'Auuk,' the man cried. He grabbed the bones of his right arm and bent over in agony.

Without delay Nat Quinto stepped forward and slung his fist upward into the man's jaw. The man went down into a little round pile.

Nat watched the man to see if he would move. He did not move. Quinto turned to his son and gestured with his head, and together they began pulling Jane Tercer's possessions back out of the wagon. Only when they had removed everything of hers did they pick the man up by the arms and feet and dump him into the back. He lay there, breathing snuffily.

Nat went up to the head of the wagon. The driver was a young slave boy. Nat pointed at his chest. 'You drive this wagon back wherever the hell it came from, doubletime. You get me?'

'Yes sir,' the boy said amiably.

'And when that son of a bitch wakes up, tell him that if he comes back I'll kill him. Jist like that, simple as that.' Young Jude let out a laugh.

'Yes sir,' the boy repeated. 'If he comes back, you'll kill him. Here we go, doubletime.' He popped the reins over the mules' backs and they set off up the road.

Flora was kept indoors. She haunted her room, that great round word still stoppered behind her lips.

Her mother believed there was a medical cause for her behavior. Jake Primrose knew better but allowed the fiction to go on. The county doctor was sent for; he was expected any hour on his tall white horse. Flora waited for him to come. She disliked the man and took every chance to mislead and belittle him. The doctor enjoyed treating the pretty blonde girl so much that he never noticed, and Flora could twist him toward any diagnosis she wanted. That was how she was prescribed the bottle of brandy which she had emptied the previous week.

Around five in the evening a rider came up. The trot sounded too quick to be the doctor's, but she went to the window anyhow. A stranger dismounted and hurried up to the house. It was a squat man with black hair. Right down the middle of the face was a broad, raw scuffmark. Flora watched him come up the porch, then went and pressed her ear to her door.

Jake greeted the man with professional courtesy but in time his tone turned harsh. Soon Flora heard him asking, 'What do you mean, you couldn't take her?'

'Mister Primrose, I'm as mad as you are. My God, look at my face! I've been assaulted.'

Jake went on talking. 'A widder, you couldn't take a widder. And one that's all soft in the brain, at that. It's the saddest thing I've ever heard.'

'Mister Primrose, I've told you, it wasn't Miz Tercer that stopped me. It was some big dumb goddamned Cracker. I don't know what his game was, he wasn't even kin to the woman. He just—' The man made a traumatized little pantomime of how he had been thrown down.

Primrose saw how the man was and eased up. 'Well. What are you going to do different this time, Mister Rapp? Lord forbid you git foiled twice. You know how important it is, to so many people, that the lady be placed in good care.'

'Yes sir, I know. What am I going to do different this time? Well, we've already sent the sheriff for the man who struck me, of course. When they get the bastard I'll make sure they wrap him up tight. And when I go back for the woman I'll take a couple of marshals, you'd better believe I will. Yes, an armed guard, to help me take up a little old widow. Lord have mercy.' He almost sobbed. 'And they told me Florida would be an easy country. Devil take my foolish heart.'

Nat Quinto was unsaddling his horse in the shade when the officers came up.

He'd been agitated all day after he and Jude returned from the Tercer place. Jude was buoyant and grinning, jubilant as if he was the one who'd whipped the man. But Nat balanced his son's jubilation with glumness. When he spied the three riders coming down the road, he exhaled as if relieved.

He turned to his son. 'Go on up to the house,' he said. Jude just looked at him.

'I say git up there, and don't come down. Keep your mother inside too.'

'What?' said Jude. 'What's wrong?' He still didn't see the lawmen riding toward the yard, fanning out as they approached the treeline. 'What's got you, dad? What's—'

Then he saw them coming. Understanding came quickly. 'Why, that little bastard,' he started to say, the blood rising to his face. But his expression shifted when he saw his father still standing horseless and hatless in the middle of the yard, waiting on the riders' approach. Just waiting, his long arms hanging lax.

Jude watched him for a moment. Then he turned and went into the house. He told his mother what was happening. Together they went to the window, with not a word to the children. The sheriff, a man named Ellis, had taken off his hat and was explaining the situation in an apologetic tone. 'They're pretty het up about it, Nat,' he was saying. 'I don't know just what you did to the fellow—you must have whipped him smartly.' He grinned, a little queasily, to try to make the thing light. One of the other two men was a young deputy, similarly embarrassed. But the third was not smiling and kept one hand resting near his waist, the gunbelt there. Nat for his part was looking mostly at the men's horses.

'Well. Then I guess I'd better come now, eh, Ellis?' Nat said at last.

'Oh, I guess you might as well.' The man seemed glad Nat had said it first.

Quinto got his hat and got his horse. Jude came out from the house; Nat eyed him but saw that he was ahold of himself. 'I'm going to Newnansville. Tell your mama I'll be back soon.'

'I'm riding with you,' Jude said.

'No,' said Quinto.

'I'll foller after, then,' Jude said, and would not move from that. Nat said nothing but mounted up and joined the other riders. They seemed glad to be getting away from the Quinto homeplace, out from under the eyes of the wife, the sons. Nat started up the road first and the other three men fell in line behind him.

II.

THEY REACHED NEWNANSVILLE by evening. The town was sinking into darkness even as they arrived, the lamplights snuffed in the few decent businesses, the few decent businessmen heading homeward through tavernlight and stewlight. There was very little illumination except where the drunks and doxies called, but luckily the sheriff's office was near all those places.

The deskman and a moustached third deputy looked up when the party came in, lifting their heads with a studied languor. As if they hadn't been expecting them. The deskman carried the lie even further, asking for every detail as if he did not know them all already. 'Name?'

'Nat Quinto.'

'Age?'

'Fifty.'

'Occupation. Besides everlasting bullhead, that is, Nat.'

'Heck, Ellis, that's my old occupation, I'm bullhead no longer. Farmer.'

Jude Quinto came inside and stood near the doorway. It was obvious by his features who he was, and it was obvious from his silence and his demeanor that he would not be removed from the place. The deskman looked at him for a moment, then pressed on. 'Where was he apprehended.'

Sheriff Ellis let the young deputy answer. 'Suspect was gathered at his own place of residence.'

'Charges to be levied.'

Sheriff Ellis made his way outside now. It seemed he did not want to be present for this part. 'One charge of assault and battery,' the younger deputy said, 'and one charge of criminal mischief.'

Nat made a sort of half-laugh in his throat. 'Mischief, you said? Hell, I remember assaulting and battering someone, but I don't remember much mischief. What's it mean, deputy?'

The young man was waiting on just such a question. 'You can hear all about your charges at your arraignment, Mister Quinto, but we are not responsible for answering legal questions with a case in progress. I'd advise against pressing me or trying to tamper any more, for that's another charge, and a heavyun.'

Quinto looked at the man for a moment. Then he nodded slowly. 'I follow you,' he said.

Jude came back at two o'clock the following afternoon with the bail money. Nat left the sheriff's office with a tip of the hat. They made some purchases at the store, since they were already in town, and then headed south late in the day. Jude had a lot of questions to ask about jail. His father was not quick to answer them.

'Was it cold? Were ye chained? Did they feed ye? What did you think about all that time, jist sitting inside a room? What did it feel like, how you couldn't leave?'

The older man shook his head. 'I wasn't in there long, Jude. I didn't quite get the hang of it. I guess I'll know more about it iffen I go back.'

'Go back?' Jude asked. He turned on the man suddenly, as if the idea had not crossed his mind.

'Sure, go back. After the trial, if they decide to send me. I think there's a pretty fair chance of it.' He spat.

'But,' Jude said. He shook his head. His eyes lost the far-away look they'd had. 'But it ain't fair, Dad. It ain't a bit fair, you've got to do something, fight em, git a lawyer, or—or don't even come to their damned court, stay away somewheres, hide—'

'What was that?' Nat Quinto asked. He turned in his saddle and stared at Jude. 'What was that you said?'

The young man looked away. 'Nothing,' he said.

'What was that you said, Jude,' the man asked once more.

Jude rode on a few more paces in silence. He gazed off down the trail, returned to himself. 'I said you should go and hide,' he repeated calmly.

'Right. And do you think that's what I'll do, Jude?'

'No sir.'

'No. And I'll tell you why, even though I think you know— jist to make sure it gets through your hard head. I done a crime. I whipped a man. You kin argue whether I had a good reason for it, but that ain't the issue. There was a law, and I broke it, and they'll show I did in court. And by God I won't despise em for it. I don't repent of doing the thing, and I ain't saying I wouldn't do it agin, but when the law comes for me I'll take the medicine. Run, and hide away? Hell. That's a coward's game, boy. A coward's.' He coughed the word coward with disgust. He had expressed himself, and was silent a moment, the horses continuing their quick walk.

In a moment he went on, quieter. 'It's like this,' he said. 'A fire comes thew and it burns out all your scrub. Then you've got the best graze that there is, there's no graze better than after a burn. So you celebrate it, and are glad that it came. Now, what if a fire goes and burns a corner of my parcel, ruins a piece of my crop. Will I suddenly go and cuss fire, jist because it caused me a spot of trouble once? No sir. I would not cuss it then. I tell you I would not cuss fire if it burned over all the living I have, and all my life, I would not cuss the fire even then.'

Jude had his head down. The man went on. 'The law is one of God's things. Like the sun, like rain. Like fire. And I won't cuss it no matter what it does to me. To defy it, to try and run from it, that's the same thing as to cuss it. And I won't, not on my life.'

They rode a ways further. Then Nat Quinto gave a sudden, sharp sigh. 'But all the same. Thinking about that room and pissing in a bucket for a week makes me want to cry. This world's a confusion sometimes, Jude, ain't it though.'

Jake Primrose woke up late one frosty morning and stretched his limbs and hitched his suspenders up over his shoulders and declared to the silent house that Yes, yes, he would go to town today. He went to his wife's door and repeated this, then strode out into the sitting room, where he declared it again to the manservant who was feeding the fireplace with wood. Then the cattleman went to his daughter's door and rapped twice and sang out, 'To town, to town, dearest. Dress smart. We gonter make a trip of it.'

If Primrose had examined his intentions even for a moment he would have seen that she, Flora, was at the root of his wish to go to Newnansville. On one hand, there was the possibility that she would refuse, leading to a loud battle. This would be vivifying, good for the lungs and circulation. On the other hand she might agree to go, out of some notion that Newnansville would be better than war at the Primrose house. Then Jake would get his true wish: to parade his daughter around the dusty little borough. He wouldn't get many more chances. Yes, Jake Primrose would take his lovely sullen maiden to town and let the country boys groan for what would soon be out of their reach forever, as if she had ever been within their reach to begin with.

As fortune had it, Flora agreed to go. On the way, Jake talked about the various things they must do that day: a man to see about indigo prices, a new bureau to buy for the spare chamber—that was what he called Hadjo's old room—and arrangements to make for the wedding. They pulled into town from the southeast.

Approaching the center of that pinebox grid, they passed the courthouse. There was a larger-than-usual jumble of sitters, standers, slouchers, and passers-by in front of it. 'Court day,' Primrose exclaimed. 'Hell, I'd forgotten. The first day of court, sure enough!' And with that all the other plans for the trip were dropped and Primrose called for the coachman to find the stable posthaste.

Court was an important holiday. It came twice a year, when the circuit-riding judges arrived. The trials made up the best entertainment in town, they were big doings. Soon after the wagon was parked, the Primrose family was walking into the building and being ushered to a seat near the front. They were late but the cattleman took his entrance slow, not yet removing the new felt hat pinched to the top of his head. He led his wife and daughter with grave conspicuousness, showing everyone that he'd come to observe the wheels of justice, and now those wheels could turn.

This day was for preliminary hearings. It offered a quick sampler of all the cases on the session's docket. As the Primroses came in, the judge was just hustling the previous case out of the box. 'There is no evidence to support the claim that Mister Williams has been trespassing at the house of Mister Botkin. And unless Mister Botkin wants to bring a case of fornication and adultery against his wife and the accused, there is no basis for a trial. Case dismissed.'

The alleged victim shot up. 'But he comes ery other day,' the man wailed. 'I see him coming crost the field, but by the time I come running they've hid themselves in the shrubs or gone. I cain't leave off my crops just to watch for that devil! I cain't!'

'Fornication, Mister Botkin,' the judge said from the bench, tapping his gavel brightly. 'Fornication and adultery, that's what we're facing here. Amass the evidence and I should love to hear all about it. Until then, please leave this court.' He went on tapping as the bailiff took ahold of the man to move him out.

'Oh, sir! Don't make me wait til there's evidence! Don't make me wait for that! Oh please, Your Honor—'

At last the man was taken out of the place. The judge watched him go, unsmiling. He was a long, lean man, a transplanted Yankee appointed to the Florida court during the territorial days. He had stayed on into statehood, enjoying his high station in the backwater, as certain perverse men always relish power in a place they consider to be beneath them. Still, he was always in a bad humor when the court circuit brought him to Newnansville. It was the stop after Saint Augustine: the transition from that ancient city of harbor breezes and Spanish servantgirls to the piney boomtown always left him temperamental. Primrose knew this. 'Old Jedge Fawnce is in one of his bad weathers today,' he whispered to Pauline. 'A right bad one. He might not git out of it before the proper trials start, and then we'll really have a show.'

As he spoke the next case was moved into position. Among the participants Primrose saw his associate, Mr. Alonso Rapp. The scuffmark down the middle of his face was still scabbed and discolored. 'Ah,' Jake hissed excitedly. 'I near forgot! They're going to try the man who whipped my Rapp! Oh, good! And who is it, now? I cain't quite see—'

The bailiff came to the side of the bench and cried, 'Gentlemen of the court, the State of Florida versus Nathan Quinto.'

Jake Primrose raised his eyebrows. He leaned back in his seat. 'Quinto,' he repeated. 'Old Nat. My, my.'

The preliminaries moved quickly. It seemed like Judge Fawnce wanted the hearing finished in time for a good midday meal. Florida was a federal state now, but it still had frontier courts, which always broke for long lunches. The lawyer for the state shuffled forward. He was a thick man with heavy eyelids, which did not quite hide his bloodshot eyes.

'Y'honor,' he said to the judge. 'The case we have before us is of the most saddest kind. It is infamous to all true souls. A gentleman was aiding a fellow woman, and for his charitable act he was dashed to pieces. The victim is named Mister Alonso Rapp. Mister Rapp was law-abidingly going through his goverment work of the State of Florida. He works with the government, y'honor. But then he was attacked suddenly and without warning. He was attacked by an animal, an animal more dangerous in the world than a tiger or a snake or a—a whalefish or a alligator. This animal was a man named Nat Quinto.'

The man puffed for a moment. 'Y'honor, what occurred was on the twentieth of Febry. Mister Rapp was on his duty when the defendant attacked, and beat him extremely well. But he did not stop there. Y'honor, I will show that the defendant did everything he could to undo, defy, derange, and deface the good works of Mister Rapp, by taking all the goods out of the cart. Yes, he undid everything he could get his hands on, and foiled the works of this goodhearted angel of a man Alonso Rapp, who is a person of angelic hands, and a virgin to evil, and a friend of God, and an employee of the State of Florida.'

'Evidence,' the judge said. 'Evidence, sir.'

'Evidence—yes, there is some of that. We have the physical markings on the exterior of Mister Rapp's person. We have his own testimony. We will also have the testimony of a few witnesses.'

'Identify your witnesses, please.'

'Yes, y'honor. These witnesses will include a Negro boy named Charles, who was driving the wagon. There will be Miz Jane Tercer, who is not present, she is at her new residence at Tallahassee. There is a written deposition from her, though, for the court. And we have the defendant's actual son. Name of Jude. He'll be testifying as to his father's actions.'

Jude was sitting in the gallery with his arms crossed. He sat perfectly straight, letting anyone look who wanted to look. As the proceedings continued, some eyes remained on him.

The judge made notes with his quill. 'And does the counsel for the defense have anything to add, which will either preclude the need for a trial or emphasize it?'

Quinto's man was a public defense attorney. He was much like his opponent, heavy and bleary. He labored upright and announced to the magistrate that he had nothing to add.

Judge Fawnce took a few seconds to write something on his tablet. At last he stuck his quill into the well. 'Trying of the case will commence four days from now, this coming Monday.'

The judge then adjourned the court and the audience stood. Many people hurried outside for the midday meal but Jake Primrose remained seated, rubbing his jaw, looking hard at the back of Nat Quinto.

After the court let out many people stayed milling and talking in the square. Jude Quinto stood by the hitching posts, as was his habit. There was a small circle of acquaintances standing around him, as people tend to linger around a person who has been in the public eye, looking left and right, not saying much. They all wanted to be near him, but none wanted to look him in the face. Jude leaned against a post with his hat set back on his head, seeming loose and careless despite himself.

A young woman broke through the circle and rushed up to him. It was Flora Primrose. Her blue eyes were fiercely lit and she spoke to him with a quavering edge in her voice.

'How kin you just stand here?' she said. 'How kin you just sit there? Are you gwine to let this happen to your father, your own father?'

At first Jude was genuinely startled by the girl, her terrible eyes, how close she seemed to physically attacking him. But he recovered and forced an amused smile. 'And what would you have me do, darling?' he asked.

'I don't know. I don't know. But you cain't just sit there and let them say these things about him. It's lies, I know it is. The man who's accusing him is with my father, so I know it's all a lie, it's all one of his tricks. You've got to stop this, do something.'

The smile on Jude's face went away. Her anger had finally touched him. He took a step forward off the post and spoke in a low voice, his eyes almost as fierce as hers. 'Now, listen,' he said. 'I don't know you, and I don't know how things look to you up in the gallery chairs. But I'll tell you what's happening to my daddy. He knocked a man on the head and foiled him, and now he'll take the consequence of it, if he has to, like a man. And not try to worm his way outen it.' His finger was up at her face, jutting at her. Then he realized what he was doing and backed away. He looked at his fellows and tried to smile coolly, like he had before. But it was not easy. The furnace of her anger, the dousing blueness of her eyes.

'And anyway, what do you care?' he scoffed. 'You're Primrose's daughter, ain't ye?'

Her eyes flared and she opened her mouth as if for a loud terrible word. But just then a slave woman sailed in and caught her by the waist.

'Yes, she's Marster Primrose's daughter,' the woman said, beginning to move her away. 'Though she sure don't always act like it.'

Snared, Flora struggled a little, like a bird caught in a net. But she never took her eyes off of Jude and never turned his gaze loose. Step by step she was led away, to where she belonged.

'Pardon us, excuse us,' the servant woman said. Jude's friends were chuckling, but he was not. He was watching her go.

The rest of the day Jude was touchy, queer. He had the queasy look of a man who has let a fight pass. The blood had come into him too late, as it often will. And so all he could do was try to grin his fury down and gaze after the opponent, thwarted and throttled.

Jake Primrose toyed with the string of the rolled map. He fussed with the knot, almost undoing it. But he stopped himself and stepped away to pace the floor. It was not time, Gallatin hadn't come yet.

The cattleman was nervous. But it was not the bad, fretting nervousness he had known so much of lately. It was more like the giddy thrill that had filled him during his early years in cattle work. The return of this youthful feeling embarrassed him somewhat. But there was no resisting it. He folded his hands behind him as he paced, as if this grave gesture might counteract his gladness.

Eventually he could not stop himself anymore. He undid the string. The map unscrolled and he flattened it to the table. Florida had a squat, potatolike shape. His land lay in the center. The property was now perfect, square, like a space for a legend.

An announcement at the front door. Mister Gallatin had come. Primrose called for him to be let in: 'John, John,' he said. They greeted each other in the doorway. The Pennsylvanian attempted to return Primrose's embrace, feigning Southern warmth as best he could. 'Jake. Ah. My dear man.' He was not getting any better at it.

Then he looked around the room. 'But, Flora,' he said, suddenly afraid. 'Is she poorly again?'

'Oh—she's improving,' Jake said, moving the man toward the map. 'She'll join us shortly. But first come, look at this. There's been developments in our section, John, there's been developments.' They stood over the map. 'There's been developments,' Jake said once more, in a graver tone. 'All sorts of things is befallen. First, look at this.' He traced his finger along the edge of the square. The piece that had once been dented by the Tercer property was now made whole.

'Yes. Hum,' he said. 'I see.'

'That orful little section, it's come in now. The widder who was there jist had to be helped along, like you said. We saw to it that some folks came in to take care of the sweet old lady. Lord knows she needed someone, she hadn't a soul in the whole world. Anyhow, she's in comfort now. Her land got auctioned for her benefit, and it so happened that I was the high bidder. So there you have it, man, there you have it. Easy as you please.'

'Yes, indeed,' Gallatin said.

'But that ain't all,' Jake went on. 'No, that's nice enough, but that ain't all.' He picked up a piece of blue chalk from a tumbler on the side table. 'Tell me what you think of this right here.' And he traced a section which protruded from the Primrose-Gallatin square in just the same way that Tercer's had once diminished it. It stuck out south and a little east of the previous blemish. It was an area of springs and small creeks. Gallatin leaned in to examine it. Then he reached into his vest for a fine-chained little monocle, put it to his eye, and leaned in again. 'Hum,' he said. 'Hum, umph.'

'Yes,' Primrose said, nodding. 'Yes sir. Now that there is a whole separate concoction. That there is an old friend of mine who come in back in the territory days. Name of Quinto. He done pretty good with that land, proved it up. But he's fell on some hard times and will have to sell out quick, for dimes on the dollar. Did I say fell on hard times?' Primrose said, suddenly louder, indignant. 'No—not hard times, fool decisions. He made fool decisions, is the fact of it, and always has. He's a cussed stubborn old bullhead, this acquaintance of mine, and won't listen to sense. Queer, stubborn fellow. Jist look at this!' Primrose jabbed the chalk at the paper. 'The damned clayeater is sitting on a stream like that, and he's never thought to build a mill dam. And look here! He's right on the road to Picolata, west of the river, and he's never thought to put in a trading post. Why, some men must think they're jist too good for the world, not to take advantage of a thing when they're sitting on it.'

Gallatin was still lensing in and out with his monocle. 'Yes. It's good. Very good, I think. It's an excellent parcel, isn't it? Yes, there's opportunity.' At last he stood up. In his way he was as excited as Primrose. 'Now, Flora. If she is here, I would like to see her.' This was a bold statement for him, and he knew it. 'Forgive me. It's just that I am feeling so very—hopeful, so very joyful, about our future together...all of a sudden...you understand.'

'Of course, my dear man,' Primrose said. He went out into the common room. 'Flora. Flora.'

But she was out in the pasture. The milch cows had to be moved to a fresh field and Emily was driving them. Flora helped. She had not done this in a long time: she started out waving the switch at the cows' haunches as if to dispel a daydream. But the cows moved, and she awoke and her blue eyes tacked down onto the task. She brandished the switch with alacrity and her part of the herd moved in a neat bunch. Old Oscar was passing by with a strip of broken leather for mending and stopped to watch. He smiled, not with his mouth but with everything else on his worn face. He watched her all the way across the pasture. Then he turned to another man and lied to him somberly. 'Go run to Marse Jake. Tell him not to hire a new cowman, there's a fine natural one on the place already.'

It was possible that the young woman heard her father calling her name Flora Flora Flora in the house but she did not turn from her task. She must certainly have heard him when he came outdoors and called her name again Flora Flora and then Fl— the last repetition catching in his teeth as he spotted her across the field, nearly through the gate with her tight bunch of cows.

There were no more calls from the porch. A young slave was sent running to tell Emily—not Flora, but Emily—what they must immediately do. Flora just shrugged, too pleased with their finished job to argue. They went out to the bend in the road and sat on a log to wait for the carriage holding Primrose and Gallatin. In a minute it came around the bend and they got in, accompanied by the distinct odor of cow.

At last Gallatin spoke up. 'Fine roads though, aren't these? Good and flat. Good and graded.' Primrose made an affirmative sound in his throat, but he was looking elsewhere. The wagon brought them around a springhead.

'Look at this,' Jake said suddenly. 'A good freshwater spring. Why, he could water five hundred head in thisyer. And look!' he said as they came along a creek. 'He could dam that creek and put a mill upon it. He could crack the whole county's corn. Look at what the bastard's sitting on. What land, what waters! It's criminal, criminal!'

They exited the bottomland near the spring and came into the forest proper, browned and frostbit, and beyond that a burnt-over field. They passed more fields and came to a wooded area, where a house stood. The sunshower had fallen here too. The rain appeared to be sitting on top of the ground like a sheet of diamonds. Their gleam was on everything: the trees, the distant cattle, a standing plough, a shed, a fence, a house. And the young man, Jude Quinto. He had been wetted by the rain but not soaked; like the fields, he shone. The dark hair was slicked to his forehead. He had been tending to his oxen but he looked up to watch the wagon speeding past his yard.

The carriage drove past several more fields, threaded through with streams, then turned back toward the highway road. 'Ain't bad, is it, John?' Primrose asked.

'No, it surely isn't,' said Gallatin. 'I could see myself living on such a place as that. After all of the right improvements, of course, and constructing a suitable house.' He turned timidly to the girl. 'What do you think, Flora?'

She was staring hard through the window. 'Yes,' she said. 'Yes. I think it looked like a right pretty place to live.'

The Quintos used the days before trial to prepare for planting. Much of their land was in corn, big swaths of it. There was a vast garden also, near the house. It had grown as the family had grown: it was now about eight children wide. Lucy worked this plot meticulously. In times of great activity they would all be out there, all the children, squabbling, laughing, fighting over the most prestigious jobs, playing games with Muscovy drakes and chasing off any crow that had the gall to eye the bags of seed.

This week the weeds needed to be torn out and the manure laid and mixed. But there was not as much shouting and fighting as usual. The children worked quietly, and like their mother they looked up at Nat every time he came near on a row-cut in the cornfields. Nat was ploughing with the oxen; Jude followed after him with a harrow to smooth out the mounds. In the few days before trial they hardly made a dent in the work.

At the end of each day Nat would not come straight in for supper but would stay outside awhile, pacing the fields. He did not have to say what he was thinking, what he was fearing. Any length of time in the county jail during this season would mean irretrievable loss. Planting time loomed but the prospect of that square cell darkened everything. After a while Nat would quit his pacing and come in to eat a little supper—not much, as if saving rations for a later time.

When the day came to go back to court, the man treated it like any other trip to town. The children knew better. Nat tried to tell his wife that she could just stay home. He and Jude were the only ones required to go, it would be tedious anyhow, and what was the point? Lucy just laughed, mirthlessly. They hitched up the wagon and the whole family piled in.

They were early for the trial but there were already people milling on the courthouse steps. Many of these men knew Nat Quinto to greet him. A bulge-skulled man named Goolby shouted to him, 'Ah, it's Quinto, Quinto, the bludgeoneer! Here he comes, start up the dirge! What say, Nat, will it be the gallows today?'

'I don't know yet, Gool,' Nat responded. 'Though if these lawyers drag on like they're looking to, I might request a hanging. Jist to get things over with.'

He got his family seated in the gallery. It was cold; mittened men were feeding stoves at the back and front of the room. Jude sat next to his mother. He put his arm around her. The young man had made sure to get the seat by the aisle, knowing he would be called forward.

When the general public was admitted, the place began to bustle and creak. People jostled for seats. A murmur became audible: Fired the old lawyer for the state. There's a new prosecutor on the case. Lawyer out of Georgia. A sharp blade. Primrose's man. A sharp blade.

The crier announced the State of Florida versus Nathan Quinto and the new prosecutor stood to give his opening statement. He was short and slightly built; the clothes he wore were fitted accordingly, trim around the chest and back. Before speaking he faced the judge as straight as a pin, showing reverence for the bench, the seal, the magistrate, the mahogany magnificence of it all. Then he began to speak, moving swiftly across the floor. His voice had a rapid-pattering rhythm of a kind Jude had never heard before. The difference between him and his predecessor was glaring. The lawyer for the defense frowned as he listened to the newcomer.

'Gentlemen of the jury, you have been called to hear the details of an unsettling case. It is an instance of wanton violence falling on a most undeserving victim—a man doing charitable work. It is the kind of crime that makes men cringe or makes men boil. Sirs,' he said, facing the jury. 'It took place on the property of a certain widow, Jane Tercer. I'm told that she will be known to many people in this room. She is a sad victim of the late Indian savageries which visited this state.

'But, gentlemen, she was at this time living in misery. Alone, and cast aside by her country. Various entities in Tallahassee heard of her tragic case and determined to bring her there to the state capitol to live comfortably, as an emblem of our hardy settlers' enduring spirit. She was to be given a fine habitation and a handsome pension. She would serve as an honored reminder of that brutal period, lest we forget.

'And yet an individual named Nathan Quinto sought to undo this charitable work, and did so savagely. He attacked Mister Rapp and beat him unconscious. He then did every other kind of mischief to undo his mission. Gentlemen, it will not be my work to uncover the strange urges that might drive a man to such an act. Indeed, I doubt my ability to plumb such dark intentions. But I will show the plain fact that he did do it—and this, I believe, will be enough, in the court's eyes and in the eyes of Justice.'

There was a long pause before anything else happened. The whole room hummed with acclamation and commentary. It took a long time, but finally the public defender stood up and eased his way to the floor, a little off to one side. His eyes were glassy under the heavy lids. 'Gentlemen of the jury, people of the state,' he began. 'What I must say is that, well, this is a great wonderful country we live in. America. And every American man in the world is under the protection of innocence, and that's jest what Nat Quinto is, innocent. Until proved guilty. He got caught up in a quarrel, that's all, without meaning nothing by it. Because, well, y'see—' he raised his hand and made a rhetorical gesture, while he tried to think. 'Y'see, there was a struggle that day, and perhaps one fellow made it out a little worset than the other, but I'm here to tell you that my client didn't mean nothing by it, and so it's not assault and battery, not quite. And as far as the other charge—well, it weren't that either, and I'll show that too. There's reasonable doubt about it.' He made to sit down but seemed to realize that he hadn't said enough, and so went on. 'Now also, look at it this way, friends. There's something happened that day, the twentieth of February. But no man can go back and say jest what it was.' He looked around the room importantly. 'And there's nowhere known jest what happened, except in God's ledgerbook.' He raised his right arm and pointed toward the ceiling. 'And cain't nobody look into it, not until the end of time. And so we'll jest have to talk it out, until then. Because that's the way of things.' He lowered his arm. 'Because Nat didn't do it, gents, as I said before. He ain't that kind of fellow. And he's pled not guilty.'

The court kept quiet this time. A minute later the prosecutor came up again. He strode to the floor with a sheet of paper in his hand. 'Your honor, I would first like to call forward Mister Alonso Rapp.' Rapp came to the front of the room, smiling falsely and nodding in acknowledgement to no one in particular. As if his nice manners would make people not see the rash down the middle of his face. 'I call Mister Rapp not yet as a witness,' the prosecutor said, 'but first as an exhibit of evidence. The marks you see on his head are the wounds he received on the twentieth of February.'

Rapp sat down in the witness's chair, with a nod at the judge and a 'Your honor.' Then he spoke to the prosecutor, still grinning. 'Before we start I want to thank you, sir, for all those kind words before. Here I thought I was just a government man, but it turns out I'm an angel of charity—make sure and write my superiors about that!' He grinned lamely at the courtroom. The prosecutor was stonefaced and did not even acknowledge the man's out-of-turn talk but pressed forward.

As Rapp described each step of the struggle, he was made to show the mark on his body that corresponded to it. By the end the man's smile had gone away and there was sweat on his brow. He was glaring at the prosecutor as if he was the one who'd beaten him. Finally the lawyer had gotten everything he wanted. 'Nothing further,' he said, and turned away.

On most days this jury of peers would have already been planning to reach a No Verdict. But today things were somehow different; they felt that they were under more scrutiny, that there were powers and interests at play which they did not fully comprehend. For once they might actually have to decide the case on the legal merits, rather than by simple commonsense gutwork backfitted with some lawyerish trimmings.

The prosecutor went on to read a deposition from Charles, the young wagon-driver, and then he presented the statement Jane Tercer had given in Tallahassee. The statement was in a stilted language nothing like Jane Tercer's. It explained that she was very comfortable and well looked-after in a tenant building of the city. It went on to say that Alonso Rapp was a kind and capable gentleman, and that Nathan Quinto was a former associate but had made himself abominable that day. It ended with a short description of the fight.

'Now I would like to call Jude Quinto to the stand,' the prosecutor said. All the faces turned toward Jude. He went forward, his mother gazing after him as if he too were going to judgment. When he reached the witness's stand, both Quinto men were together at the front of the courtroom. There was some comfort in that, for Jude. He took the size of the crowd, and they in turn took the size of him: a tall youth, quick-eyed, smooth-jawed, regarding the audience with curiosity. He put his broad hand out and swore on the Bible.

The lawyer stepped to his desk and looked at a piece of paper. 'Young man, what is your connection to Missus Tercer? Describe it, please.'

'My connection to her? I don't know.' He thought awhile. 'I known the Tercers as long as I've known anyone. They was our neighbors. It's like I was born knowing them.'

'How far do you live from that residence?'

'Oh, a good piece. I'd say about twelve thirteen mile.'

'Twelve or thirteen miles. So you are not very close neighbors, then,' the man said. 'By geography.'

Jude just frowned. 'Well. Not so very close, I guess.'

'So, given that you were not very close neighbors, can you explain for us what exactly you were doing on the Tercer property that day?'

'Well, we'd come to burn her land.'

'Excuse me,' the lawyer said. He squinted. 'Will you repeat that? You were going to burn—to set a fire?'

'Yes, a few of them. You know. To get her land good for berries and sich, and to keep a wildfire out.'

The lawyer's eyes darted to the judge, as if to ask for help. 'Could you elaborate a little further, for the jury?' he asked

One of the jurors was Teek Geyer. He shouted out. 'Peas, sir Lawyer! We know why to bring a fire through.'

The judge stood out of his chair. 'Order! Order. The jury will not interfere with the conduct of this trial. On my oath, I'll expel the next man to talk.' Geyer shut up and put his knuckles to his mouth, suppressing his titters. He was drunk, of course, as were several men in his corner of the jurors' box. But he did not want to leave jury duty, which provided a wage and a good story for later, so he smiled ruddily as his fellows held him down.

Jude continued helpfully on the topic of prescribed fire. 'We lay the fire carefully, so it stays low. Jist let the fire back its way out, so it burns the scrub. Then it'll grow. Nothing'll ever grow so well as after a fire, it's a material fact.'

'And the lady allowed you to do this.'

'Sure. We used Mister Shay's old mules.'

'Well. Well,' said the prosecutor, again glancing to the judge. 'And yet you did not actually set fire to anything that day, as you claim you intended. Why?'

'Well, we found that strange wagon there.'

'And what was your reaction when you saw the State's wagon?'

'My reaction? I don't know. I jist wanted to see who that man was, what he was doing. Because I didn't know. And I still don't quite know, though I've heard it five different ways.'

The attorney smiled tightly. 'As we've heard, Mister Rapp was there to assist Missus Tercer in her move.'

'I heard that,' Jude said. 'But I'd like to know what made anyone think Miz Jane wanted that assistance to start with. Matter of fact, it always looked to me like that house was all she cared about, and staying in it, and waiting there for her son Ab to come back, as she thought he would come back, and—'

'We have heard Jane Tercer's deposition,' the prosecutor interjected. 'And as we heard, Mister Rapp was doing the lady's will, as a compassionate friend.'

'A friend,' Jude broke in. He squinted at the lawyer. 'What made him a friend? Sitting her down a chair, while he took everything outen her house?'

'Order, order,' said the judge, and rapped his gavel.

'Jude,' Nat Quinto muttered from his seat. Probably no one else heard him say it. The young man met his father's eyes and the anger in him fled, abashed though not quite defeated.

The audience grumbled for a moment. The prosecutor paced, waiting. 'Now. Young man, will you describe what happened after you saw Mister Rapp's wagon?'

'Shoot. You already heard it.'

'Are you saying that Mister Rapp's version of the events corresponds with your own?'

Jude sighed again and looked at his father. Nat was looking back at him, smiling faintly as though curious what the boy would say.

Jude looked at his hands. 'It happened like he said it did. They argued. The man kept on carrying things out. Then Dad picked him up and hucked him off the porch. As ye can see for yourself.' He nodded toward Rapp. 'Dad went down there in the dirt, and the man swung but couldn't find him, and then dad tetched him on the jaw one time. And that was it.'

The prosecutor walked in a circle, nodding. 'And was there any further conversation with the agent?'

'Conversations? Lord, no. He weren't conversating much.'

'And then the wagon departed? We know that the wagon eventually left the scene.'

'Yes. Well, no. Dad and I got all the things outen it first. Then we set the fellow in the rear, and they went away.'

'We have heard the statement from the Negro boy Charles,' the lawyer said. He picked up a piece of paper from his desk. 'He stated under oath, and I quote—Nat Quinto instructed me to tell Mister Rapp he would kill him if he returned. End quote. Did you hear your father say this?'

'I heard.'

The prosecutor turned to the judge. 'Nothing further,' he said, and sat down.

Mutterings across the room. The judge rapped his gavel. 'This court is adjourned until one-thirty. The defense will have its chance to question the witness after the interval.' Then he headed for the door to his chamber.

Jude made his way to his father's table. 'Dad,' he said, unable to look at him straight.

Nat stretched. 'You did good up there, son.'

'Dad. I ruint it. I stepped right into his mouth, I let him chew me.'

'Hey, boy. What do you mean? Hey.' Jude would not look up, so the man snapped his fingers at him. 'Hey there, friend. What are you talking about? You answered his questions truly. Was there someaught else you should of done?'

'I feel like I slapped you.'

'Oh, hell,' Quinto sighed. He turned in his chair.

Jude looked around. 'Damn this place. I hate it here, this whole town. I'm on go find some tobacco to smoke.' He went out.

In the press around the courthouse steps Flora Primrose stood apart. With her height and the straightness of her carriage she could see out across the crowd. A group of court-watchers were arguing in a tight ring. Drunks were wagering cups on Nat Quinto's sentence. Flora's own parents had gone off to a better part of the courthouse square, where the gentry mingled. She turned to Emily. 'Will you walk with me?' she asked.

The woman glanced at Flora's face. 'Of course,' she said. Flora took one last survey of the square and then they slipped away.

A minute later they found Jude at the back of the court-house, sitting on the stoop with a corncob pipe. When he saw a female coming, he quickly hid the pipe under his leg; it stayed there, still smoking, as he looked to see who it was. When he saw it was not his mother, he took it up again and began puffing nonchalantly.

'You agin,' he said as Flora came up.

He had put on his meanest expression but the girl was not put off; she kept coming. She sat down on a barrelhead near him and folded her hands. Her companion sat next to her. She was looking at Jude very intently.

Jude's stoniness faltered. 'You ain't as talkative as you were last time,' he said. 'Are ye.' He was prepared for her fury but not for this.

'I want to talk to you,' she said.

Jude scoffed. 'I don't even know your name.'

'Flora,' she said. 'And this is Emily. She's the one watches to make sure I don't do nothing wrong.'

The woman did not take her wary eyes off of Jude. 'I ain't managed it yet,' she said.

'Fine. Fine.' Jude took another draw on the pipe. Then he looked at it distastefully and set it down. 'Well,' he said, as if tired. 'I guess they're going to find him guilty, before long.'

Flora stood up like a shot. 'A stay, you've got to request a stay,' she said. 'I've seen it done before. It'll hold the case over until a later session, and then you can work up a defense aginst this new lawyer man they've got, and you kin find out why they're persecuting him, and all of it.'

'What, and then do this all over agin?' Jude actually chuckled. 'No ma'am. They ain't no time. Planting season's coming on—shoot, it's already here. We've got to get this over with. He knows they'll find him guilty, he's not of a mind to spend time messing around in the lawbooks—might as well hurry and get the thing done with.'

She took a step toward him. 'Then find another way. I heard them talking at the front of the court. They say the sheriff, he hates this whole business. They say if your daddy jist runs away, the sheriff probably won't even chase him. He could run home and they might never come follering.'

Jude shook his head. 'Darling, you heard wrong. Sheriff Ellis is friendly enough with us. But he won't let my daddy go. No, he'll set him in that jail if they tell him to, make no mistake.'

'Then break him out.' Her voice dropped to a harsh whisper. 'Break him out, if you see no other way. Git a hammer. Bust a hole. Pull the wall down with a mule. Free him, bust him loose, cain't you do it?'

Her eyes had come alive again with that awful fire he had seen before. But this time Jude stood apart from her passion, observing it, and even smiled. There was genuine pleasure in the smile, and admiration. 'Miss Primrose,' he said. 'You don't understand me. I could do as you say, I could bust a hole in that wall big enough for him to walk through. And do you know what would happen? He'd walk through it, all right—far enough to come out and whip me raw. Then he would walk right back in thew that hole and make a spot for me in the cell.

'I don't speak for him, now,' Jude continued after a moment, taking up the pipe thoughtfully. 'But I say it's the law's doing, like it or not. And the law ain't something you cuss or fight. No, it helps you sometime and hurts you othertime, but you've got to jist honor it, either way.' He pointed with the reed of the pipe. 'Consider it. Who spites a thing the Lord is made? A man's got to take his lumps.'

'Do you mean that if you landed in jail for nothing, you'd go happily?' It sounded like mockery but it was not. She was watching him intently.

'Happily? I don't say that, now. I don't want nothing to do with no jail. It's no place for me. I expect it gets terrible lonesome, for one.'

'I'd visit you,' Flora said simply.

It had come out very quickly. A kind of fear spread over her face. 'Well, that'd be kind of you,' the young man said slowly. 'Though it might be one of them things that she's supposed to keep you from doing.' He nodded at Emily.

He had said the right thing. Flora stood up again, haughty. 'I'd do it, if I wanted to,' she said. 'If I wanted to come visit you in jail, I'd do it. I don't care what no one says.'

'I don't doubt that a bit, darling,' Jude said, smiling. 'And now you've half got me thinking of which law to break, to get in that jailhouse quickest.'

Emily intervened at last. 'Flora,' she moaned. 'Let's go, we got to go eat. Come on, before they come looking for us.' She took Flora by the wrist and began to walk off with her. 'We're sorry for disturbing you, sir.'

Jude stood up. 'You ain't disturbed me. You've taken my mind off things admirably.' He took a step after them. 'Miss Flora,' he said.

She turned around. He spoke quietly. 'Please come meet me here, after the next break. Will you?'

Her eyes were averted, but he stared into them anyway. 'No, I shouldn't,' Flora said, shaking her head.

'Psho. After all that about how they cain't hold you nowheres?' Jude said.

A smile almost appeared on her lips. 'You must think you know me pretty well, don't you.'

'Not well enough. Is the point.'

'Flora!' Emily cried.

'All right,' said Flora. 'I'll be here agin.' Then they were gone.

Back in the courtroom the spectators were subdued after their midday meal. But they did not fail to murmur at the sight of Nat Quinto sitting alone at the defense's table. His public defender was gone. After Judge Fawnce came in and called for order, Quinto stood up and explained that he'd have no lawyer anymore.

'With many thanks to Mister Hilton for his help,' he added. 'I told him to go take some relaxation. I hear there's steak and eggs at Missus Lattner's.'

The judge looked him up and down. 'You choose to represent yourself.'

'Yes, y'honor, if that's all right. I'll represent myself.'

The judge grimaced. 'That is your right, if you feel you are advantaged by it.'

'Well, I don't know whether I'm advantaged by it. I feel led to do it, that's all—I get such fancies sometimes, though they don't always play me fair.' He rubbed his jaw. 'The only thing I'm worried about is that I might speak out of turn in some way, y'honor. Because I confess the way you good people talk here is uncommon to me, and I feel almost a foreigner to it. If I was a Spainiard, you'd forgive me for speaking Spainish, or so I'd hope—well, you'll have to do me the same courtesy today, for I'm as good as a Castilian here, with my poor tongue.'

'And yet you're committed to this course.'

'I am, your honor. I feel answerable in this matter. And I figure if it's my own reputation under the gun, I might as well do the talking. Might as well.'

'Granted.' The judge took up his quill and made a note. 'Well, as it happens, it is now the defense's turn. You may call forward any witnesses.'

'Hum. Let's see now,' said Nat. He squinted into the audience. 'I'd like to talk to Mister Rapp.'

'Objection,' said the prosecutor. 'The victim has already been examined. He should not have to be called up again.'

The judge shook his head. 'Overruled. The defendant has changed counsel. He has the ability to reexamine Mister Rapp if he sees fit.'

Rapp had no choice but to come to the front. He sat down, smiling sardonically as he had before, though it was a pretty thin thing this time. Eventually he had to look at Nat, and then nothing could keep the shadow of animal fear and hatred from his eyes.

Quinto saw the effect he was having on the man and moved a few paces off before speaking. 'Well first of all, sir, how do ye feel.'

'I feel fine,' Rapp grunted. There was quiet for a moment, and the real import of the question seemed to dawn on him. There were scattered chuckles throughout the room. He swallowed, glared. 'I am feeling fine,' he said, more seriously.

'I know you was the one who emptied June's place. Did you also take her up to Tallyhassee?'

'I escorted her there, yes.'

'So you saw her in her new place. Is it like they said in that statement? Did she really seem happy and content, and all of that? Does she have a good place to stay, and a berry patch, and—'

The judge rapped his gavel. 'Missus Tercer's current welfare has no bearing on this case. None.'

Rapp broke in. 'And anyhow, it's just like I said before, I don't have to tell you nothing,' he said. 'You weren't kin or guardian then, and you sure as hell ain't one now.'

The judge roared at Rapp but Rapp smirked, glad to have spoken out. Then Quinto turned on him, friendly no longer, and he shrank back.

'Then I'll keep to the events of that day, Mister Rapp. And your mission. I ask you this. Who sent you to go see about Missus Tercer that day?'

'Well,' Rapp said drily, trying to sound professional. 'There was various communications received in the capital about her. They said there was a helpless woman who had survived the Indian fighting in Alachua County, and she was indigent. Alone.'

Quinto broke in. 'Jane Tercer was not alone, she had vis-
itings most every day. She wasn't helpless, she had the helps of
half this county at her fingertips. Every man or woman who ever
knew Shay Tercer would have done anything—'

'We object,' said the prosecutor. 'This is argument, not
examination. The witness is being disputed against.'

'The objection is sustained,' said the judge.

'All right then, all right.' Quinto was walking back and
forth in front of the witness's stand. It was not an attorney's
thoughtful stroll; he was prowling like a boxer in a ring. 'All
right. I'll put this as a question. Had every woman who is alone
and helpless ought to be taken out of her home and carried
away to another part of the earth, and her land sold to the high-
est bidder?'

The prosecutor looked livid. 'We obj—'

'It was voluntary,' Rapp shouted, meeting Nat's dark gaze.
'She was convinced of it before I ever got there. Another person
had prepared her, got her to sign papers. She wanted to go. She
wanted it. She believed if she went to the capital the government
might find her sons and bring them to her, and they would be
reunited.'

Quinto turned away. 'And everlasting shame fall on whoe'er
told her that lie.'

A baleful murmur, almost a moan, went up in the courtroom.

'We object,' said the prosecutor.

But Rapp was up from his seat and shouting louder than the
prosecutor. 'I didn't know any of it, I didn't know.'

'Order,' the judge bellowed, louder than anyone. He
slammed his gavel. 'The objection is sustained. Order, by God.'
He struck his gavel six more times, even as the courtroom went

silent. 'Mister Quinto,' he said. 'You will confine yourself to questioning, and no other species of statement, or I will hold you in contempt of court.'

Quinto surely heard the judge. But he did not look at him. He did not shift his eyes from the agent. 'I ain't got nothing more to say to this man,' he said, and went to sit down.

There was silence on all parts for a time. Soon Rapp dismissed himself from the stand. The audience began to whisper and shift. The jurors were murmurous in the box. For a moment it looked as if the proceedings might just come apart. Then the prosecutor stood up.

'Your honor, I have half a mind to ask that the entire last testimony be stricken from the record as utterly irrelevant and contemptuous. But I am equally convinced that the exchange was empty of any material that might free the defendant from his guilt, and so not worth even the effort to strike it.' He sniffed. 'I myself have no need to question the witness again. He has suffered more than enough for Mister Quinto's sake.' He sat down.

Nat was expressionless. He remained silent in his seat, and once again the courtroom began to unravel. The judge addressed Quinto. 'The floor is the defense's,' he said hurriedly.

Quinto didn't get up. 'I ast everything I wanted. I've got nothing more.'

The judge looked at his papers. 'Sir, the prosecution has already rested its case. If you say that you rest also, then we will move to the closing arguments.'

Nat made a gesture with his right hand. 'Move on,' he said.

At a nod from the judge the prosecutor stood up to his utmost height. He took a turn across the floor in silence, as if waiting for the muse to visit him. But when he started speaking it sounded like he was reading off of a page.

'Gentlemen. You have sat and listened, you have sat and observed. And I believe that if you have the normal organs of sense, you cannot doubt what has happened here. You have met a humble civil servant hoping to carry out his work in peace. You have heard the sad case of the wounded widow who was placed in his care. And then you have met the individual who blasted this whole enterprise to splinters. An individual unaccountable to order, as he sees it—unaccountable to law. A man who believed, in a moment of strange passion, that he could see down to the bedrock of Mister Rapp's intentions and remedy their imaginary ill with blows. What right did he have, what authority did he wield to take this action? Why, the oldest one—brutal strength. Gentlemen, you know what sort of man this Quinto is. We have all met them. The sort who lives his life content in his own judgment, happy with his own powers, unconcerned with human society, seeing no need to consult with the sources of goodness and fairness which make up the gridwork of most men's lives. I guarantee you, this man has no thought for the powers of this edifice where we now sit.' For the first time his thin face showed clear emotion, flushed and strained. 'This edifice of law, which can remedy the imbalances which corrupt human life. This edifice, which is the one sure way to bring men together in pure symmetry, without nature's unequal and capricious favors. Nathan Quinto may be a strong man, sirs, but here in this house he is no stronger than the weakest man, who is no weaker than a king. This is, in short, the most wonderful place on earth, and yet, and yet, I tell you'—he pointed a finger roofward and thundered—'I tell you that if this man was able he would break, and burn, and pull this entire structure to the ground.' A child whimpered near the back of the courtroom.

'So,' the prosecutor said, pacing. 'So, what did he do, exactly? First, he came and struck the victim unconscious. Then he undid all the man's work for that day and sent his vehicle away empty. Doing this he cost the state valuable monies. You have heard all this, sirs, in every different way. It points to an easy conclusion, guilty on both counts.

'There's only one thing which worries me,' the prosecutor said, his pale face once again clear of emotion, 'and that is the accused's wide popularity in this country. Mister Quinto is well known to many of you the jury, and I believe that even those who do not know him directly are acquainted with his name, or have ties with people who know him. It is unavoidable, with this place's small population and the intimacy of all ties here. I was aware of this concern before I took the case. But now, being here and seeing things for myself, my fear is increased—I believe that Mister Quinto may be able to use his popularity, mixed with a certain native cleverness of speech, to prejudice this jury. I warn you gentlemen to be careful. The man will seek to use your neighborly spirit to distance you from the law. He will sway you against this court and magnify the bonds of friendship above the bonds of justice.

'You must not allow this. It would squander and pervert the progress of this young state. Sirs, from time to time a community has to gather itself together and decide just what it intends to be—where it will build its fences and where it will set its walls. I suggest that this is just such a time for your young state. This is the season when the yearling colt—for Florida is in truth a yearling, or not much more than one—must stand up and decide what sort of creature it will be. Will it be a dray, a pack animal, wayward and brutish, requiring the whip? Or will it be a galloper, a gallant thing, racing under the master's hand, the nobility of its heart as visible as if it wore it on the outside of its chest? That is Florida's choice, and it is a choice you have a hand in making, as agents of justice in the very heart of this state, at the very dawn of its existence. You have a deciding vote, sirs. Your hand will twitch the reins.'

The prosecutor nodded to the jury and went to sit down. The room stayed very quiet. Nat Quinto was at his table, seemingly lost in thought. Then he looked up, looked around. A sheepish smile came over his face, as if he was just realizing this silence was for him.

He stood up and took a turn around the floor, casually. He had picked up a thing or two about lawyering. At last he cleared his throat. 'Well, gentlemen,' he said. 'That man can turn a word, cain't he? I confess—he got so het up jist now that I was ready to whip the scoundrel he was talking about. Then I remembered it was me.' He ran his fingers through his nearblack hair, smiled a brief smile. 'But that gets me to worrying. If the fellow can make me want to whip myself, why, the rest of you should be easy enough. I'm the toughest sale he's likely to make.

'But then I step back, fellows, and I ponder all this. And I find I do not recognize the man he's painted for us. That Nat Quinto is not the one I'm acquainted with, not quite, and I'd like to set up a few fences between the two. The first and awfullest misunderstanding he's made of me is to say that I am a clever speaker. Fellows, I declare it isn't so. Very plainly I tell you that all day I have used only the first words to come into my mouth and am doing the same thing now. What use is clever talk in sich a muddle as this? None, and that's why I ain't used it.

'The other thing that Mister Prosecutor accused me of is knowing the people I live among, and being known by them. I suppose he is closer to the truth on that, though I wonder why he needed to mention it. And the way he brought it up is odd to me, too, as if it was something snakeish I done beforehand to get in your good graces, or something you'd oughter be ashamed of and put out of your hearts. But I won't apologize for knowing these men, no. They're my neighbors, and I will be neighborly. I know the quality of man in thisyer county, and so I know that our lawyer has nothing to fear. I believe that ye will do justice to the matter at hand, no matter what the relations between us. I have faith in that. I believe that ye will even conduct your duty better, knowing a little of my life outside of this great room. Of course I understand Mister Lawyer's idea that we should all jedge one other as if we was strangers. But I feel like I know every man I ever laid eyes on, at least a little—he's a creature of the same materials as me. That's why I do not understand sich men, who want all justice to be done in a room outside of life. No, I'd rather have my fate held by a group of fine men who'll jedge me in the fulness of things, as a countryman, as a neighbor, as a fellow-creature of their same materials. Find me guilty or find me innocent, boys—I kin take it, I promise ye. I came here expecting to have it so. It was either this or run off for some foreign place to evade you. But I view this whole business as a sort of tax, for the pleasure of continuing to live amongst you. If that's what the law is, then I'll bear it.'

As the judge gave his final instructions to the jury, people were already leaving the courtroom, talking the trial over in loud voices. Flora waited for a moment, anonymous in the burgeoning crowd. Then she drew Emily with her around the side of the courthouse. When they got to the rear corner of the building she took the woman's face in her hands and said, 'Please, please wait for me here. I won't be long, but don't come no closer.'

Jude was sitting with his elbows on his knees, staring straight ahead. Flora came very close before he ever looked up. And even when he did look up it seemed he did not quite recognize the girl. She stood for a moment, wavering, then she sat next to him on the step.

Eventually Jude managed to call himself out of his reverie. 'Well, I guess it won't be long now,' he said.

'Jude,' she said. 'Why'd he get rid of his lawyer?'

'Why?' he said. 'So he could stand up and talk awhile. Seemed more entertaining than jist sitting there, I guess.'

She smiled a little. 'It was. They cain't stop shouting about it on the front steps. Said it's the best trial they've seen in a year.'

'That's fine, that's fine,' Jude said, scowling. 'I'm glad them boys enjoyed their day.' He snapped a twig. 'Lord, I don't understand how folks can be happy, sitting in a room, watching people talk. Ain't they got nothing of their own to do? I swear, I cain't wait to get home. I cain't stand thisyer city.'

Flora raised her face skyward. 'Me neither.'

'It's got too many dratted people running around everwheres.'

'Too many dogs, too. Running around everwheres.'

'And they all smell like pig. The people and the dogs, both.'

'And the pigs smell like spiled cabbage.'

'Cabbage, Lord help us. Do they eat anything but coleslaw in this place?'

'I think they eat the pigs, eventually.'

'Yes, after they've gorged em on the cabbage. It's all one big hoop.'

'Hoops? You don't know hoops until you see the dresses on these parlour ladies.'

'I hope I never get the chance.'

'If you do, you'll know you're really stuck. Teatime takes four hours, in this city.'

'I feel like ever time I get in here I'll never get back out.'

'I feel like ever time I get out I'll never go back in.'

'Then why'd you come?' Jude asked. There was silence, and he let it draw out. 'Why'd you come here today?'

Flora narrowed her eyes. She looked away. 'My papa made me.'

'Hogwash,' Jude said. 'I've seen you. Nobody makes you do anything.'

Flora was still looking down. 'Sometimes they do,' she said.

Jude watched her face. 'Well. Whoever does must have a devilish powerful hand to play.'

Flora's mouth was beginning to go weak. 'Devilish powerful,' she agreed, her voice shaking.

Jude saw a single tear-stain darken the blue front of her dress. He reached out an arm to put it around her. Then he drew back, as if stung. Another drop darkened her dress. Another.

Jude watched for a full minute, utterly helpless. Only three more tears fell but each one shook him. Finally, Flora wiped her eyes. 'And here I came out to comfort you,' she said with a laugh.

'Naw,' said Jude. It was the most he could manage.

She looked at him harder. 'Jude,' she said. 'You ain't got to be so—strong about this. You kin be a little afraid. You kin be angry.'

The young man recovered himself. 'This ain't anything,' he said calmly. 'Don't worry. We're going to be all right. My family is.'

She looked up, her face reddened by the tears but still resplendent. Her eyes were the color of the late-winter sky, exactly that color. 'What makes you this way, Jude?' she asked. 'What makes you so—unafraid?'

He smiled. 'It's just a little show I put on. When I'm talking to a pretty girl, mainly.'

She drew away a little. But then his smile began to creep onto her face, a reproduction in a paler material. They had fixed their eyes on each other. They were very close.

A bell rang at the front of the building. The crier's voice. 'The jury has exited the chamber! The jury will read the verdict!'

Flora continued looking into Jude's face, but it had gone suddenly clouded. He looked straight through her now. And he stood up slowly, and turned away, and stepped past the broken barrels and the hogs.

Flora went to Emily and together they went to the court-house. The jury was coming in, more quickly than they had gone out. They wanted this finished; they wanted to go home. One of the tipplers, a redheaded man, stood up to read the verdict before the judge even asked for it. He informed the judge and the members of the public that Nat Quinto was guilty on both counts.

He sat down again. The audience let out a gratified breath. Whether or not it was the outcome they wanted, it was the one they had expected. The judge cleared his throat and looked down his nose at Nat Quinto. He was not actually looking him in the eye, but no one knew that except for the two of them, and the effect worked on the audience. The judge declared that he was sentencing Nathan Quinto to thirty days in prison and a fine of two hundred fifty dollars, payable to the Clerk of Court. He tapped his gavel.

The surprise started quiet but grew. There were shouts of disbelief around the room, dumbfoundment—the noise crested into a general din as Nat Quinto was put in bonds and led out the back door. A man stood up on his seat and hurled an insult at the judge, who gathered up his papers and hurried to his ante-chamber. The jurors seemed unwilling to leave their box.

Outside the disbelief resolved into specific points of contention. Flora came out and stood among them, listening, frantic. 'Thirty days? Thirty days! For fisticuffs!' 'A fine, too.' 'Never mind the fine—thirty days! Why, he'll miss March.' 'And into April.' 'By God, you're right. He'll miss damnnear the whole planting season. He has fifty acres in corn down there, Quinto has. They'll never git it planted.' 'He'll be ruint by this.' 'What're they going to do? What're they going to do?' 'Ruint!'

Then the condemned man's family came outside. Folk stopped their discussion, out of respect. The smaller children stayed close to the mother. Jude was at the back. The young man had regained himself fully; his face was calm and even defiant. He was supporting Lucy with one arm and wrangling a small sister with the other and fending off the press of sympathizers who would have the swallowed the family whole. Still, he found the strength to look out across the courthouse steps and meet Flora's gaze, and meeting it to not quite nod and not quite wink and not quite smile and yet to convey a thing which summed up all such gestures and surpassed them all. Then he was down the steps and gone. But Flora stood and the sorrow and fear and anger fell from her as she watched him all the way down the dusty street.

III.

THE WAGON RIDE HOME was quiet for the Quintos, as was home itself. It was a strange quietness, very empty: something missing, someone. Lucy moved about making a supper that was one portion too small in a house a half-size too large.

Jude and Lucy each had their reasons to be unafraid. Lucy knew that the family could pay her husband's fine without trouble. It might have surprised the cityfolk, but they had plenty of money—they acquired it in the same piddling quantities as the urbanites but lacked ways to spend it. So the stuff just accumulated in a cracked waterpail under their bed. The years of coins would cover the extraordinary fine. There would be enough left over to hire a hand or two to get them through Nat's absence, with only one sacrifice: Lucy and Nat had promised each other long ago that if they had money at such a time in their lives, they would send some of their children up to the school in Middleburg. Samuel, nine years old, seemed likely for it—he had a grave and priestly air, and had taken to all of Lucy's basic reading lessons with ease. But now that plan would have to be jettisoned, for the sake of all their stomachs. Lucy understood this and accepted it and was calm in that knowledge.

Jude for his part did not know about the waterpail full of coins. He had never thought about his family having money, just as he had never thought about his family lacking money: he had never needed to consider the topic one way or the other. His calmness came from another source. He simply knew beyond the last dead doubt that he could apply his strength to the land, plough it and harrow it flat and sow it full entirely by himself, and the family would suffer no shortfall. He would take up his father's implements and accomplish alone the thing which they had meant to do together. That was his certainty, and his calm. That was why he ate in such thoughtful silence, chewing slowly.

After supper Jude and Lucy sat on the porch together in the cold lamplit dark. Jude was patching a hole in a seedbag. Lucy was doing the same, and sighing.

'I'll go see him the day after tomorrow,' she said at last. 'I'll see how he's eating and how he's sleeping. Take him another jacket. They'd better let me in.'

Jude glanced at his mother's face in the candlelight glow. 'They'll let you in. But you ain't got to think about him freezing. He'll be warmer there than here. I'd be more worried about him catching a heat stroke. That jail cell's jist a room next to the sheriff's office, and they keep that place right cozy. The danged mary-boys.'

Lucy went on, needing to talk. 'I'm gonter buy the two ox we been talking about, while I'm up there. And I guess I'll see about finding someone to hire on.'

'Hire on,' Jude said. He quit with the needle and the sackcloth. 'You're going to hire someone on.'

'Well, yes, Jude. I'd say we've got to.'

'Hire a man, and pay him?'

'Yes, son. We've got to get some help on this place.'

'Ma,' Jude said. 'Have we got the money for that, and the ox, and dad's fine too?'

'Yes,' said Lucy. But then she said, 'No,' and her face crumpled. She tried to say the word yes again but was overcome, and the young man held her as she began to weep. Her sobs were deep and musical. Not yet asleep, Samuel came outside at the sound. Jude nodded back toward the inside of the house. The boy kept watching for a moment but then withdrew.

Soon Lucy was drying her eyes; she never cried for long. She apologized in a thick voice and told Jude about the pail of coins, and also about what she and Nat had told each other they'd do with it. Jude listened, his arm still around her shoulders. Then, when she had fully gathered herself, he went back to his own chair and sat down again. He stretched his legs out in the murk and cracked his knuckles cheerily.

'Ma,' he said. 'We don't have to hire nobody and spend that money. I'll jist do it.'

She was silent awhile. 'You'll jist do it,' she repeated at last. As if the words had taken that long to reach her through the cold and humid air.

'Yes,' Jude said. But Lucy did not say anything, so he had to go on. 'I'll plough the fields, the north and east and south, and I'll harrow them, and we'll do the planting. That's all.' Still she said nothing. Her silence grated on him. 'I'm nineteen years old,' he said.

'I know how old you are, boy.'

'So I'm a man. A man, like he was, when you two first came here. When you got the land open, and did everything by yourselves, and lived. And if—'

'And if he did it, so kin you,' the woman helped.

'That's right,' said Jude.

'We almost starved, Jude,' Lucy said. 'We didn't know it then, but we almost starved.'

'I know, you told me how hard it was. But you've got the place open now, and humming. And you've got children now. The children help.'

'Yes, Nat got himself some children to help around the place. And do you know what else he got? New tools, at a price. New livestock. And a contract to fill for a thousand bushels of corn to the hogkeeper. And more land to do it all on. Do you know how many acres we was planting, when we first come down? In the big old religious days, in them times we've told you about over and over agin? Eight. Your father struggled and most died trying to make eight acres work. Do you know how many we plant now?'

Now Jude was quiet. So she answered her own question. 'Fifty.'

'Fifty,' Jude said at last, 'and I've walked ever last one. And I've dropped a creek of sweat in ever last one myself. Mama,' he said, and turned to her. 'Simeon grew up, and jined the cowhunters. Samantha grew up, and left with Hooper. They grew to adults, and you saw it, and let them do what they wanted. Well, this is what I want. To stay here and help us through this. With my own work, and not with the money you've earned and saved. And I kin do it, too.' He was standing up, he discovered, and addressing his mother with a kind of furious boldness which was not his own. Lucy had never seen this from him. He had not seen it from himself. But now it had emerged and would not withdraw.

'I kin do it and I will do it. You see that, I know you do. They've got him in jail but that ain't a cause for you to spile your fortune and give up what you planned for Samuel, for the schooling. It's a cause for me to step forward and do what I'm fixing to do. And that's all there is to say.' His anger began to falter but still he did not move.

'Who's got you talking this way?' Lucy said at last, in a low, knowing voice.

'Ma'am?' said Jude.

'Who is it?' she asked again.

The young man opened his mouth but said nothing. He turned to lean on the railing of the porch and breathed in as if injured.

Lucy watched him for a little while. Then she got up. 'I'll talk to your father about all of this tomorrow,' she said. She touched him on the shoulder. 'Good night, Jude.'

No response. The woman might as well have touched a piece of warm marble. She went inside and left the young man lolling his head against the night.

Flora took her tongue-lashing stoically. Too stoically. Her mother joined in the game, but still she held up. This lack of a reaction unnerved both parents. After half an hour of it they backed away and retired to their separate rooms, perturbed.

They didn't know what to make of her the next day either. When she came out of her room Jake looked at her with concern. Her blue eyes were swimming, full of some bright secret. 'Papa,' she said. 'Papa, I want to tell you something.'

Primrose was taken aback. There truly must be something wrong with the girl. He came up the steps to her. 'What's the matter, dear? Something's the matter.'

'Yes, Papa, it is. Something horrible. I only hope you'll understand.'

'Of course I'll understand, darling. I'm your father. Now, what is it?'

Jude was harnessing the two mules when his mother came to him. She was looking at something up the road. 'Well, son,' she said. 'You've talked about being the man of the house and all. Now, here's your shot. Go head, boy, aim true.'

Jake Primrose was coming up the road on a big grey horse. A gloved child on a mule rode beside him, struggling to keep up. Primrose rode straight up to them. He stayed in his saddle.

'Good morning, Jake,' Lucy said, to start things off.

'Good morning, Lucy,' the cattleman said, touching the brim of his hat. But then he turned his gaze to Jude.

'And you're Jude,' Jake said.

'That's right, yes sir.'

'My name's Jacob Primrose, as I guess ye know.'

'Yes sir.'

'And I guess you also know,' the man said, 'that I am the father of a young lady name of Flora. Nineteen year old, tall, yaller headed, eyes blue, right pretty. You know this, I think.'

'Yes.'

{ 297 }

'I guess I ain't got to tell you what all else you know, that she is set to be married to Mister John Gallatin of Harrisburg, Pennsylvania.'

'I didn't know that,' said Jude.

'Well, now you do. And so I'll bid ye leave off your chasing and let the girl be in peace. Your actions along them lines is offending to her sense of honor, and so you must quit. I thank ye, young man.' He nodded and pretended to turn to go, though his head remained cocked for Jude's response.

It took a moment, but Jude got it out. 'Me, sir? Chasing?'

Primrose paused and looked down at Jude over his left shoulder. 'That's right. And there ain't no need to deny it. How you done sought her out. Full of outrageousness. Followed her through the streets of Newnansville, making heart-confessins.'

Jude looked at the cattleman a long time. 'But who—who said that?'

Primrose smiled down on the lad. 'She did, son.'

'She?'

'She, I say it agin! Why, she done told her dear pappy everthing. How you pursued her in town, during your father's trial no less! How you sought her at the court, and distraught her with your passionate talk, and your eye-looks, all while they was deciding your poor daddy's fate! And you may even have made some worse statements to her in time, but they called out the jury, and so she went inside. Thank God! Because your passionate talk—that's how she said it—might of all the way overwhelmed her senses—that's how she said it.'

Jude blinked. 'And she told you all this, to tell me?'

'That's right, to pass on to you,' Primrose said triumphantly. 'To cut this foolishness off at the root. So take your tight trousers and go make sheep-eyes at someone else, son, Flora'll have none of it.' He turned to go again but remembered something else. 'Ah, and by the way. She told me that when you had her a-cornered, and she said she wanted to see you agin, very soon—well, that was jist a lie to get away from you. She told me to inform you of that specially.'

Something in Jude's face made Primrose soften. 'Now, boy. Now, don't go getting all mournful about this. Take it as a lesson. You ain't fer Flora. You're a handsome enough lad, though, and fine on the muscle, jist like your old pa. Do yourself a favor and find ye a girl a little nearer to you. A little more of your own material—do you follow? There's plenty of them around, trust me.' And with that he turned and started back up the Quintos' drive, trailing the Negro child who had served no purpose whatsoever apart from being a human token of Primrose's wealth. They were not out of earshot before Primrose started saying to the boy: 'Well! What do ye say to that? Looked like he'd been hit with a brickbat. Stunned, the poor ruffian.'

When Jake Primrose was around the bend in the trail, Lucy threw her hands in the air. 'Jude!'

Her son turned. 'Ma, listen. I don't know what he's saying, I never chased her at the court. We spoke together, but—'

'I know, I know, I know,' Lucy moaned. 'I know, drat it all. I know a love trick when I see one. O Jude, Jude—the Primrose girl? The cattleman's daughter?'

'Ma,' protested Jude. 'Ma, nothing's happened.'

'That's what you think, you thickheaded Quinto,' the woman half-wailed. 'But she knows better. And now I know better too, and ain't got to be told who's got you acting so—bunched up, lately.' She pressed a hand to her forehead. 'O Lord, help me. My husband's in jail and my son's come a-cropper a Primrose. The world's gone mad. I'm going to Newnansville.' And with that she got up onto the bench of the cart and harried the horses away from the house at an incredible speed.

Flora paced. She did not pace outdoors; she paced in her room. That was the change in her. In seasons past she might have been found in some far woods or by some farther creek. But now she was containing herself. She walked back and forth from the window to the bed, talking to Emily, being talked to by her. Finally the woman put her finger to her lips and said *Hush*.

Flora stared at her, and then at the window where the woman was looking, listening. There was a horse coming up the drive. Flora brushed her hair until it hung straight. Instantaneously she emptied her face of all its earlier emotion. She stepped in front of the looking glass, to confirm that this was so. Satisfied, she walked out into the common room.

Jake Primrose was coming in. He saw his daughter standing right where she was supposed to be, and a smile of pleasure came over his face. 'I'm back,' he said.

'Yes, Papa,' the young woman said.

'Well, Flora, you done lay a bruising on the boy.' He shook his head, removing his jacket. 'You ought to of seen his face.'

The girl kept her composure. 'What—what did he say?'

'Well, first there was a little hemming and hawing, of course, like he didn't know what I was talking about. But then a change came over him, sudden,' the man said. 'Sorter sad, but— maybe not—I don't know, he didn't say much. He looked like I'd hit him right square in the stomach, the poor boy. Anyway, he's sorted out now. He won't be coming around here with them sheep-eyes, I promise you.'

Flora had not moved or shown a smile or a frown all the time he talked. Jake saw this and looked her over. 'All the same,' he said, more quietly. 'The boy may be poor, not worth a chip off of old Gallatin's bootheel, but—he's fine-looking, and mannish. There's some girls would be led into foolishness by him. I applaud ye, Flora, you've kept your head. You've done as you were supposed to.' He leaned and kissed her forehead. 'It warms your pappy's heart.'

He hung his jacket on a peg and sighed. 'A fellow's almost got to feel sorry for the boy—that look on his face, fah! But it's the way it had to be, it's all the way it had to be.'

The man went into his sideroom. Flora remained where she was. She had never let her face waver, but now it reddened, flushed with the blood she could not control.

Ox teams were hitched to both the walking plough and the harrow. His mother gone, Jude came to give the animals a last handful of feed. He spoke to them for a time, explained what was before them. He explained what the challenges would be, explained his own deficiencies and weaknesses. He explained it all. 'But we're gonter get it done, despite me. Won't we. We will.'

He went and fetched Dan, his next-younger brother. Jude told the boy—still a boy, still skinny, fifteen and moonfaced— what they must do. 'I'm on set out with the plough. Ten minutes later, foller after me with the harrow. Jist foller right on the row I made and let the harrow level it. Make sure to look down plenty and see that the teeth are dragging true, and nothing's caught in them. All right? And make sure you wait that ten minutes before setting out after me, otherwise you'll run up on me with that harrow. All right?'

'All right,' Dan said quietly. He looked out across the fields. The boy had run the harrow before, but only once or twice. And never during the real work, the work of spring, which had such immense repercussions.

Jude touched him on the shoulder. 'Hey. Dan. Look, you'll get out there and you'll bungle for a while, but then you'll find your step, and the whole thing'll go by before you're ready for it. Just remember what Dad says. Don't hurry and don't worry, but make ever stroke count. All right?'

Dan looked up. He nodded.

'All right. Jist follow my line. I'll see you after a while.' And Jude put his hand to the plough.

Out in the field Jude followed the oxen on their course. The bright share cut through the groundcover and rolled it open to the greyish sandy soil. The mouldboard scoured clean of its endless rush of earth. By noon the sun fell straight down into the open tilth and Jude was dropping sweat in the blustery cold. At the butt end of that field was a trickling creek and he let the oxen off to drink from it. He called for Dan to go home and eat. For himself he had packed a cotton cloth with four biscuits and one big slice of fatback. He ate it in the shade with the oxen. Not fifteen minutes later he was up again and looping the beasts back into their yokes. They bellowed and complained but he cut a switch and made them go.

When he went inside at the end of the day he found the older children involved in making some greens, hoecakes, and salt fish out of the brine barrels. Lucette, sixteen, was taking great pride in corralling the children and making the meal in her mother's absence. It came time to sit down and eat, and Jude said a mumbled grace. There was something a little cold in the meal without either parent present. They rushed through it, eager to be away from the table. All except for Jude, who lingered, eating every last scrap of food on everyone else's plate, and Dan, whom he urged to do the same. 'You'll need this,' he told the boy. 'Eat all you kin.'

The moon was up by the time Jude finished his supper. He went outside and stood in the brightness. He drew out two of the oxen which had not been worked that day and yoked them and set to harrowing. In the cold light the work was easily done. The wooden teeth sifted through the thick sand with a shushing sound and lay the earth down flat. He finished the field in a couple of hours and without pausing moved down the forest path to the next. The oxen did not seem to mind the night work any more than Jude, their surroundings familiar and yet transformed, the pale field inverted by the moonlight. Finally he finished harrowing everything that had been ploughed during the day. He whooped once like a bard owl, yawned, and undid the oxen. He rode back to the barn drooping from their shoulders and fell straight into his bed. Dawn seemed to hold off a while but when it came at last he got up loudly, stretching his arms out halfway across the little room.

Lucy came back midday. She had been crying, though she had stopped it before she arrived at the house. She found Jude finishing the tillage of the second field. 'Good Lord,' she said to her two sons. 'How? I didn't think you'd finish the first one.' Jude didn't say anything. Dan smiled but was quiet too.

'Did you talk to Dad about what I said?' Jude asked.

'Yes.'

'What'd he say.'

The woman pursed her lips. 'He said it wouldn't be no harm to hold off a little while before hiring somebody,' she said. 'A little while,' she repeated. 'And then we'll see. He left it up to me.'

Jude watched her. 'So we're going to hold off a while.'

'And then we'll see.'

'All right,' he said. He turned to his brother. 'Come on, Dan.' They returned to their work. Their mother stood watching.

John Gallatin arrived at the Primroses' at noon, as scheduled, with his top-heavy face shining. Primrose eagerly told him what the meal would be: they'd planned a light lunch, a little seated conversation, perhaps a walk in the orange grove or a ride in the wagon. But then Flora emerged from her room.

She swung into the parlour with her eyes wide. 'Papa, Papa, oh, Papa,' she said. 'Look.'

She was holding a small wooden box. It looked to be carved out of persimmon or some other hard wood. She came and set it down on the table and stepped back as if it might explode.

'Flora, what's wrong? What is that?' Primrose asked.

Gallatin put his hand near the young lady's back, worried she might swoon. She had a swooning look.

'That thing, that thing,' the girl said. 'Oh, Papa! That loathsome boy.'

'Who? What? What is it?'

'One of his little scamps come up to my winder,' she said, moving past Gallatin's outstretched hand. 'Said I been sent to give you this from old Jude Quinto. I tried to say No, I won't have it, but he jist tossed it in my room and ran away. Oh devil!

Oh Papa! Look.' Flora threw open the lid. Inside was a piece of folded paper. 'It's a love letter.'

Both men recoiled from the cream-colored thing. It took a moment before either one could speak. Primrose found his tongue first. 'Why, the sonofabitch,' he sputtered, forgetting himself.

Then came the Pennsylvanian, in a harsh whisper: 'Treachery. Infamy. Devilry. Black devilry.'

Flora observed them both with a haughty look. 'Yes, devilry. But I won't have it. I've got to send it back, to spite the beast—send it back jist as it came. He must have his pretty box thrown in the dust, and his love letter flown at him. Why, I've got half a mind to go and do it my ownself—'

'No,' cried Gallatin.

'No,' cried Primrose. 'You mustn't, Flora. You mustn't venture nowhere near the creatur. I'll go and deliver it back to him, with thanks.'

'No!' exclaimed Gallatin. Both Primroses turned to him. 'No,' he said again, his jaw trembling. 'I shall deliver it to him. I am—the only man to do it. No other. I shall go.'

Flora looked excited, a little surprised. 'Yes, Mister Gallatin,' she said. 'Why, yes. If you give it to him, it'll jist be that much better. He'll see you and know what type of man he has to deal with.'

Gallatin nodded once. He strode over to the box and picked it up. 'I shall return it immediately. I shall leave no doubts in his mind. But first, let us read what he dared say to thee.' He took the letter out of the box, feeling for the wax seal.

'No,' Flora shouted. 'No—my dear man. God's sakes, don't open that seal.'

Both men squinted at her. 'But—whyever not?'

'Don't you see? He'll think I've opened it. A lady must never open sich a letter. It'd show him that I'm curious, that I want to see what he's written about me. It'll show that my soul is open to his ugly praisings and flattery. No, Mister Gallatin, take it back to him unopened. That way he'll know that my heart ain't a bit friendly to his ways.'

Gallatin stared at her. A bald look of joy spread over his face. 'Yes. Of course you're right. You are quite perfectly right—your virtue has seen straight through to the correct path. I'll do as you say.' He put the unopened letter back in the box and closed the lid. 'I'll go at once,' he said. 'This cannot be delayed. This foolish passion must be snuffed before it can progress another inch.'

Jake seemed alarmed by the rich man's attitude. Perhaps he was considering how the gentleman might fare against the strong Quinto youth. 'Well, now, John, oughtn't you wait a little while?' he urged. 'Cool off jist a whit—I mean, sit and eat a little lunch, first. Look, it's laid out already. Lookee there, fried chicken.' But the man was already heading for the door.

'I shall return when I have set this nonsense right,' he said.

Jake threw up his hands. 'Well, go if ye got to,' he sighed. 'But hold, take Frank. He knows the way to Quinto's, you don't know where to head.'

'Yes,' said Gallatin, frowning at this unwanted practicality. 'True enough. Give me a man.'

Emily's brother Frank was sent for, to escort the Pennsylvanian on the long ride to Quinto's. At last they came up to the cornfields, where young Jude was ploughing with the oxen. 'There, there,' Frank said, pointing. 'That's your man, marster. That's your scoundrel.' Gallatin nodded grimly and set his horse forward, clutching the wooden box tightly, almost jealously.

Jude saw these visitors and waved, though he kept on ploughing. At the edge of the field the gentleman dismounted and waited while Jude came up. Where the row ended the young man let his oxen step and came up wiping his hands on his trousers. 'Hidy,' he said. Gallatin did not say a word but produced the wooden box and threw it in the dirt at Jude's feet.

Jude looked down at the box. Then he looked up at the stranger. It was several seconds before he could speak. 'What's that?'

Gallatin turned his chin up. 'You dare not ask that question, rogue. No, thou darest not.'

Jude squinted, trying to form another question. 'Who're you?' he managed finally.

'I am John Gallatin. Yes, John Gallatin, the very same.'

Jude looked down at the box again. He bent and picked it up.

'Yes, yes, you self-deceived deceiver. Open it and see your billet-doux returned, flung back in your face.'

'Billet—what?' said Jude. 'Speak plainly, man, I cain't bear this.'

'Open it!' Gallatin demanded.

Jude opened the lid. There lay the letter.

'Yes, fiend. There is your billet-doux. And do you see— unopened! She did not wish to taste your evil flattery. She pleaded with me—yes, me, her betrothed!—to return it to you immediately. She did not wish to sully her fingers with your filthy work.'

'She?' said Jude.

'She, yes, she,' the man said. 'She, your sham love, my true one, Flora.'

'Oh, Lord,' Jude said, and covered his eyes.

The man looked upon him in triumph. 'Yes, man, yes. Your scheme has come to nothing. Your game has been undone. You loved her for her beauty and comeliness, maybe, but you for-got—ah, fool! you forgot the maidenly virtue which is the crown of her beauty.'

Jude just stood there, rubbing his neck and looking down into the box. After a moment of this Gallatin relented. 'Now, do not think that I altogether condemn you. Your action was vile, but your motives are plain to understand. You were entranced with a creature who is incomparably spirited, graceful, beautiful.'

Jude nodded. 'She's all of that,' he said.

'Beyond any other! Beautiful, and truehearted, and pure.'

'And clever,' Jude added.

'Clever, yes! She is clever—yes, you are correct, man.'

'Right clever,' Jude said, peering at the man's face. 'But—she's troublesome too, sometimes. Don't ye find?'

The Pennsylvanian smiled a dreamy smile. 'Troublesome? Oh, perhaps, perhaps. But only in the most innocent, girlish, harmless of ways. And in the end, she always does well.'

'Yes, I spect she does,' said Jude.

'Well,' the rich man said with a deep, satisfied breath. 'I have done my duty. I told her I would ensure her honor, and I've done it. I applaud you for bowing to my superior claims.' The man sniffed.

'No, thank you, sir,' Jude said. 'For setting me to rights.' He gave a stiff bow.

With that acknowledgment Gallatin got back on his horse and rode off toward the road. The slave followed him on his mule. And all the way across the field Frank was a-spasm with such poorly suppressed laughter that it was amazing the rich man did not hear him and turn around.

My Dear Jude

I guess this letter might surprise you. Both in what it says and how I have sent it. But I pray you ll understand me and what I have done. Though I must certain seem never so rash and foolish please belive there was no better way to reach you and waiting for another chance would be death to me.

I am in bondege to a father I detest in a house I detest and am doomed to a even worse thing which I cant even bare to think of let alone tell. My fate is sealed in the space of a month. Of course I would refuse it but my father is unspeakeable coldhearted and has made threat against someone dear to me if I do not obey. Despite the risks of failure I had decided to run away from my home to escape this al together.——Yet I no longer wish to run away. for I have found something dear to me and do not wish to depart from it. O do you not undestand?——Dear Jude in our meeting there s a chink in the dark and cheerlessnesse of the world and am I a fool to see it? Am I a fool to think that life is someway not lost to me forever? Jude I get strength from the few minutes of our meeting and survive upon them like others have bread——

If you have any mercy in your soul do send word
someway somehow. I would see you again.—

Forgive my forward ways but something tells me that
you of all souls will not scorn me

Flora.

Jude read the note, slowly, laboriously. Then he replaced it in its
wooden box and set the box under a tree. He went back to the
plough and started down the next row and did not pause again
until noon. At the end of every row he looked at the box where
it sat in the shade.

He ate his meal in silence that night. He had much less
appetite than usual, so he ate like a normal person, spooning
his stew listlessly. His mother looked at him from time to
time.

After supper he lingered on the porch. When young Samuel
came outside, he took him under the arm and told the boy to
come on. Glancing all directions for Lucy, he took the boy out
to the trees. He crouched down before him, staring him in the
eye.

'Samuel,' Jude said after a silence. 'Do you know how to get
to the Primrose place?'

'No,' said the boy. 'Are they far?'

'Not so far,' Jude said. 'I'll tell you the way. And I'll tell you
jist what to say when you get there.' He sniffed. 'If you're up to
the job, that is.'

Flora lay down on the bed. Emily had just told her everything
that her brother Frank had recounted. It was a cool day and the

window was open and the breeze dallied her dresshem and the curtains, and for a while those were the only things in the room that moved.

She emerged dry-eyed at suppertime. The great round word which had been pursed in her mouth for so long was gone. Now her mouth could open, and breath went in and out.

'You ain't been eating enough,' Jake Primrose said to her as they sat down to the meal. 'Finish your food. I don't want my daughter looking skinny on her marriage day.'

'Yes, Papa,' Flora said, and devoured a catfish whole.

It was night when the boy wandered onto the property. It was too dark and he was too small for anyone to notice or care. In the shadows he inquired after Flora's window and then he came right up to it and tapped on the frame.

She opened it and looked down on the boy with his dark eyes and honeycolored hair. He spoke his piece. 'Jude says he'll come to you after he ploughs our east field. He says he's gon finish them in three days from today. He says he could never scorn you because—because you're all he thinks of. And so on the fourth night from tonight he'll come.'

'No,' said Flora. 'Baby, tell him no, he'll not come all the way here. I'll come out toward you—halfway down the New Smyrna road. At the big oak at the crossroads, I'll meet him there. All right? Will you tell him that?'

'Yes, ma'am,' said the boy. He turned to go.

'Wait,' said Flora. She leaned so far out of the window that her hips balanced on the sill and took the boy's face in her hands and kissed him on the forehead, beneath the curling hair. Then she let him go and he sprinted off into the darkness.

* * *

It was an hour's swift ride to the crossroads oak. Flora approached the tree with caution, swinging a wide loop on her little jaded marshtackie. She had left off riding the animal four years ago, when her father explained that horseback was incorrect for a young lady. She'd been confined to carriages and wagons ever since. Still, the horse seemed to remember her.

There was no one standing near the tree. She dismounted from the marshtackie and let it graze, holding herself in the cold. Her breath was visible and it came a little quick.

A rider came galloping up the road. Jude. He heeled his horse to a stop at the tree and vaulted out of the saddle. He saw her riderless horse grazing a little ways off, ran toward it, stopped, turned all the way around, and froze there for a moment, his feet akimbo, just breathing.

Flora stepped out from the trees. 'Jude,' she said.

He jumped, and actually let out a shout. Flora stepped farther out into the moonlight. Jude remained where he was as she came toward him. He relaxed, hung his head, drew a breath. She approached him smiling.

'Sorry,' he said.

'Hello, Jude,' she said. 'You're acting funny.'

'I know,' he said. He looked around the clearing. 'It's this meeting in the woods, the dark. When Samuel told me you said to meet here, and that he didn't say no—I about killed him.'

She took a step forward. 'Why, whatever's the problem? Was you worried about me? I got my gun, you know.'

'You do?'

She smiled mildly. 'Yes sir, a pistol. A knife too. Or did ye think I would go to meet a strange man at night unarmed?'

Jude looked her over. 'But—where?'

She shrugged. 'Girls' skirts are funny places, Jude,' she said, and smoothed the fabric over her knees. 'Anyway, there wasn't much choice. You could either meet me out here and be scared. Or ye could meet me at my house and get a skin full of buckshot.'

He snorted. 'Or I could of stayed home, and you could come all the way to my winder. You could put on some trousers and do the courting proper, pistoleer.'

Flora tilted her head dangerously. 'Or we could jist not meet at all,' she said.

'I wish you wouldn't say that,' Jude said simply.

'I don't mean that at all,' Flora said, almost simultaneously.

'I've thought of nothing but this,' Jude said.

'You've been in my mind all day,' Flora said, overlapping him again. Then she put out her hand, as he reached too, and they pressed them together like partners in a pavane. They stood like that for a moment, looking at each other.

Then Flora moved away a few steps. 'Come on,' she said. 'Let's go where I was afore. I liked it there.' And she wheeled around and started for the trees.

There was a log there, beneath an overhang of laurelcherry. Flora looked like she might be starting to regret such intimate quarters but the young man came in chatty. 'Well, it's been good hearing so much from you. Lately.'

'What? Oh. Yes.'

'You've been clever.'

'Hum. And I've almost been caught.'

'Caught? Pshaw. Not by that elder fellow. He believed it to the hilt.'

Flora nodded.

'I couldn't figure him out.' Jude laughed. 'He was jist steaming mad at me, and I couldn't see his meaning. He threw that box down at my feet. Kept calling you his beloved and sich, that bony old—' But he trailed off. The girl was not looking at him.

'He's the fellow, isn't he,' Jude said.

Flora did not make a single sound or motion.

'Flora—' Jude began. 'I'm sorry, but—how did that happen?'

It took her a while, but finally she spoke. 'I ain't sure I feel like telling you.'

'I want to know.'

Flora let out a cold hard laugh. 'I liked him, at first,' she said. 'Mister Gallatin. The way you'd like an uncle. And he had a pianoforte in his house, that made it nice. And so even after I knew he, he, he wanted me, I let it go on. Because of that cussed pianoforte.'

Jude shook his head. 'But—what happened?' he asked.

'What happened is my father needs him, someway. Needs him badly. My brother got wise and ran off, so there's no man to be my father's man but the one I bring in. And no other one will do but Gallatin.' She sighed. 'The awfullest, rawbonedest railroadman to ever live.'

'But what happened? He proposed to you—didn't he? And you said yes, didn't you?

'No. I didn't.'

'What?'

'He asked, and I didn't say nothing. Jist broke down and started crying.'

'Shoot. And what'd he do?'

'He started crying too.' She shook her head. 'He was happy, I was ruined. There was no one there to notice the difference.'

But this was still not enough. 'Flora,' Jude exclaimed, and rose to his feet. 'Why don't you jist tell me what happened? All this that you've told me, it'd work on some girls—they'd marry a bony old rich man if someone leaned on them hard enough. But you, Flora—I bet you'd marry a man jist to make your daddy poor on purpose. It don't make sense. What is this devilish hand you say he's playing? What is it?'

When he grew quiet again her eyes pooled with light from the moon, filled with it, until she dropped her head and let the tears fall straight down.

'Hadjo.'

'What?'

'Hadjo,' she said again. She was sobbing.

He looked on, fearful, uncomprehending.

'He's got my brother's life in his hand, and he don't even know it. There's charges on Hadjo and a reward out for him, and my father says he'll turn him over. Says if I buck him, he'll give him to Addison and them. Jude! He'll let them have him.'

'His son,' Jude said. 'He wouldn't let them bastards take his son, would he?'

Flora balled her fists over her eyes. 'He don't call him son, don't think of him that way no more. All he sees is one more way to get me to do what he wants. And he's right, too, oh God, he's right, I couldn't live with myself if Hadjo got hurt on my account, if Addison got him because of me—' she broke off, her face contorting. 'But you don't understand. My brother. My only friend, most of the time—you don't understand—'

'You're wrong,' Jude put in quietly. 'I do understand.' He moved to her, put his hands on her shoulders. 'You cain't let him be hurt. I see that. And your father saw it too. He got you, good and hard. He knew jist where to stab.'

It was minutes before her sobs stopped. He put his hand on the ridge of her spine, ran his palm up the length of it. At last she spoke.

'You're right. He has me. I cain't even struggle like a—a trapped animal would. I've got to jist stand, and smile, and blink my eyes, and try not to talk. And I cain't spy a way outen it. I ain't strong enough. I ain't clever enough.'

But Jude shook his head. 'Like hell,' he said, and stood up. 'Like hell you ain't. Is this Flora Primrose? Are you yourself? I don't know you much, but Lord I know you better than that. You the one fooled two grown men with a love letter beneath their noses. Not clever enough? Not strong enough? Why, you must not know what you've done. You've kept me upright for days now. I'd never have the heart to do what I'm doing if you weren't in the world. I'd of flipped belly-up after my daddy got taken away from the planting, like any sensible person would. It's meeting you that's turned my head this way—you're the stubbornest, gunpowderyest girl I ever known. Don't you see?' He stepped back, shook his head. 'But, enough. The tilling don't matter, I don't matter. You're the one who's got to know. We jist need to figure a way.'

She looked up. 'We?' she said quietly.

Jude took a breath. 'We,' he said, slowly. 'We, yes.' And then they came together in the near-dark, and hid their faces from the moonlight.

In a moment Flora pulled away. 'But, Jude. We won't see each other. You're ploughing. I'll never see you til the fields are done.'

'Yes, you will,' Jude said. 'You'll see me the night after next.' He pointed. 'Standing right over there, by that oak. Do you see?'

Flora smiled. 'Yes.'

Again Jude leaned in to kiss her, but this time she broke away and ran out toward the road and the horses. 'Night after next,' she cried when she was good and gone.

Jude stood clutching at the air, gasping it. He could only watch as she went to her horse, mounted up, rode away.

He stood there a long time. But eventually he went out to his horse also and headed south. Each of them half-slept in the saddle then, or sat and dreamed, letting the horses walk them to their homes.

Dan could not keep up with Jude in the harrowing work. He would probably be capable next year; next year he could take up Jude's old role and harrow behind his father. But this season he could not quite hold up. Sometimes he would do only half a day and then be spelled by Lucette or young Samuel. Lucy took up the harrow when she could, but she was more often marshaling the children to prepare the vegetable beds, tending to the calving herds, or preparing the huge cribs of seed corn for planting. Some days Jude would harrow his own rows after he ploughed them, so that they would not stay open to dry and leach in the sun.

Many of Nat's old friends came by the place. They came out of love, yes, and to help if they could, but they also came out of morbid interest. They came to see—and say they tried to prevent—Quinto's famous catastrophe. But they found no catastrophe. By the middle of March the fields were two-thirds tilled. Fields which would sustain a family of ten and fulfill a buyer's contract for one thousand bushels were being cultivated by a lad of nineteen, with the sometime help of his undergrown brothers and sisters and one hardy goodwife. The men came, and saw, and marveled, and hurried away—back to their own fields, which possibly were not so well advanced at that date. The smoothness and straightness of the rows convicted their own wayward hearts. Before they hurried away, some men would run out to Jude with a cup of cool water and hand it to him and watch the boy drink, gratified, glad to do something. Then they would clap him on the strong shoulder and smile with him, saying You do what you can, boy, I'll be back agin at sowing time to make sure it's all right. And Jude would drink and smile back, seeming somehow not to hear them—not discourteous, merely distant. He's like a sleepwalker, they would say to Lucy. And yet good God amighty look at them fields.

Lucy would nod and murmur her agreement: He does seem a little tired, doesn't he. She would smile, and say nothing more, though she knew the truth. Knew that at night the young man hardly slept for love. That sometimes the vision of the girl kept him awake and sighing atop his bed, but that other times it was the real girl, solid and bodily, twenty miles from home under the crossroads oak. That during those late-winter nights with the waning moon and the fields too dark for tilling he'd go to the appointed tree and spend his soul out with Flora Primrose under the blueblack sky, talking and talking, laughing and talking, crying and talking, kissing and kissing, visible to each other only by the tracework faintness of the failing moon.

The young man promised himself he'd sleep a month when this was over. If it ever would be. His father had been in jail twenty days out of the forty. In ten more days, after the new moon, it would be time to plant—whether they were ready or not. The young man talked to his brothers. He talked to himself. He sometimes fell unconscious over meals. Other times he ate more than they had in the house. The children looked at this strange Jude, asleep at the table or wolfishly devouring, and they whispered to each other behind their hands.

Things turned unseasonably hot after the middle of March. It displeased everyone to be sweating all of a sudden. Things were amiss on the Primrose estate. Jake did not like how his herds were yielding. Pauline was fretful about the wedding, only three weeks away. She had never had a wedding herself—she and Jake had been married by a chaplain in Carolina, happy and quick, like normal people—and since Hadjo was gone, this was her only shot. She was mortally anxious about it all and making everybody else anxious too. Gallatin stopped in sometimes but he only made things worse. He learned to stay away.

Then there was Flora. Flora, in the center of it all, the maiden for whom the flowers were gathered, the heiress for whom the herds were counted. She stood still while it spun all around her. She answered questions with short, helpful responses. What did she think, a string band or choir singers? 'String band.' What for the main course, beef, fish or pig? 'Pig.' Yellow tablecloths or blue? 'Yaller.' False silver on the table or false gold? 'Gold.' Did she care if the Henleys were invited, from up in Jacksonville? 'No, I don't care, they kin come,' she said. 'Let everyone come, Mama. I hope they all come.'

And so the girl went right along, mild-mannered, a little aloof, answering questions, letting things be arranged, not angry anymore, not even tearful, though sleeping quite a bit during the day. Jake Primrose was surprised. He had always believed that he could make her marry Gallatin, but he had expected it to be harder than this. Outside observers felt cheated. It was as if they had paid admission to a tragedy and the female lead had simply decided not to drown herself. It was astounding, and a little unnerving.

The only tense time came when they traveled to Saint Augustine to fit Flora for her dress. She specifically asked for Saint Augustine, for the latinate fabrics there. Newnansville would be much less expensive, as Jacob said, but Flora raged against the ugly silk and tulle of that city. At last her father bowed to her demands, privately pleased that she was beginning to take such interest in the particulars of her wedding. They got up a carriage and headed for the coast.

There was a dressmaker on the central street, and Primrose led his daughter toward it from the stables. They were nearing the place when a voice called out from inside of a saloon.

'Jake, Jake.' Primrose turned. It was a man of about his age, but ragged, with a gap in his teeth and dull piggish eyes. 'Jake, old boy, it's Pete Smith. Your man Smith, don't you know me?'

Primrose allowed his hand to be taken, shaken. 'Smith,' he said. 'Yes.' He did not quite stop walking.

'I hoped to meet you here, Jake,' the man said with a grin, as he hurried to fall in with them. 'Yes, I told these chaps around here I had a lookout for you. Said to them Don't I know Jake Primrose? Why, we're old friends, stewed in the same pot. You remember them old time days, Jake, around Missus Monroe's good table, and hiding in trees, and running them cows up out of Indin territory, and—'

'I remember,' Jake said.

'Of course you do. But look here, Jake, I got a piece of news. Listen now. I was down in Punta Gorda, and I met a feller. Young feller. Looked at him and looked at him. And I'll be damned if—I said Look here, I'll be damned if you ain't a Primrose. Young feller, so high. Favored just like his pappy. He was running under a different name, but I was never missing him. So I goes up to him and say Look here, I'm Pete Smith, don't you know me? Says I, I'm one of your pappy's very oldest friends, stewed in the same pot. But I said Hi now, your old man's the biggest grandest cowman in Floridy, what are you doing down here running under a different name? And he didn't seem to like that too much, but—'

Primrose had his daughter's elbow and pushed her toward the shop. 'Go on, Flora,' he said. 'Get inside.'

'But I—good day to you, young lady—anyhow, I said Something tells me old Jake will be glad to hear tell of his boy. Ain't you, Jake? And I'm going back down there in a week, for a bit of business. So what do you want me to tell him for you? What should I bring him from his old pappy back home?'

'Not a damned thing,' Primrose growled. He had Flora inside of the shop, and pushed in after her.

'Now hold on, Jake. That ain't—' But Primrose closed the door behind himself and slid the bolt.

The old Minorcan dressmaker looked up from her needle-work. 'We need a dress,' Primrose half-shouted. 'Whatever's your best stuff. The yellow—yellow? No, white.'

Flora watched out the slatted window as Smith moved back along the street, cursing. 'Whatever she wants, but in your good fabric. None of the middling stuff you give to these Crackers around here. Flora, your mother will be back soon from the confectioner's, make sure and have something to show her.'

She was taken into the back of the salon. Jake stayed in the front, pacing. Almost wordlessly, the seamstress showed Flora a set of models for her to try on, to get a feel for a style. Flora dully picked a continental dress and was left alone to change. She stood surrounded by a bank of mirrors, lit by lanterns. But there was also a narrow chink of natural light in the room. A door at the rear of the shop.

Primrose was pacing the floor at the front of the shop. Flora checked the privacy curtains, to see they were drawn tight. Then eased the door open. She slipped out as quickly as she could and was out in a reeking alleyway. Flora hurried to the main street and then to the saloon, halfway down.

Every eye in the place turned to her as she came inside. But she moved too quickly to let them fall on her for long. She walked along the sodden bar until she found him. Smith was already sitting down, already had a cup of rum in hand. He was the last to notice the young woman and he looked up at her startled.

'Well,' he said. 'The daughter.'

'Pardon me, sir. But I need to talk to you.'

He turned back to the bar, resumed a speech she'd interrupted. 'It's just some folks got no sense of history,' he said. 'No tenderness for old times or the folks they passed them with. Now I know it weren't all pretty. Weren't all fine and noble. Far from't. I seen days with old Jake that he wouldn't care to speak of now. Seen him begging coppers, begging cornbread. I known how he got his start of cows and I known the Seminole that gave it to him. Had you heard of that, little lady? Few's left that have. He owes that Indin his life, his whole livelihood. Spoke of naming a son for him, haw, can you imagine that today? Well, I know what he did instead. Ran them off the land, as soon as he was able. That's gratitude for you. About the same as he shown old Smith.'

Flora was casting urgent glances to the front of the shop. She couldn't wait any longer. 'Pardon me sir, but are you really going down there again, to see my brother?'

'Surely,' the man said. 'I'll be meeting a ship from Hispanola, and the boy's down there working on the old Forty-Four brand. Ranges all the way down to the sawgrass. Found the ends of the earth there, I suppose. Seemed as though he liked it.'

'Tell him to leave,' Flora said.

The man peered at her. 'Leave? Why, he's just getting started. He's—'

'Tell him to leave,' Flora repeated. 'You must go straight-away. Tell him that our father is going to send people after him there. Tell him to leave, please tell him. It's to save his life and my life both.'

Smith looked at her carefully. 'Jake intends to send people after the boy, you say. But the flip side now. What happens for old Primrose if he cannot get him?'

'He's counting on being able to hunt my brother if he needs to. He's counting on it as a way to keep his finger on—everyone else. If he can't do it—' Flora closed her eyes. 'It would be trouble for him. It might be ruination.'

The man peered at her a while longer. Then he smiled. 'I like the sound of that,' he said. 'I'll tell him.'

'Tell him it's from Flora, with love.' She was turning now, walking out. 'And tell him too what you said earlier, about how our father got his start with the cattle and all. He'll like you for that story.'

Flora reached the front of the rumshop and was about to pass through the sheet of daylight out into the street when she saw her mother coming along the plank sidewalk, accompanied by Emily. Pauline did not deign to look at the saloon to her left, and so did not see her daughter standing inside of it. Emily did, however. They met eyes. The slave woman had to stifle a shout when she saw her. All Flora could do was press a finger to her lips and wait for them to go down the street and turn the corner toward the dressmaker's.

Only then did Flora come out of the saloon. She hurried along the fetid alleyway until she'd come to the back door of the shop. She slipped inside, the latch sounding loudly.

Her father's voice from behind the curtain. 'What the hell is she doing? Been back there for ages. You should go in, Pauline.'

'Oh, darling, leave her be. It's hard business for a woman to choose a dress. Flora, Flora. Sweetheart, have you seen anything you like? Are you all right?'

Flora was breathing heavily. She picked up a wedding dress and held it against her chest, as if to stifle the sound of her heart. At last she opened her eyes and saw herself in the mirror. A long dress, white, with fine lace. 'Yes, mother,' she said. 'Yes, mother, I'm going to be all right.'

The night before the new moon, she rode away from the house. At the oak she found Jude waiting. They were together for hours, they walked the unlit forest, they kissed by a creek. Eventually morning mist began to form in the low places and it was time to leave again. 'When's the next time?' Flora asked. 'Night after tomorrow?'

'No,' said Jude. He was holding her.

'The night after that, then?'

'No.'

Flora sat very still.

'We've got to sow,' Jude said. 'It's the growing moon now. I kin see by the moon to plant, so I'll work all night. It'll be a week before I kin leave it agin.'

'A week,' Flora repeated.

'Yes.'

'Jude,' she said. 'Do you know that I am to be married in ten days?'

'Yes,' said Jude. 'Yes. And do you know that my daddy is in jail for another twelve?'

'I know that, man. But—'

'And when he gets out I intend to have kept my promise. I intend to have his land tilled and planted for him jist as if he'd never been gone. That's what I mean to do.'

'Ah,' Flora said, and laughed drily. 'Ah, good. A man jist like all others. Needs to have his battle, his challenge. Can't live life otherwise. Yes, needs to have all the time a sporting challenge in front of him.'

Jude let go of her. 'You kin call it that if you want,' he said.

'So you'll do all this,' Flora said, 'and git your fists good and bloody in your big prizefight and win the bout. But what are you going to do about me? Jude? Which way are you gonter go? What's more important to you? This thing you're doing for your papa, or me?'

'Don't ask me that,' Jude warned.

'I cain't help it, Jude, the question can't wait. Which is more important, me or them fields?'

'I told you don't ask me that, damn it, don't.'

'Well, it's asked. Now what?'

'I cain't answer what's more important in my mind, Flora,' Jude said. 'Because I don't know. But I don't have to know. All I kin tell you is what I'm gon to do. And what I'm gon to do is finish working my father's fields and sow them. However long that takes. And as soon as that's done I'm gone to look up and see you. You, as you've always been. A rich man's daughter. Set to be another man's wife.'

When Flora spoke, it was in a monotone. 'That's all you see,' she said, 'because it's all you dare to see. You ain't bold enough to see me any other way. You're too scared to see things other than jist as they are. That's the truth. That's the truth about you.' She watched him for a moment. Then she turned away.

'All the same,' she said, as she went toward her horse. 'I hope you come call on me next week, when you're finished with working. I could use some more easy fun before I'm married away.' She got on her horse and left.

She came in weeping so hard that Pauline woke up. When Pauline woke up, she woke Jake up. They lit a lantern and came to her room. They found her struggling with her shoes, which were covered in dirt, as was the hem of her dress. It was three in the morning. Pauline immediately began to scream in despair.

'Oh! She's ruint, she's ruint.'

Jake told her to shut up and then started to scream himself. 'Ah, you've been out helling agin. What a fool I was to think you'd not turn whore. Who is it, who have you seen?' But she shut her mouth against him furiously. 'Who? Who?' He began to shake her.

She struck him on the face, almost a reflex. It was what he'd been waiting for. He backhanded her hard across the jaw. Pauline screamed.

'Aw, quit howling. Tweren't but a tap. She's a good strong Cracker filly, she'll heal by daybreak. You'll never see the mark.'

Flora lay still, sprawled across the bed, silent.

'I kin let this go,' he told her, satisfied. 'You could mount ever man in Florida, I don't much care. Gallatin won't never guess, the poor sod, you could be Sally Salisbury for all he'll know. But hear me, girl. Your fun is over in this house. You've got ten nights till your sweet marriage, and that's ten nights in this room with a watchman outside the door. And another watchman outside the winder, too, hussy, don't think I don't know the game.' He took the lantern and left the room, leaving his wife weeping and his daughter silent in the dark.

It took Jude one more full day to finish the ploughing, beginning at dawn. One full day, in the sudden heat. When it was finished, he came inside and went straight to his room. He spent an unusual hour alone there, barechested on the cool bedspread, immobile and silent in the blue dusk light seeping under the shutters. It took three calls for supper before he came.

The garden plot was finished and so the entire family was freed to help with the sowing. Beginning the next morning, they moved in waves across the fields, dropping seed in the dirt and hoeing it under. Jude no longer kept the outrageous pace he had maintained for almost thirty days. Now he hung about even with his siblings and mother. Sometimes he even lagged. But it didn't matter. The work was being done, it would be finished in time. Jude had assured it, with his month of furious activity. Still the young man kept working long after he should have stopped, into darkness, through half the night, listlessly, as if unsure what else to do. He slept more than before but seemed wearier. Lucy saw that he was not sneaking out at night anymore and heard real sorrow in his sighs.

At the end of the week, the Quintos had forty of the fifty acres of corn planted. Jude went to his mother. 'Ma,' he said. 'I'm taking this day off. Y'all kin keep planting well enough without me.'

She looked at him. 'Yes,' she said.

He turned. 'I'm taking the paint mare.'

'All right,' she said. She watched him as he went to the stable. 'Jude,' she called at last, as he led the horse out into the yard. 'Are you going to come back?'

He told her yes, he would be back that afternoon. Then he got up on the horse and set off at a steady canter.

Flora was bending over the berry bush, eating ravenously. She had not been joining her parents at mealtime, and so the berries were how she did not starve. Her father was angry about her missing meals, but her mother calmed him down. She hinted that the dress they'd bought her was, if anything, a stitch tight in the bust. Missing dinner was one way to train her full figure for the garment. This idea pleased them both. Though of course the real reason Flora did not eat with her parents was to avoid all conversation about the wedding, which might make her scream and not stop screaming. That was why she was out here on her knees in the dirt, eating berries as fast as she could pick them. Her fingers were stained like a dyer's.

But then she stopped. Someone had called her name, once, from a distance: 'Flora.'

She looked up. Standing at the fenceline was Jude Quinto. In the broad daylight. Flora jumped to her feet and looked around frantically. She could hear her father's voice from the other side of the house, talking to a foreman. She gestured wildly for Jude to go away, then for him to come near, then for him to go away again. He made no movement, just stood. At last, with a frightened look toward the house, Flora ran out to the fenceline.

'Jude, what are you doing here?'

'Come to talk to you, of course.'

'Jude, you've got to go away. If he sees!'

'I have to tell you something.'

'Jude, go out yonder—jist go out yonder in the trees! I'll come out—'

'I won't be long here.'

'Well speak quick then,' she said, desperate. 'Speak, fool.'

Jude took off his hat. 'You was wrong about me,' he said. 'I ain't scared. I am bold enough. And it's because of you—you, nothing else, no one else.'

She put her hands over her face. 'Jude.'

'Look at me. Please. I will not let the world carry you away from me jist because it sees fit. Before I met you I would have allowed it. Not anymore. You're the one I needed to change for and the one who's changed me, both. Both at the same time. Ain't it a marvel? Only God could make a contraption sich as this.'

'Jude. Jude.'

'I'm going now. I don't know jist what's going to happen yet, but if you love me, stay ready.'

'But Jude,' she said. 'I'm being watched. Daytime. Nighttime too, now.'

'I know it,' Jude said. 'We'll come up with something. It might take a while—'

'A while? Jude, there's two days left.'

'Aw, that's plenty of time,' he scoffed.

Flora averted her eyes. 'I'm scared of this,' she said.

He reached across the fence, took her hand. 'Flora, you got nothing to be scared of save ideas that you put in my head yourself. I'm going now. Kiss me.'

She shook her head. 'No. You kiss me, and make it look like it's your idea.' She grabbed his hands and put them on her shoulders and pulled him halfway over the fence. Only from a distance could the kiss have looked like his idea.

Jude took a northern route along an ancient road. It had been blazed so long ago that the sawn stumps had been worn down smooth by horseshoes and bootheels. They resembled round puddles now, flush to the surface and buffed to a sheen.

It was the way to Mrs. Monroe's roadhouse. When he started the trip, he only had the faintest glimmer of a plan. But as he rode, the young man rehearsed what he'd say when he got there, and by the time he reached the place he was in full spate. An idea had taken form, and it carried him galloping right up to the entrance of the roadhouse.

Jude came in through the door which had never been closed since the day it was hung. A waft of rabbit stew and Spanish tobacco. It was just a few days before the cowhunting season began, and yet the place was only sparsely occupied. That was how it had been, lately. There were other roads now, other road-houses. Soon there was going to be a railway, too, cutting across the countryside, bearing people along from one point to another with little need for the blank country between them. In time the establishment would dwindle down, alone and adrift in the middle of the forest. As it had been in the beginning. The rare traveler who happened to pass it might wonder aloud who had ever decided to put a public house in such a place. They might remark that it looked like it had been set down by the receding of the Flood.

But for now there were still patrons. Some who still needed the place. They sat around in small quiet circles of good con-versation, as in the latter hours of a gathering. They all looked up when Jude came in through the door. A few people there knew him, called for him to come and take a drink. Those who didn't know him had the young man's name spoken in their ear. Quinto. That's that Quinto boy. The one what hazed the hell out of those fields when they took his papa. He sown thirty acres. Fifty acres. A hundred acres. Hell, I don't know how many. But that's the one, no doubt to look at him.

They all assumed the young man was there to rest after his work, and be foolish awhile. He surprised them by seeking no such thing. He accepted a cup of rum a little sheepishly and then set about his real business. Moving from chair to chair around the room, he asked each person if they had any griev-ance against Jake Primrose the cattleman. And if they did have a grievance, would they take part in an action against him.

A big-skulled man named Goolby was the first, and he kept on crowing and clapping his hands long after others had settled down. 'Oh yes, old Jake, beloved countryman. The lord of the manor, the cock of the walk! What a friend he's been in times of need! Do you remember the big fine fort he had built for us to live in, and the little commotion he started with the Indins to bring us all together in it? We was close back then, weren't we? Damned close! Old Jake! How I'd treasure to see him again.'

There were two fat men jammed into a little table, both out-of-work lawyers. 'Primrose the cowman, yes I know him,' the first one said. 'Sure, I know the son of a bitch. He had me took off of the trial up there in Newnansville, then saw to it that I didn't get my fee. That was bad enough. But worse is, everone who saw that new banty bastard he put on the case decided they needed to get themselves a Georgia lawyer too. A fellow cain't get hired no more unless he's from Georgia, or spent time up there someway.'

'It's true, it's a goddamned craze,' grumbled the heavylidded man in the next seat. 'Don't know as I'll ever get another case.'

A bawdy woman was hovering around the lawyers' table. A rough old bird, with borrowed red plumage. Her name was Miss Tamaryn. She'd been in negotiations with the two men, but Jude's plan drew her in. 'Primrose, you say? Primrose, scrap of a fellow, yellowhaired, works in cows? Oh, the scoundrel! I'll hang him! He done me worset than he done any man here, I guarantee it. With you fellows it was money, but with me it was love. Love! Six years ago in Jacksonville—I was twenty-three then— he shared a whole fortnight with me, and many tender promises, and were they any good? No, and neither was the necklace he gave me. False diamints! If I see him, boys, I'll climb on his back, and damn me if I come back down while he's still got hair on his head.'

A farmer named Teek Geyer was there too, but he got very few words out. It was mostly tears. He'd been on the jury in Nat's trial, helped deliver the guilty verdict. 'If I knew what'd come from it,' he moaned, 'if I knew—' Jude held him around the shoulder and said he didn't need to apologize, but the man kept trying anyway. At last he indicated his intention to help Jude in whatever way he could, and lowered his head down to the bar.

The old rumhouse veteran Herb Nail was in the next seat— he'd been comforting Geyer even before Jude arrived; it was a long job. Nail was less inflamed for the conspiracy than the others. Jake Primrose had not been inside the roadhouse in many years and Nail had rarely left it, so they hadn't crossed paths. But he mused and mused, and finally agreed to take part. 'Ah, why not? I'll join in, just so I don't have to hear the rest of you rattle on about it forevermore afterward. The exhaustion of that! I'll go, just so I can say No, friend, you needn't tell me the story again, I was there. It will save my ears.' And he sat back, happy with his decision.

On the other side of him was a small man with black hair going silver, Ziegler. He was very drunk and just as overwrought as Teek Geyer. Herb Nail had his hands full that day. Nail leaned down to the little man and asked whether he would join. He murmured the details. 'A grand plot. This Quinto lad. Three days from today. Something to look forward to, a higher cause. Might do you good. What do you say, my dear man? Yes? Yes.'

There was one more patron in the place, a figure in the corner. Jude had not noticed, but now Herb Nail directed his attention there. It was an exceedingly thin and exceedingly old man, propped in a chair and staring dead ahead. Nail introduced them in a loud voice. 'This here is one of Jake Primrose's longest friends in this territory. Aren't you, Old Rouchefort? Yes. And it'd been many years, many years since we last had him in the place. Since before the war. He just walked right out of the woods the other day, gave us all a surprise. Looked a wee bit worse for wear, but we been doctoring you, hain't we? We been fixing you up, hain't we, old man?'

Jude looked at this half-skeleton. Someone had barbered his wiry hair and cut his white beard square at the breastbone. They'd been feeding him, or at least offering him food—a big tray of cornbread and a rasher of bacon sat on the table. A whole tankard of rum, too, as if that might restore him to life.

'Yes, old man, we was surely glad to see you here again. Now did you ever meet this lad right here? If you did, he'd only been a child. It's Jude Quinto. Quinto.'

The old man looked up at the sound of that name. He regarded Jude for the first time. Eyes staring out of a tremendous depth. He lifted one arm up off the table and stretched it out for Jude, who took the gnarled hand and shook it.

'I knew your daddy,' the old man said. His jaw kept working after that, as if he was saying words. No more words were coming out. Jude released the hand.

Herb Nail took Jude and led him back to the center of the room. 'Well now, young Mister Quinto. I believe you've got the ear of every person present on the subject of Primrose. Now give us your plans for him.'

'Well, it's like this.' Jude put one foot up on a chair. 'Primrose is planning a mighty large wedding tomorrow. But the bride don't want no part of it, not a damned bit. I don't like that. Do you? It so happens that I love the girl, but I figure I'd be angered anyhow. So, my intention is to go and do something about it. Flail it apart. I'll go alone and do it my damnself if I have to, please believe that. Only, it'd be an honor to have you good people be a part of it. And I don't mind saying it'll make it a sight easier when we're trying to run away.'

'Run away? You're running away, at the end?' Miss Tamaryn asked, breathless.

'Well, yes. If she wants to go.' The young man rubbed his neck. 'And I believe she does want to, as it's moreless her idea to begin with.'

There were whispers, hoots. 'Crazy bastard,' Herb Nail murmured approvingly.

'How do you aim to do it?' asked one of the unemployed lawyers.

'Well,' Jude said. 'I guess there isn't much of a trick to it. We cover our faces, conceal ourselves. Then go in loud and frightful. The place will be full of billowy folk, old ladies and senators and such, and if we make a big enough noise they'll start to carry on awfully. I'll turn their horses loose in the middle of the shouting. If there's enough confusion it won't be no trouble to run away again once it's all done, and they'll have no horses for chasing. And me and Flora will be gone.'

There was silence. 'That's it?' Herb Nail asked.

'That's it, yes, that's the plan,' said big-skulled Goolby. 'The best plan I've heard in a century!'

'Sounds like the plan his daddy had for the trial defense,' murmured one of the lawyers.

Teek Geyer had picked his head up off of the bar. 'Speak about Nat, will ye?' he growled. 'Speak on Nat Quinto's name, will ye?'

'The lad looks like he can handle this business, though, doesn't he,' murmured Miss Tamaryn, regarding Jude. 'A likely enough fellow, isn't he.'

'I'd follow him,' said Ziegler.

'A damned Lancelot of a chap,' said Herb Nail. 'Oh, won't we have a time, tomorrow?'

The talk went on, and Jude said no more to try to sway anyone; he just stood there in front of them, letting it be discussed, staring at them with fierce dark eyes and waiting for the outcome. Then Mrs. Monroe emerged from whichever part of the tavern's shadows she'd been occupying.

'Here, you'll need these,' she said. 'I've got a whole box of stage clothes from some playactors what passed through here, years ago. They went off in a rush and left their trunk of costumes. Cavaliers. Savages. Sultans. All of it. You take them and wear them and it will all come off right.'

Something in this tipped the room. Mrs. Monroe dragged the chest out from the back room and threw it open. The patrons crowded around, pulling out cloaks and capes and stage jewelry. Nail made the cheering suggestion that Mrs. Monroe come along with them. It was not serious, of course— the lady did not desert her establishment, not for any reason. But the next day, she hefted all of the boxes up on to the tailgate when they went to depart, and she blessed the road in front of them as the cart rolled away.

The Quintos' acres were all planted, and that night the family celebrated with a tremendous meal. But the day to come loomed for Jude. All afternoon he paced the yard, while the others took their rest.

His mother called to him from the porch. 'Won't you come sit, boy? You told me you'd plain collapse if you ever finished them fields. Well, they're finished—now, collapse.'

He nodded and tried for a while to relax in the shade. He found that he could not.

'What is it?' his mother asked. But he just shook his head and turned to walk down toward the springhead, where many of his siblings were swimming.

Around dusk he told her everything. She nodded, unsurprised. He pushed on, encouraged by her steadiness. 'I'm gone away, likely,' he said to her. 'Tomorrow. For a while. Maybe forever. Could be I'll come back someday, but I—I cain't promise it.' He took ahold of his mouth with his left hand. The woman just kept nodding.

After that he had to tell his brothers and sisters. The younger children listened impassively. They had come to accept such things. Three older siblings had already left home; they saw it as a mechanism of nature, like the seasons, beyond their comprehension. The older ones were less understanding. They tried to argue.

'You're going before daddy gets back?' Lucetta asked.

'That's right.'

'Why now?' Dan asked. 'Why won't you wait?'

'Because I don't have a choice.'

But the younger brother was very hard and would not accept it. Eventually Jude took him out around the side of the house. They talked awhile, those two closest siblings, and Dan wept. But eventually he scuffed his eyes with his sleeve and said he understood. In reward, Jude took him one step further from the house. 'I'll tell you what else, man,' he said. 'I'm going to let you come along with me tomorrer. You'll be my righthand partner.' The fifteen-year-old's eyes lit up. Yet he did not shout or do anything unseemly—he nodded once and spat mannishly, though there was some mucous in it from the weeping.

Lucy called them to supper. They ate, and talked, and Lucy brought out a bottle of porto wine, and the elder children of the brood all got cups of it. Eventually the youngest ones were excused from the table. The remainder stayed up late into the night by candlelight, laughing and talking and retelling their stories.

Before noon the next day Jude and Dan reached a bend in a creek just below the Primrose house. This was the appointed meeting place. No one else was there. They waited and waited. Jude did not dismount—he paced his horse up and down the trail, glowering. He rebuffed his brother's questions with stony silence.

Then there was a team of horses coming up the road. Three Morgan horses, to be exact. It took that many to pull them. It was a whole party sagging the axles of an overloaded cart. They were loud, cheerful, boisterous, like any wedding-goers. Herb Nail was driving it with a riding crop. Little darkhaired Ziegler was there, and bawdy Miss Tamaryn, and Old Rouchefort. The two unemployed lawyers had changed out of their tatty suits into more comfortable clothing and were hanging off of the sides of the cart, each waving a rum bottle in his free hand and hollering.

Herb Nail got down to greet him. 'Ah, here's our young squire. A nobler soul you won't find anywhere on thisyer spit of sand. Ain't he, dearie? Ain't he though? A damn Lancelot of a chap.' Miss Tamaryn cooed in agreement. Ziegler nodded along blithely.

They helped Old Rouchefort down from the cart, as Teek Geyer rode up from the direction of his homestead. They got the stage trunk and began to spread its contents out on the ground. There was a wealth of options, the vanished troupe's whole repertoire lay about on the wiregrass.

'How to make a big enough fright?' Geyer asked. 'We could all go in yowling like Highland Scots—put on those tartans there.'

'No, no,' said Herb Nail. 'That ain't frightful enough. Let's put on these—' he hefted a Roman helmet— 'conquistador headpieces and take up some cutlasses. Go in shouting for a matanza.'

'Hell, they won't scare for Spainiards,' Goolby said. 'Those boys haven't made a peep since Twenty-Two. No, if we really want to scare some senators we'll go in as Seminoles. Make them think a Red Stick war party has done snuck up the coast.'

There came a hand on Jude's shoulder. It was Miss Tamaryn and she was welling up. 'I wanted to be a French lady,' the woman said. 'I found the most wonderful dress in the trunk. There's a masque with catty eyeholes, and I'd paint my lips red, like Marie Antoinette.'

'Me too,' Ziegler breathed rummily. 'I'd dreamt of going as a chevalier.'

'All right. All right,' Jude said. 'Ain't no need for us to all wear the same thing. Just find the getup that suits you best and put it on.'

They did. Shirts flounced and stage-jewelry clanked. They availed themselves of the makeup kit. Some got a thick layer of white powder. Others got a full-face rouge. The lawyers elected to simply strip down half-naked and coat their ample torsos in blue paint. They wanted freedom of movement. To cover their faces they each got an Attic mask, plaster grin, and plaster grimace.

Someone put a cape and hood over Old Rouchefort. His face was not covered, but he did not need a mask. He already looked like a death's-head. They daubed some white paint on his face but it was hardly needed. He stretched out his arms and moaned.

'Oo, sinners,' he said, in a quavering voice. 'Oo—o—o, sinners.'

'Yes, yes, it's perfect,' said Nail.

Jude looked up at the sun. 'All right. Are we all set up? We got to hurry, friends. The time—Lord, we cain't be late.'

They made their way through the trees toward the estate, leading their horses. They stopped before the fenceline, under cover of the trees. Jude alone had put on no costume. There was no need. He would pursue this action undisguised. Let them look at him and know his face. If he succeeded they would never see it again.

He stepped out of the cover to observe. The Primrose yard was arrayed with carriages, arriving mostly from the north. Guests ambled toward the backyard of the house, where an altar had been set up within a trellised arbor. They checked their coats and other encumbrances before going in. A string quartet droned. Jude observed the scene with care. 'Look— they're all bunched up in that garden place, like we said. And look—they're checking their pistols with the coats and all. There'll be no shooting. And look—their horses, all paddocked up. Simple enough to manage them. Simple enough.' Herb Nail was standing behind him, with little Ziegler. He raised his eyebrows at the young man, then he took another pull on the rum bottle.

Jude kept looking over the scene for a while, making sure of the positions. But before turning back to the woods he looked across the open space, to the room where he knew Flora was now putting on her own costume.

She stood with one foot up on an ottoman and her dress hem hiked all the way up her leg. Her mother's voice was frantic in the hallway. 'Flora, let me in.'

She could not let her in, not yet. She had a roll of ribbon and a sharp knife. She was cutting lengths of the ribbon and using them to tie things to her bare leg. Not many things—she didn't have the time. Only a few. A favorite comb. Several rings and several earrings, threaded through. A letter she'd gotten from her brother Hadjo. High on her left thigh, several necklaces: old amethyst, mother's cameo, silver cross. They hung down and jounced against her knee. And then, with one last length of ribbon, she tied up the little silver knife itself. The door rattled in its frame.

'Open up, you hellion. I'll break the door down.'

'Coming,' Flora cried, and threw the dresshem down over her knee and ran to the door. She unlocked it and came out nonchalantly, stepping past her mother. The woman was half-mad with fear and anger but said nothing.

Two blank-faced little girls whom Flora did not know came and took ahold of her train. 'Thank you, darlings,' Flora said. 'Forgive me if I walk fast, but I oughtn't be late.'

They hustled out the front door and onto the porch. Flora shaded her eyes and scanned the treeline. There was nothing out of the ordinary. A signal was passed around the side of the house and the music changed. Her father appeared. His eyes were a little puffy; he took her tenderly by the arm.

At last father and daughter came alone down the side walkway, around the corner, through the arbor threshold. They entered into the chapel area. Fifty faces turned to see, they all fixed on the diamantine beauty in her high-necked suit of lace.

Father and daughter took a few slow steps down the aisle. But then Jake Primrose stopped and so Flora stopped too.

The attendees all stared. They could only wonder why in the world Primrose had halted there at the top of the aisle with such a queer look on his face. But they could not see what he was looking at.

Primrose dropped his daughter's hand, still gawping dead ahead. One by one the audience began to turn in that direction. A creaking sound came from the altar facade. It was rocking back and forth behind the bald minister. Gently at first, but then less gently. The minister noticed it too and peered over his shoulder at the shadow growing there, perturbed. He was halfway turned around when the thing collapsed on top of him with a clatter.

There were all the usual gasps and shouts that follow an accident of that kind. But the gasps and shouts didn't last long. Because soon the audience got a glimpse of the real catastrophe: there, behind the fallen altarpiece, a brace of painted harlequins leering at them. The noises changed. They turned from gasps into bellows, shrieks, and the clatter of fifty people leaping from their chairs.

But they were wrong to all look one way. The catastrophe was behind them, too. A half-dozen invaders rushed through the entrance at the rear. Chortling, whooping, they came, bowling over chairs and throwing ornamental flowerpots. The crowd wailed and tried to escape, but the harlequins brandished bits of splintered altarfront. Here and there the guests' shrieks resolved into actual words: 'Uprising! Uprising!' 'O Christ, the Spaniards!' 'Someone call the militia!' 'Is that Chief Osceola? Oh, help!' But the words were disconnected, and no one heard anyone else.

They ran for the side exit which led to the banquet area. They pressed for it, but the door was terribly narrow. They shoved more frantically. A holy terror menaced them from the back of the crowd, a gowned figure with its arms raised skyward: 'O—o—o, sinners! O—oo—oo—o, sinners!'

At last, with a long, ripping crash, the trellis wall gave way. The attendees fell into the next chamber like a tumbling surf. But this was no deliverance, they were not saved. The assailants were waiting here also: The two lawyers had snuck into the reception area to start on the roast pig and the pies. At the toppling of the wall they turned around and with impressive strength each one tore a legbone off of the pig. With these they began laying into the nearest attendees, landing blows with meaty thuds.

Some people tried to rush for the main entryway but met Goolby standing there with a meat cleaver. Miss Tamaryn was snatching the hair out of a banker she'd mistaken for Jake Primrose. There were pockets of resistance: Judge Fawnce and the slender Georgia lawyer were fighting back to back and fending off all comers. Elsewhere, a tremendous yellow-haired woman named Miss Cook was swinging a punch ladle all around herself with whistling speed. But mostly it was desolation. Calamity and ruin. Several old ladies were borne aloft on pewter plates and told they were going to be fed to a chieftain. A fur broker was praying on his knees to Herb Nail, who brandished a dull breadknife over his scalp. The mask of tragedy and the mask of comedy were taking turns thumping a railroadman like a drum. There was a great effort at the dessert table as the wedding cake was lifted—it took three people— and thrown. It accordioned through the air and landed heavily on top of a circuit judge. He was flattened to the ground with a thump of spongecake. Immediately one of the lawyers leapt on the inverted delicacy and began to eat out the bottom with both fists.

There were five quick pops from outside the wedding arbor. Whipcracks from the stable. With them came the sound of hooves. 'Our horses, our horses,' said a bald man crouching underneath a table. There were more whipcracks, and whinnying. The man wailed. 'Oh God, our horses, gone away.' A new horror in the guests' cries now, no escape.

Flora stood alone in the middle of the garden, neither chasing nor being chased. The fracas flowed around her. No one looked at her there, in her wedding dress; she was too strangely still. She stood alone, not quite waiting: watching.

She moved around the arbor. She came across John Gallatin. The man was partially submerged in a big punchbowl with his cravat stuffed into his mouth. He was dazed, had been beaten. He looked at Flora with a sweet innocence.

'Mister Gallatin,' Flora said.

'O a,' said the rich man.

She shook her head. 'I'm sorry,' she said. 'It just weren't meant to be. Ask my daddy why, sometime.' She kissed her fingertips and reached down to press them to his forehead, then stepped away. He watched her go, his face shining with bliss.

Flora's mother had been treed. She was perched at the very top of a young peach tree with besiegers at the bottom; it was astonishing that she had gotten so high in such thick skirts. Two conquistadors were now rocking the tree back and forth, to get at the peaches. Pauline held on tight, wailing as it swayed. Flora shook her head sadly, walked on.

There were four more whipcracks, and more galloping of horses. Then Jude appeared at the entrance on his marshtackie. He rode straight into the place, looking for Flora. He found her and jumped down at her feet. They gripped each other by the arms. Perhaps a word passed between them—no more than that, just a syllable perhaps. Then Jude got back up into the saddle and Flora swung up, too. Jude turned the horse toward the exit. Then she saw her father.

The cattleman was seated in a chair in the corner. Pairs of painted and clawed and gauntletted hands held him in place. His clothes were torn; he had been beaten as badly as Gallatin. But that was nothing compared to what was afflicting him now. A figure in a black cloak was hunched in front of him, face to pallid face, speaking in low tones. Primrose was trying to worm away from the specter but could not. The voice was harsh and insistent.

'Oh yes, Jake, I died, I died out in them woods. Died alone and rotted slow, and the dogs tore at the body. And I blame you for it, Jake, yes I do, ever bit of it.'

Primrose was fighting to get free, screaming No, no please

old man, leave me alone. But the cloaked figure kept its wretched alabaster death's-head evenly in front of him as the captors held him down. 'Yes, Jake, and Little Tom's coming along after me, for he's not dead like I am, he's alive as ever, alive and biding his time where he's gaithered to his people down there in the sawgrass. Yes, they're damned unhappy with you, Jake, for how you done em, and there's no telling what they'll do when they get here—though I may not leave you alive for them—' The figure reached two bony hands to the cattleman's throat.

'Papa,' Flora cried.

They all looked up at her, all except for Primrose himself, who was still staring into the face of his old subordinate risen from the dead to visit him. 'Please,' Flora said. 'Leave him alone.'

They looked at Jude and then back again at the bride.

'No more,' she said. 'Enough.'

Hand by hand released its grip. One of them pulled Primrose's chair roughly and he tumbled to the ground.

The assailants moved away, Old Rouchefort included. Primrose was splayed out on the dirt. It seemed the short fall had knocked something straight in him, returned the man to himself. His eyes lost some of their glazed terror. They turned up to fix on his daughter and narrowed. He stared at her from the dirt.

'Flora,' he said. 'Darling.' He slowly began to raise himself up.

'Jude, go,' she said. 'Go.'

Jude reeled the horse. They pushed out of the garden. In a moment they were galloping across the open yard, the young man in his plain clothes and the young woman in her wedding dress, the sweep flying out behind her, Jude spurring the horse, Flora spurring Jude.

They galloped the rest of the way to Newnansville on Jude's strong horse. They made good time, knowing pursuers would not be too far behind them. Once in the city they rode toward the courthouse. But before they reached it Jude turned aside.

'Hold on,' he said to Flora. 'How would you like to meet my daddy just once before we go?' He pointed his horse toward the sheriff's office, the jail cell.

'I already did meet him,' Flora said.

Jude shook his head. 'When?'

'The last time I was here,' Flora said. 'I slipped away and came to the sheriff's office, found the jail winder. I tapped right on the bars. I said Hello Mister Quinto, I'm Flora Primrose. And he said Ah, Miss Primrose, I known you since you was small. I always predicted you'd be pretty. And I said Thankye. And I said Mister Quinto, I'm in love with your son, I hope I'm on marry him. And he said, Marry a Quinto? There's some that will recommend it and some that won't. I jist hope you don't like being rich. I said I haven't liked it yet, much. And he said Good. Said But he'll work for you, Jude will. I said I know. And he said He'll keep faith with you. And I said I know. And then I said Mister Quinto real quick can you tell me any good stories about him before I leave? And he said Oh, I expect you'll have some better stories than mine before long. Then I had to leave, my mama was calling me to look at wedding shoes.'

Jude rode on for a moment. 'Well,' he said. 'I guess that's good enough for me.' And he turned the horse back toward the courthouse. Just off to the east there was the sound of horses-men hurrying to the sheriff's office, shouts, pursuers' curses.

Flora and Jude galloped to the courthouse. They went around to the back of the building and tied up the horse. Hand in hand they ran in through the door and down the hall. They hunted through the corridors for the clerk of court, found him. Big desk, meek little man. He asked the relevant questions. Your name, ma'am. Your name, sir. Your age, ma'am. Your age, sir. Your place of birth, ma'am. Your place of birth, sir. From the front of the building came an echoing slam. 'Do you think you can hurry it up?' asked Jude. The man shook his head, looked amused. Young people, always in such a hurry. He went on. Your occupation, ma'am. Yours. Your current residence. Yours. Thank you. And now I come to the real question, and will you tell me the truth? Will you take this contrary scrap of Creation, to hold, to use? Will you drink deeply of them? As if there was no more water in the world on a dry noon? But here now is the difference. This girl, this boy, this soul, this life, they are not made from water. You cannot cup or contain them; they do not as they should. But they will make, and speak, and love, just as they were made, and spoken, and loved. Such is their high glory and their peril.

Bootsteps down the hallway. 'Hurry,' said Flora.

I conclude. In short, God-resemblers, will you be what you are? Will you see in the soul that stands before you the stamp that you too bear? Will you recognize your selfsame shape in theirs and uphold both halves wholly? O holy, do you know what it is you do?

'I do,' said Flora.

'I do,' said Jude.

The clerk nodded at them both, smiling, and stamped the certificate.

Jude dug in his pocket for the court fee and threw it down on the desk. There were shouts coming closer. Jude and Flora kissed, and kissing they burst out of the office. Hand in hand they ran off down the hall and out the back door, and were gone. But they left their names behind them on the paper.

ABOUT THE AUTHOR

JAMES CHAPIN'S WRITING has appeared in *Slate*, *Catapult*, the *Los Angeles Review of Books'* Marginalia channel, and the *Tampa Bay Times*. He is from north Florida, where he lived while writing this novel. He currently lives in Georgia with his wife and their animals.